Praise for *The Company You Keep*
by Neil Gordon

Voted one of 2003's Best Summer Reads by *USA Today*

"Rousing, cerebral. . . . Gordon's plot is a doozy—a trio of doozies, in fact—yet utterly credible. He projects wrenching political and personal drama onto a slightly futuristic version of where we stand now as a people. In so doing he shows how we got here. . . . What makes this novel compelling is not only the ideological spectrum it covers but its emotional chiaroscuro. . . . It bids well to enter the company of our best fiction about the Vietnam era."

—*The New York Times Book Review*

"*The Company You Keep* works as a thriller, but the adventures . . . are grounded firmly in larger political and moral issues, in this case the passionate conviction that the radical opposition in the '60s to the Vietnam War represented the high point of American idealism, the best dream America ever had. . . . The characters speak with passion about serious moral issues, and they admit us to the intimate moments of their lives where the political and the personal intersect. The result is a compelling story." —*Los Angeles Times*

"As compellingly as the best nonfiction accounts of the '60s and '70s, Gordon's novel shows why so many of us took to the streets to fight social injustice and what Martin Luther King Jr. called 'this immoral, unjust war' . . . Gordon has intertwined fact and fiction as seamlessly as Don DeLillo did in *Libra*, his 'factional' account of Kennedy's assassination. . . . [A] precisely written swashbuckler, a serious, sometimes brilliant, always protean tale . . . lively, energetic."

—*The Washington Post*

"Gripping." —*Chicago Tribune*

"Neil Gordon's *The Company You Keep* is an astonishing tour de force, at once an intellectual, emotional and political thriller. . . . [A]n American novel in which plot, characters and ideas are in perfect balance. By bringing the past alive, Gordon enables us to see more clearly where America stands now." —*San Francisco Chronicle*

"Gordon skillfully interweaves the voices of his fictional narrators with many of the most important totems of the era: Vietnam, the shooting of Kent State students by Ohio National Guard members, and the bombing of a townhouse in Greenwich Village. . . . His characters are so skillfully drawn that they remain likable and interesting, and their missives to Isabel are sincerely felt and compelling reads until the very last page." — *The Boston Globe*

"[A] hybrid of political novel, love story, cat-and-mouse thriller, and French bedroom farce . . . entertaining . . . *The Company You Keep* becomes an addictive page-turner of a book."

—*Seattle Times*

"*The Company You Keep* is an important story that's at once a compelling yarn and an exhumation of issues the '60s generation would prefer to dodge. . . . [It is] close to the bone, an American saga that captures a poignant moment in our history where the war at home was as real—if not as deadly—as the one in Vietnam. Gordon's story is about a revolution that never really happened, in a time that never really ended." —*Times Union* (Albany)

"Gordon . . . writes with precision and understanding about the political and personal psychodramas that beset the radical left thirty years or so ago. . . . [He] skillfully weaves an intricate narrative. . . . *The Company You Keep* isn't a standard historical novel. But it certainly is a novel that tells a history."

—*The Capital Times* (Madison, Wisconsin)

"Gordon skillfully combines a tense fugitive procedural, full of intriguing lore about false identities and techniques for losing a tail, with nuanced exploration of boomer nostalgia and regret."

—*Publishers Weekly*

"Compelling and intricately plotted. . . . Well-rendered and engaging political drama." —*Kirkus Reviews*

PENGUIN BOOKS

THE COMPANY YOU KEEP

Neil Gordon was born in South Africa in 1958. He holds a Ph.D. in French literature from Yale University, worked for many years at *The New York Review of Books*, and is currently the literary editor at *The Boston Review* and on the faculty of Eugene Lang College at the New School University. His journalism has appeared in *Tin House, Tricycle,* and *Salon* and he reviews regularly for *The New York Times Book Review* and other periodicals. He is the author of two previous novels, *Sacrifice of Isaac* and *The Gunrunner's Daughter.*

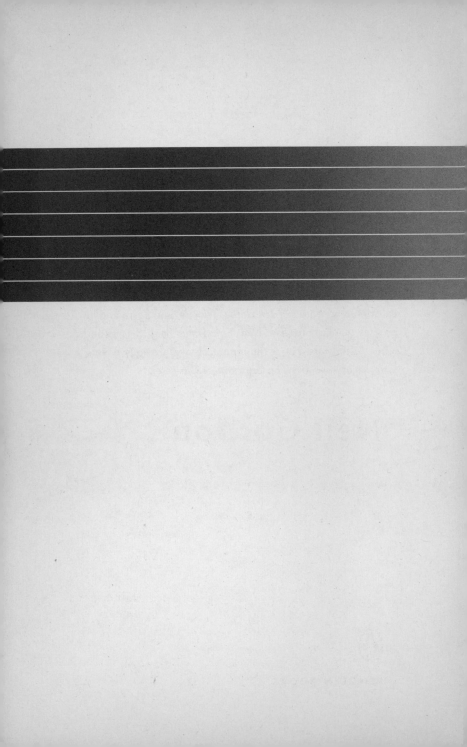

THE COMPANY YOU KEEP

Neil Gordon

PENGUIN BOOKS

PENGUIN BOOKS
Published by the Penguin Group
Penguin Group (USA) Inc., 375 Hudson Street,
New York, New York 10014, USA

USA | Canada | UK | Ireland | Australia | New Zealand |India | South Africa | China
Penguin Books Ltd, Registered Offices: 80 Strand, London WC2R 0RL, England
For more information about the Penguin Group visit penguin.com

First published in the United States of America by Viking 2003
Published in Penguin Books 2004
This edition published in Penguin Books 2013

THE LIBRARY OF CONGRESS HAS CATALOGED THE HARDCOVER EDITION AS FOLLOWS:
Gordon, Neil, 1958–
The company you keep / Neil Gordon.
p. cm.
ISBN 0-670-03218-1 (hc.)
ISBN 978-0-14-312387-3 (pbk.)
1. Weather Underground Organization—Fiction. 2.Revolutionaries—Fiction.
3. Radicals—Fiction. I. Title.
PS3557.O677C66 2003
813'.54—dc21 2002044905

Printed in the United States of America
10 9 8 7 6 5 4 3 2 1

PUBLISHER'S NOTE
This is a work of fiction. Names, characters, places, and incidents either are the product of the author's imagination or are used fictitiously, and any resemblance to actual persons, living or dead, businesses, companies, events, or locales is entirely coincidental.

To my mother and my father,
with admiration and love

PART ONE

Hush little baby
My poor little thing
You've been shuffled about
Like a pawned wedding ring
It must seem strange
Love was here then gone
And the Oklahoma sunrise
Becomes the Amarillo dawn
What's important
In this life?
Ask the man
Who's lost his wife.

—Chrissie Hynde,
"Thumbelina"

Date: Saturday, June 1, 2006
From: "Daddy" <littlej@cusimanorganics.com>
To: "Isabel Montgomery" <isabel@exmnster.uk>
CC: maillist: The_Committee
Subject: letter 1

My dearest Izzy,

All parents are bad parents. This is the first thing I want to tell you. All parents are bad parents, and the sooner you understand this, the easier it's going to be to decide what to do.

I mean, how can we possibly be anything else? Everything we tell you from the day of your birth is such bullshit. We tell you that Mommy and Daddy love each other, that there is a difference between bad and good, and that everything, always, is going to be all right. Then you grow up and find that Mommy and Daddy can't stand each other; that nobody cares if the rich are bad or the poor are good; that most of the world is at war and that everything is in fact looking like it's going to be coming out all, entirely, completely wrong.

We didn't tell you about that part. We didn't tell you that we don't have the faintest idea where we came from, we don't have a clue about why we're here, and as for where we're going, God knows. Except we don't know if there is a God.

See? And so we lie, and therefore, are bad parents.

Right? I'm not arguing with you, Isabel. I don't want you to excuse me, understand me, or sympathize with me. I lied to you, I deceived you about the very fact of who I was, who you were, and then I abandoned you, and all this by the time you were seven. You can't, I think you have to agree, get much worse than that, parent-wise.

The single point that I want to make, in fact, is that *all* parents are bad parents. We in fact *decide,* very early on, to lie. And the fact is, we make that decision because the truth would have been worse.

If you think that's defending myself, fine. You can trash this e-mail and miss your plane, that's your choice. But in fact—in fact, now, whether you believe it or not—the truth would have been worse.

I mean, what the hell were we supposed to tell you? Think about it. *Hey, darling, you know what? After you go to bed, Mommy and Daddy can hardly sit in the same room without starting to fight, bitter fights, where they say horrible things specifically to hurt each other as deeply as they can. And guess what? Chances are 50–50 that you and some lucky man, one day, are going to make each other just that miserable too.*

See what I mean, Isabel? Or how about this:

My dearest girl, bad people are murdering each other horribly from Sierra Leone to Bethlehem, sometimes with machetes, sometimes with guns, and sometimes by torture and starvation. They do it for each other's money, they do it because they don't like what each other believes, and in some places—Ireland, Israel, magical lands over the seas—they do it because they just don't know how to stop.

Then you run off and play with your Legos, right? Right. More likely, after that, you go play with a semiautomatic in a school cafeteria.

Therefore we lie, and we do so because the truth would have been worse.

Isabel. You are all grown up now. Seventeen, and filled with the knowledge of good and evil. I didn't mean to brutalize you with the truth when you were a baby, and I don't mean to brutalize you now, either.

I can see you, as you are now, in this spring of 2006. Here in America it is two in the afternoon, the sun distant behind cloud, the field outside my room turning the palest green in the early spring. Where you are, England, it is evening, 7 P.M., the season already in leaf, the night kind with still, warm air. I imagine you in your dorm room, reading this as you sneak cigarette smoke out the windows—in England, I know, school is still in session, and in England, I know, people still smoke.

What I don't know, but I imagine, is that this e-mail isn't any big surprise to you. You've always known it was coming. June 27, 2006—the date has been in your mind as long as you can remember. You have, I think, long been expecting us to contact you. The Committee, your mother calls us. She's entertained you no end, I'm sure, with stories of what we had to go through to get this to you. Group decisions. Pointless arguments. Criticism–self-criticism sessions. You have been waiting for June 27, 2006, for years, and now that it is only weeks away, you are not surprised, I think, to hear from us, nor are you surprised to hear what we are asking you to do.

I see you by the window, your delicate face illumined by a setting sun, the same sun I see outside my own window, right now, from such a different angle on the planet. You are a slight person, seventeen years old. You are, as you have always been, a denial of both of your parents: my round-nosed, high-cheeked daughter with her nut-brown hair; the olive-skinned, brown-eyed daughter of blond Julia Montgomery. And in each way that you do resemble one parent, you deny the other: the intensely studious daughter of the woman who makes European gossip columns every month; my cynical daughter, although I am, if nothing else, an idealist. What do they call you now, Isabel? The Naught Generation, right? The Millennial Generation. No politics, not even antiwar, no ideals, no drugs. The first generation since I was a child, nearly fifty years, not to use drugs! See, I have not seen you in a long time, Isabel, but I know you.

And I can hear what you're thinking, too. You're thinking, You know me, Dadda? I don't think so. Or better yet, Dadda, I do not think so one bit.

Okay. I admit, maybe it is a little girl's voice that I am remembering. But memory is telling, isn't it? Because I think I understand also that if I want to get Isabel, the young woman, to do what I want her to do, it is still a little girl I have to convince.

Yes, my dear. We *are* going to ask you to do it. We *are* going to ask you to leave one of the nicest places on earth, three weeks from now, and fly to one of the worst. Detroit, Michigan. We are just what your mother says we are: the "Committee," a bunch of balding ex-hippies, at least, I am bald, and I am an ex-hippie. And we are in fact contacting you—and that by e-mail, so as to avoid your grandfather and your mother—to convince you, just as you have always known we were going to, to do something very public, very exposed, and very awful indeed.

We want you, on Sunday, June 25, to escape your grandfather's security, those bodyguards who are there ostensibly to protect Ambassador Montgomery's granddaughter from kidnapping but in fact to keep you from doing exactly what we have contacted you to ask you to do. We want you to take a flight from your picture-book little school for rich kids in England to a maximum-security state prison in Michigan—note the difference—and there to testify at a parole hearing, and in so doing, to commit a horrendous act of betrayal.

I won't blame you for saying no.

And still, I am going to try to convince you to do it.

This is why.

Because while it's true that all parents are bad parents, there is something else true also. That as bad as we were—and we were very, very bad—we were also as good as ever we could be. Given the circumstances of our lives, which were dramatic, and were not circumstances of our making.

And that's the point, Izzy. That's the point. I don't deny that I was a bad parent. I'm not writing to excuse that fact. I'm writing, and so are the others, to tell you why.

We're writing to tell you why, in the summer of 1996, ten years ago, your good, kind, just father, a man widely admired in the picture-book little town where you lived, was revealed to be someone altogether other than who he said. We're writing to tell you how the world he had constructed around you—a kind and just world; a world filled with sun and snow and water; a world of rich colors and high adventure; a world of safe interiors and long, fearless nights—how that world was all revealed to be a lie.

We're writing to ask you to understand that not just your parents, but all parents are bad parents, and we are that because we have no choice.

That one day, you will be a bad parent too.

Okay. That's *why* we're writing. And we all agreed on that. *How* to write, on the other hand, was harder for us. The finer points of how—that required the extended debate that your mother, no doubt, would have found amusing. See, we agreed to tell you the truth. But as to what was the truth, that was not so clear.

First we thought we'd write it together. Billy Cusimano got his computer geek to give us all e-mails on his Web site, so people like Ben and Rebeccah don't have to use their work e-mails, and none of us have to worry too much about confidentiality: apparently Billy—who doesn't quite understand that Cusimano Organics is actually a legal business—uses some pretty far-out encryption. So I get started, write a dozen pages, send them to the Committee. Not ten minutes later, Rebeccah IM's me, that damn little AOL Instant Messenger window popping up on my screen. "This a walk down amnesia lane, Pops? Or are we trying to tell the girl something about what really happened?" Pops, for Christ sake. Then Jeddy chimes in, wondering whether I'm drawing on a Trotskyite historiographical framework, here, because he wants to know how to interpret my blatant falsifications of fact—propaganda or Alzheimer's. Then Ben, always useful, asks if we're trying to get Isabel to help us or to hurt us, 'cause from what I've written so far, it looked like we should *all* be jailed without parole, and soon it's clear that no one is going to agree on anything. Until Molly suggests that we just each take turns, the five, six of us who played direct roles in what happened the summer of 1996.

Here's her plan: we'll each tell you a piece of the story, and then hand it on to the next one, and like that we won't have to agree with each other, but just let you see the whole thing. And furthermore, we each do it alone, so whatever contradictions there might be in our accounts, you can hear them yourself. I'll go first, and when I've done as much as I can in one sitting, I'll e-mail it to you and cc the rest of the Committee, then someone else will take the story a step further. And like that, unless you start blocking our e-mails, little by little, the whole story will come to you, and all you have to do is read.

So everyone agreed to that, and everyone agreed that I had to start, and so the problem then became, Where? The day you were born? The day I was born? The day civil war broke out in Spain? I fretted over that for a good few days of Michigan spring rains. And then I thought, the hell with it, we are telling the truth, aren't we? And trying to tell it in the way it actually happened, aren't we? Well, if that's the case, it all really started in Billy Cusimano's Sea of Green in June 1996, and it is, therefore, with Billy that I am going to start.

2.

Today you know Billy Cusimano as the owner of a national chain of organic supermarkets that he runs from a loft in SoHo, runs with a vengeance: he's paying three college tuitions, and still has one more to come. But in 1996, when I became Billy's lawyer, he was a very different man than he is today.

For one thing, he still had some hair. Not much, but enough for one of those phony little ponytails guys our age wore in those days. For another, he was enormous, with a huge fat belly that stuck out of his T-shirt: at forty-seven, before his first heart attack, Billy had not yet learned it was eat better or die—a phrase, believe it or not, he once tried to adopt as his supermarket's slogan before his advertising firm told him to lose it, and quick. Last, but not least, in 1996 when he became my client, Billy had either not yet had the brilliant idea of opening Cusimano's Organic Markets, or America wasn't ready for them. In either case, he was not a successful and legitimate businessman but a criminal defendant in a federal case. Billy, you could say, came a long way in the past ten years.

Ostensibly, in 1996, he ran a fleet of six small trucks delivering to New York City greenmarkets for a dozen or so Hudson Valley organic farms. In fact, he made his living the way he had since the mid-sixties: by growing pure, hybridized, state-of-the-art marijuana in an underground Sea of Green.

Yes, Isabel, marijuana, a substance to which I'm sure you are an utter stranger, right? Well, as you're going to see throughout this story, I'm emphatically not, so if that shocks you, just think of it as another way I was a bad parent.

Anyway it was from this career path, you may have guessed, that stemmed Billy's need for my services as a lawyer.

There are policy mistakes in the world of criminals, and performance ones. Nine times out of ten, surprisingly, what causes a criminal to be caught is not in fact performance, but policy. Billy's policy mistake happened the autumn before, and consisted of not letting one of his drivers know that under a truckload of sweet corn bound for the Union Square market he was carrying a late summer harvest: thirty kilos of cured, hybridized, hydroponic marijuana, so seedless it could never be reproduced, so resinous that your fingers got dirty rolling a joint, and so strong that a hit had you spending the next three hours staring, ego shattered, at the cat.

The upside of this policy was that the driver could neither rip you off nor turn you in, and besides only cost a fraction of what Billy's real mules—the ones who moved bud across state lines and who knew the risk they were running—got paid.

The downside was that because he knew nothing about his cargo, the driver was smoking a joint while heading downstate at 80 miles an hour, all the while listening, get this, to the Grateful Dead.

Which, in turn, gave the state police probable cause to shovel the entire load of corn onto the side of the road, where the gophers feasted on it for a week. The joint, I mean. Gave them probable cause. Not the Grateful Dead, who, contrary to what people like your grandfather thinks, were still legal.

Now, despite what a bad parent I was and a bad person I am—you need a refresher course on that, Izzy, hop up to London and my ex-father-in-law will be glad to oblige—the fact that I had even taken on a criminal client like Billy may just seem to you like another of the many lousy things I did that summer. In fact, it did look pretty odd to a lot of people at the time. See, James Marshal Grant did not soil his hands by defending criminals. James Grant, it was well known in the little world of Albany law, worked only for principle.

What you have to understand, though, is that in the summer of 1996 my little moral universe was changing pretty radically, and what was changing it was that I had to earn a living. And to understand that, you have to know that when your mother and I got married, it was clearly understood—check with her, Izzy, she won't deny it—that I was going to practice law exclusively in the public interest, given that the Montgomery fortune needed some kind of expiation.

It did make sense at the time: we were in love, and the fortune was enormous. Your mother inherited from her grandfather, as you will inherit from yours, and even at the time of our marriage she was so rich that any thought of doing anything other than public-interest work was absurd.

When I left your mother, of course, I also left the Montgomery fortune. The reputation of the most idealistic lawyer between Miami and Montreal, however, remained mine, as did a full docket of pro bono clients, many of whom had no hope of a decent defense except for my services. On the other hand, your grandfather's lawyers had ensured that I had no income from the family, none at all, despite the fact that I had a little girl to take care of.

Billy Cusimano, in the summer of 1996, therefore looked like a very good client to me: an old hippie with closets full of cash, and in fact he constituted my entire source of income between the winter of 1995, when your mother went into rehab, and the spring of 1996, a year and a half later, when she sued me for custody.

Custody, I mean, of you. Because in the summer of 1996, your mother had just announced her intention of suing me for full custody of our daughter. Bet she didn't tell you that part, Iz, did she? That she was barely out of rehab, and already her father's phalanx of high-powered lawyers were starting to bring legal action against me?

Still, Billy would not be so important to my story if not for the fact that, at the worst moment possible, he got his criminal present all mixed up with his political past.

This was on a June afternoon in, as it happened, Billy's underground Sea of Green itself.

3.

Picture pitch-blackness: an absolutely lightless space, in which the sound of a steady spring rain is hissing endlessly down. It is an all-encompassing noise, and as you listen, you can hear its depth, for it is composed of thousands of tiny little jets of water: When it stops, all of a sudden, the sound that takes its place is that of millions of drops of water falling, dripping, and gathering into little rivulets that, in their turn, run down a distant, hollow storm drain. For a time, the dripping is everything. The air is thick with moisture, nearly tropical, and a loamy smell rises in it. Then, with a sudden electric buzz, a switch is thrown, and a low ceiling of brilliant light floods the room in which a thin concrete border surrounds a lush, thick carpet of tall, lush, glistening cannabis plants, sweating resin, absolutely without seed, hydroponically planted in a sealed basement chamber, blazing with a bank of gro-lights.

For the past three months the room has been sealed, taking in carbon dioxide from canisters, feeding oxygen out into a vent that connects with the furnace burning in the basement, getting twenty-hour days of blazing UV light and four-hour pitch-black nights, all controlled by a computer on a workbench next to the back wall. Juice for the whole thing comes from a Honda generator, off the grid so consumption can't be detected, held in a concrete bunker so it makes no sound. If you must know, gas for the generator is supplied from Billy's fleet of trucks, each of which is always full up when returned for the night to Billy, and somewhat less than full when taken out the next morning, a fact disguised from the drivers by a cunningly altered fuel gauge. Entry is provided by a hole in the bricked ceiling—bricked three layers thick with two layers of insulation, to obviate the possibility of airborne heat detection—through which Billy and I have climbed in for this, the single inspection of the four-month growing cycle, and which will duly be bricked in again when we climb out.

When we came in, I took off my jacket and opened my shirt, sweat breaking out on my chest in the moist air, then sat back in a vinyl string lawn chair, briefcase in lap, at the side of the Sea of Green while Billy pinched off a hairy bud from one of the plants and dried it in a little toaster oven hardwired—like the computer—into a circuit breaker, and rolled it into a joint. Then Billy joined me in the second deck chair, and we passed the J back and forth while I told him where his criminal case was at.

Now, if you wonder how I remember the conversation that ensued so exactly, it's not a mystery. The fact is, virtually the entirety of Billy Cusimano's life was bugged that year—the FBI turned out to know all about the Sea of Green—and virtually every conversation he had—in his car, in his kitchen, in his bed—was recorded. That, for the record, is how Billy was ultimately acquitted: all of the wiretaps were ruled illegal, and made inadmissible the existing evidence. To that extent, the bugs were very useful to us. And they were useful to me again, when I started putting together this story. Which is all by way of saying that my reconstruction, I assure you, is pretty good.

In any case, call it fact or call it fiction, but what you have to picture is the pair of us sitting there and talking to each other, going over business, neither of us with any idea about what was about to happen.

"So, Billy boy, I filed for a continuance Friday; with luck we don't come up again till Sonny Carver's in. If not, fuck Evans, that dickhead. We'll appeal before he's done ruling, and there's not a damn thing he can do. The only immediate risk—immediate, right?—you face is sitting right here under these gro-lights, friend. Sign here."

Signing off on some court documents, Billy answered in one of those tight little voices, holding smoke in his lungs.

"I swear, Jimmy, in three weeks I harvest. This load sells, I'll even be able to afford you."

"Get out of this business, boyo, you won't need me."

"Hey, counselor, I'm not only sending my four kids to Steiner school, I'm sending your Izzy too. So don't be in any hurry getting me out of the game."

It was reasoning that had to make a certain sense to me, I admit. And so, rightly or wrongly, I shrugged off the fact that my client was about to harvest and sell what looked to be twenty keys of marijuana. I drew on the J myself, leafing through some papers, then blew the smoke, a hanging cloud, into the wet air, talking all the while.

"Good God, man, maybe this shit *should* be illegal. It's like you hybridized this poor little plant to produce LSD instead of THC."

That got me a withering look: I was smoking the joint like a cigarette, wastefully, and Billy knew the value of his product. He picked the roach out of my fingers, took a long last hit, and flicked it into the hydroponic bed, exhaling while he spoke. But his pride showed even through his concern. "Know where I'm selling this? California. Hardest market in the country—that's how good it is. And, by the way, why they aren't going to catch me. Last place in the world they'd expect me to be shipping East Coast product."

Then Billy changed the subject, and this—these precise words—was where it all started.

"Hey, Jim? You know who Sharon Solarz is? Or you too young?"

4.

It wasn't the first time that my lives had, so to speak, met. Once I'd run into Jeff Jones in the Albany State building, I taking a deposition from a state senator, he, in his role as environmental lobbyist, on his way to buttonhole another one. He'd looked at me with that piercing eye, and for a moment my heart tumbled. Then he'd walked on. Other things like that happened. I met Bernardine at a conference on juvenile justice. I ran into Brian Flanagan at a bar. I even once sat in the Bedford Hills visiting room with a client while Kathy Boudin was in there with a visitor. It was inevitable.

Still, in retrospect, Billy's voice that day is imbued, for me, with the sense of an augury.

I answered, watching him close, "Yes."

"Yes what?"

That stopped me. "What?"

"Yes, you know who Sharon is? Or yes, you're too young?"

"Both, of course."

For a moment we watched each other in confusion. Then, for a long time, and to my surprise, Billy began to laugh—the easy laugh of the stoned, comfortable, happy, like someone who is used to laughing and someone who is used to being stoned, an infectious laugh that even I could not completely resist. And while he laughed, I understood how to respond. Smiling too, I rose.

"You know, I recognize an exit line when I hear it."

Billy looked up with surprise. "What's that mean?"

"It means, I got enough problems without taking a walk down memory lane with an aging, fat old hippie."

"Jimmy. She needs a lawyer to negotiate her surrender. I—"

But I interrupted, speaking in a voice that quieted Billy down right away. "Billy. Call Lenny Weinglass. Or Michael Kennedy. Or Ron Kuby. Or Gillian Morrealle. Call anyone the fuck you like. But anything you know about Sharon Solarz, keep it away from me."

Billy hesitated, thinking. "Mind telling me why?"

"I do mind, Billy." I looked at him directly, no longer enjoying being stoned. "I mind because I shouldn't have to tell you. Christ sake, you know that Julia's suing me for custody of Izzy."

"Sure." Speaking slowly, as if trying to understand. "I also know Julia was a terrible mother before she got into a drug and alcohol problem as big as the Catskill State Park. And I know you're as good a father and as stand-up a guy as exists in the country. She's not getting custody of anyone."

"Well, it's nice of you to say so, but if you'll pardon me, you're a babe in the fucking woods. You think me being a stand-up guy will counterweigh Julia's father being an ex–U.S. senator and the current ambassador to the Court of St. James? Not to mention that I am supported exclusively by an overweight, unrepentant dope seller, and the Montgomerys have most, if not all, of the money in the world?"

Billy nodded stoned agreement. "I'd say that more or less evens the score. I mean, Julia's shitty history, on one hand; her father's money on the other. I think you're still coming out ahead."

"Okay." Sounding like a lawyer now, I went on. "Now, what do you think it does to that balance if I start defending a cop killer who's been running from the law for twenty-five years?"

There was something cold in Billy's response. "You tell me, counselor."

"With pleasure. It gives Montgomery and his lawyer a public relations boost so massive, I might as well just avoid the trauma and send Izzy off to England today. That's what it does."

"Jim. So you let Sharon twist in the wind? That doesn't sound like you."

"Bill. You're talking about my daughter. You're talking about letting Julia Montgomery raise my daughter. Remember? Julia Montgomery's the one who forgot Izzy in a car overnight while she was smoking crack. On Warren Street. In Hudson. An open *convertible*."

I was kind of shouting at this point. But when Billy didn't answer, I went on in a quieter tone. "Tell Sharon to call Gillian Morrealle at Stockard Dyson, Boston. I'll give Gilly a call. And forget we ever had this conversation, okay? Ever ever ever."

Slowly, laboriously, Billy rose. "Okay, man. If you're sure." But his voice was quiet—disappointed, in a way that actually hurt. Remember, dope wasn't a business for people like Billy Cusimano, it was a political cause—one in a spectrum that included Sharon Solarz. And he was silent while he followed me up the ladder and into the kitchen, then out the kitchen door to where two cars and a truck were parked at the top of a dirt road.

See, Isabel? I can't ever do anything to make myself, in your memory, into a good parent. But I can stop lying. And I can try to ensure that no one else does so, either. If that conversation with Billy had not been tapped by the FBI, everything would have been fine. Sharon would have found a lawyer, I would have defended my custody of you on the grounds of your mother's addiction, and life would have gone on.

But the FBI did listen to that conversation. And on the basis of it, before it was even over, they had gotten a warrant on Billy's premises, and were activating a surveillance plan long since developed. And even worse than that, worst thing of all, they let the story be known outside of their own agency, which meant that, later that night, it would all be told to the press. The press, that is, in the person of one Benjamin Schulberg, a beat reporter at the *Albany Times*, barely older, then, than you are now.

And Benny, as we've all come to expect from him, would proceed neatly and directly to fucking everything—everything—up.

And now I think you see, Isabel, why I started my story, which is your story, that day in the early summer of 1996, when you were seven, in Billy Cusimano's Sea of Green.

Date: Saturday, June 1, 2006
From: "Benjamin Schulberg" <benny@cusimanorganics.com>
To: "Isabel Montgomery" <isabel@exmnster.uk>
CC: maillist: The_Committee
Subject: letter 2

That your daddy, Isabel, still retains the ability to accuse anyone else of messing everything up, I admire him. Larger than life, he and his peers. At least in their capacity for self-delusion.

Next: I understand you to be, now, seventeen. In June of 1996, I would like you to know, I was, despite your father's recollection, twenty-seven. I had been working at the *Albany Times* for three years, was a beat reporter, had a master's in journalism from Northwestern, and was soon going to be offered a Porter Fellowship at Yale. So let's just bear in mind that all parents might be bad parents, but your father, in particular, is also an asshole.

Now then. It seems to be my turn to pick up the thread of this little narrative, so let me clue you in to one important thing: when, on that June day in 1996, your father and Billy Cusimano came out of their little rabbit hole, I was a busy and happy person and had no need of either of them in my productive and useful existence. Or at least, to stick a little closer to the facts—yes, yes, J, I see the irony—I was busy. General Electric was getting their ass sued for dumping a planet worth of dioxides into the Hudson, Empire-Besicort was trying to divert millions of gallons of water out of the Esopus River, and some bozo had come up with a plan to get a few Native Americans to file a federal claim and turn the Rondout Valley watershed into a casino. In 1996 there was plenty of important work in the Hudson Valley, and I didn't know either your father or Billy Cusimano but by reputation, which was just fine with me. My time of innocence, though, was dwindling fast: by the night of June 14

I would be part of this story, and in the weeks to come I would learn more about the pair of them than I had ever wanted to. And one thing I would learn was exactly what happened as they walked out onto Billy's lawn—as exactly, in fact, as if it had been videotaped by hidden surveillance cameras and, later, shown to me.

Which, of course, it was.

I can watch it whenever I want, right here on my computer screen, as I write to you. In the video of the lawn, brilliant spring light is angling in from a pure blue sky. Big clouds are rolling in from the north, throwing a shadow that runs from the peaks of the Blackheads, over North and South Lake, across the valley of the Katterskill and then over the plateau of Platte Clove. On Billy's lawn they stood a couple of minutes, watching the clouds on the wind: two old-timers, too stoned to talk, almost comically various: Billy with his ponytail and massive stomach in an old T-shirt; your father slim, bald, and in a suit and tie.

James Grant, at forty-six. I can freeze the frame and zoom in, close enough to see his eyes, pupils huge with Billy's weed, focusing on distance. It is a clean-shaven face I'm watching, still showing a few freckles, a rounded nose bent remarkably to the left, a funnily winning smile, winning enough to support the fact that his still faintly red hair had thinned to just this side of the vanishing point. Nonetheless, there was still enough of it to make it something of a surprise when you saw his eyes. The freckles, the red hair, the round face and broken nose: clearly, what you had to do with, here, was a mick. The eyes, however, were brown: a big, dark maroon that had nothing Irish in it at all, as if his mother had really been raped by a dago, as he liked to say. In a white shirt, open now to reveal the red hair of his chest, which had not thinned, he stood most of six feet, and while his body did not have much left of the nervous, infectious energy that had characterized James Grant for most of his life, it was beginning to have the slim solidity that was going to be the mark of his middle age.

After a moment, the camera followed him to his car, a Subaru Outback, not new, and after exchanging a few words that the camera didn't pick up, your father drove away.

Billy went back into the house once your father was gone. He emerged some minutes later, accompanied by a dark-haired, middle-aged woman, angular of face and wearing a gray skirt suit. The pair climbed into the remaining car and drove away.

Next, and last, to emerge from the house were two Mexican workers, perhaps a quarter hour later, carrying mason's tools. Presumably they had closed the Sea of Green to finish its growing cycle, and now they cleaned their mason's tools under an outside tap, then climbed into the cab of the truck and in turn drove down the dirt road, leaving the house locked and empty until, in an hour's time, Ruth Cusimano was to return from the Steiner school in Woodstock with her four children.

Or almost empty. Because, after a stage wait, a Greene County Telephone Company van came up the drive and parked.

As such, it was the first of several extremely serious things that were going to happen that night to Billy Cusimano, your father, and by extension, you.

2.

We now know that while your father was driving down the mountain to pick you up from Molly Sackler, who was baby-sitting you; and while Billy Cusimano was driving down the other side of the mountain toward Rosendale with his mystery guest; and while, in fact, Ruth Cusimano was picking up her children from the Steiner school in Woodstock, each and every one of them was being followed by a vehicle containing FBI agents.

We know it, of course, because I, Benjamin Schulberg, beat reporter for the *Albany Times,* spent the rest of that summer of 1996 writing about your father, and how I knew everything I wrote was a subject of some speculation at the time. For what I knew about those FBI agents was very precise indeed—so precise that I could only have known it if the FBI was leaking it all to me while it happened.

Which, oddly enough, they were.

And therefore, I knew that each of the cars following Billy and his friends was reporting to the Greene County Telephone Company van in Billy's driveway, one after the other. The first, following your father, reported that "Bleeding Heart"—your father—"has passed Katterskill

Falls," the second that "Jerry"—the agents weren't blind to the resemblance either—"is on Sixteen," and the third that "Mrs. Garcia is in the school." And I knew that having received these messages, three uniformed telephone workers exited the van, entered the house, and filed directly into the living room, where they began dusting for fingerprints.

In hindsight, it always struck me as kind of funny, though exactly what's funny, in hindsight, only comes clear when you know what was ahead. If you did know, though, you'd have thought it funny that your father wasn't being followed because they were suspicious of him. At that time, although Jim Grant had FBI files, they were only the normal ones that end up being held on folk who tend to bring suit against the government.

That the FBI was following your father tonight, however, was in fact part of an investigation of Billy Cusimano—with whom, you remember, your father insisted on starting this story. Following your father was absolutely pro forma: when a subject's premises are being searched, and the subject is known to have a personal relationship with his lawyer, it's only common sense to keep track of that lawyer during the operation.

And that, in fact, was the story: Billy Cusimano's premises in Tannersville were being searched under a federal sneak-and-peek that afternoon. And when, twenty minutes later, your father had been followed all the way to Molly Sackler's house in Saugerties, and the agents following him heard that the search of Billy's premises was completed, they pulled out of their parking spots in a neighbor's driveway and went back north, their job done.

If this surveillance had nothing to do with your father, however, its consequences were to come to mean a lot to him. It's worth explaining, therefore, a little bit about what we now know to have happened behind the scenes that night, and how I learned about it.

3.

It was a Friday afternoon when your father and Billy met in his Sea of Green and, later, Billy's house was searched. And it was in the very, very early morning of Saturday that my telephone rang at my desk in the *Albany Times*'s newsroom, and I answered.

Calling was a man with a reedy voice and a slightly western accent, the kind upstaters like to assume for no real reason. And what the man said to me was that Sharon Solarz, a federal fugitive of twenty-five years' standing, sought by the FBI and U.S. marshal on charges of accessory to murder, was known to be in the region.

I listened carefully, though with some suspicion. Now, of course, I am a staff writer at *World News New York* and am always being used for government leaks, but in the summer of 1996 Benjamin Schulberg was not yet a household name, incredible though that might seem, and I was not at all sure why I had been chosen for this tip. I listened carefully, but all the while I listened, I was logging the name Sharon Solarz in the *Times*'s electronic archives. While the computer worked, I tried a question.

"What is she doing in the region?"

The voice answered readily. "We think she came to see an old friend."

"Called?"

"Billy Cusimano."

That name was familiar to me, as to anyone who followed the court docket. "The dope dealer? Why?"

"You ever heard of the Brotherhood of Eternal Love?"

"Nope."

"Well, why don't you go find out what it is?"

That pissed me off. "Save me some time, Deep, will you?"

"Why should I?"

I answered conversationally. "Because otherwise I'll hang up and forget whatever bullshit this may be about."

The voice chuckled, then spoke in a singsong. "Let me put it this way. Billy Cusimano and Sharon Solarz are old friends from the Summer of Love in Mendocino. No one knows that but you, boy. Run with it, is my advice."

On my computer screen, hits were coming in on Sharon Solarz, and I read while I kept the guy talking.

"Are you planning to identify yourself?"

"No, sir."

"Okay." I did not have to simulate the boredom in my voice. "Thanks for the tip."

"Mr. Schulberg?"

"Yes?"

"Do me a favor, would you?"

"Sure. If it doesn't take me more than the next five seconds."

"Okay. Inform yourself as to who Sharon Solarz is, would you? Then start doing your job. Dimes to doughnuts says you'll be printing a story about Sharon Solarz tomorrow night, and if you do it right, you'll be out in front of a national story. With me?"

"Um-hmm." I answered as noncommittally as I could. "That was twelve seconds."

The conversation over, I returned to work, a back-page article about the new cement works in Athens. And only toward dawn, when the article was filed and done, and when I had stepped to the window to smoke a cigarette—the newsroom was deserted now—did I think again about the call.

On one hand, it was nearly dawn, and there was no real reason why I couldn't go home and go to bed.

On the other hand, if I went home, there was nothing to do *but* go to bed. And once there, the most likely scenario had it that I would be lying in the dark feeling my heart beat out the nicotine and caffeine I had been feeding it for nearly twenty-four hours, and waiting for dawn, when I could start ingesting more caffeine, and more nicotine, and go back to work.

Until then, of course, I could while away the time thinking about the bills I hadn't paid for months, the exercise I hadn't gotten in years, the laundry I hadn't washed for weeks, and other less important things. The girlfriend, for example, I hadn't found in the year since a certain ex-colleague who had seen fit to share my bed for a time and whom I shall never name to protect her virtue—Dawn Mahoney, late of the Style Section, now resident of Sunnyvale, CA, and, I can tell you, in the phone book—decided that the love of a small-town beat reporter with a penchant for low-profile environmental stories was less important than a new job at the *San Jose Mercury News*.

In her defense, I should say that she only finally dumped me when I turned down a five-figure raise to cover the movie business for them, which would have allowed me to move west with her.

In fact, given the facts, an impartial observer could reasonably conclude that it was I who had in fact put work over love in that situation—a fact that would not be lost on me as I lay in the dark thinking about how much less important the bills, the laundry, the gym would seem if Dawn Mahoney's naked body were next to mine.

Which was why, as was often the case, I shortcut the entire process by simply not stopping working. I went back to my desk, switched screens, and read more carefully through the Nexis yield I had gotten in response to my computer query about Sharon Solarz.

Then, dutifully, I flipped through my Rolodex and placed a call to the Albany FBI duty desk.

Which was the point that this stopped being business as usual.

Twenty minutes later, having been interrogated brutally as to the identity of my source, lied to, threatened, and cajoled, I had agreed with the Albany FBI to withhold my story about Sharon Solarz in return for an exclusive first publication on the manhunt that was going on that night. And the first installment of that exclusive was given to me when, twenty minutes later, in the early dawn of an upstate June, I arrived at FBI headquarters in Albany and was greeted by a black-haired man the size of a refrigerator who introduced himself as Kevin Cornelius, and proceeded to take me into the operations room while explaining the progress of the biggest manhunt New York State had undertaken since the Brinks robbery.

4.

The search papers on Billy's premises had been served at the request of the U.S. Attorney's Office, acting, in turn, on behalf of the FBI. The court had been less than perfectly happy about it. For one thing, Cusimano's case was under the state's jurisdiction, as was his care and feeding. As a felon awaiting trial who had made a $150,000 bond and still didn't seem to be going begging, there was enough reason to keep an active monitoring in progress, the judge saw that, but they didn't need the federal court to authorize a sneak-and-peek for that.

What did fall under federal jurisdiction was the fact that the FBI was requesting license to search at discretion and take fingerprints on other evidence altogether: evidence that was gathered during the state's surveillance but was immaterial to the state's specific prosecution of Billy Cusimano on marijuana charges. In other words, the FBI wanted to investigate Billy's house for a federal crime that had nothing to do with the state's drug charges. The crime was harboring a federal fugitive.

This evidence was moreover very scant: a woman had arrived at Billy Cusimano's house the night before, and left somewhat after Jim Grant's visit. During a conversation between Cusimano and Grant, the name of Sharon Solarz had been mentioned. On those grounds, the FBI teams surveilling Cusimano and his associates requested and received from a federal judge based in Syracuse permission to take fingerprints from the house. While they did so, they in addition followed the woman, traveling in Billy's car, to Rosendale and observed that Billy dropped her off at the summer house of a New Yorker, currently unoccupied. She had, they observed, known where to find the key.

Now, who was this woman, and why did she need to meet with a dope grower and his lawyer? This was the question Kevin Cornelius set about to answer that afternoon after your father left Billy Cusimano's house. First, he eliminated known prints belonging to Billy, his wife, his four children, his maid, his lawyer, and his lawyer's daughter, who was a frequent visitor. The five remaining latents he sent to West Virginia, which would in turn notify relevant field offices of any hits. Seattle, Washington, was, some hours later, the surprised beneficiary. Four were unknown. But they believed a thumb partial to be that of a resident of Port Angeles, Washington, who had been arrested and fingerprinted during the Seattle protest against the WTO. The duty officer in Seattle, in turn, called in a favor from the state police, who—a neat symmetry, I thought—used contacts in local law enforcement to identify the woman as a quite recent arrival in town, a new hire at a small Internet advertising company, who was said to have left on a car trip some days previous.

From here, it was all very simple: you want to learn about anyone in Port Angeles, go to the single café and wait for the first chilly, lonely local to come in and start to chat. By six o'clock that evening, Kevin Cornelius had a social security number, and was running it through what was known as the "array"—a series of different electronic sources that included databases as banal as Nexis and PACER Legal and extended to the Internal Revenue Service and, literally, thousands of medical records storages.

As always, the array gave out a lot of garbage: minority percentile hits, doubles, self-contradictions, errors. Thousands of databases relying on tens of thousands of input sources had been visited. Cornelius, in this as in all investigations, used more art than craft. What he noticed was not the garbage but the fact that one of the few 90-percent-or-over hits was the IRS, which reported that the social had no other trace and was less than six months old.

That didn't necessarily mean anything—social security numbers are not terribly reliable. But Cornelius knew that by the FBI's own analysis, it was a datapoint that had been shown to be over 65 percent reliable in the identification of fugitives.

And therefore Cornelius was more than interested enough to start assembling a full surveillance routine on the house in Rosendale. No known fingerprints existed of Sharon Solarz. But if they could find grounds for probable cause, they could stop her and question her. This, in fact, was what they planned to do.

The record is crystal clear. Albany field office logged Seattle's call at 6 P.M. and notified Special Agent Cornelius immediately. Surveillance on the Rosendale home, which was found to belong to a New York City labor lawyer and his psychologist wife, was quadrupled by nine. By morning parabolic listening devices had been put on the kitchen windows, and the telephone had been redirected through an FBI switchboard. The woman spent the entire day inside, talking to no one. At

5 P.M. she got in her car and drove northeast, apparently returning to Cusimano's. When, however, she bypassed Billy's and headed up toward 23, agents began to have doubts, and a roadblock was set up on the Catskill Thruway entrance. She stopped for an hour in Catskill, talking on pay phones, but due to her frequent changes of telephone, no reliable trace could be set up. She could, however, be digitally photographed, the image sent back to the office and computer enhanced, by means of comparison with photographs taken in the early seventies, before Sharon Solarz went underground, to remove the effects of aging. These results, Kevin Cornelius felt, were unambiguous. And therefore, when she went for the Thruway, which was of course the road to Canada, the roadblock was deployed, and at eight o'clock that evening Sharon Solarz was quietly, smoothly—and, Cornelius noted with satisfaction, in time for the *Times*'s deadline—arrested from twenty-five years as a federal fugitive.

And I, who had by now been along for the ride since the night before, wrote the story.

Now, I have just to add one more detail, Isabel, and I think we can consider the scene appropriately set—even to your father's satisfaction—for what we have to tell you.

And that detail is this. When finally Sharon Solarz had been read her rights, formally arrested and handcuffed, taken to Albany, and booked, she was then offered a chance to write and sign a full confession.

And when she declined that opportunity, she was at last permitted to contact her lawyer.

The lawyer she called was, per her instructions from Billy, Gillian Morrealle, a criminal defense lawyer at the Boston firm of Stockard, Dyson, Freeh and Kerry; one who had made something of a specialty of representing supposed "political" criminals, many from the sixties and seventies.

There was nothing private about the call. It was overheard by the guards attending this high-profile prisoner, it was taped, and it was reported, verbatim, to Kevin Cornelius and, through him, to me.

What she said, was, "Ms. Morrealle? My name is Sharon Solarz. Jim Grant told me to be in touch with you."

And now I think you see why, Izzy, I was suddenly, and deeply, curious. I hope you see why. And I think you see why. Because I know how smart you are, which is very, very smart indeed. Smart enough to understand that suddenly, this stopped being Sharon Solarz's story, or Billy Cusimano's, and became, in fact, your father's.

Date:	Saturday, June 3, 2006
From:	**"Daddy" <littlej@cusimanorganics.com>**
To:	**"Isabel Montgomery" <isabel@exmnster.uk>**
CC:	maillist: The_Committee
Subject:	letter 3

It's good to know some things never change. Benjamino, for instance. His little account of how he got involved in all this, it got to me this morning around one, and if I didn't know it was impossible, I'd swear that the e-mail smelled of bourbon, no matter that little Benny's supposed to have given up drinking years ago.

But I promised Molly I wasn't going to get pissed off. I understand that everyone on this story experienced it from their own point of view. That some of those points of view reveal the excessive intake of alcohol and a warped sense of history, that need not detain us. I mean, I haven't the slightest doubt that you read right beyond little Benny's nonsense and understood how deeply, how profoundly, he had let himself be manipulated.

Right, Izzy? I mean, you know your grandfather. Does it make sense to you?

In any case, that Saturday, June 15, 1996, was a big day for a lot of people in this story. And my movements during the day would later come under some serious scrutiny. At the time, however, the only thing remarkable was the perfection of the spring morning, a blue sky empty but for wisps of fading night clouds, the silence of a sleeping neighborhood inhabiting our little corner of Saugerties like the dew hung in the air. In that silence, in your bed by the light-flooded window, you slept.

Izzy. Do you know, all your childhood, I kept buying the newest video cameras available, and never once did I take a film? I'd lie in bed at night berating myself—your childhood was fleeing, and I was letting it go. But

I could not make myself even try to capture it, and each new camera would go, like the one before, unused. What it was, I'd have a vision of myself watching those films at eighty, and I didn't think I could bear it. Love and loss, for so long, the two had been inextricable to me. How could I stand to look, then, at what I could barely face now: the beauty of this tiny being who had taught me everything I knew about love and who, with each second of her life, was vanishing before my eyes? And yet now, after all these years, I find that it doesn't matter whether I filmed it or not, because we lose our children not once but over and over again. That loss, I can feel it now, yesterday, tomorrow, every minute, and I promise you, I do.

Shit. I swore I wasn't going to say this sort of thing to you. But I swear to you, now, sitting here, I can see every inch of that house I have not been in for ten years, just as it was that morning. I can feel the early silence of the suburban street, the chill spring air moist with the dew from the lawn, the shafts of light through the kitchen windows with their stained oak and bull's-eye molding. Your room. Your room, which I visit in dreams. The sun flooding through the blue Dr. Seuss curtains Molly gave us when we moved in, the curtains moving in the breeze, your body supine, so perfectly relaxed, arms around your head and head in a pillow of brown hair.

I can see you, waking in the silent room, opening your brown eyes into the morning light and, after a moment of recollection, sitting up on the side of the bed and delivering yourself of a wild, arms-akimbo stretch. Isabel Miriam Grant, seven years old in the spring of 1996. Your face, which was very round and distinguished by Julia's cheekbones, was of enormous vivacity; your eyes, huge and intense. You had, in fact, a particularly American type of baby-boom beauty, the union of the regularity of your mother's long-standing American features, which had participated only in British and Protestant bloodlines since the 1600s, and your father's European irregularity, a long Mediterranean gene line, also protected by community, at least 500 years back to Spain. You had what is called a "rosebud" mouth, full lips always pursed, but the speed and intensity with which you talked mitigated against its roundness, for you had to tighten its corners in order to get out all the words you wanted as quickly as possible—in this, too, you showed both of your parents, both of whom were, in their ways, primarily verbal people. Your hair, also brown, fell far down your back, and already you had the tic of brushing it out of your eyes.

I can close my eyes and see you. Quickly you registered what was going on in the house—the early morning, your father still asleep. Then, moving silently and with determination, you dressed in bell-bottoms, a tank top tight over your still baby-round stomach, sandals. Perhaps you came to my room, watched me sleeping for a moment. But you did not wake me. For the fact was, what awaited you in your father's house on a Saturday morning was a bowl of granola and a book, whereas if you could get out the front door without waking me and across the lawn to Molly's, you would be able to avail yourself of a wide-screen color TV with satellite service, eggs and bacon, and possibly even a little time with your hero, Molly's son Leo, in the event that Leo had both gotten home from his night's adventures and not yet gone to bed.

So, with the faultless egocentricity of a seven-year-old, you beat a quiet retreat and, still in your bare feet, ran lightly over the lawns to Molly's house.

I only woke, that Saturday morning, when the sun slipped over the eave of the roof and cast light over my face. Then I, in turn, finding your room empty, went out the front door in my bare feet and across the lawns to the next-door house. Here, I found Molly sitting on the front steps, smoking and reading the paper, while inside the screen door you were watching Pokémon. Without a word, I corrected both of these infractions: first I entered the house to turn off the TV, kiss you, and serve myself coffee. I came out the door again, removed Molly's cigarette from her hands, and threw it into the bushes. Then I leaned back against the doorjamb with my coffee.

"Godammit, Moll. Leo's going to get you hooked again."

Molly did not look up, and her black bangs, reaching to her big glasses, made her face, from this angle, impregnable to me. As for you, you had by now wandered outside and sat down next to her on the steps, regarding her open paper with curiosity, the pair of you united in your absolute lack of interest in me. Silence reigned while I drank my coffee, watching the two women in my life, then you, entirely disregarding the fact that you had willfully disobeyed me and been caught, asked, "Dadda, who's George Bush?"

"He's a governor, doll. From Texas."

"Why does he have thirty-five million dollars?"

"Well, he wants to be the next president. After Clinton's turn is up."

"Is he good or bad?"

"Well, not so good. No better than he has to be."

You thought about this for a moment. "Moll likes him."

"Really?" I carried my coffee to the stairs, steering an exaggerated path around the pack of cigarettes sitting on the top step, then sat down so you were between me and Molly. "I don't believe that, darling. Bush is a criminal maniac bozo. Molly's way too smart not to know that."

"Iz." Molly spoke from behind her newspaper, her low voice without emotion.

"Yup?"

"I like Bush just fine and plan to vote for him so he can become our next president, which he'll do very well. Lots and lots of people agree with me, win or lose."

Now she lowered the paper to reveal a round face behind owlish glasses. "See, you don't have to hate your opponent in this country, you just vote for the person you think best. That's called democracy, which people like Jimbo here don't understand so good."

"Democracy's just another word for nothing left to lose." Lifting the paper out of Molly's hand to read the front page, I sang the words, absently. "W's an out-and-out Reagan Republican, Molly Wolly my dear. That means he's a radical and an activist. Ideological radicalism, judicial activism, the heart of the Bush regime. And you know it."

"No, J. *You're* the one around here who *knows* things."

The silence that followed, you observed with interest, turning from one to the other. Then you stood between us and stretched your body, a perfect curve, like a comma with a belly, and when you were done, lowered your arms around my neck.

"Be a gladdy daddy, not a saddy daddy."

I hitched you into my lap with one arm around your waist, letting my face go into your hair. For a long moment, I sat like that. Then I shifted.

"So, what's the plan, Stan? Let's hit the road and feel the wind in our hair."

"And where are we going?" Molly, too, was watching now.

"Well, I just got to drop some paper off at the courthouse in Albany. You all stay here, get packed up, then I thought we could camp up in the Blackheads. Spend the night, hike out, go to Colgate Lake in the morning? It's going to be perfect weather."

"Dad-ee. You said you weren't going to work today."

"Just a delivery, doll, up to Albany. Won't take an hour. Moll?"

Molly was hesitating—seriously hesitating, because everyone always wanted to go into the woods with me due to the fact that I knew them like almost nobody, anymore, knew the Catskills, even many of the old-timers. Yet another fruit of the moneyed life, was what I told people, having the time to explore the woods, but in fact there were spots I used to take you to that probably hadn't been visited since, well, since my father took me when I was your age. Not just dinky little spots, either: waterfalls, scooped-out rock baths in mountain streams, pine groves, ginseng hollows, caves. Old Charlie Thorpe up to Haines Falls used to look at me sideways and say that I had Esopus Indian blood in my veins. I don't believe he meant it as a compliment.

But finally Molly shook her head. "Not me, guys. Not while Leo's here. I'll meet you at Colgate Lake in the morning."

She meant that while her son, Leo, who had just finished marine corps flight training and was about to be posted to Italy, was staying, she was too scared to leave the house at night, and in fact, I knew she was too scared to go to sleep, too.

"Well, doll." This was me, to you. "Just you and me, then. I nip up to Albany, come back down, go camping."

You looked at Molly as if for permission. And she, in turn, shrugged.

"So I baby-sit till you get back?"

"You mind?"

"I don't mind. If Iz doesn't."

A look passed between you and Molly in which I read the following exchange: TV? TV. Then you turned back.

"Oh, okey-dokey. *Baddy* Daddy."

More TV. I hated to give in. But I had something to do.

2.

Later on, a lot would be made of what I did that trip to Albany. Some of it was known, and some—well, there were folk who had me more or less plotting the World Trade Center attacks, that day, even though the attacks and all that followed on them were still five years off. In fact, there was a time when some of the main evidence for jailing me was to do with that trip to Albany. So for the record, let me tell you exactly what I did when I met you that Saturday morning.

First, I packed a Sportsac bag with clothes and toiletries—mostly yours—as well as some books and a few little toys. Then I threw it in the trunk of the car and drove up to Albany. When I got there, I went to a Mailboxes Etcetera downtown and bought a large cardboard box, some packing tape, and some labels. I packed the bag of clothes in the box, then addressed it to John Herman, care of General Delivery, Clayton, NY 13624—Clayton being a town on the St. Lawrence River, just across from Canada. I did not need to look up the zip code, having done so long before.

I took the box then into the store and express-Mailed it, paying by credit card. Then I went and bought a tank of gas with the same credit card.

Later, that would look like a serious mistake.

When I'd finished that, I left back down the Thruway for home.

And that's all, Izzy. Later, they tried to say I met with people from Fidel Castro to Saddam Hussein, communed with the ghost of Timothy McVeigh, and joined the Taliban. But nobody ever proved that I did anything other than what I just told you, and they never will.

And in fact, not three hours after I finished, you and I were parking at the trailhead to the Dutcher Notch trail, then hiking in on the trail to where, finally, I led you down through thick growth, bushwhacking a good half mile in from any known trail, ignoring your complaints and looking forward to your gasps of surprise when, as you soon did, you emerged onto a pool in the little stream that flows down Thomas Cole Mountain.

3.

While you marveled at this perfectly formed, and perfectly secret, swimming hole, I pitched a tent and unrolled the sleeping bag. After I'd uncovered a fireplace, hidden under leaves since the last time I was here, I settled you down with a book and a bottle of water, changed into my gym shorts and a pair of well-used trail-running shoes, and then, giving you one of two Motorola shortwave receivers, set out for a run while there was still enough light.

This was a well-known routine for us: you, who had grown up in the woods, were unafraid of holding down the fort for the hour of my run, and I, like many single parents—and I had been, to all intents and purposes, a single parent for your entire life—knew how to find the time I needed for myself within the context of the things we did together. This, the six-mile round trip to Dutcher Notch, was a very familiar one to me—believe me, I run it again and again in my imagination, these days, now that I cannot run it for real—and for the first mile or so I ran easily, thoughtlessly, watching the long afternoon shadows play in the little pools of thin light, all under the vast green canopy of the woods, shifting in the breeze. And only after a mile, as if my mind had moved backward through the events of the past couple days, searching for purchase, did I arrive back at my conversation in Billy Cusimano's Sea of Green, and my anxiety come back.

Sharon Solarz, Christ. How that fucking name came up. It seemed like people got a thrill out of just saying it. There were other names like that. Bernardine Dohrn. H. Rap Brown. Mimi Lurie. When ex-Movement people gathered—and in the Catskills, not unlike the French and their heroes of the Resistance, everyone over fifty was ex-Movement—it was only a matter of time till one of those names came up.

But now—I cannot tell you how emphatically now was not, repeat not, the time for Sharon Solarz's sexy name to enter my life. Should I have seen how suspicious it was? I'm not sure. The fact is, it had been just a few days earlier that Norman Rosen had called to say that his firm had been retained by Ambassador Montgomery concerning the matter of Isabel Grant, aged seven, the single child of the fifteen-year union between James Grant and Julia Montgomery.

That had shocked me into silence, which, Benny will tell you, isn't that common an event. Your grandfather and I, I thought, understood each other: for the two years I'd had you since Julia went back to England, it had been clearly understood that our relationship was governed by a kind of nuclear parity. I, for my part, did not tell anyone that Julia was a hopeless drug addict and a criminally negligent mother. He, for his part, left me alone with you.

Now, incredibly, Norm Rosen was telling me that Julia was no longer content with the original divorce settlement, which allowed her unlimited access to her child as long as she was willing to come back to America from London, where she had gone to rehab under her father's care after I left her.

Finally, I got my voice back. "Norman, come off it, will you? She can see her daughter whenever she wants."

"She's seen her twice in the past year, Jim." He had one of those phony western accents upstaters like to affect, and a reedy, annoying voice—see what I mean about Benny's manipulation by your grandfather?

"That's because she's been too whacked out of her gourd to come to America."

"That was then. This is now."

"So now that she's clean and sober, she's decided that taking away my house, income, and reputation weren't enough? She wants my daughter, too?"

"Her daughter, counselor."

"Norm." I couldn't believe he knew what he was saying. But then, I couldn't know how much your grandfather had actually told him, could

I? Nor did I know, then, that Norm was Benny's anonymous tipster, putting Ben on my tail in the first place. So I temporized. "The only positive thing Julia ever did for her daughter was take her shopping at Anna Sui rather than Donna Karan. Or was it the other way round? There is no way I'm letting this child leave the country."

His answer told me that your grandfather had told him a lot. Perhaps all. "Jim? You know what I'd do if I were you? I'd listen real carefully. You fight this, we're taking you to the *show*. You understand what I'm saying?"

Okay, I admit, it is hard to shut me up. This did it. For a couple seconds, I was like a fish out of water, gasping for air. Then I said, as carefully as I could: "Norm, I thought that Senator Montgomery was looking to be named ambassador to the Court of St. James in the next Democratic administration."

"No, sir." He answered without a beat. "Not looking. Planning on it. Better get used to something new, counselor. You don't have any more standing in the senator's plans. That's all over."

"And how exactly did that end?" I wasn't being sarcastic. It was a real request for information. And in the pleasure that came into Norm's thin little voice when he answered, you could understand why, despite his lifelong liberalism, your grandfather had chosen Fratelli and Rosen, house lawyers for George Pataki, who hated me only slightly less than they hated abortion rights activists—though slightly more than they hated the ACLU—to represent him in the matter of his granddaughter's custody.

"I should have been a little more precise, Mr., uh, Grant. It hasn't quite ended yet. But, counselor, there is no doubt at all that it's over by the end of the week."

At the time, a discouraging statement, I think you agree.

At the edge of the field, the trail dipped right into the woods, and I passed into shadow and onto an uphill at the same time, an uphill that broke my heart each time I did it, long and even and steepening over perhaps three-quarters of a mile. As always, as I worked into the first pain of the run, my thoughts darkened; as always, I failed to note the connection. Rather, panting hard toward my second wind and breaking into a sweat, I thought I was looking at the question before me with calm, reasonable, and experienced legal eyes, the eyes I'd been using all week, trying to figure out what Norm had been talking about.

Because, Isabel, you are a grown-up person now, and you know as well as I that when I sent her to England, your mother had had a drug and alcohol problem the size of a house. You do know, right? You know that she had virtually abandoned your upbringing, and let her compulsion for white powders take over her life, filling the space her dwindling career left empty. She had let you spend a night in an open convertible on the main street of Hudson, while she very, very nearly overdosed on smack in a dealer's apartment. And once—just once, the last time she saw you until her first exercise of supervised visitation rights after rehabbing in London—she hit you, hard enough to leave you with the little scar you have on the bottom right of your chin.

See, all that was true. And all the time it was going on, your grandfather and I had, each time, nursed your mother out of whatever kind of strung-out horrors she was going through; covered the trails of her crimes; called in favors from cops and judges; and ensured that no one knew. See? My father-in-law, at the time, was my partner in trying to save my wife, your mother, his daughter, whom we all adored. And it was only after a week when I thought she was clean but she had, fooling me completely, been snorting a stash of coke she had hidden in the pool house, she ran out, and got strung out, and while strung out hit you in the chin with her fist, that I drove her to Kennedy airport and left her at British Airways, and then, before I could be kicked out of the Woodstock house, took you down to our new house in Saugerties.

At the time, it was very clear.

I said nothing to anyone about Julia. I let Senator Montgomery keep his career; he let me keep my daughter.

Except that now, he had found a way to take both, and leave me with nothing.

I crossed Fresh Kill, the grade evened, and I let my step loosen, and lengthen, into the slow downhill past Beaver Pond: I was, now, sinking into the little hollow formed by Stoppel Point, to the east, and Thomas

Cole, to the north: properly a "clove," but one that had not been named. An easy mile of downhill. I increased my speed, enough to keep up my respiratory rate, but not too much to negotiate the long mud puddles as the sodden ground let up its water, which converted the trails into runoffs. While I ran, I checked on you on the Motorola, then got back into a careful rhythm: if I knew nothing else, I knew I could not, right now, afford a fall.

So what was I to do, Isabel? Was I to let you go live with your mother? How were you to understand, at your age, that your mother was abusive and addicted? Should I have told you that Julia was an unfit mother because she let you watch too much TV? She should be denied custody because she fed you junk food? None of that meant anything, nor would it mean anything if I told you the truth, which was that I would not give you over to your mother because your mother, simply, did not know how to love, and had never known how to love, and if knowing how to fuck was a fair enough way to hide that fact from her husband, for a while anyway, it just wouldn't do for a child. Especially a fiendishly verbal, precociously observant, and prematurely cynical child, who had been hit and left out in cars and whose only hope in the world was to be loved and loved well all the days of her childhood and on beyond too.

And it was in this spiraling suite of thoughts that I arrived at the big expanse of what the local kids from Tannersville and Hunter call Strawberry Field, and paused.

From here, the run's steepest uphill did the last mile to Dutcher Notch, a grueling uphill in which steady climbs were interrupted by hills so steep as to seem a personal insult. At the edge of my vital capacity—I had failed to pace myself, for being lost in defeatist thoughts—I leaned over, hands on knees, panting hard. If I was going to abbreviate the run—six miles was nothing to be ashamed of—this was the time. But then, I never abbreviated my run; only when a muscle was in real danger of injury, real enough to keep me from running again. And so I turned and pushed up, taking my respiration into rarefied territories.

For a time, accelerating my heart into the uphill, my mind was clear, the first thought to articulate itself being simply to ask, Where the fuck was the notch? The trail was mounting alongside a true moonshine gully, a mountain stream running a deep, thickly wooded gash in the forest, typical of the vast Appalachian range of which the Catskills were four hundred miles south of the northern edge in Canada and the Tennessee Cumberlands were a thousand miles north of the southern edge in Alabama. Unlike the Cumberlands, the Catskills had never been still country—vast, now exhausted supplies of hemlock had served a local tanning industry and kept the locals out of the moonshine business. Now, however, both gave serious shares to the marijuana breadbasket, with Tennessee quoting pot as its biggest cash crop. And the same exact qualities that made these woods so apt to hide marijuana made this trail a heartbreaking run. Until I at last came to a stop, bending over and spitting, at Dutcher Notch, I did not think at all. Not, in fact, till I had started again, with abandoned speed, down the path.

What did it mean, Norm's call? And how was I to respond? Izzy, I was a lawyer. My job was to go to court and oppose my will to that of others. I argued for what I felt was right, publicly, without protection. Often I did it at great personal risk. Some thought that I was, for this reason, a hero. No one mistook me, however, for a gentleman. You're not required to be a gentleman to defend the Constitution, because whatever else the law is, it's a dirty business, and like it or not, it's appropriate for a lawyer to be properly dirty too.

Now, running the downhill from Dutcher Notch, I asked myself, how ungentlemanly could I be to retain custody of my daughter? My ammunition, remember, was good. I could prove your mother's every affair in a Woodstock summer house, her every episode of steroid psychosis caused by self-medicating for cocaine-induced sinus polyposis, her every miserable meth-induced bedroom tantrum, and her every failed attempt to detox at the Lucy Freeland Clinic in Saratoga Springs. I could prove her two abortions of planned pregnancies that unexpectedly turned out to interfere with acting roles. I could, moreover, prove that all of this, which involved several serious run-ins with the police, had been effectively concealed by the ex–U.S. senator, Julia's father. And I could leave Bobby Montgomery waiting for his next incarnation before he got into politics again.

No—Rosen was bluffing. Evening out into the long, gentle downhill back to the campsite, I concluded again: Rosen was bluffing. The stakes were too high for Bobby. It was a nice try, but the stakes were simply too high.

And I found you—as if proving my reassurance—lying happily in the tent with Bun Bun, your stuffed rabbit, singing a song and kicking your legs, on which, through the nylon roof, trees nodding above cast lazily shifting shadows.

4.

As the afternoon lengthened, the two of us—as you used to say—"hop-rocked" up the stream to where a waterfall dropped down a mossy face in the rock perhaps thirty feet high, me throwing handfuls of dirt or sticks in front of you to scare away any rattlers that may have come down thc mountain looking for water. So infrequent were visitors here that we saw two snapping turtles clatter away with their always surprising speed and, when we returned to camp, scared a hawk into flying off with a half-eaten chipmunk in his claws.

Having repossessed the campsite from the hawk, we ate dinner, watching the thin fall of water into the shaded pool—already, that year, the rivers were low, and later that summer there would be some severe drought. I had packed artichokes, chicken salad, Bread Alone bread, iced tea. And slowly, the air turned grainy and the evening fell softly down.

Well before dark, I led you back down the river to the little pool, washed your hands and face in the icy water while you sang variations on the Pete Seeger song Molly'd been playing to you that day:

Here's to England
Here's to France
Here's to Leo's crazy rants
And here's to the lovely Izzy Grant's
Brand new purple un-der pants

We climbed back up to the tent; I changed you into pajamas and a sweatshirt, then watched you brush the hair around the soft curves of your face, your cheeks, your massive brown eyes with their endless lashes. Changing into pajamas, your little body's perfect balance on bare feet was as enticing, as perfect as a wild animal, and I watched you with enchantment, with fascination, in the silence of evening's fall, as if all the forest were hushing for you. The sun was setting, and next to the little fire I sat cross-legged with you in my lap while I read you a book. Then I cajoled you inside the tent, and you lay, watching through the tent's star window the wind moving the leaves above in the thickening grain of the dusk while I sang you the real Pete Seeger song.

Here's to Cheshire
Here's to cheese
Here's to the pears and the apple trees
And here's to the lovely straw-berries
Ding dang dong go the wedding bells

At last, heavy on my arm, your hair creeping along my shirtsleeve, while I watched your face in the dim light from the tent's star window, in that hour of pure silence in the woods when the sun first goes down before the nocturnal sounds come out, you fell asleep.

And did I think, that night, how much I would one day give to see that sight before my eyes? Did I think of the absolute unrepeatability of what was before me, a vision of a single nexus of so many confluent paths of change—the fall of the evening, the turn of the seasons, your steady climb out of childhood, my steady growth through middle age—an intersection of so many things that would never appear again in the same way, ever again, in all the millions of years of our species' life?

You may say that beauty is everywhere, Isabel. But never before, and never again in this life, have I ever seen anything as beautiful as my sleeping daughter. You slept, and for that long first hour of darkness, when the night animals wake and the woods, as if worshiping the moon, come out of their sunset hush, I watched you.

And for perhaps the single last time of my life, watching you that night, Izzy—the ten years to come until I sat down to write you this—I felt peace.

Date: June 4, 2006
From: "Molly Sackler" <Molly@cusimanorganics.com>
To: "Isabel Montgomery" <isabel@exmnster.uk>
CC: maillist: The_Committee
Subject: letter 4

Izzy, because I couldn't go camping with you, it was I who got the news of the Solarz arrest first, very early that Sunday morning.

This is because, while you were sleeping that night in your tent with J, I was sitting up, waiting for my son to come home.

And while I was waiting, I was beating the delivery boy by reading the paper on the Web.

Just like insomniacs do all over the world.

You know my whole story now, my love. You know that in 1996 I only had my son, and that by the barest of luck. My husband never even knew he'd gotten me pregnant during a one-week leave in Okinawa, a few weeks before he was killed in Vietnam. By the time Leo was a megabyte of cells big, Donny was dead in the jungle at Songbe. Then the war ended.

You know what they told me once? They told me that the Vietcong firing squad that executed him, it had only three members over fifteen.

Don't ask how old Donny was.

J and you came to me just when Leo followed his daddy into the marines, and as I think you know, Izzy, you stepped into a place in my heart as empty as a tomb. Aviation Guarantee. For God's sake. Grown men promise an eighteen-year-old that if he enlists, they'll guarantee him flight training. Just what they did to Donny. What the hell *can't* you get an eighteen-year-old to do after you promise to let him fly supersonic jets? Donny they baited and switched, forcing him into CID, Criminal Investigations, which is how he got captured. At least Leo, they kept their word. Now it's 2006 and I'm still up all night, with the single damn difference that now I sit around with hot flashes watching the webcasts of Greater Persia, where Leo's commanding a stratospheric firefight, rather than waking up barfing with morning sickness and listening to the news from Nam. Oh, and in between? In between was me, sitting up all night, reading the Web to see that Leo hasn't wrapped his damn car around a tree in Woodstock during his leave in that damn, damn summer of '96.

Alright. The hell with it, I'm up all night right now, too, reading your daddy's version of that Saturday night in 1996, the night Sharon Solarz was arrested while you two camped out on the Dutcher Notch trail, and I can watch Frank Smyth reporting from Baghdad in a window on my screen all the while I write this, as I promised your father I'd do, so let's get it done. I am Molly Sackler. I took care of you for the couple years between the time your dad left your mother and the spring of 1996, and I hoped I was going to take care of you the rest of your life, but it didn't happen that way. And this whole thing, it might be the way your father and his friends try to talk you into going to testify at the parole hearing, but for me, it's just a way of explaining to you that I love you as much as if you were really mine, Izzy, and I love your father too.

You were too young to know it, by all rights we were an unlikely pair of friends. Your father a lefty lawyer married to one of the most glamorous residents of Woodstock. Me the principal at Mount Marion Elementary, a resident of the wrong side of decidedly unglamorous Saugerties, the widow of a marines intelligence officer perished in Vietnam, and get this, a *Republican*. The fact is, Donny Sackler, my late husband: when we were kids, he would sooner have taken a baseball bat to your father than speak to him. And as for me, in those days, makeup and bouffant hair and get this, an actual cheerleader, as far as your daddy was concerned, I could have been from Mars.

Now, 1996, we sat out our evenings on the upstairs porch like two aging sweethearts, and even the two-three shouting matches we once had about the war never made as much difference as the fact that once, we both lost everything that meant anything to Vietnam. Just like thousands and thousands of other Americans. And at the time, of course, I was about the only one who knew exactly how much your father had lost, and how dearly he had paid for it.

We had met in '94 when you were five and J represented Mount Marion Elementary in our strike against the state regents over our refusal to use state-mandated pass-fail criteria. I had adamantly opposed your dad's selection as attorney until it turned out that no one else would take the case on for free. And because we had to work together so much during the trial, I didn't have to admit that I liked being with this person who was so abhorrent to my every principle. When it turned out we both were training for the Albany Marathon, however, we started running together, and there wasn't much business excuse for that.

Now, I didn't know it then, but Julia was around less and less, in '94, and your daddy was taking care of you more and more, and in fact, the time we were spending together made up most of his life outside working and taking care of his daughter. In fact I knew nearly nothing about him: so little that I had no conception of how he lived. I mean, I knew who Julia Montgomery was about as good as any other *People* magazine reader, but I hadn't ever really put together how *rich* they were.

I found out because we used to run a trail your daddy knew on private land up to Meades, just outside Woodstock, and one day when we had pushed on an extra mile we emerged suddenly in what looked to me to be an endless expanse of mowed pasture, in the middle of which sat a sprawling ranch house. When I realized it was his, and in fact, the whole trail we'd been running on went with it, I couldn't help myself.

"Jim, my God, you *own* this."

He shrugged. "I don't own anything. I'm just the token Jew here."

Though I guess he was enjoying my shock, because he took me in and gave me the tour: a living room as big as the auditorium in Mount Marion Elementary, a sunken couch area, a wall of windows looking out over the mountains to the north. Huge bedrooms decorated in Arts and Crafts, no reproductions. A swimming pool in a glass geodesic dome. Then he explained that Julia had inherited from her maternal grandfather, and was in fact richer in her own right than her father—as well as far more willing to spend the money.

I may as well tell you, seeing we're all friends here, that I remember that day not just because it was the only time I was ever in Julia Montgomery's house, but for a couple of other reasons, too.

One was because, in the tour of the house, we unexpectedly came upon you, Izzy, in your room, playing on your bed while a baby-sitter sat reading a magazine, and when you saw him, I swear, I don't think you even touched ground on your way into his arms. And your father is surprised, but he pretends not to be and asks where Julia is in this offhand voice. The baby-sitter answers, without even looking at him, that Julia had gone out. What time? Nine o'clock, which you had to figure was right after your father left for work. A silence greeted that. Then your father told the baby-sitter she could go; he'd stay home now. "I'll need pay for the whole day, mister," was the baby-sitter's response.

The second reason was because watching your father with you that day was when I fell in love with him, because as you know, that's what happened. He had a gift with you, and let me tell you, as a teacher, I have been watching parents screw their children up for a long, long time. Watching him, this man who could not have been more different from me and my husband, I found myself thinking: This is how Donny would have been with Leo, Leo whom Donny never met. And that was the first time I felt desire for him.

So we became friends. Either out running or, as Julia started disappearing for longer or longer periods, hanging out down at my house—I didn't want to visit his place again, nor did he invite me to. And then, one day when you were perhaps six, we're sitting at my kitchen table rehydrating from a run and Leo, who has just finished basic training and is waiting assignment to flight school, is practicing dives into the swimming pool, and I hear a sound precisely like an underinflated basketball slapping a concrete surface, and thank God your father had been lifting weights for ten years because Leo is on the floor of the pool in a cloud of red and he didn't wake up until J had hauled him right out, 170 pounds of inert adolescent, and started CPR. He swears to me, he can still taste that blend of blood and chlorine in his mouth, these many years later.

Know what? When someone saves your child's life, you don't need any more excuse to be friends. And so I made the first friend of my life who wasn't a Republican, and your daddy made the first friend of his life who was. Not the second, not the third. The first. And in fact, it was kind of a kick hanging out with him in front of various Saugerties dignitaries, who tended to congregate together depending on whether they'd been at Woodstock or Khe Sanh, or rather, whether or not they remembered which was which.

I may as well tell you, Izzy, now that you are a big girl, that although he insisted on keeping his own house, and making sure you didn't see, because he thought it would confuse you, your father and I had become lovers by the spring of 1996. And I may as well tell you, also, that before he ever got into my bed, your father told me everything there was to know about him, all of his secrets, and I believed in him then, and I believe in him now.

And if I have to say it explicitly, then I will: that's why I'm writing. Because I think you should believe in him too.

2.

Alright. It is the summer of 1996, I live in the little clapboard house next to yours in Saugerties, which in fact I'd found for your father as soon as he left Julia. It was a change from what you were used to, my love, believe me. But in retrospect, it does seem that you should have been there all along rather than Julia's Woodstock. I, for one, am convinced that you got something richer down there than you ever had up to Woodstock with the Montgomery money, and I like to think that I had something to do with that.

So this had been my routine since early that summer Leo had come home from his first tour in the marines. Wait for him to wake up in the afternoon, sit and talk with him through dinner, then lend him the car to go out with his high school friends, and then, the high point of my day, wait for the 4 A.M. update of the paper on the Web so I could check the police blotter for car crashes and arrests. After that, a luxurious two hours of sleep before you came over in the morning, little ray of sunshine that you were.

Christ. Leo had been around the world with the service by then. He had been in "combat" in the Persian Gulf, where he had served as private first class in a reconnaissance unit. Then he became a pilot and after that a strat commander. But nothing he had done then or was to do afterward terrified me quite as much as what he could get up to with his old high school buddies in Saugerties, or Catskill, or Hudson: depressed and hopeless places, rife with liquor, drugs, and guns. But of course there was nothing I could do or say, and so I had long resigned myself to sitting up all night, my stomach clenched with anxiety, waiting for the morning paper to be posted and listening to WDST Woodstock.

Sharon Solarz. I remember the very layout of that computer screen. Once I had assured myself that by the *Albany Times'* electronic deadline my son had neither been killed nor maimed nor shot nor robbed nor arrested—so far that night at least—I clicked back to the Solarz story and read it through: during the period Sharon had been famous, I had been the young wife of an active-duty marine, and the politics of the antiwar movement had been very alive to me. There was a vivid account of the manhunt and arrest, and I was by no means blind to the fact that it all started in Billy Cusimano's house, where, the paper reported, Solarz had come hoping to connect with a lawyer to negotiate her surrender. I remember that vividly, because I remember thinking, Christ, her life must be awful for her to prefer a decade in jail. Then I read the summary of Sharon's career: SDS member in Chicago, founding member of Weatherman, underground after the town house bombing, arrested briefly on explosives charges after Weather broke up in '75, then jumped bail and underground again as part of the MDB—Marion Delgado Brigade—and not seen again until the Bank of Michigan robbery. She was named by Vincent Dellesandro, the only person arrested after the crime, who also named, in addition to Solarz, the other two members of the MDB: Mimi Lurie and Jason Sinai.

That Dellesandro, whom the article implied had been, rather than a revolutionary, a crazy homicidal vet, had named his partners was no surprise. There was some suspicion that later, one of the three fugitives had given Dellesandro up, shocked by his willingness to shoot during the holdup. After all, there had been no proven casualties in any Weatherman action, although other Weather-inspired groups had not been as skillful, and three Weather members had been killed in the town house bombing. When he was arrested, apparently, Dellesandro claimed he'd been working undercover for the FBI all along. For all anyone knew, this might have been true. But before being tried for Bank of Michigan, he was extradited to New York to face prior charges and killed during the Attica uprising—strangely, because the article pointed out that surviving inmates told the ACLU that Dellesandro had been nowhere near the actual violence.

The paper concluded by observing that with Solarz's arrest, Mimi Lurie and Jason Sinai were the last two fugitives from the Vietnam era remaining at large, which was also untrue. A where-are-they-now sidebar listed, as they always do on such occasions, a roundup of ex-fugitives. This time they got Katherine Power, Bernardine Dohrn, Patty Hearst Shaw, and Silas Trim Bissell, of whom only one had actually been in the Weather Underground at all.

It was dawn when I got through this, and the dim light through the window washed the computer screen of colors. That struck me as appropriate to the black-and-white newspaper archive images on the screen. Those people, in the days when I had a husband in Vietnam, my blood had heated every time I'd seen their images. And now, for God's sake, peering across twenty-five years from my computer screen, I found that they looked so vivid to me: real people, not these strange, ugly, shaved-headed, pierced and tattooed kids of today in their big baggy clothes—real people who might have believed in the wrong thing, but who at least believed in *something*.

And I guess I was lost in thought, because I found myself at the kitchen cabinet by the window, now, and with a mental maneuver that was growing all too familiar, I managed to open a drawer, extract a Marlboro, and light it without quite admitting to myself that I was doing anything other than looking out the window, down the driveway, watching for my son's headlights. The smoke hit the back of my throat with an intimate familiarity. Mother's milk. J was quite right. I was hooked again, through and through.

And it was then, at that thought, that the meaning of the reference to Sharon having come looking for a lawyer at Billy Cusimano's house struck me, though the coincidence with the first wave of nicotine electrifying my brain, disguised, to some extent, the shock.

Not so much, however, that I was not able to pronounce, out loud: "Oh, my God, he's talking about J."

And then I said, louder, again: "For God's sake. It must have been Montgomery himself who had that one leaked."

And I thought, if this damnable paper keeps this up, they might as well buy you a one-way flight to London, Izzy, because you were never, ever coming back.

Now I've gone this far, so let me finish off what happened, that Sunday morning, and then let me get back to the webcast because there is a State of the Union address in half an hour, and whether my son stays in Kabul or comes back home depends on what our fine president has to say. In this respect, let me tell you, no matter how big a decision you have to make next week, you may bear in mind, there are bigger things happening still. Far bigger.

By the time Leo got home and bestowed on me a boozy kiss before ushering a woman who appeared to be all of sixteen up to his bedroom, it was way too late to go to bed. So I put on a swimsuit and drove down to Woodstock to get muffins at Bread Alone, then up the mountain to Colgate Lake to meet you and your daddy, and to tell J the news.

But I was too late. By then, your father and you had hiked out of the woods, changed into bathing suits, driven the quarter mile or so to Colgate Lake, and settled down on the grass, where I found J lying on a blanket, deep asleep, and you involved in a mudcastle-in-progress group project by the water's edge.

It was a perfect Catskill morning. A perfectly cloudless Sunday, wind softly blowing, late lilacs in bloom. Already the grassy beach at the lake was filling with its particular summer mix: weekend New Yorkers, Jewish and Italian; all kinds of Eastern Europeans from the Ukrainian and Latvian resorts up Platte Clove; canoes going into the water, and dogs, and children. Sharon Solarz would have to wait: I wasn't taking this sleep away from J. So I lay back next to your daddy, the sun on the front of my body and the warmth of his skin on the side, and let the murmur of mixed voices and languages around us lull me to sleep. Russian in the group of pretty young girls next to us. A dog's feet padding by, water shaking on my thigh from its fur on its chest. A voice in a canoe, far out on the lake, calling to another. Next to us, two couples with New York accents were talking in what sounded, to me, like middle-aged friendship. And what they were discussing was the arrest of Sharon Solarz, the night before, in Rosendale, of all places.

And your daddy must have heard too, because when I turned my head on my neck to look at him, his eyes were wide open, staring at the sky. The air, suddenly, was thick with heat. Quickly now, I looked over at the group talking next to us, then back to your dad, studying the afterimage against the pink of the sun through my eyelids.

It was a fifty-something foursome, two sets of parents up from the city, and now three of them were listening with interest as the fourth, lying on the grass with the *Albany Times,* gave a summation of the article, pausing after each sentence for discussion. He read next that it appeared that Solarz may have been in the area seeking to make a negotiated surrender. At this one of the wives snorted. That was the way they always did it, said the other woman, this one apparently a lawyer herself—a surrender would mitigate in favor of the defendant, so they always went for the arrest rather than the surrender, in order to get the harshest sentence they could. None of them seemed to have any doubt who "they" were.

Your daddy and I listened. What next? Eventually, someone would say that Sharon to some degree deserved what she was getting: this wasn't a Weatherman bombing, where only property was destroyed, but an actual armed robbery in which a guard was killed. And someone else would say that Sharon—they would all use her first name—Sharon's only crime was having anything to do with Vinnie Dellesandro. And from there someone was sure to say how they knew Billy and Bernardine, only they knew them under their fugitive identities when they lived on the Upper West Side; or someone would say how they had dropped blotter acid with Susan Stern out in Seattle, or Chicago, or recently seen a letter from Jeff Jones in the *New York Times*, or had a friend who had a friend who had a friend who knew David Gilbert . . . A lulling, gentle conversation, four middle-aged ex-hippies discussing the familiar, comforting righteousness of their youths, of menace to no one.

Except us.

Because instead of the thousand things I could have predicted these guys would say, they said the one thing they shouldn't have.

". . . says here she was coming to consult a lawyer in Saugerties."

"Lawyer? In Saugerties? What kind of lawyer would practice in Saugerties?"

"Hey, babe, that's where Jim Grant is. Must have been him. Who else could it be? The local bankruptcy lawyer?"

By now, little adrenaline shots were running through my whole body and, I knew, your daddy's too. We didn't move, of course, and in time the foursome waddled off to the water, and we sat up.

First, your daddy made a big show of looking at his watch. Then he glanced over at the paper they had left lying with their towels and books. The paper was open to the Solarz coverage, and he pulled it over and we looked together. The byline was Ben Schulberg.

Now this Schulberg character, I was relieved to see, had not actually named your dad. That was because what he was talking about was an actionable offence: in New York State, concealing information on the whereabouts of a known felon was tantamount to being an accessory in that felon's crime—and this felon, Sharon Solarz, was wanted for murder, which has no statute of limitations. If Schulberg had actually named your father, then the police would have been waiting at his door when we got home.

But that was the only good news, that he had not been named. Everything else was disastrous.

J pushed the paper back and, still without a word, looked at me.

And suddenly, as if a gray ceiling had moved in over the sky and a sodden rain begun to fall, it was not such a perfect Catskill Sunday anymore.

Date: June 5, 2006
From: "Benjamin Schulberg" <Benny@cusimanorganics.com>
To: "Isabel Montgomery" <isabel@exminster.uk>
CC: maillist: The_Committee
Subject: letter 5

And while, at Colgate Lake on Sunday morning, your father was realizing how very, very right he had been not even to discuss Sharon Solarz with his client, Billy Cusimano, and how, nonetheless, very, very little help that was going to give him now, I, up in Albany, was starting in on what was to be twenty-four hours of uninterrupted work.

Now, on this matter, let me say this: What else is new? Right? Working a night, a day, then a night again—this did not in any way indicate any interest whatsoever in your father, or Sharon Solarz, or Billy Cusimano, or the Tet Offensive, or Earth Day, or Birkenstocks, or marijuana—well, I was interested in marijuana, but that had nothing to do with these bozos. This was merely the kind of work expected of junior staff at the *Times*.

The only difference, in fact, was the actual content of my work that Sunday and Sunday night. Lately, if it was happening in a town bigger than 200 and involved something more controversial than a farm animal, it went to someone else, which gives you an idea both of my status at my place of employ that summer and of the newsworthiness my editor ascribed to the Sharon Solarz story. Now I had not only been taken off my regular beat to spend a few days researching three in-depth stories on the meaning of the Solarz arrest, but had actually been ordered to read up on the very particular history that had started three decades ago and ended with Sharon Solarz being arrested the night before.

• • •

I wasn't working enthusiastically. My bargain-basement status at the paper was due to a fresh graduate from Columbia J School having just been hired, and given preference for anything I might have gotten otherwise. And then, the fact is, I am not so big on research, if you want to know the truth, Isabel, though if you happen to be at the National Press Club, if you don't mind not mentioning this, that would be fine. What I had going for me as a journalist was primarily luck, and secondarily a gift.

See, people like to talk to me. Why, I can't tell you. Rebeccah says that it's because I'm so foolish looking, and God knows she's right about that—I am too tall, and too thin, and the main reason my face inspires confidence is because it is incapable of inspiring fear. But the fact is, you put me in a room, or at a bar, or on a checkout line at a supermarket, and I'll come back and tell you the most intimate details about the person nearest to me. It's not skill, exactly. In fact, it's nearly politeness: I have to listen, because I can't stop people from telling me things.

But let me not be modest. In 1996 I was a beat reporter, and I went out and got subjects to talk, and although it seemed to them as if it was just by chance that I happened to be there and they happened to be baring their souls, everything they had to say—everything relevant, that is—was in the paper the next day. And—at least before the eminent graduate of Columbia J School came to do a better job than I—the halls of power in Albany, New York, were filled with people who wished they had never met me or that, when they met me, they had kept their mouths shut tight.

When, therefore, my editor, Richard Harmon, told me to spend a few days researching who Sharon Solarz was and what she had done, I experienced an instant regret at having gotten involved in the story in the first place. The hell with that geek who called me with his anonymous tip, was my feeling. What I said to my editor, however, was:

"Rick, they're about to put a generator in Saugerties that's like to raise the ambient temperature of the Esopus enough to kill the entire trout population. Let me get to that, will you? You're wasting me on some ancient hippie history."

It was not a good choice of words. For one thing, my editor promptly made a mental note—at least I believe he did—to assign the J school graduate to write on the ambient temperature of the Esopus, which he'd known nothing about till I mentioned it. For another, however, my editor, at fifty-five, defined himself precisely by the time that I had called "ancient history," in particular by the reporting he'd done in Saigon when his father edited the *Times*. And, like a lot of people around Albany at the time, in 1996 Harmon was already looking toward Kathy Boudin's 2001 parole date, and planned to use every chance he got to keep the Weather Underground in the negative glare of publicity.

But lastly, and most importantly, Rick knew something that I, as it turned out, was too young to know: that an important portion of the paper's demographic—forty-five to sixty—would read anything connected to the antiwar movement, which, for or against, had played a central role in their lives, and that stories of the last radical fugitives always sold issues. So and therefore, in the face of my disagreement, Rick let a moment of thought play behind his gray eyes, and then inquired politely whether or not I actually wanted my job, because if I didn't, there were plenty of others who did. To my shock and embarrassment, he used not one, but two four-letter expletives in this sentence, both beginning with an *f*. Nonetheless, I took the man at his word, and seriously entertained the issue, to no small effect. For in fact, a few moments later, it emerged from our conversation that yes, I did want the job, at least enough to sit there quietly, agreeing with a man whose sole qualification to do his job was having inherited the goddamn business from his father, who was also an idiot. In brief, having enthusiastically agreed to research the Sharon Solarz story, I left my editor's office and returned to my desk, vowing to go to business school, build up a multinational communications empire, buy the paper, and fire his ass.

But only briefly. Some of Harmon's sources were so old that I couldn't even get them on Nexis, and I had to go for the first time in my career to find actual printed sources in the document morgue. By the time I returned, sneezing, the question that most bothered me was how I was going to stay awake through the research.

But in the event, this particular history I was learning that night, it turned out not to leave much room for sleep at all.

For one thing, it didn't seem at all like it would be on the final, you know? I mean, I know how they teach this stuff in American schools: a week on civil rights, a week on Vietnam, then wham! it's Watergate, and everything's alright again. Jowly old Nixon humiliated on a global scale, the system has "self-corrected," and democracy is safe. Never mind that there's not a damn thing Nixon did that everyone else hadn't done before, and hasn't done since—in which, oddly enough, his story and Clinton's have a lot in common. Maybe it's different at Dothegirl's Hall, wherever the hell it is you are. I hope the Brits are honest enough to teach Vietnam in the context of the cold war, are they? You know the word COINTELPRO? Or do they give it to you as part of the history of imperialism, pardon me, the Great Days of Colonialism?

But this stuff I was reading now, no way I had learned a word of it in school, and I became very interested, very quickly. Not only because it was about the fairly recent past, but also because it was filled with sex, which I'm for; drugs, a couple of which I'd tried; and rock and roll, which was invariably spectacular. And the fact that while I'd worked that night, I'd been listening on my always-on computer feed from WMVY to the Beatles, Hendrix, Dusty Springfield, Joe Cocker, Joni Mitchell, and wall-to-wall Dylan—precisely the music that the subjects of my research had listened to while conducting their failed revolution—was by no means lost on me.

So in the event, I had had no trouble at all spending the night smoking, drinking coffee, and learning the history Rick Harmon had sentenced me to.

2.

I started with a group called Weatherman—a little group of middle-class white kids who, during the Vietnam War, tried to play a leadership role in the antiwar and civil rights movements.

You with me, Isabel? Listen—if you aren't, then do me a favor: do a little Web search, will you please? Get a sense of what I'm talking about, then come back—take you ten minutes. See, if I try to teach you too much history, the Committee gets pissed off—they say I'll lose your attention.

Because, when you come right down to it, if you're going to make a real decision about what you're going to do later this month, you'd better understand what the issues are. What exactly your father did in the summer of 1996. And when. And to understand that, you have to go back another twenty-five years and more to the summers of the early 1960s.

What you have to understand is that up until the war in Vietnam, for the first time in history, there were more people under twenty-one in America than over. This was the famous baby boom. And this overflow level of young people, of which the whites grew up in towns and cities where there was plenty of money and plenty of fun, created a generation of kids who thought anything was possible. It was a happy time in America, and although it's pretty hard for you all, who consider cynicism the only proper response to any politics, to understand today, these kids actually took the ideals of American democracy seriously.

When these clean-cut types like Eisenhower and Kennedy came up on their TVs and said they were building the greatest, fairest, richest society in human history, these kids believed it.

And when they found out that Eisenhower, and Kennedy, and Johnson, and all those great men were lying to them—lying deliberately and with premeditation—they were pissed.

Really pissed. Pissed like only disappointed children can be when they realize that despite everything they've been told all their lives, their parents are not good parents, but bad parents.

You see what I mean?

Take SDS. The main political organizing group of young people working for civil rights in the early sixties and, a little later, organizing to oppose the war. Know what SDS stood for? Students for a Democratic Society. You see? Not Students for a Violent Marxist-Leninist Revolution; not Students for Undermining the American Way of Life with Sex and Drugs and Long Hair; not Students for Glorifying Charles Manson and Eldridge Cleaver. Bizarre, right? All that demonstrating, fighting—at one point Nixon called it a "civil war." But what were they actually demonstrating for? When you think of it, they already existed in a democratic society.

And that's my point: at the beginning, all that this great movement of American youth was asking for was for the adults around them to make good on the promises that had been made to them all their lives—on TV, in commercials, in their public schools. All they were doing was asking the adults around them to put their money where their mouths were, and be the good parents they had always said they were.

But it's like your father told you, isn't it? All parents are bad parents, and as the sixties went on, a lot of young folk began to wake up to the fact that American Democracy wasn't happening the way that had been promised. No one denies this, Izzy, left or right: the long march from McCarthy to Watergate proved to everyone in the country that somewhere the idea of democracy and the idea of government had diverged, if they had ever been what they said they were. Let's just look at one simple, easy fact that I learned that night in 1996: the Voting Rights Act was passed in 1965. Think of it, Izzy: it took until 1965, a century after the Civil War, for the government to enforce the constitutional right of all Americans to vote. Imagine how you'd feel if in England today, say, Parliament had to be forced, by popular and often violent protest, to guarantee the right of Arab citizens to vote. Think you'd be going to class and studying calculus so you can go to university? I don't think so. I think you'd be at Piccadilly Circus right now getting your ass arrested in a protest.

Now imagine this. Imagine that you were also being told that when you turned eighteen, if you weren't in college and you weren't sick, you could kiss your ass good-bye because the government had the right to force you—to *force* you—to go to this little country in Southeast Asia and shoot ferocious big bullets into people who, likewise, were going to shoot ferocious big bullets into you. And you weren't allowed to raise your hand and say, uh, Mr. Kennedy, or Mr. Johnson, or Mr. Nixon—two Democrats and one Republican, note—I wish to be excused from this part because I didn't volunteer for any army, I don't want to kill anyone, and I sure as hell don't want to be one of the 58,000 of us who are about to be killed in Vietnam—*58,000 Americans*. Be excused? Fuck you, kid. And if you're not white, then fuck you twice, because when you turn eighteen, you are going to be cannon fodder.

Now, relax. I'm not going to go on in this vein. All I want to tell you is that this massive group of organized young folk developed during the sixties, SDS, and some of the biggest hearts and best minds of the times put everything they believed into it. They gave up school, they gave up careers, they were arrested and they were beaten, and you know what? The more they went on, and the more they grew, the greater the number of people all over the country and all over the world who came to agree with them. Don't make any mistake, Isabel: the opposition to the war in Vietnam was massive in this country, and all sorts of people were in it, from mainstream television newsmen like Walter Cronkite to big-time athletes like Muhammad Ali to Martin Luther King to white middle-class Americans all over this country. Americans wanted out of this war. You ask people if they went to Vietnam to fight communism, know what they'll tell you? Nine times out of ten, the reason Americans went to Vietnam is because of the company they kept: their friends were going, and they weren't going to sleaze out of what they saw to be their responsibility. But you come right down to it, they didn't want to fight, they didn't want to win, and they sure as hell didn't want to kill.

But you know what? Pay attention now, Isabel, 'cause this is the kicker, and if you don't get this, you won't get anything, and then all these bozos'll have wasted their time sending you e-mails. The bigger the opposition grew, you know what? This odd thing happened: the war didn't get any *smaller*, it got *bigger*. They didn't send *less* soldiers in, they sent *more*. And the government didn't get more *responsive* but more *oppressive*. In fact, as they declassify the papers of Nixon's secretary of state, Henry Kissinger, we learn even today that they had used the same tactics against the anti-war activists that they used against Communists, only worse, in a big FBI program called COINTELPRO—the counterintelligence program—and most of what they did was so illegal that one president, Nixon, was actually, for the first time in American history, kicked out of office for it!

Isabel, I'll tell you. I was twenty-seven in 1996, and I was a reasonably well-informed person, but I swear to you, when I went into this stuff, I couldn't believe it. A couple times that night I actually called my father and asked him if this was all true. Which amused him no end, I can tell you.

Anyway, to cut to the chase—and to get your daddy to stop instant-messengering me mean notes asking me why I'm taking so long on this:

by the end of the sixties, when SDS had not only failed to diminish the level of racism in our country and failed to stop the war, but to the contrary, three different presidential administrations had increased the legal and illegal pressures on American blacks and escalated the war into outright illegal and secret activities—once again, Isabel, I'm not (as you can imagine) giving you any lefty line here, just the facts, on which everyone, including the people who ran the war, agrees—a group of people in SDS start growing, shall we say, impatient. And fueled by a whole lot of speed, and helped by Black Panthers kicking the shit out of selected members of the opposition—who knows, maybe they deserved it—a gang of four took over the organization and renamed it Weatherman, from a line from a Dylan song.

Maggie comes fleet foot
Face full of black soot
Talkin' that the heat put
Plants in the bed but
The phone's tapped anyway
Maggie says that many say
They must bust in early May
Orders from the D.A.
Look out kid
Don't matter what you did
Walk on your tip toes
Don't try "No Doz"
Better stay away from those
That carry around a fire hose
Keep a clean nose
Watch the plain clothes
You don't need a weather man
To know which way the wind blows

That's where they got the name. Dylan, to these guys—and quite a few other guys—was God. But, as a man called Shin'ya Ono put it, it turned out that a lot of people felt you *did* need a weatherman after all:

> The whites in this country are insulated from the world revolution and the Third World liberation struggles because of their access to, and acceptance of, blood-soaked white-skin privileges. In large measure, this insulation from the struggle holds true for the radicals in the movement. The whole point of the Weatherman politics is to break down this insulation, to bring the war home, to make the coming revolution real.

He went on to say,

> I am confident . . . that in the near future . . . [Weatherman] will come to occupy a widely recognized position as the revolutionary vanguard of the entire movement in the white mother country.

Well, he was wrong about that, of course. There was to be no revolution, and no vanguard, and as for how people on the left saw Weatherman then, and how they see them today, Ono could no more have guessed that than he could have guessed that his cousin Yoko was going to marry John Lennon or that, before all the Weather fugitives would have even surfaced, Lennon would be shot dead on a street in Manhattan and everything anyone had ever hoped for in the days—everything good, everything hopeful, everything peaceful—would be ruined, and no one would ever try to change the world again.

Now. That's some of what I had learned that night, and I'm already in trouble for telling you this much. But because this is, my dear, the history that defines you, and I highly doubt you have ever heard it before—because of this, I am going to go on a little more, and let me inform the Committee here, including your own father, who have abrogated to themselves the right to dictate what I say, that they can go to hell: I'm the big-time journalist now, and I think Isabel wants to hear what I'm saying, and I think she's paying attention, and therefore I am going to go on, for a few more minutes anyway.

It's not easy to talk politely on the subject of Weatherman. For one thing, there's a lot I've agreed not to tell anyone, and if you want to know it, you'll have to find out from someone other than me. What you need to know about Weather was that one of the major differences between SDS and Weather was that SDS was a resolutely anti-Communist organization, whereas Weather was essentially Marxist-Leninist. This made a massive difference. It meant for example that the same army that executed Donny Sackler, Molly's husband, in Vietnam in 1972 hosted our little buddies from Weather on several occasions in several countries. As did Fidel Castro, and several heads of Soviet satellites during the cold war.

You hear what I'm saying? That makes them a properly treasonous organization. And there's a lot else you can say about them. Like, for example, the fact that because a Marxist-Leninist revolution has also to be a revolution within, Weatherman lived in collectives, with a centralized leadership so strong that they could order couples apart and together, homosexual, heterosexual, whatever. A great innovation, right? Destroy monogamy, all that? Add that to things like their criticism–self-criticism sessions, in which they ganged up on each other and tore each other's livers out, and the "acid tests" for loyalty—self-explanatory, no?—and the fact that some of them were and indeed are highly manipulative people who, like so many on the left, are pretty convinced they have a monopoly on what's right, well, you have a portrait of the American Weatherman Revolutionary. Bunch of pricks, for the most part.

Charles Manson, for example, was a big hero to them for a while—fucking college kids praising the murderers, for fuck's sake, who buried forks in the pregnant stomach of Sharon Tate. Talk about *épater les bourgeoises*.

But it wasn't all attitude. No one knows exactly how many actions they were responsible for, though it's clear that they bombed dozens of government and corporate targets across the country, including the Pentagon. And there were other things they did, such as the thing my anonymous tipster referred to: in 1970 the Weather Underground was contacted by the organization called, if you will pardon me, the Brotherhood of Eternal Love. The Brotherhood was a network of marijuana growers and smugglers out in northern California, and what they wanted—and were prepared to pay for—was to have one of their heroes, a man called Timothy Leary, broken out of jail.

Do I need to explain to you who Timothy Leary was? I hope not. What I will tell you, though, because for some reason very few people know about it, is that Weather succeeded in removing Dr. Leary from jail and spiriting him all the way to Algeria. True, it was a minimum-security jail. Nonetheless, to remove a convicted felon from the possession of the law and take him out of the country to freedom—and that not as insiders with government connections, but from the platform of being sought-after fugitives themselves—you can, Isabel, say a lot about the Weather Underground organization, but you can't deny that they did what they did, and they did not, in general, get caught.

What they're best known for, however, was not what they did to others, but what they did to themselves. In March 1970 three members of Weather, building a bomb in the basement of a house at 18 West Eleventh Street, crossed the wires of a timing device and blew themselves into pieces so small that one of them was identified only by the print of a single surviving finger. Ted Gold, Terry Robbins, Diana Oughton, none over twenty years old. You can see it now, next time you go to New York: just west of Fifth Avenue on the south side of Eleventh Street, the only new house on the block. See, the old one was leveled.

In the aftermath of the bombing, some thirty of the group, most of whom faced various conspiracy charges, using carefully prepared false identities—identities prepared long in advance—disappeared in a way that hadn't been used since the forties, when the Communist Party formed an underground. And from then until the end of the Vietnam War in 1975, they evaded capture and, far from retreating from that unsuccessful experience of bomb building, built dozens more, blowing up governmental and military targets all over the country.

See? And do you understand, now, why the history lesson? I mean, yes: this was a bunch of spoiled little kids, just like they say in all the papers; they were babyish, cruel, and violent. But what I need you to see is that when Sharon Solarz first went underground in 1970, passions were running pretty high. And from a distance, those passions seem a little ridiculous, but I swear to you, they weren't ridiculous then, and they hadn't died down much by 1996, when all these things happened that were going to change your life. Just think of, say, Molly Sackler watching Sharon get arrested. Molly, when Sharon first went underground, was sending her husband to his first tour in Vietnam.

These aren't passions that die down, Iz; they were high then, and they're high now. Most of the people who lived for and were defined by that history are still alive, and lots of others will bear the scars well into this century. Leo Sackler, for example. Or Rebeccah Osborne.

And—and this is the point I am trying to make—you.

Okay. Your father is filling my screen with instant messages, and I do believe the telephone ringing is him calling to yell at me—the caller ID says it's a Michigan number, anyway, so just to be on the safe side, I'm not going to answer. But let me tie it up. When the town house blew up, Weather held a big meeting out in northern California and adopted a couple of ground rules, of which the main one was: No human targets. It was not unanimous, but the peaceniks won, and for the rest of their career together as Weather proper, as far as anyone knows, they were successful in bombing only property, with never a casualty, often through great effort. Hardliners twice formed splinter groups. The most famous, after the war was over and Weather was done, formed a group called the May 19th Collective, and went on to infamy in the early eighties, when some of them participated in a famous robbery of a Brinks truck in which two policemen and a guard were killed. Of the participants in the Brinks robbery, all but one are still in jail today, June 2006, twenty-five years later. But it is the other group we're interested in here. The other split off before the end of the war—in 1974, to be precise—and formed the Marion Delgado Brigade. And the MDB achieved fame when, in 1974, they robbed a bank in Ann Arbor, Michigan, and killed a guard.

The Bank of Michigan robbery was led by a career criminal called

Vincent Dellesandro, and included the three ex-Weatherman members. And while Vinnie was caught soon after the robbery, extradited to New York, where he was wanted on prior charges of murder, and killed in the Attica riot, the three Weather members, who were living as fugitives at the time in any case, all succeeded in evading capture; succeeded so well that in the summer of 1996, when virtually every single other Weather fugitive had either been caught or surrendered, they remained at large.

The first two were called Jason Sinai and Mimi Lurie.

The third was Sharon Solarz.

I'm finished now. And I'll go back to the job I've been assigned by the Committee. Where was I? Oh yes, at dawn. June 16, 1996. Armed with the knowledge, now, of who Sharon Solarz was and why anyone cared, I turned off my desk lamp, powered down my computer, rose, and with a massive stretch, knocked over my desk lamp. Then I sat down again.

It had been an interesting night. So much to learn. So much to write. And if I had started out pretty unwilling, now I was fairly convinced that I had fallen upon a chance to do a series of articles that would show my elders and betters a great deal about who Benjamino Schulberg was and what Benjamino Schulberg could do.

And yet I was not planning on starting writing. Not just yet.

First I was planning, as I now did, to sit back in my chair, drawing on an unlit cigarette, and think about what it was that was so bothering me about this story, not in the past, but in the present.

3.

So, I knew who Billy Cusimano was, to some extent. I knew that Billy had settled down in Tannersville in the eighties to begin screwing up the genome of the marijuana plant—at one time he owned an electron microscope and employed a botany postdoc out of SUNY Albany. As to where he came from before that, well, that Sharon Solarz, founding member of Weatherman, had come to see Billy Cusimano, was pretty good stuff, in my journalistic opinion. You with me? It was a good hint that Billy, maybe, had roots in that common ground between the Brotherhood of Eternal Love and the Weather Underground. And it suggested that Sharon had been involved in the Timothy Leary escape, too, and even that perhaps Billy had been a source of the money, which for all I knew could still lead to criminal charges. Was there a statute of limitations on jailbreak from a federal prison? "Note to self," I thought to myself, and laughed heartily. Then I went back to work, which meant, under the circumstances, that I stopped laughing and closed my eyes again.

What else was in this fact? Well, how about that Billy could have been part of the extensive aboveground support network that Weather had: lawyers, doctors, academics, many of whom are prominent members of their professions today. That was also good stuff. But it wasn't addressing what was bothering me.

So I tried another question. Why had Sharon come east? Well, here was a no-brainer: my new close personal friend from the FBI, Kevin Cornelius, had, the night before, told me that they had traced calls from the pay phones Sharon was using before she was arrested to Gillian Morrealle, the leftist lawyer in Boston. Clearly Solarz was looking to follow what Katherine Power had done a few years before, that is, negotiate a surrender. Katherine Power had spent eight years in jail, which was severe, but a hell of a lot less severe than what would have happened had she been arrested.

So what was bothering me? Years later, and for years later, your father would grill me on this. Why, in all of this story, was I so like a dog with a bone with this question? There was so much to write, so much story, just with what I had there.

But it wasn't enough for me, and never did I have an explanation why. I was just built that way. Drives Rebeccah crazy. Like when I see a movie and everyone else is sitting around wiping tears from their eyes, I'm totally stuck on the fact that before he died saving the girl's life, the hero's dog appeared on either side of a cut with different collars, or during the chase scene that cost five million dollars to produce and had lead articles devoted to it in the *Sunday Times,* a license plate read the wrong state.

And so now, after all the work I'd done, and all I'd learned; now, with the chance to sit down and write a career-making story—I still couldn't stop myself. What was wrong with this picture? Once again, starting with the first anonymous call, what seemed now like weeks ago, I went through the story step by step, detail by detail. And once again, I kept feeling, like an elusive sneeze, the thing that didn't make sense.

I'll never stop wondering at that process.

One minute, I couldn't for the life of me conjure it up.

The next minute, it was sitting on my tongue like my own name, and I said it, aloud: "Why didn't Jim Grant represent Sharon Solarz?"

That's all there was. That simple question.

I mean, I didn't know about the divorce, and the custody battle, or any of that. If I had, would I still have asked the question? It's impossible to answer.

And if I had known the answer to the question, would I still have published?

I don't know, Isabel. I don't know. The question comes down to this: If I had known how much my work, that spring of 1996, was going to fuck up your life, would I have gone ahead?

But see, I didn't even know that you existed, then, and if I had known, I was too young to understand. What the hell did I know about children? What the hell did I know about the fact that next to a child, nothing political matters a good goddamn?

Not knowing that, on June 16, 1996, it became, for me, the most urgent matter in my life to answer that question.

Jim Grant was the kind of lawyer who should have gotten moist over the chance to negotiate Sharon Solarz's surrender. It had news value, it had political value, it had moral value, it had historical value. And what did he do? He handed it over to a competitor.

Why?

I stood, stretched, and knocked over my desk lamp again. This time, however, I didn't bother picking it up but instead pocketed my car keys and cigarettes. Then, leaning over my keyboard, I looked up Billy Cusimano's address and telephone number in an on-line phone book, and walked out of the newsroom.

It's worth noting, by the way, that on my way out, while quite a few people said hello to me, none of them seemed to expect me to respond. And none were disappointed, either. Benjamino Schulberg, it was quite clear, was more or less expected to live in his own world.

4.

Arriving in Tannersville toward midmorning, I found Billy Cusimano in his front lawn, kneeling in a flower bed. With some trepidation—the guy was *huge*—I approached, and he looked up, a questioning look on his face.

"Mr. Cusimano."

"Yes, child." He spoke in a baritone and, as he spoke, began the slow process of rising while I, trying to absorb that I had just been called "child," tried to find my tongue.

"I'm Ben Schulberg. From the *Times* in Albany."

"Well, well. You're the only paper on the eastern seaboard who doesn't seem to have concluded that I'm guilty of supplying half the minors on the East Coast with marijuana all the while harboring dangerous fugitives. That your doing?" Cusimano was standing now, hands on his hips, and I had a chance to appreciate just how massive he was—in all directions.

"Well, I like to think so. I mean, you haven't actually come to trial yet."

"That doesn't seem to bother anyone else." Cusimano paused, still staring down. "So?"

"Pardon me?"

"So what do you want?"

"Well . . . where do you know Sharon Solarz from?" Knowing how lame that sounded, I struggled for control. But once again it eluded me as this monstrously large man, without expression, stepped out of the flower bed and began to walk away, out of the driveway and across a very large, very green lawn. And because he was talking, I had to follow if I wanted to keep listening.

"You don't really expect me to answer that." It was a statement, not a question.

On the lawn, I became aware in quick succession of three things. The first was how enormous the lawn was, sloping down a gentle series of hillocks to a line of trees. The second was the size of the sky, a flood-lit blue, above the range of mountains that stood away over the trees, the colors nearly fluorescent with early summer sun. And finally, the fact that a row of poplars now ensured that, just at the spot where Billy stopped and turned around, forcing me nearly to walk into his huge belly, no one could see us from the road. Then he went on.

"I mean, if you have a Nexis account and you're not a fucking idiot, then you know how I know her. And you do have a Nexis account, don't you?" Cusimano peered with evident curiosity into my face, as if trying to see if I were a fucking idiot. Then he laughed, briefly, which I did not appreciate.

"Alright." I spoke now without—as you see—much caution. "You know Sharon Solarz from Mendocino in '71—sounds like a Joni Mitchell song, doesn't it—when she was in the Weather Underground and you hired her to help get Timothy Leary out of San Luis Obispo. Now, either you've stayed in touch for all these years, which was stupid of you, because that means you've protected a federal fugitive, or she's just come to find you for old times sake. What's amazing is that you're so arrogant as to let her into your house while you're under federal surveillance. So there's my first question. Are you really so arrogant?"

I could see Billy's cheeks reddening just slightly under his beard. He answered in a straightforward voice, though.

"I didn't invite Sharon to come here. She came unannounced. And I didn't have any—any—way of knowing that the FBI would be doing a black-bag job on my house. What, they exhume J. Edgar Hoover for this?

"They had a warrant, Mr. Cusimano."

"Listen, kid. First of all, Mr. Cusimano was my father, who ran a greengrocery in Brooklyn. Second of all, as for their warrant: that warrant'll stand up in court for about seven seconds. That doesn't matter one bit, though, 'cause they've already done what they set out to. My lawyer says they wiped out my whole prosecution with that warrant. A blatantly illegal search warrant."

"Your lawyer," I answered right away. "So that's why Sharon came. To meet him?"

"No. He refused even to meet her."

It was funny. This guy, I could see he wasn't stupid. To the contrary, he was evidently an extremely smart man. And yet I had gotten him in less than three minutes. I let the pace slow a little, now, by lighting a cigarette.

"Really? Why's that? Isn't this Grant's kind of case? I mean, the most fundamental issues of the lefty pantheon, I would have thought."

Now he seemed to be taking me a little more seriously, squinting at me through the sun and speaking in a lower tone.

"Listen, Sharon came here looking for a way to surrender herself. If she'd been able to do it, she'd have at least had a little control over her life. Now she's facing spending the rest of her days in jail. If you had any part in that, then feel bad."

"And why do I feel bad about someone complicit in the murder of a policeman going to jail?"

But his answer surprised me. Less for what he said than for the tone in which he said it, which was not mad but sad. "Complicit? Complicity's a big word, boy. For example, what are you, right now, complicit in?"

I thought about that. Then: "I don't know. You tell me."

"Nah." Cusimano was turning already. "You wouldn't believe me."

"Wait. What are you talking about?"

"That's your job. Go figure it out."

But he didn't turn, speaking as he walked away.

"Mr. Cusimano. Bill. Stop."

Now he turned and shook his head slowly. "No. You're not going to listen to me. Kids never do. See, it's our parents' revenge on us."

"But it's my job to listen."

"Yeah, that'll be the day. I'll tell Jim to expect you. Take 23A down to Palenville, your car doesn't look like it'll weather 16."

And after watching Billy Cusimano walk—or rather waddle—away, I went back to my car and started down 23A to Palenville. I knew the way to Saugerties, and I didn't need Cusimano here to tell me my car couldn't make it down 16.

And I guess I knew that your father was the next logical person for me to talk to.

What I didn't know was why Billy Cusimano's tone was so hopeless.

Like I was about to do something very bad to someone who didn't deserve it, and if I only understood why, I too would be sad.

Okay? That good enough for you, J? It's like two in the morning, and I'm just sending this now, so you got to figure you'll be up at least another half an hour reading, right? Well, when you finish, reflect on this: you woulda gotten this story four hours ago, except you pissed me off so much with your incessant IMs and phone calls that I went out to dinner just to get you back. So in the future, you just remember: you don't like the way I'm telling Isabel this story? Then tell her yourself.

Date: June 6, 2006
From: "Daddy" <littlej@cusimanorganics.com>
To: "Isabel Montgomery" <isabel@exmnster.uk>
CC: maillist: The_Committee
Subject: letter 6

So now it's Tuesday, for Christ sake, and thanks to Benny's nonsense I fell asleep before I even got his e-mail last night, or I should say, this morning.

About time someone takes that boy out back and shoots him.

Then, I'm that annoyed, I can't get myself to sit down to work on this, which is making me feel a little desperate because it's already the sixth of June, and we're on, like, day two of this story. So listen up, all of you—from now on we write faster, smoother, and sleeker. I mean everybody, and especially you, Benny, you little shithead.

I, for one, am going to cut to the chase. So it's Monday, the day, come to think of it, just a week or two shy of ten years ago when I was first annoyed by the little shithead, I mean Benny. My business that morning was a bail hearing on a court-assigned hit-and-run case, a young man whose conviction, I'm sorry to say, I was going to overturn on technical grounds to do with probable cause. Sorry, because the little bastard had been drunk as a lord when he left the Ace of Spades in Palenville and promptly plowed into a minivan containing six adolescents from the Harriman Lodge, putting four of them in the hospital. In my opinion, he deserved a harsh and punitive sentence, which perhaps wasn't a very good attitude for a defense lawyer. And worse yet, he wasn't going to get it, because the arresting officer had violated the little asshole's constitutional rights. The way I looked at it, it was the arresting officer who should have been on trial.

I was going to do what I had to. But I wasn't going to be happy about it, and in fact, when the hearing was finished and the irate judge had recessed until the afternoon—yet another member of the Judicial Friends of Jim Grant Club—I didn't have the heart to go back to the office. Instead, I walked over to have an early lunch with you and Molly. When that was done, and you had gone out to play in the yard with Kate Carlucci from next door, was when Billy called on my cell to tell me to expect a visit from an *Albany Times* reporter. That was not unexpected, but it was still a major blow, and I guess how major a blow could be seen on my face, for Molly, turning from the window, frowned and said, "Now what's up with you, Little J?"

"Ummm . . ." I put a hand through what I liked to call my hair, my eyes closed, and rested like this a moment. "This reporter from the *Albany Times*. He's been to see Billy, now he's coming here."

Molly answered this one more softly. "That's not bad news, J, that's good news."

"And how do you make this good news?" My eyes were still closed.

"Oh, come on. You needed to get proactive sooner or later. They're going to smear you with this Sharon Solarz thing and eat you up in court. You tell this reporter the truth about Julia and her father and get it over with."

I could have cried. Even Molly had no idea how impossible that was. She knew my secrets, but she didn't even imagine Bob Montgomery's. I mean, how the hell could I have told her that? And without knowing that: the truth? Ha ha ha. But what I said was: "Okay, I know."

"But you're not going to do it, are you?"

"I don't know."

"I don't understand you." Molly spoke calmly, as if to inject a note of reason into madness—quite a frequent tone of hers with me. "You have to do it, you know."

I nodded, as much as my head in my hands permitted, but I didn't say anything. I couldn't. So I nodded, and didn't say anything, and after a moment she spoke more gently.

"Can I help?"

"You already have. And are."

"Uh-huh." She came close now and put a hand on my shoulder, a gesture of companionship that struck me, at the time, as infinitely sexy.

"Come on, J. I know you don't want to assassinate your ex-wife in the papers. I admire you. But now's not the time for ideals. Izzy needs you. She needs to stay with you. With *us*."

"Okay." I was just shutting her up now. Her hand on my shoulder was unbearable, unbearable, and I wanted it never to move.

"Good. Get going now, boy. And remember what my father used to say."

"What was that?" Willing her hand to stay put, to just stay put.

"That your problems aren't likely to go away just because you forget about them for a few minutes."

Her father. In those days, whenever someone my age mentioned their father, I felt like crying. As if, now that all our parents were dying, mine was a whole generation in mourning, still shocked by the ridiculous truth that our parents could be taken away forever. I lifted her hand to my cheek and shut my eyes. And then her hand was gone, and I was a grown man again, not a child, even though while I was walking out the door my heart was in my mouth.

2.

Do you remember my assistant, Izzy? Michael Joseph Rafferty Jr.? Works for Hillary now? He was this kid who came to me straight out of Exeter, Princeton, Yale Law School; drives up to my single-room office in Saugerties when the rest of his class is out doing tequila shots and lines to celebrate their first jobs at Chase Manhattan, or Salomon Smith Barney, or Bear Stearns; asks to work for Jim Grant, unpaid. Friday afternoon, not hours after graduation.

I say, You shitting me? You turn right around and don't stop until you've got a forty-thousand-dollar-a-year entry-level job in New York.

But this kid is not going anywhere.

"Mr. Grant, there's the strongest economy in thirty years in New York. I published in *Yale Law Journal* first year, and my starting offers, for your information, run into the low sixes. You think I'm turning that down on a whim?"

"Don't call me Mr. Grant. Go intern for Ron Kuby, then."

"No way. Case by case, you're doing more interesting work up here than anyone in New York." The kid was actually unpacking his briefcase as he spoke. "I'm staying right here."

And so he had. It had been two years now he'd been working for me, and we'd even expanded into a second funky little office in the horrible little suite above the Saugerties Center antique store, and he'd been so good I had to pay him a few bucks of Julia's money, first, and now of Billy's. Mikey. He'll be at the parole board, and you'll see him there—if you go. When I first paid him, it was in cash. For a moment he looked truly downcast, poor kid: this was far from what he had bargained for when he decided to go idealistic. Then he brightened up and said: "Hey, Mr. Grant, tell you what. Fire me, I'll get unemployment and work off the books. I could go as high as the low five figures this year!"

Now, coming upstairs at 9:15, I found Mikey and the kid from the *Times,* Ben Schulberg, sitting in his office, Mikey chatting merrily—as if the whole world were his friend—and the kid from the *Times* clearly noting every word.

I kicked Mikey out and put the kid in the client's chair on the other side of the desk, facing the morning sun. In the light, I had the time to see that my persecutor had a long face and aviator glasses that looked out of the seventies, nice looking without being anything that could be called handsome. It was, I saw right away, a face that inspired confidence, which is, depending on the circumstance, either a dangerous or an admirable quality for a reporter. Admirable when he's after someone else; dangerous when he's after you. He wore a white shirt, sleeves rolled up to show thin forearms, a badly tied tie, and khakis, and sat with his hands loosely clenched between his knees.

"Mr. Grant, can you confirm that you were consulted by Sharon Solarz on the day of her arrest last week?"

That was an easy one. I did not have to feign the bitterness in my answer. "Why should I? You already printed it."

"I printed that she met with a 'public interest' lawyer in Saugerties. Not that she met with you."

At that, I reached over to pick up the phone book from where I had it filed on the floor, then tossed it onto the surface of the desk so it slid over a few layers of paper and into his lap, carrying the papers with it.

"There are thirty-nine lawyers in Saugerties. Thirty-eight do accidents, thirty-eight do deeds, thirty-eight do closings. Then there's me. Now, who did you say she met with? Asshole." That last word I improvised, though I admit that I had rehearsed the first ones after Billy called saying Ben was on his way. A short silence followed the question, while we glowered at each other. I, personally, felt I had made a point. So I pressed on.

"So, Benny. Someone's been leaking you information. Who?"

The answer was automatic. "I protect sources, Mr. Grant. If you were a source, I'd protect you."

"Yeah, yeah." I let my eye steal to some papers on the desk, then up again, like I was bored by him. "The difference is that your sources are violating the law by speaking to you. You understand, don't you, that you're being used?"

"I suppose." Ben answered carefully, and in his answer I saw that he had done his homework. "You mean that since Sharon Solarz's arrest the FBI's leaking information to the press in the hope of flushing Mimi Lurie and Jason Sinai out. Like they did with Kathleen Soliah from the Symbionese Liberation Army, feeding info to *America's Most Wanted*. I'm sure that's true. That's not my problem, though. My job is to learn what I can, and it's constitutionally guaranteed. So I'm planning to keep doing what I'm doing, Mr. Grant, and just so there's no misunderstanding, this conversation is on the record now."

Leaning first downward into his briefcase, then forward, Ben placed a tape recorder on the desk and turned it on.

"Don't call me Mr. Grant," I answered automatically, thinking, not many kids his age knew the FBI used the media in that way. Not many kids his age, I thought, knew who Mimi Lurie and Jason Sinai were. Looking back, I saw that the kid had a box of Marlboro Reds in his shirt pocket. Not many kids his age, I thought, smoked. Finally, I went on.

"Well, here's something on the record for you, Benny. The wire they had recording Billy Cusimano's business was illegal. Get it? They gave up their whole marijuana case on Cusimano for this, and they know it—

all they've done is issue a bench warrant for Cusimano for cultivating. I'll have it thrown out of court next week. But Sharon Solarz is still in custody, and there's no doubt at all that they developed an alternate chain of evidence to defend that arrest in court."

Ben, listening hard, answered slowly. "Okay. They traded a marijuana dealer for one of the longest-standing federal fugitives in America. What's wrong with that?"

"From my point of view? Nothing. They've virtually freed my client. From the point of view of the American taxpayer? Plenty."

"And why's that?"

"Because if you believe that the greatest crimes should get the greatest weight of law enforcement, then you have to ask why they let a serious, known criminal free in order to arrest a minor accomplice in a quarter-century-old crime who's probably been leading an exemplary life ever since."

Ben nodded understanding, and when he answered, I had the feeling that he had been in control of this conversation all along.

"Is that all she is? I thought she was a dangerous accomplice in a violent armed robbery who had eluded the law for a quarter century."

"Sure, kid. That's what they want to you think."

The kid went on without a break, his voice suddenly very tired. "But, of course, if I understood the context, I'd know that it was different."

I didn't answer that one. A slippery little fellow, this. And frighteningly good at his job. I tried one more time to get in front of him.

"Okey-doke, Benny. So I won't tell you about the '68 Democratic National Convention, I won't tell you about Woodstock, and I won't tell you about Kent State. Why don't you fuck off now?"

He smiled. A wide, intelligent smile. "You mind if I ask the question I actually came to ask? Or does your support of the Bill of Rights end when it's you in the hot seat?"

I couldn't help but smile back. "Go ahead."

"So, why didn't you represent Solarz?" Without asking, he lit a cigarette.

Jesus. Thank God he was smoking, because it gave me something to do. I went over to the window and opened it. Then I walked back to

Ben, took the cigarette out of his fingers, and threw it out the window. Then I returned to the desk.

"I felt that Solarz deserves a defense that I can't give her."

"How's that?"

I hesitated. "I'm not ready to answer that question at this time."

"No? How interesting. Well, do you believe she is guilty in the Bank of Michigan robbery?"

"What I believe isn't the issue."

"Um-hmm." Ben seemed—seemed—satisfied with the answer. But he also seemed as if it wasn't entirely what he cared about. "Tell me, Mr. Grant. How did Solarz know you?"

"She didn't. Only by reputation."

"Did you know who she was?"

A tiny pause. "Sure."

"How?"

"Doesn't everyone?"

"Really? How old are you?"

The question surprised me. "Thirty-nine."

"Thirty-nine." Ben calculated ostentatiously, eyes up at the ceiling. "Then the Bank of Michigan robbery took place when you were, what, seventeen?"

"I guess." I answered slowly.

"And you remember it?"

Now I raised a single eyebrow. "How old are you?"

"Twenty-seven."

"Really? Well, let's see. Iran-Contra happened when you were, what, fifteen? Ever hear of Oliver North?"

"Mr. Grant. There's a difference between a crime that was a pimple on the ass of the sixties and Oliver North's constitutional crisis. I studied Iran-Contra in college."

"I don't see that at all, Benny." I made my voice sound very, very reasonable, rather than pissed off. "In the seventies, for the second time since 1776, white Americans defending the ideals of democracy took up arms against our government. That might have slipped by in your education. It didn't in mine."

"Yeah, yeah." I did not seem to have impressed him with the point. "Thomas Jefferson didn't fund the revolution by writing home to Daddy and Mommy in Larchmont, and neither did John Brown. It didn't slip by me at all."

"Well, if you want to argue the antiwar movement, I'm all yours."

Oddly, that seemed to be precisely what the boy wanted to argue. "What were you doing during it?"

I narrowed my eyes, not at all sure I believed we were actually having this conversation. "Why is this your business?"

"Why is it a secret?"

"There's no secret. I'm from Bakersfield, California. I went to the University of Chicago, Yale University Law School, and came up here to practice. The war ended in '75, which was my freshman year of college."

I had the feeling that this guy knew, already, most of what he was hearing. "That's when you met your wife?"

"Yeah. I met Julia Montgomery at the U of C. She was there because of the Steppenwolf Theater. Her father had just been elected senator from New York State. He was very, very good to me. He helped me through my college, then law school. It was incredibly generous."

"He's valued at seven billion dollars." Ben's voice went dry once again.

"Today. Doubt that he had more than half of that, in those days." I smiled, not my most, but perhaps my second most disarming smile. "It was still a wonderful thing to do. Changed my life."

"Though, of course, it did give his daughter's foundation a perfect employee."

I shrugged. "If you want to put it that way, I can't stop you. Myself, I loved him."

"Uh-huh. What about your own parents?"

"My parents died in a car crash when I was a baby."

"Okay. Then Julia left you in 1994, and moved to her father's place in England."

I paused. Then I shook my head. "I have no comment about my wife, about her life, about where she is now."

Now the boy let a little bit of dead air sit between us before asking, "Had any contact ever with Mimi Lurie?"

"What?" My voice rose.

"Mimi Lurie. Sharon's Solarz's partner."

"I know who she is. Of course I've had no contact with her."

"Jason Sinai?"

"Nope."

"Any idea where they are?"

"Oh, fuck off. Benny, would you?"

He smiled suddenly and switched topics.

"What's going to happen to Sharon Solarz?"

"She's going to be sentenced to many, many years in jail."

"And what do you think should happen?"

"That's up to the judge, isn't it?"

"Oh, come on, Mr. Grant. I know you think she's some kind of hero."

"For participating in a bank robbery where a guard was killed? Come off it. I doubt even she thinks she's a hero."

Now he shook his head, emphatically, and for the first time I had the feeling I was seeing him speak honestly. "Oh, I don't believe that at all. A hell of a lot of people had a lot of sympathy for those guys, in the days. A hell of a lot of people'll fall over themselves to prove they blew a joint with Weatherman in San Francisco when they were underground. Sharon, Mimi, Jason: good revolutionaries fooled by a bad person, that's what people like you think."

I interrupted. "How do you know all this?"

The question surprised him. "Why shouldn't I?"

"Kind of strange, a kid your age so interested in an event that was over twenty-five years ago."

"Hey, you're the one with the bullshit about Weatherman and 1776."

"Yah." I nodded. "Only, Sharon Solarz wasn't in Weather. Not during the Bank of Michigan robbery, anyway."

"Weather, MDB, BLA." Ben let contempt into his voice. "May 19th Collective. What's the difference?"

"All the difference in the world. No one in Weather has ever been convicted, so far, of killing anyone, for one thing—except themselves. Nor did they ever practice violence against people, only property."

"What about the Army Math bombing? Kids who blew up that lab at the University of Wisconsin?"

"Wasn't Weather. Was independents. But that's beside the point."

"Which is?"

"Which is that you're stereotyping me. You're trying to associate me with a kind of radicalism I had nothing to do with. I'm a lefty lawyer today, sure, but I was a child in 1974—we already established that—and I was in the mainstream of American politics, not the revolutionary fringe. Please don't interrupt."

Ben had been trying to talk, but now he stopped. "Moreover, you're drawing me into an argument that's not worth having. That was then. This is now. There are real battles to fight, now, today. There's the RRA transfer station on Route 32. Do you know the Empire-Besicort recycling plant proposal in Saugerties calls for drawing ten *million* gallons of water out of the Esopus *per day* and raising its temperature a full degree? And all up and down this county there are people, in the system, with constitutional rights being stomped on. See, that's what you have to understand. I don't want to talk about the battles of thirty years ago, I want to talk about the battles of today. And that's why I turned down Sharon Solarz. She needed a lawyer who did want to fight that fight, and that was Gilly Morrealle. Get it?"

"I guess."

Standing now, suddenly, I walked to the door. "Enough. I'm due in court. Go away now, Benny. Mikey'll see you out. Mikey"—As I walked out, I spoke in a stage voice to Mike—"come watch this man so he doesn't steal any office supplies."

3.

Outside, across the sun-flooded street, I waited for a moment in a doorway to see Benny leave. When at last he did, I called up to the office on my cell phone while I began to walk toward court.

"Mikey, Jim. What did you and this Schulberg cat talk about?"

"Talk about? When?" Mike sounded truly surprised by the question.

"Before I came in this morning."

"Nothing. In particular."

"Mi-*key*." I used my slow-speak-for-idiots voice. Come to think of it, I learned that voice from you, Iz. "*Dad*-ee. *Did you or did you* not *buy Fig Newtons?*" "Did he or did he *not* ask you any questions?"

"Yes." Mikey had gone defensive now, and committed himself to nothing more.

"Were the questions about me?"

"Yes."

"Could you characterize them as his business or not his business?"

"Well . . . as an investigative reporter, it's his business to go outside his business, isn't it? Fourth estate? First Amendment? All those little things you're constantly going to court about?"

I know Mikey, and when he gets mad, he can be pretty cutting. But I managed to keep my tone even.

"Would you consider telling me what some of his questions were?"

"Public record stuff. Where you come from, where you went to school, what you do with yourself."

"And you told him?"

"Let's see—where you come from, where you went to school, what you do with yourself."

"I see. Hey, Mikey? You ever speak to a reporter about me again, and you're fired."

"Hey, Mr. Grant? Go to hell."

My cell gave that horrid beep it gives when the line goes dead.

I wondered if Kunstler's assistants spoke to him like this.

And while I wondered that, I saw myself surrounded by merciless young men: efficient, idealistic, bloodless young men who had no idea the damage they were going to do in the name of their ideals.

And yet I had to admit to myself that if anything I'd ever believed in was worth anything—which, right that moment, I rather doubted—I could not criticize them for it.

Head down, I walked slowly to court, pinching my lip and thinking.

When I got there, it took me several long minutes, standing in the lobby, looking at the floor, to remember why I'd come.

4.

So I got my hit-and-run defendant dismissed, which may have satisfied the Constitution but earned me no friends at all. Afterward I hung around the courthouse, wasting some time. A couple lawyers made some reference to the *Times* article—Norman Bailey, who was helping Sharon Naylor buy a large portion of the Adirondacks with her Enron stock; Wayne Curry, who was doing a title search on a packet of land off Route 23C—but neither of them cared too much. Chances are, they believed that Sharon Solarz had in fact come to find me to negotiate her surrender—why not? I had handled First Amendment cases, labor cases, and was well known to have worked hand in glove with the ACLU on capital cases. My father-in-law was Bobby Montgomery, the third in what William Buckley once called the "Tristate Troika" with Bob Torricelli and Joe Lieberman. My soon-to-be ex-wife was always inviting people like Paul Newman up to her Woodstock home, or Katrina van den Heuvel, or Alec Baldwin. And Hillary Clinton had twice asked me to meetings with her committee exploring a run for the New York State Senate, which up in the Saugerties courthouse passes for very lefty indeed.

Mostly, however, my colleagues didn't care: the more work I took on for free, the less was assigned to their pro bono dockets by the court, and the more they could focus on getting rich, which, in the nineties, anyone with an opposable thumb could do. Bailey said to me, in passing, in this syrupy voice with his eyes half shut as if he were stoned, "Like, Sharon Solarz, wow man. Miss Days of Rage herself. That's some far-out heavy shit." And Curry said, hey, if the Hollywood Radical Chic was footing the bill, could he sit in as cocounsel? "Cause ah got to git me a new telescopic .22 and git my pickup outa hock in time for deer season, boy." Of course in fact Bailey's wife was a gynecologist down in New Paltz, and he probably sat on the board of the Metropolitan Opera.

It was not lost on me that when four o'clock rolled around and I knew Molly was warming up for our afternoon run—leaving you with your hero, Leo—I suddenly found myself too busy to go: even running with Molly was a pensive activity, and I found myself entirely unwilling to think. Nor did I have to: not until that evening, after I had picked you up and fed you, played with you, gotten you to bed, cleaned the dinner dishes, and swept the kitchen floor, and put on the laundry, and paid a couple bills, and watched *Ally McBeal*, which only tragedy on the international level could make me miss, did I have to face my thoughts. Then, sneaking a can of Coke from its constantly shifting hiding place—always just one step ahead of your search—I turned on the computer and found that without my having to ask, Mikey had done research on Schulberg and e-mailed me the results, and the time stamp on the e-mail showed that the poor guy had been in the office till 10:30.

Ben had been at the *Times* for a year. Originally, he was from New York, where he'd attended some fairly fancy private schools. At the *Times* he had been promoted three times but was considered, Mikey's friend Andrew told him, an oddball: solitary and moody. Mikey had included the Nexis URL of Ben's major stories, all of which were muckraking: a shabbily built school in Margaretville, an iffy land sale by a town alderman in Schuylerville, Medicaid fraud in Hudson.

I thought about that for some time, wandering the living room, listening to the night outside the screens. How far was Ben going to look into the Sharon Solarz story? As if I could actually discern the answer in the night, I found myself standing by a window, squinting through the screen. And yet no matter how hard I looked into the future, I simply saw no way to predict what was about to happen, and no way to prepare.

I remember that moment very precisely, because as I watched through the window, a recollection of my own father so profound, so detailed, came to me—my father in his fifties when I was in high school—and I must have been worrying about something, because my father was calling me by my family nickname and reciting the Hebrew proverb, *Al tegid lilah*, "Never say night." *Never think about your problems at night, little J. Night's just a big lie, and you can't find the truth until morning comes.*

But which was the lie and which was the truth? As that spring night in 1996 dipped into its blackest, I could find nothing, nothing to show me the difference, because night or day, the fact was that a period of my life and your own little life was coming to an end, and when it was over, I knew I would look back at it as a time when I was happier than I had ever been or would ever be again.

Date: June 7, 2006
From: "Benjamin Schulberg" <Benny@cusimanorganics.com>
To: "Isabel Montgomery" <isabel@exmnster.uk>
CC: maillist: The_Committee
Subject: letter 7

As for me, I very nearly fell asleep at the wheel, driving back from Saugerties after interviewing your daddy. Maybe I should have—certainly would have simplified life for a lot of people to have me wrap my car around a tree. After a while, though, the way it will, my tiredness evened out into a kind of low-level cogitation, the impressions of the day—and night, and day before, and night before—following one another with their own logic, or lack of logic.

It was quitting time when I got back—or close enough. Certainly time to retire to, as we liked to call it in the newsroom, the "other office"—namely the Shandon Star Lounge over on Western Avenue. Nonetheless, I went back to my desk long enough to run a Nexis on James Grant. The yield was copious, but it wasn't until I reached a short item from, of all places, the *London Star,* that I paused. The rag—I mean tabloid—had a May 25 dateline, and here it is, pasted in from Nexis:

> Actress Julia Montgomery, daughter of former US Senator Robert Montgomery, now the chairman of Dreamworks UK, has filed in New York State Court to sue her former husband for custody of their seven-year-old daughter. Ms. Montgomery, who was reported by the *Daily Mirror* to have been brought to London by her father to recover from a long-term addiction problem, declared that her former husband was

"unfit to raise her daughter," although she declined to define the precise reasons behind her allegation.

That interested me, and I thought about why for some time. That is, I thought about why it interested me for some time, while I paced the little concrete courtyard outside the paper's offices, smoking. So Jim Grant was involved in a custody battle with his ex-wife. So what? So what, so what—I repeated the words to myself like a mantra, and while I did, I tried to list the reasons that it bothered me.

That the custody suit had not been mentioned anywhere in the American press, including my fine paper, didn't particularly surprise me: you could call the *Albany Times* neoconservative, or neoliberal, or you could simply notice that Rick Harmon's father and Bobby Montgomery dined together at the Century Club each time Montgomery was in New York, but either way, it was not in the habit of publishing anything that reflected badly on Robert Montgomery. And that Julia Montgomery apparently had a drug and alcohol problem? Well, that was the kind of thing that was harder to conceal, and besides, if it were true, Grant would have used it to quash the custody suit, wouldn't he? I ran a quick check on PACER and learned that the custody suit had in fact been filed, whereas a Nexis on Julia showed no stories about her supposed drug addiction—that's the *London Star* for you.

But that wasn't quite it, was it? For a long time I paced and smoked. It bothered me badly. It bothered me that Jim Grant had not mentioned his custody battle. It bothered me that two newsworthy things—Solarz and a high-profile custody suit—were happening to him at the same time. It bothered me that I had learned about Solarz through an anonymous tipster—one who clearly had some access to the FBI. Alright. In the end I decided that it was time to cut to the chase.

See, somewhere, while I paced and smoked, without really noticing it, I had decided that I was going to go after this story. In fact, I decided that I was going to go after this story at any cost. And if I was going to go after this story, this would be my last chance for several weeks to do laundry, pay my nearly hilarious backlog of bills, and clean my apartment, among other matters requiring urgent attention: grocery shopping, finding a girlfriend, calling my parents, working on my novel, going to the gym, opening an IRA, doing my taxes, getting my car inspected, paying the tickets that resulted from my car having not been inspected, cleaning my bathroom, and getting some much-needed sleep.

Of these imperatives, the first and the last got done, that Monday night. I did laundry and got some sleep.

That is, I dropped my laundry at the Laundromat, gave the owner a sizable portion of my life savings, then sat in the Shandon Star drinking until my laundry was done, picked it up, then went back to the Shandon Star to celebrate my laundry being done, then went home, then went to sleep.

Tuesday morning, on the other hand, all I needed to do was wake up, step over my clean laundry where it lay on the floor in a neat pile and into the shower—a cold shower, because during the night my electricity seemed to have been cut off. And after that, my main challenge was to ignore the fact that the surface of the kitchen table could not be seen for the weeks of unopened letters in which bills and junk mail vied for majority status, drink a refreshing glass of tepid tap water, and walk out the door. The temperature, fortunately, obviated the need for a jacket—I had no clean ones. On reflection, though, I turned back, shuffled through the envelopes on the kitchen table, and extracted an electricity bill, easily recognizable by the large announcement in red ink that my power was about to be suspended. This, I knew, I'd better pay right away to get the refrigerator running again, a task that, considering the last time I opened it had been to put in a half-eaten bagel with lox, rose to the level of civic duty.

Sometimes I think, looking back, that the whole reason I had a job in those days was to prevent me from thinking about what a mess my life had become. For so long had I lived with a feeling of dread at the pit of my stomach—classes unattended in high school, incompletes not finished in college, retirement accounts not cared for, superiors not stroked, cigarettes not given up—that I'd come to question whether I actually could live without that feeling. Everyone, I know, simplifies life somehow: booze, television. Everyone, I know, has to find some way to direct their minds away from the horrible disappointment of adulthood, the horrible disappointment of finding out that you've been lied to all your childhood, that nothing you were taught to care about actually matters. An all-consuming job, a consistent feeling of remorse, for me, those worked just fine. Nights, of course—at least those nights when I went to bed sober—my dreams showed that nothing ever worked that fine. Nights, the past showed its face, and large, liquid feelings filled my stomach. In the day, however, there were the simple moves: step over the laundry, take a cold shower, pay the electric bill, leave the house. As for my refrigerator, for all I knew at that point, Jimmy Hoffa was in there.

Tuesday morning I found my car where I'd hidden it on a side street, hoping to avoid another ticket for my overdue inspection. Once again, the strategy had failed. I removed the ticket from the windshield—it was rare that I avoided one, no matter where I parked, which I had to admit implied a certain efficiency on the part of the police—and was soon behind the wheel, driving to the office.

And yet, as I drove, I found myself thinking again about Julia Montgomery. For a time I argued with myself about what I knew I had to do. And when I was done, I wheeled out into traffic and toward the highway, speeding to make it up to Great Meadows Correctional Facility in Comstock before the morning head count.

2.

I remember that drive so vividly. On the highway, the thick sun of June flooded the windscreen, the day's air drenched: nine o'clock in the morning, the heat was stifling. Above was a pastel sky, blue with clouds developing like an overexposed photograph. Tentatively, as my heart picked up its pace to its morning dose of caffeine and nicotine, I felt a little excitement replace the dread in my belly. Dread, I knew, never went away. Fortunately, excitement was its flip side.

Up at Comstock, Darryl Taylor, whom I had interviewed after his 1995 conviction for selling heroin to a seventeen-year-old model and her forty-five-year-old agent in Woodstock, was happy to be called down for a visitor just before the daily count. Sure, he knew Julia Montgomery. Yes, he used to sell to her, and yes, he was happy to give me her shopping list, which was headed by crystal meth and followed closely by coke and Klonopin, a monstrous strong kind of Valium, and just about the only recourse after the kind of amphetamines your mother had taken, Isabel—if you want ever to sleep again, that is. The reason he was so happy to spill all this was because he, Darryl, thought Senator Montgomery should have done more to protect him after his arrest. Like he was some kind of big-time insider because he had once sold drugs to a senator's daughter. I tell you, Izzy, you want to find out how easily people fool themselves? Interview a few real, genuine jailbirds. Like Darryl Taylor, doing fifteen to twenty at Comstock. His first parole date comes when he's sixty-five, and he's HIV-positive from a gang bang his first week in. Now he's eagerly spilling Julia Montgomery's shopping list to a reporter because he thinks a U.S. senator should have protected him, and somehow this is going to get him out. But nothing's ever going to get him out, and not five years after I visited him he was dead, unloved and forgotten, of AIDS-related lymphoma.

I knew all about it. I knew that everyone's got some vicious little illusion protecting them from their own utter obscurity. One of the first things you learn as a newspaper reporter is the degree to which people live in fantasies of their own importance, and how necessary those fantasies are for most of them.

Darryl ended his monologue by suggesting that if I was interested in Julia Montgomery, I should check out the Lucy Freeland Clinic and speak to Alistair Bates, Hank Anderson, and Billy Friedman, whom, back in Albany, I saw in their respective lairs early that afternoon, one in his editing suite at his production company, one in the State Capitol Building, and one in SUNY Albany. Only the first had not been, pardon me, Isabel, intimate with Julia Montgomery, but knew a great deal about the many who had from his work as a news producer. The other two—simply could not keep from bragging that they had. That didn't surprise me either, not one bit. I knew that nine times out of ten, men over forty won't even have an affair if they can't tell anyone about it. Instead, they'll get drunk and go to bed, hope actually to sleep rather than, as usual, lie awake all night thinking about how they've been wronged and how they've failed. Hank Anderson actually said to me, "This is off the record, of course." Oh, absolutely off the record, I'm thinking. It'll be off the record when, one day, I tell every soul I know in Albany politics about this little conversation, you mini-dicked, smirking shithead. Or words to that effect—this is only a reconstruction, of course, not a verbatim transcript. I might have thought, micro-dicked.

As for the Lucy Freeland Clinic, I didn't bother trying to hack the medical records, which was illegal and therefore kind of inadvisable for print, but I did social-engineer a night guard for confirmation of Julia Montgomery's three dryouts there. Not a pretty picture. Her third admission had been after a hospitalization for hepatic failure. The guy said her eyes were as yellow as fog lights.

Finally, late Tuesday afternoon, I went to see Lorraine Jellins, our entertainment editor. Julia Montgomery's career had peaked, it appeared, just before her daughter Isabel was born in 1989, with a single lead in an indie opposite Mark Wohlinger. After that, for no apparent reason, her star more or less waned in the business. Maybe it had to do with her living on the East Coast, maybe it had to do with having bombed a key audition with Jonathan Demme, maybe it even had something to do with a lack of talent, though that last explanation, to me, seemed pretty far-fetched. I told Lorraine what I had learned about Julia's drug use, and she shrugged.

"Benjy my boykie, what do you think actually happens to all these people after they have their moments in the sun? It is a rough world on talent. Think of them all out there: all the people who starred in movies, or television shows, or rock bands, and then disappeared? We never hear about them again, but somewhere, on some private stage, they have to be playing out the drama of their disappointment."

I asked Lorraine if I could quote her on that for my new study of celebrity, *A Moment in the Sun,* but I was thinking, Does every failed actor do so much damage on their way down? Does no one practice an art for its own sake? And don't these people recognize what stereotypes they are? Then I thought about the 118 pages of novel manuscript about an intrepid small-town investigative reporter and thought, Well, maybe not. Lorraine showed me some pictures of Julia, a lovely woman, slim and gorgeous with skin so pale the word *alabaster* came to mind. With yellow eyes, I thought, she must have looked out of *Alien*.

In the early evening, sitting in the sunshine outside the *Times* plant smoking a cigarette, I found myself, for the first time I could remember, actually excited. Exhaling smoke straight into the still June air, my neck stretched taut, my eyes closed against the dazzling light of the low sun, for the first time I allowed myself to assemble the pieces of the story I had fallen into. It made the original assignment—a complex, ambiguous story about a fugitive from a twenty-two-year-old crime—look insignificant. Jim Grant, Senator Montgomery, Julia Montgomery—an ex–U.S. senator protecting his drug-addled daughter, using dirty pool to take custody of his granddaughter from her rightful father . . . It was a big, sexy story, just right to send Ben Schulberg, boy reporter, zipping down the Thruway to the *New York Times*. And in New York, I knew, everything would suddenly become better: my health, my sleep, my gym attendance, my lack of girlfriend. Hell, I could even escape cleaning my refrigerator.

As I often did, in order to keep smoking, I walked over to my car and, engine running so I could get juice from the cigarette lighter—I never remembered to charge the battery—used the cell phone to call, in turn, directory assistance, Jim Grant's home, directory assistance, Jim Grant's office, and finally, using the number that Jim Grant's assistant gave me, Jim Grant's cell phone, which was answered by, of all people, you, Izzy, who finally agreed to find your father. It sounded as if you were outside somewhere, perhaps on a farm, because I could swear I heard goats bleating. Here, when your father finally came on the telephone, I asked him.

"Mr. Grant. You didn't mention to me you were going to court with your wife over your daughter's custody."

"Ben?" Your father's voice paused.

"Yes?"

"When are you going to stop calling me Mr. Grant?"

"I'm sorry."

"You should be. It's a fucking outrage."

"Mr. . . . Jim. Surely it's not that important?"

"Yes, it is. I deliberately asked you not to call me Mr. Grant. It's rude."

"I apologize."

"Now, what the hell business are my marriage and daughter of yours?"

I paused, reminding myself that I was being manipulated; reminding myself that I was, as a reporter, de facto my subject's enemy.

"So, how'd she get as far as filing suit?"

"What's that mean, Benny? She hired a lawyer, he filed papers—not a lot of mystery there."

"No, I mean, why aren't you taking her to the cleaners? It's a no-brainer, her record of drug addiction and abuse."

Now he was actually silent for a few seconds, and when he answered, I actually felt bad. "How do you know about that?"

"It's my job, Mr.—Jim."

"Well, I have no comment on that."

Now I didn't feel bad anymore. "No? How about this, then: you think your custody battle has nothing to do with the fact that I got an anonymous tip about Sharon Solarz?"

"And why should it?" He knew the answer, of course. What he wanted was to see if I knew it too.

"Your father-in-law is a former U.S. senator, Jim. He has a lot of clout in Albany."

"So?"

Just to show him I understood, I said patiently, "So, if I were Julia Montgomery, and I were taking you to court for custody of my daughter, and you knew that I was incompetent for reason of drug addiction, well . . . getting Daddy and his lawyers to tie you to a cop-killing radical fugitive would seem like a good start."

"Very good, Benny." There was resignation in your father's voice now. "Thanks a lot. You got it all right. Now go publish it."

"Mr. Grant."

"Ben, for God's sake."

"Jim. I'm sorry. Jim. I'm giving tons of goodwill here. You have all the chance in the world to respond."

A pause, and a shift in his voice. "I appreciate that, Ben. I'll tell you what. Come by my office, tomorrow afternoon. Say, four o'clock. And I'll explain."

I looked at my watch. "I have a deadline this evening, Mr. Grant."

Now your dad's voice shifted again, and I had a sense of what he was like in court. "Listen, if I'm in the paper tomorrow, don't bother coming downstate. You want the story, miss your deadline."

The line went dead. I flipped my cigarette onto the ground and went pensively back to my office.

Now, as you know, I got the Pulitzer in 2004, reporting on the fundamentalist revolution in Turkey before Turkey joined the war. I like to tell people that it was only the purest luck that had me in Istanbul in the first place—I'd been kicked out of Israel by the Jewish fundamentalists, and Turkey was the closest U.S. allied border.

Apart from that, however, the single other greatest piece of luck in my life was what happened that Tuesday afternoon in June, when I went in to my office.

I didn't have any question about waiting to write my story until I found out what Jim Grant had in mind the following afternoon. Certainly I was going to wait. Why not?

What I could do now, however, was see what else I could learn about Jim Grant. I could check with the American Bar Association. I could call friends in the Albany courthouse. I could run a PACER Legal search, and a Lexis, and look at past cases he'd been involved in.

And, nearly as an afterthought, I could do a background search.

Like most reporters, I had an investigator to call on.

Unlike most reporters, mine was a friend—Bill Taylor, a private detective in Connecticut I'd met researching one of my first articles.

I spent a good hour on the phone with Bill, catching up. Then another few minutes giving him the specifics of Jim Grant.

Bill listened quietly. Then he said, "Okay, bubba. I'll see what I can find. Page me Wednesday at twelve-hundred-thirty. I'm out of pocket till then."

And then, at last, it was time to check into the other office, where, it seemed to me, scotch and soda was the people's choice.

My reasoning was, essentially, homeopathic: treat like with like. Good scotch for the good, good work I'd done that day.

And soda because the effervescence would exactly mimic the feeling of excitement growing in my stomach and chest.

Date: June 8, 2006
From: **"Molly Sackler" <Molly@cusimanorganics.com>**
To: **"Isabel Montgomery" <isabel@exmnster.uk>**
CC: maillist: The_Committee
Subject: letter 8

Should I have noticed something wrong when J came home early that day? It was all so normal, my love. You'd spent the morning at my house, waiting for Leo to wake up, playing on the lawn and swimming in the pool, you little beauty, slim-limbed and lithe in the chlorine blue. That your father should have come home early wasn't exactly usual, not at that point when he was working hard, needing money. But it was not so strange this particular June afternoon, a summer day in the Catskills. Particularly given what he wanted to do, which was simply to go swimming up on the Katterskill with us.

I remember that day so well. I remember how present J was with you, fully engaged, listening carefully and responding with a gentleness that for me, in fact, defined him at his very best. I remember watching his slim, muscled body, warm in the sun, and under its fine tangle of red hair as he lay on an elbow, his brown eyes focused totally on you.

In retrospect, I realize the courage that it took, to be so present with you that day.

As we left the river in his Subaru, I remember clouds sweeping in from the west, high up, casting fast shadows across the thick midsummer foliage. Driving up 23A to pick up some cheese at the goat farm under the shifting shadows from the sky. You visiting with the goats while your daddy and I bought the cheese, your body hitched up on the fence in shorts and a swimming suit, while the little beasts gathered to the fence, bleating for food, and a barn kitten rubbed against your foot.

It was while we were there that J got a call from Benny, and then the tone of the day shifted again.

I remember afterward, taking 28 south through the Ashoken Reservoir to Kerhonkson, your father winding down the little roads with his eye on the rearview mirror, then up the long private road, where we had dinner with Charlie Miles and Naomi Freundlich and their kids while the sky got ready to rain. While Naomi and I took a run up Haver Road, your daddy sat with Charlie, watching you and Hannah and Clara, intently peering into the little pond, hunting for frogs. I remember leaving and driving through the night, you asleep against me in the backseat, and the car warm with the heat of our bodies, and intimate, and the black night all around infinite, and safe, and the menace of distant storm.

And I knew we were anything but safe, and your daddy knew it too. I could feel it, the sense of helplessness in him, a sense of lostness, and not just once but several times I found myself thinking of my own father. As if buried inside us for all these years was still the impulse, when things got bad enough, to call home. But there was no home to call to, and had not been for a great long time, and driving through that night with your father I think that we both, each in ourselves, felt the bitter and unheroic solitude of adulthood as we had never felt it before.

Your father, your father. Your father pulled into my driveway and sent me up into my own house, watching while I tiredly climbed the stairs to begin my night's vigil. Perhaps he longed to come with me, up to my bedroom; perhaps he told himself that that avenue of comfort, the last, was closed to him now too. Perhaps driving across to his own driveway, pulling in, and turning off the car's lights, it was easier for him to think that I did not understand what he was about to do.

For a long time, at the window of my bedroom, I watched him sitting there. Knowing, knowing, and still wishing it wasn't true, and still knowing there was nothing, nothing I could do.

You sleeping in the backseat.

The storm approaching through the night.

And then I watched him pull out of the driveway, headlights still off, and make his way slowly along the road, lit only by the moon, past my house and back to 32.

And it was only then, as he got clear out of our neighborhood and onto the main road, that I saw his headlights turn on and accelerate out of sight to the north.

Date: June 8, 2006
From: "Daddy" <littlej@cusimanorganics.com>
To: "Isabel Montgomery" <isabel@exmnster.uk>
CC: maillist: The_Committee
Subject: letter 9

Oh, God, Isabel, that night. I drove north under the shifting sky, north and west, and didn't stop until Watertown, where a one-story motel lay in a hollow of rolling hills.

I remember the smell of curry in the office of the motel, a Hindi satellite broadcast sounding from a TV. I remember carrying you inside a little room, limp over my left shoulder, through the mosquitoes under the neon lights lighting the outside of the little rooms.

Because I knew the thunder would wake you and scare you, I sat with you while the storm rolled in, watching your face in the dim light through the curtain on which big moths threw shadows, unwilling to leave. You slept on one cheek, your face composed in nonnegotiable gravity, but with a total lack of effort, a sleeping Buddha. And as always, at the sight of you sleeping I felt a regret that sat heavy in my belly, a regret that seared.

What good is beauty when it never appears but as an adjunct of loss? What good is love when it is entirely powerless? I left the bedroom door open and went out onto the little concrete porch where under the motel's eaves I sat, watching the curtain of rain. I closed my eyes and saw myself surfing a wave of flame, balanced on the heat itself. My stomach was flooded with the awareness of loss, past loss, imminent loss. I tried to tell myself that my perch in life was not nearly that precarious. I tried to tell myself that life has a way of righting itself. I tried to tell myself what I've always told myself: that my life was a story with a happy ending, and that the plot twist I was in now would only make that ending all the happier. I tried to let my mind melt into the thick tapestry of falling rain.

God, I was scared. A paralyzing, debilitating fear that seemed, now, to stretch each second out to an unbearable length, an unendurable stretch of time to be traversed. Regret searing through me. Sharon Solarz, Julia's lawsuit, Ben Schulberg. Everything I most feared was coming home, just when I needed a quiet, calm, obscure life in which I could, alone and unencumbered, try to help my fiendishly smart, precociously verbal daughter—the daughter of a drug addict—become a human being. No one knew the damage Julia had done, no one except me and Molly. Even you don't know, Izzy. The night terrors, the phobias, the early childhood stammering—no one knew the enormity of the heart, the solitude, the patience that you needed, and no one knew how much progress you had made in the past two years.

And now the whole wide world was conspiring to take away my chance to make you whole.

I sat up nursing my anxiety, as hard as a bowling ball in my stomach, until midnight, while the rain came and passed. And finally, when I could stand it no more, I stepped out of my clothes and, stark naked, dropped into the motel pool.

Here for a time I floated on the surface, staring up into the sky, where waves of clouds moved over a quilt of stars and a half moon was rising. I must have dozed, for through my body passed a memory of my father as a young man, swimming with me at Colgate Lake. For a time I felt my body as light as a boy's, a boy's in the strong and safe care of his father. Then, vividly, a recurrent dream came to me, and I watched myself walk into the woods and lift my infant daughter from where she lay on the ground. Then I came to myself: a middle-aged man with a dead father and the grief of a lost daughter in a black night.

Back at the room where you slept, I sat on the porch again. A full cloud cover was over now, and a growing breeze made me shiver once or twice. I did not move, though. I sat, watching the darkness at the bottom of the night while the winds rose and the summer storm at last came in from the mountaintop, dumped its water on the river flats with its roaring complexity of tiny drops, and then rumbled away to the distance, leaving in its wake thin rivulets of water running toward the creek.

And then it was light, and I must have slept in the deck chair, because you were standing next to me in your nightdress, your body still warm from sleep, your face artless in its awakening. And I noticed, as I did every morning, that no matter what kind of night I had had, or what kind of pain I was in, before you, before your reality, it seemed that all horrors were an illusion and that everything was going to be okay.

But which was the illusion?

No decision had been made, no understanding had been accomplished, no clarity achieved. But with the vision of your face, smoothed by sleep and softened in early light, I slowly, with saturnine unwillingness, acknowledged that what I had for so long feared was here.

Bobby Montgomery and I, our little game of nuclear parity was at an end.

As long as the threat I posed to him—my ability to ruin his chances of becoming ambassador to the Court of St. James by exposing his daughter's years of drug abuse and trouble with the law—was balanced against the threat he posed to me, everything was stable.

But now Sharon Solarz was going to trial, and somehow, somehow, your grandfather had gotten Ben Schulberg on the case and caused him to put Jim Grant's name in the press. That changed the whole equation. Because Ben Schulberg, whether he knew it or not, was on the story of his career, a story that would be followed not just in Saugerties and Albany but by the *New York Times,* by *60 Minutes,* by reporters like Douglas Frantz and producers like John Marks, and these remorselessly intelligent, infinitely energetic people would focus the same energies on me as they did on embezzlers, dictators, and murderers, and when they did, they would find out the truth.

Watching you, with an unwillingness as big as the big blue Catskill sky, I began the long process of finding the words to describe, to a seven-year-old, the absolutely incomprehensible thing that I was about to do.

Date: June 9, 2006

From: "Benjamin Schulberg" <benny@cusimanorganics.com>

To: "Isabel Montgomery" <isabel@exmnster.uk>

CC: maillist: The_Committee

Subject: letter 10

"Kid?" The voice in the telephone receiver, when I got to work on Wednesday morning, was hard to place—particularly through the fog of hangover: I had spent the evening at the Shandon Star the night before, and tested, not for the first time, Hemingway's statement that a bottle of wine was the best dinner companion. Of course, the wine, in this case, was bar scotch and soda—at some point I dropped the soda—and dinner was sliced turkey and gravy on white bread from the Shandon Star's steam table. Memory serves, I believe instant mashed potatoes had also entered into the picture. Nonetheless, Hemingway was not entirely unrelated to the evening, if only because now, this morning, I felt like shooting myself.

"Yes?"

"Billy Cusimano here. Have you been in touch with my lawyer?"

I looked at my watch, which I had been avoiding in order not to know how late I was to work. It was ten. "Yesterday I was. I'm due to see him at four this afternoon."

"I see." There was a silence.

"What's up, Mr. Cusimano?"

There was real ambivalence in the man's voice, but at last he answered. "He hasn't shown up at my arraignment."

Foggily, I tried to figure that one out. "You're in court?"

"Christ, you should know. Remember, those fuckers had a bug in my Sea of Green? Caught Sharon like that?"

"I thought you said Mr. Grant would have that thrown out of court?"

Cusimano seemed a bit testy this morning. Perhaps he was hung over too. "First he has to show up *in* court. Then he gets it thrown out *of* court. That's the way it works. You seen him, or not?"

I was stammering a little. "No."

"Okay, kid. You'll see him this afternoon, then. I guess."

The call had come in as I sat down at my desk. Now, thinking about it, I checked my messages and found that it was the third time Cusimano had called that morning. I booted my computer, launched my phone book, and called your daddy's house, where there was no answer, then his office, which picked up right away.

"Mike? Ben Schulberg, up at the *Times*."

"Hey, Ben." Jim's assistant answered in what struck me as an anxious voice.

"Mr. Grant in?"

"No, he's not."

There was a silence. I found myself holding the receiver with both hands.

"Mike, tell me what's up."

"Nothing's up."

"Yes, something is. Tell me. Off the record. I can help."

I listened to the silence of Mike's struggle for a moment, holding his breath. Then he spoke.

"Well, the woman who takes care of Jim's daughter? This morning, Jim and Isabel don't come over. So Molly goes over to his house, and finds that they hadn't slept there."

"Is that unusual?"

"Well, yeah. She's . . . she's kind of Jim's girlfriend. They're very close. It's very unusual. Look, we're badly worried."

"And why?"

"Because . . . look, you know the kind of work Jim does. And he's been under a great deal of pressure. We're extremely worried."

"Okay. Could you keep me in the loop? I'll see if I can find something."

Ten-fifteen. I was standing before I even hung up the telephone, and my cigarette was lit before I got out of the building lobby. Still, it was only half smoked before I was back at my desk, on the edge of my chair, dialing the number of the Albany FBI field station and speaking in a voice that, since I'd last spoken to Cornelius, I had not yet used.

"Mr. Cornelius. Listen. I've got something for you. The terms are that I get exclusive coverage, and the fullest disclosure the law allows."

This time, Cornelius was prepared. "Mr. Schulberg, if you have evidence of a crime, you are legally obliged to tell me. And don't give me any privileged-source bullshit, my bosses are itching to take the question to court."

"Okay. Send someone over to arrest me. Because I have solid suspicion of a serious crime, and I'm not telling you anything. And by the time you even get me handcuffed, it'll be too the fuck late."

I hung up. There was a pause of perhaps two minutes, during which I kept my hand on the receiver.

I wanted to smoke.

At last, the phone rang. "This better turn out good, Schulberg."

"It will."

"Go ahead then."

"Okay. I'm on the way to your office. While you're waiting, you know Jim Grant, Billy Cusimano's lawyer? James Marshal Grant. Run a check on Jim Grant's recent credit card activity, EZ Pass usage, and cell phone. I'll be right there."

"Wait. Why?"

It was like my whole body was on the way to the door while the phone tethered me to the desk.

"Because Jim Grant's kidnapped his daughter to escape his wife's custody suit."

Date: June 9, 2006
From: "Daddy" <littlej@cusimanorganics.com>
To: "Isabel Montgomery" <isabel@exmnster.uk>
CC: maillist: The_Committee
Subject: letter 11

Clayton, New York. Midsummer sun, rich with the potamic hues of the St. Lawrence River. The shores of Canada a virtually neon green in the distance.

At 10:00, I parked at the bottom of the highway exit ramp and listened to the hourly news on NPR, all the while carrying on the game of "I Spy" I was playing with you, buckled in the backseat, over the sound of the radio. When nothing on the news made me nervous, I drove on into town and found the post office.

On the street: vacation families in shorts and sandals and T-shirts advertising various products moved under the high, hot sun, overflowing out the door of the breakfast joint, the drugstore, the sporting goods shop. I watched the scene through the windscreen for a time. No one was hanging out casually watching the post office front door, no vans were parked, no pedestrians passed, then passed again. Finally, instructing you to stay in the car, I pulled on a baseball cap from Jam's Café and Pancake House in Haines Falls, climbed out into the heat, and went through the front door.

Wearing the hat on my head and my heart, I swear to you, Izzy, in my mouth. Right between my teeth. Red, and beating, and dripping blood.

The post office doubled as a convenience store, and I noticed, in passing, that Sharon Solarz was on the front page of the *New York Times*. I didn't buy the paper but went straight to the counter and picked up the package of clothes I had express-mailed to John Herman, care of General Delivery, in what seemed like another life. The woman behind the counter gave it to me without a second glance, but it was not until I was walking out that I allowed relief to flood through me, like a drug. I went back to the car, and I remember, I lifted you out and hugged you like I had not seen you in six weeks.

God, I was scared.

I locked the car and, carrying the package, walked with you down the main street to the little Greyhound terminal, announced by a neon sign surviving from the 1940s. With the sun already up for hours, the temperature was in the high nineties, the air laden with moisture. In the station, there were two ticket booths, and I approached the left-hand one, then hoisted you into my arms so you could see in the window while I bought two tickets on the 10:30 to Montreal, an adult and a child, the adult wearing a hat reading "Jam's Café and Pancake House," across the border to Montreal.

The bus was leaving in ten minutes. Plenty of time, I assured you, for you to go to the bathroom. You asked me, what if we missed it? Then there was a 10:50, I told you. You didn't, of course, think to ask how I knew this schedule by heart. Your daddy, you still thought, knew everything.

And I didn't, of course, think to tell you that I had memorized, long before, virtually every bus leaving that station, any morning of the week.

Date: June 9, 2006
From: "Benjamin Schulberg" <benny@cusimanorganics.com>
To: "Isabel Montgomery" <isabel@exmnster.uk>
CC: maillist: The_Committee
Subject: letter 12

Albany, New York. I arrived at the Albany FBI's office by 11:00 to find Kevin Cornelius in the situation room with a task force of four. Three were on the telephone, one before a computer screen. Kevin took me directly to the wall, where a state map was hung.

"Grant's credit card paid a motel room in Watertown last night. This morning his EZ Pass paid a toll on I-84."

Watching the map, I nodded. "Canada."

"Yep. More important, he express-mailed a package to himself in Clayton last Saturday, from Albany." There was thinly veiled satisfaction in Cornelius's voice. "Must have been a change of clothes for his kid. Used the same credit card then. Not smart. Not smart at all. For such a smart guy."

Cornelius laughed—a laugh I recognized as the one a sixty-five-thousand-dollar-a-year cop laughs when a Yale-educated lawyer makes a mistake. When he was finished, I said, "That's the day I first went to see him."

He nodded happily. "Never fails. Use the press, make the criminal make a mistake. Clayton police already found Grant's car on Clayton Main Street, right near the post office."

I watched him now, mouth open, which seemed to satisfy him. "Did he pick up his package?"

"Sure did."

"Have you checked the bus station?"

"Better yet, we have a middle-aged man with a daughter buying tickets on the 10:30 to Montreal. Bus left thirty minutes ago. Canadian police are searching for him."

"You mean, they don't have him yet?"

"No, buddy." He said it in a singsong, with a western lilt. "The bus made four stops in Canada before we traced him to it. There's a dragnet out already. Won't be long, Ben. And when we get him, we'll get him on the other side of the border. That's international flight."

"Is it really?" And as I said that, Cornelius's earlier comment, about your daddy not being smart, came back to me, and I sat down heavily on a chair, as realization after realization washed through me.

Date: June 9, 2006
From: "Daddy" <littlej@cusimanorganics.com>
To: "Isabel Montgomery" <isabel@exmnster.uk>
CC: maillist: The_Committee
Subject: letter 13

Eleven o'clock. In the bus station in Clayton.

At ten-twenty, when you went to the bathroom, I left you with strict instructions to wash your hands and then wait just inside the bathroom door until I knocked.

Then I went to the men's room.

Inside, I went into a stall and locked the door. I took off the baseball cap and put on sunglasses. I took off my white shirt and blue jeans. Then I opened the Mailboxes Etcetera box and took out the nylon Sportsac bag. From it I put on a loud blue tropical shirt and a pair of white pants. I stuffed my other clothes back and closed the bag. Then I peeled the address labels off the box, tore them up, and flushed them down the toilet. Finally, I folded the box carefully and wedged it behind the toilet.

I went right back out now, a balding man in a loud shirt and black glasses, carrying a Sportsac bag, hoping I looked like a tall Jack Nicholson traveling alone, knowing I looked like an upstate loser who had just lost all his money at a reservation casino. I crossed the little terminal to the right-hand teller and bought two adult tickets to New York City, Port Authority.

Then I collected you from the girl's room.

The New York bus left at 10:40. We waited together, sitting in the little lunch counter in the back of the terminal. You talked to the counterperson, played with an activity book I had bought, drank an orange juice. I, next to you, watched the police following the trail I'd left from the Mailboxes Etc. in Albany to the bus to Canada.

This was a key time, the time at the beginning when, I knew, any mistakes you had made would come out and bite you, hard. And that was as it should be: if there were mistakes, I wanted to find out early, at the beginning, rather than later, when I would have involved other people too.

I watched—and I didn't quite watch. An unreal air hung over the scene for me. Both state cops and what looked like FBI were in the ticket booths, and after a time a few carloads left, lights flashing, in the direction of the bridge to Canada.

Then it was just a bus station again. The smell of bus exhaust and hot dogs was familiar from ages spent in bus terminals when I was younger. But nothing felt familiar. The sense of loss that had been tearing at me since early in the morning, it shocked me.

Izzy. I can't tell you how happy I had been as Jim Grant. It was like being a child. I missed everything: the kitchen of the house in Saugerties; the run to Dutcher Notch; I missed Molly. It was a feeling of mourning, a mourning nearly as intense as I'd felt when I read that my father had died in '94, and with it came shock, for I had not known that I could feel this mourning for my own life. And I asked myself, How was I, an overgrown baby feeling homesick, meant to take care of you?

And then we were on the bus, with its stale smell of gas and old smoke, pulling out and through town. At the post office, two state police cruisers were parked, and I could see that the police were searching my car, but the bus went right on by, out onto the highway, the pitch of its tires on concrete rising with its speed.

New York City. *Just like I pictured it.* From far in my mind came Stevie Wonder's voice from "Living for the City." Believe it or not, Izzy, I hadn't been to New York City in twenty years.

I closed my eyes now, tight, and all of New York—the whole city—appeared to me a strange, foreign, frightening world.

Date: June 9, 2006
From: "Benjamin Schulberg"
<benny@cusimanorganics.com>
To: "Isabel Montgomery" <isabel@exmnster.uk>
CC: maillist: The_Committee
Subject: letter 14

At twelve-thirty, Kevin Cornelius and his task force were eating sandwiches in the situation room. The subject of discussion was marriage and its discontents—particularly when those discontents caused arrests to be made, which was more often than one might have thought.

That's always the way with cops, when writers get to them. First they have to tell you what weasels all writers are. Then they have to tell you how tough they are. Only when the proper pecking order has been established, and they've proved themselves to be the purplest-assed baboon in the troop, do they start spilling their guts all over the floor. And before long, everyone is telling you about the screenplay they're writing, or the short story, or the novel, or failing that, their secret passion for needlepoint. Never fails—or hardly ever.

These guys were still at stage two. All of them had been involved in parental kidnappings before; all had war stories to tell me.

Only I, it seemed, was watching the big clock on the wall ticking.

When I could, I excused myself and went outside. Stepping into the sun, I put a cigarette in my mouth, then ostentatiously patted down my pockets, looking for matches. Clearly having none, I walked now over to my car, sat in the front seat, and turned on the engine. I lit my cigarette from the lighter, then switched to the battery charger and placed a call.

Anyone watching could have seen I was calling a pager. I punched in some numbers, then hung up and waited, smoking. In a few moments my phone rang, and I answered.

"Hey, bub." Billy Taylor's deep, rich voice sounded in my ear, and as always, I felt a little safer. Billy, as law enforcers go, was the exception that proved the rule. For one thing, he'd much rather have been a writer, and he admitted it. For another, he only enforced laws he believed in.

"Billy, how are you?"

"Better'n you, the sound of your voice."

"You haven't had the chance to run the check, have you?"

"I have not. My assistant has, though."

"What'd she get?"

"Well, bub, your boy's pretty interesting. You know that?"

I realized my hand was holding the cell phone like a vise. I changed hands and lowered my voice.

"Bill, I'm outside an FBI field station, and there's a manhunt going on. Give it to me."

Billy's voice changed. "There's three datapoints. One: your man hasn't filed taxes on his social but once, and the social was only issued in one-nine-seven-six. That's from Autovan, so it's not so reliable. But there it is. That make sense?"

Me, dry mouthed: "It could. But it also couldn't—he worked for his wife's foundation, unpaid. What's two?"

"A death certificate in the name of James Marshal Grant was issued in Bakersfield, California, where your man says he comes from, in 1959. A two-year-old boy, killed in a car crash."

"Oh, God. Dead baby." My stomach was plummeting.

"Not bad, for a college boy. But three's the kicker."

"I'm listening."

"Your man had a PSA test last year."

"PSA?"

"Prostate-specific antigen. A screening for prostate cancer."

"So?"

"The doctor's records specify it was a screening, mind. No specific complaint. No benign hypertrophy, no problem pissing, no burning, no tingling. No impotence, pain, weight loss, anemia. No—"

Billy was mid-fifties. I interrupted. "Billy?"

"Yes, bub."

"How's your prostate?"

"Sucks. Big time."

"Sorry to hear it."

"That's okay, bub. Four marriages, five kids. I'm about done with it, anyways."

"Hope so. Now, about my man."

With satisfaction in his voice, Bill answered. "In the absence of a specific complaint, you only screen for PSA after forty-five. Your man's supposed to be thirty-nine."

I let a long silence hang in the phone. "I see."

Billy, who had done three tours of duty in Vietnam, spoke with a chuckle in his voice. "You got a tiger by the tail there, bubba?"

"I believe I do."

"Need some protection? I can have a man with you in a quarter hour."

"No, it's not me that needs the protection."

"On the hunt, are we? Well, boy, remember, that's dangerous too. If it hollers, you let it go and call me tout suite. Promise?"

"I promise, Billy."

God, I felt exhausted as I walked back into the situation room. A glance was enough to see that nothing had changed except the subject of conversation, which was now sex crimes. Drained, I sat down next to Cornelius. A *New York Times* was on the table. I picked it up and turned to page 21, where I knew—I had already read the article and noted the reference to my having broken the Solarz story—there was a photo. Here, a picture ran of Sharon Solarz, sitting on the hood of a car between Billy Ayers and Skip Taube, in front of the University of Michigan campus. The caption had it at 1971, and dully I registered the mistake: it must have been before March 6, 1970, in fact, because Diana Oughton was visible in the background, and Diana Oughton died in the town house bombing. Next to her was Jason Sinai, and it was at his picture that I peered closely. Staring across twenty-five years back at me, the young man told me nothing. Then, without looking up, and interrupting the description of the apprehension of a serial rapist, I asked.

"Kevin, didn't you say you got Grant's prints out of Cusimano's house?"

"I did."

"Did you run them against anything?"

"No. Just against Grant's known prints."

"I see." Now I closed the papers and sighed. "Can you run them against Jason Sinai?"

Cornelius stared. "Why would I do that?"

I checked my watch. Nearly eight hours to deadline. It seemed like no time at all for the story I had to write.

"Because I was wrong. Jim Grant didn't run to escape his wife's custody suit."

Pause, while they watched me.

"What actually happened is that Jim Grant ran to avoid being arrested as Jason Sinai. And Jason Sinai's just evaded your capture in Clayton, New York."

Date: June 9, 2006
From: "daddy" <littlej@cusimanorganics.com>
To: "Isabel Montgomery" <isabel@exmnster.uk>
CC: maillist: The_Committee
Subject: letter 15

In New York City the summer's heat was coming in, the part of the year approaching when even Woodstock summer residents rented out their houses for criminal prices to unsuspecting New Yorkers and escaped to cooler climes, a killing heat interrupted, only if you're lucky, by vicious rains.

It was early afternoon when we arrived at the Port Authority, and I led you into the city as if into a magical forest. You had never, ever imagined that there could be a place like this, and for every moment that you found yourself, literally, squeezing my hand so hard that it hurt, you also found yourself utterly lost in your field of vision.

For seven straight hours I led you, and carried you, and had you driven, and even had you pulled by a horse in a carriage. Without ever explaining to you how I knew this place so well. I took you to a round building where you took an elevator to the top and then skipped down in circles, like on the inside of a corkscrew, you running up and down while I watched, and when you were bored of running, we looked, together, at some of the paintings on the wall. I took you to a toy store to buy presents and a jewelry store for earrings and a grand, massive hotel for tea. I took you to the zoo, to the carousel, and there, next to the carousel, I had a horse and chariot take you through a park. A taxi swept you down a wide river, which I said was the same that flowed by your house, at home, the one I always said got so small that the people in the Adirondacks could step over it. Watching it, you thought of the people in the Adirondacks, who you always thought of as Indians. Watching, you wondered how far we were from home and when we were going back. Watching, you wondered why you were being so spoiled today.

We went to a store where I dressed you in new clothes, then I bought you a whole bunch more. Then we went to a restaurant where you ate, for the first time in your life, a lobster. It was dark when we came out, and a taxi took us way into another part of the city, where the buildings were high and thin and the streets like long, shadowed canyons. In one building was a hotel, and here they were expecting us, because they greeted me by name. Admittedly, it was by the wrong name, but I had warned you they were going to do this. I had even told you the name: Robert Russell. From now on, I told you, I was going to be Robert Russell, and you were going to be little Isabel Russell. It was all part of the game.

Here, in a hotel room, I bathed you by the open window, the slow summer dusk flowing in while you chatted away about the day before with Molly. Standing, your body was like a kidney bean on a stick: still round with baby fat, but your legs already showing the slim length they would, just like your mother's, one day hold. When you were washed I dried you, first telling you to hold your hands up, then your chin up, then your legs open. Then I hit you lightly with the towel and said to go get dressed, which you did, still holding your chin up, hands up, legs open as you marched to the bedroom, until one by one I told you to resume normal stance.

I had to call down to the front desk for a toothbrush, because in all the things I had packed to send to Clayton, and in all the things I had bought in New York, I had forgotten a toothbrush. While you waited, you watched cable TV, which you had never seen before.

You argued over combing your hair, you argued over turning off the TV, I sang you a song, and we lay together in your bed by the open window, feeling the hot night wash in, smelling the sea. I told you you were just on the tip of the Island, the southern tip. It was, I told you, where sailors used to sail for the ocean to hunt whales. I talked until your eyes shut, and then I lay next to you, staring at you, until you were asleep.

Or so I thought.

Much later I found out, not from you but from someone you told, that when you opened one eye, to surprise me, you found me not waiting but crying, and surprised, you closed your eyes again to think.

Only, so long had been the day, filled with so many things, that even seeing something this strange didn't stop your descent into sleep, and the vision of your father crying, with your thoughts, turned into dreams.

While you slept, I watched. I watched, lying on the bed next to you, stroking your forehead, while you slept, and I watched while the clock passed ten, then eleven, to twelve. I watched you, in fact, until the time when the *Albany Times* posted its next morning's Web edition.

At two o'clock, I finally got up from the bed and walked down the hallway to the little office suite the Wall Street Marriot advertised having on each floor. True to their word, a computer sat with an always-on Net connection. I found and launched Netscape, then entered the URL for the *Times* and then, for a long moment, shut my eyes; longer than it took for the front page to launch, much longer.

When I opened them I was looking, of course, at a picture of myself.

Three pictures, to be exact.

One taken recently at a dinner at the Albany Civil Liberties Union, the second from a twenty-year-old wanted poster for Jason Sinai, and the third, a computer enhancement showing the effects of aging and plastic surgery, rendering it crystal clear that, as the article under Ben Schulberg's byline made clear, they were the same.

So Benny had done it. Twenty years before, Senator Montgomery had discovered who I was with the aid of the FBI's background check of his daughter's fiancé, and then he had used resources that only a U.S. senator could command to bury the truth again. Now, with a telephone and a computer, for the second time ever, Benny had figured it all out.

Only Benny wasn't going to keep it secret, the way your grandfather did, Izzy. There was no way.

First of all, he didn't have his daughter's happiness to think about, as Bobby Montgomery had, twenty years ago, when he faced the choice of quashing an FBI investigation or seeing his daughter go underground with her fugitive boyfriend.

Second of all, Benny didn't have a reason to blackmail me, as your grandfather later had, forcing me to keep Julia's drug and law troubles secret in exchange for his keeping mine.

Now your grandfather didn't need to blackmail me anymore. Now Benny had told the whole story, and all your grandfather had to do was send someone to pick you up and take you to London.

This time, when your mother remembered to look for you where she last left you, before she got high, who knows if you'd survive?

Woodenly, I stood now and walked back to the room. I did not look at you again, nor did I touch you. Robotic, automatic—numbed. I simply picked up the Sportsac, put it over my shoulder, and left.

When you woke up, of course, I was gone.

Other people were there. A woman with red hair. A man in a suit. And policemen, lots and lots of policemen, all with their uniforms on and guns out, and all pointed at you, or rather, at the bed, where they thought that I was hiding, under the covers, next to you.

See, it's like I told you, Izzy.

All parents are bad parents.

One day, I promise, I promise, you will be a bad parent too.

PART TWO

Hush little darling
Go to sleep
Look out the window
Count the sheep
That dot the hillsides
And the fields of wheat
Across America
As we cross America
What's important
Here today?
The broken line
On the highway.

—Chrissie Hynde,
"Thumbelina"

Date: June 10, 2006
From: "Amelia Wanda Lurie" <mimi@cusimanorganics.com>
To: "Isabel Montgomery" <isabel@exmnster.uk>
CC: maillist: The_Committee
Subject: letter 16

Childhood is a shadowed path into a fairy-tale forest. It's dark in there, and scary, and we don't want to go in, but the big hand holding ours is always pulling, and the voice somewhere above is always urging us to come ahead.

For a while everything is okay.

For a while, in fact, everything is even kind of good.

The woods are beautiful, filled with sparkling streams and swaying trees, with enticing patches of sun on the bed of leaves and the huge, even breath of kind wind. There are furry beasts and glowing fires, and if it's a little scary, so what? The adults around us, the kind, good adults, they're sure and strong, and they have, for us, marvelous places waiting around every turn.

It's only slowly, a step at a time, that it happens. A half-truth, a tiny disappointment, a little lie, and guess what? They never even apologize. One day they expect us just to understand their dirty little secret. Life is a shadowed path into a fairy-tale forest, and we never should have gone in because the dangers are real, there is no way out, and as for our guides, they are now, and have been since the very beginning, completely lost.

Isabel Sinai. Jason Sinai's daughter, come back to haunt us. Come back to tell us: *I am the voice of everyone you failed. I am the witness of every mistake you made. I am the little one you abandoned in the fairy-tale woods, the one you lied to and lost, and now, now, I have your life in my hands.*

Your father asked me to write to you. But what am I supposed to say? Should I beg? Should I plead? I've never even met you, but I can hear your answer. *Do you have any idea—any idea at all—what you are asking me to do? Do you have any idea who you are asking me to betray?*

Yes. Yes, I know what we are asking you to do. I know who we are asking you to betray. It's that your father asked me to write to you. The whole damn Committee asked me to write to you. How am I supposed to say no?

So let me tell you a story, Isabel-Sinai-at-seventeen-years-old. Listen, Isabel Sinai who lost her childhood when she was abandoned in a hotel room at seven, and who will never get it back. Let me tell you a story about your father and his father.

Of all the stories your father told me, the years and years that we were underground, and in love, it's the one that stayed with me. It stayed with me the way it is when someone you love tells you a part of their past that becomes a part of your own past. Stayed with me as if it were my own memory, in all its details, in all its importance. For the twenty-five years that Little J was Jim Grant and I was Tess Sanders, and, now that I am Mimi Lurie again, it stays with me still.

You may think this is a distraction.

But I promise you, when all this is done, and your decision is made, and the events of June 2006, like those of June 1996, are a memory, it is this little story that will stay with you, the rest of your life.

2.

When your father was a boy, his father woke him in the middle of the night and took him on a trip.

His memory starts in the backseat of a Dodge Dart, his father at the wheel, watching through the window as they pulled silently through the empty city, Sheridan Square, Seventh Avenue, Chambers Street, the Municipal Building with its gilded figure of justice aloft over the deserted streets. They crossed the Brooklyn Bridge, and your father remembers as if in a photograph the smooth spread of heaving black, the basin of New York Harbor, on the mouth of which the Verrazano-Narrows Bridge glittered just as it would appear to him, all those years later after he left you in a hotel room.

Even then, at ten, leaving the city made him scared for his father, your grandfather. There was a big country out there, he knew, and that big country had once put his father in jail.

That, his father told him, was the bad old days of the fifties.

Now, in this black of night, it was 1960, and by the time they hit Jersey, your father was asleep in the backseat of a Dodge Dart.

He woke in light, a place unlike any he had ever seen before. An endless vista of people composed the landscape, thousands and thousands of them in an undulating, unbroken mass. It seemed the car had been swallowed by this crowd of people, all of whom seemed to be facing in the direction of a loudspeaker, sometimes listening, sometimes roaring a response. Such a roar that, when at last the car could go no farther and its doors opened from the outside, your father drew back in fright. But his father took his hand, and they climbed out into the crowd.

It was 1960, my dear, forty-six years ago today. A lifetime. The place was the mall in Washington, D.C.; the crowd was gathered to demand the passage of a law called the Voting Rights Act—a law that protected the right of black Americans to vote, and would not be passed for five years yet—and your father's father had driven him through the night to come and demand it too.

But your father doesn't remember any of that. What your father remembers is a forest of legs, a jungle of identical black-suited legs in black shiny dress shoes, and how sweaty and slippery was his father's hand, and the slow waves of the crowd shifting ahead, and then back, and a big voice booming, disembodied, from a loudspeaker somewhere he couldn't see.

And then his father's hand was gone. In an instant, gone, leaving only the memory of its grip, its warmth, leaving your father alone. For a time he stood in shock as the black-suited legs pressed all around him, closer and closer as a great roar rose from the crowd and there was a long surge forward, and he had to move with it to stay upright, as best he could. Then the crowd surged back, and back again, and he was jogging backward away from the legs in front of him, constantly about to fall on those behind. Above him the adults were shouting, and above them farther he saw a flash of ice blue sky, a brilliant October sun, and as he struggled in the shifting mass of adults—as your father tells it, he found his gaze fixed on that blue, as if in its distance, in its utter unknowability, lay some kind of hope. And then, just as suddenly as he had been pushed ahead, he was lifted up by a pair of long hands that lifted him under his arms and carried him high up into the air over the crowd as his father, panic-stricken, struggled back through the thick press of people who had separated them, and took him back.

It may seem a small thing to you, you who were really abandoned, and really lost, what happened to your father in Washington. But your father never forgave his father that day; never. And for all the people on earth who adored Jack Sinai—for Jack Sinai was a massive figure of his times—never did your grandfather recover from the fact that even before he lost his eldest son, he lost his eldest son's trust. As for your father, before too long he was back on the mall in Washington, D.C., and he was feeling, again, rage. Rage at all the people, like his father, who had marched on Washington before. Rage at their failure to achieve civil rights, to stop the war, to change the government. Rage at their compromise, their ineffectiveness; rage at *their* rage, which had lost their battles, again and again. And in many ways, it would be for that loss—not for losing him, but for losing the battle for what was right—that your father would never forgive his father.

But Isabel—this is the part I want you to understand. Your father, too, would come to be an adult who lost a child, and when that happened, your father began to think of his father in a new way. You may say that it was because it was then that for the first time your father stopped blaming his father for having lost him and began blaming himself for having lost his own child. Maybe so. The fact remains that from that day on his memory of his father began to change, as if he had never really recognized his father when he could actually see him, talk to him, touch him. As if, because his father had died while he was underground, he had never really lost him but would find him, with the rest of his family—his mother, his brother—where he had left them, in a Greenwich Village of twenty-six years ago.

He discovered in his mind remarkable detail, remarkably vivid memories of remarkably precise times: his father under the Atlantic sun next to water at Martha's Vineyard; in the vast green woods of the Catskills, summer after summer, at the window in his offices at the Exchange Building, staring out over the East River; and in a sudden rush of longing, at the dinner table at home on Bedford Street. Food gave him vivid memories, as if his father's tastes all along had inhabited your fathers' palate, waiting to be found. And as the decisions and the dangers of his life became adult, he found very new images of his father becoming dominant in his imagination, much more complex ones than the man who drove his ten-year-old son from New York to Washington to attend a voting rights demonstration and once there, lost him. Some were historical: his father—like your father—had played big roles in his time, as a lawyer, as an activist, and once even as a soldier. Others were intimate: in memory he recognized as never before the old man's patience, his forbearance, his fundamental goodness. And some were purely physical: the quiet strength of the middle-aged man who had raised him, and whom he had never seen grow old.

And so it was that when it came to your father, in turn, to lose his child, he found it was to his father's image that he turned immediately and repeatedly to measure each step of what he was about to do.

And always, his father was there. As if his father was a voice deep in his mind, and that voice was whispering help. In a very real way, your father's father came to him more directly than when he had been alive. And perhaps that is the answer to the conundrum that all parents are, one way or another, bad parents; the conundrum that one day we will each be a bad parent too. Perhaps the more flawed performances of our lives as parents are, in the deepest sense, our practice for that more complicated job we will have to do long after we're gone, long after we're dead, guiding our children through the high dangers of adulthood, giving them directions they will not even know they need for many, many years to come.

When your father came to need so his father's example was many years after his father lost him at a civil rights demonstration in Washington, when your father lost his own daughter. And it was then, when a series of events with which we are required to reckon today, began.

3.

Now in the story your father and Ben are telling you, it is June 20, 1996, the day your father went on the run, leaving you in a hotel bedroom on Wall Street. Okay, and for me, too, it is that day. Only it is later, three o'clock in the afternoon, West Coast time. More or less. You want to know exactly, go get the Coast Guard's log of their activities that afternoon: it'll tell you the precise time they hailed the *Evelyn II,* a Pearson 49 in a racing suit of sail—a half-million-dollar yacht—practicing for the Catalina Cup some two miles off the coast of Big Sur.

A high, pale blue sky of wispy cloud was overhead, moving in southerly air at nine knots or so. When it hit the warm mass of land, it defined itself as a cloud bank at the coast, through which showed an occasional glimpse of Big Sur. We stood hove-to in, maybe, three foot of sea, waiting. Four points off the port bow at perhaps a quarter mile's distance a freighter tossed little balls of smoke into the sky.

At the Coast Guard's radioed orders, I, captaining the yacht, had hove to and waited for them to cross my bow on their way to board the freighter. At the same time a young man called Aaron, one of the *Evelyn*'s crew of six, surreptitiously gaffed the last shrink-wrapped bale of marijuana, bobbing gently in the chop, a satellite beacon made from a doctored EPIRB gently flashing orange. Aaron held the bale against the boat's side with the gaff while I spilled wind out of the mainsail, balancing the backed jib against the rudder to keep us as still as possible until the Coast Guard boat had disappeared on the portside of the freighter. Then Aaron hauled in the bale and muscled it belowdecks while the rest of us waited for the Coast Guard to let us go.

If they decided to board us, they'd find a crew of seven sailors, four men, three women, in matching red Gill Atlantic coveralls practicing for a yacht race in a million-dollar boat. The boat belonged to Mark "Mac" McLeod, an obscenely wealthy resident of Big Sur, and the crew were semiprofessionals, with thousands of hours of yacht racing between us, including America's Cup experience.

If, however, they went belowdecks, they'd find in the place of the number two and three suits of sail, and life raft, and personal flotation devices, and extra gear, and all the other equipment that any racing boat carries, twenty-five shrink-wrapped bales of marijuana, grown on McLeod's holdings in Costa Rica, carried through the Panama Canal on the *Troy*, and dropped into the ocean, marked by doctored EPIRBs that bounced signals off of a satellite to allow the crew of the *Evelyn II*, using a GPS receiver, to pick them up, casually, while practicing for the Catalina Cup. And if they found that, the whole fragile structure I called my life would come tumbling down, one lie after another after another, until they got to the big lie, the lie at the center of my existence. Standing there, staring out to sea as the Coast Guard cruiser reemerged from the stern of the freighter and began to approach us, that lie seemed all there was.

But that's fear. That's the tired, familiar, hackneyed face of fear, like a cackling demon in a children's book. Fear: ridiculous, corrosive, debilitating fear. It rots the soul, Fassbinder said, and in my life I have had ample occasion to reflect on that truth. I am one of the few people practiced enough to know, for example, how to distinguish fear from its kissing cousins, panic and excitement. Excitement is what comes at the awesome possibility of joy. And panic, well, panic was what came to me when the Coast Guard came into view and I saw that they meant to board us, and my heart launched into a tattoo inside the walls of my chest, pounding, as I felt the periphery of my field of vision disappear.

Ah, panic. Intimate like an old lover, probing deep into your body. I wanted to confess before they accused me; in fact, I had physically to restrain myself from doing so by tightening all the muscles of my stomach, chest, neck, and jaw. The calculus of my terror plateaued in an endless series of unbearable nanoseconds, each more unbearable than the one before, as a liquid regret poured through me: my disguise was weak, my ID was no good, my game plan sucked, I had made mistakes,

mistakes, mistakes a beginner would have made, mistakes an idiot would have made, a whole lifetime of mistakes culminating in the mistake of where I was, right now, right here.

And only slowly, through a vast fog, did I realize that all they wanted, the Coast Guard, was a visual inspection, which they conducted without even coming aboard, and then, with a warning to stay out of the shipping lane, they were gone.

See, it is always like that, panic. In the old days, there were those who seemed immune, but I always wondered about that. Myself, I have never, not once in the hundreds of times I have risked capture, failed to feel it go through me like a fire, putting everything I had ever believed into question.

The only progress I had ever made was to learn not to show it.

And I knew I had not shown it. I knew I could have taken tea with the Coast Guard captain and his aunt, and they would never have known a thing.

That, you must see, is why I am paid so highly for what I do, and why I do it so well.

4.

We delivered to Deetjen's Cove, a portion of the California coast invisible from the highway and which you have never seen unless Mac McLeod has given you permission, which he has not. No one ever goes there except the *Evelyn II*, when she delivers, and it is the single place McLeod—with Billy C, the last of the old-time smugglers for whom marijuana was a social cause, not the business it has become today—would use a gun. He had to: the L.A. gangs to the south had considerable Colombian connections, and San Francisco, to the north, was all mobbed up. McLeod, you could say, was an anachronism, and there was no knowing how much longer his way of doing business was going to be tolerated by those who had, since the days of the Brotherhood, taken it over.

We used a Zodiac to offload to a shack at the water's edge—Kerouac stayed there once, the story goes, having strayed, half mad, from Lawrence

Ferlinghetti's neighboring property. Later, the bales would be winched up the cliffside under armed guard and trucked one by one to a processing location. And from there, we would use a big variety of methods to deliver the product to thousands and thousands of Americans for whom smoking dope was a part of their lives: young kids, old folk, Republicans, Democrats, politicians, musicians, doctors, construction workers, cancer patients, lawyers, insomniacs, secretaries, parents, glaucoma sufferers, children. And though they didn't know it, all of those people, all over the country, would be smoking good, pure, chemical-free bud, whose production never supported a terrorist, or a dictatorship, or a revolution, or a fundamentalist, or a violent criminal of any sort.

Okay. And if, an hour later, you were on the Monterey Pier, you'd have seen a middle-aged woman in jeans and a jean jacket, a black shirt, and a blond ponytail coming out the back of a Bermuda Race cap climbing out of a Pearson 49 and heading for the street. Maybe if you came close, you'd have thought her a pretty well-kept woman, for forty-five, with a slim waist and a strong bearing, and you'd have thought, There's the wife of a very rich man, coming in from a day's cruising in the Pacific. Then you'd have gone on to whatever you were doing, without ever dreaming that you had just seen Mimi Lurie, the last surviving fugitive from the Weather Underground, and even more remarkably, you had seen her on the last normal day of her very abnormal life.

As for me, I can remember every detail of that day. As if the long Pacific sun had burned it into my optic nerve. As if I knew, already, how drastically everything was about to change. A midsummer's day in 1996. Walking out of Monterey port, the light-drenched sidewalk along the bay, cars passing busily, tourists in their sportswear with brand names on their chests, and hats, and shoes.

As always after being outside the law, I felt from a different dimension. Partly that was the way criminals think of regular people as civilians, like carnival workers consider customers rubes and hookers their clients johns. When you live illegally, it is like being in a hidden world, where the rules by which the normal lived, the rules of offices and schools, simply do not hold, and often as I passed through the real world I felt invisible.

And partly it was the fact that the real world, for me, still wore crew cuts and thin black ties, or tie-dyed shirts and bell-bottoms, and drove Dodge Darts and VW Bugs, still watched *Hootenanny* and *Laugh-In* and *Get Smart*—as if the world I'd left twenty-two years before, frozen in time, was still there, somewhere, setting all the standards for normalcy. These people around me, I did not fully understand the references of their lives, the rules, the objects. Once I tried to watch an episode of *Seinfeld*. It was like a different language.

My car was in the parking lot, a Jeep Cherokee. I drove out of town right away, down to Carmel, where I parked in the lot behind the supermarket on the Valley Road intersection and waited for my go-ahead. There was not much danger: I was a known person here, Tess Sanders, one of the people who lived up on Mark McLeod's ranch in Big Sur, some kind of personal assistant, usually traveling for Mr. McLeod. About McLeod himself there were quite a few theories: a dot-commer grown absurdly rich from some start-up company; an inventor of the Macintosh; an early investor in Microsoft. None of it mattered: around Carmel Valley in the nineties, it was harder to explain an income under six figures than one over seven, and people treated the wealthy with self-conscious indifference. In time, Gail pulled up next to me in her own Jeep and gave me the thumbs-up: she'd been following me from Monterey to be sure I was clean. I nodded and pulled out and onto the 1, down to Big Sur, and up the road to the ranch.

Now, Isabel, I understand the point of this exercise, and I know I have to be telling you the truth, and so I will tell you how I met McLeod and all that. But you will have to excuse me if it does not come easily. It is hard to tell someone the truth, after so many years of hiding it. It is harder if that person is a complete stranger, even if you feel that long bonds of love unite you. But love is not trust—believe me. If you believe me on nothing else, still, try to listen to that. You cannot live as I have a lifetime deprived of both love or trust and not come to understand them both very well indeed. Love, Isabel, is not trust. Many, many people have come to trouble by confusing them.

I learned of McLeod in 1970, when he approached the Weather Bureau through an intermediary. McLeod was part of a group of Mendocino dope growers who were known, then, as the Brotherhood, which was short for the Brotherhood of Eternal Love. Timothy Leary had just been arrested, and they offered to finance us if we could get him out of prison in San Luis Obispo. The short answer was, we could, and indeed we did, breaking him out of lockup and eventually moving him right out of the country to the Black Panther compound in Algeria. There's a secret for you. I was one of the team that got Dr. Leary out. I won't tell you, of course, who the others were. But I will tell you this: when you hear about how Weather was a bunch of spoiled brats who survived only by the grace of the FBI's incompetence, you just think about how we got Dr. Leary out to Algeria. If, that is, you're not thinking about how we put a bomb in the U.S. Capitol, and in the Pentagon, and how I had in 1996 eluded capture for *twenty-six years*, despite having been on the FBI's most-wanted list for five years and featured thrice on *America's Most Wanted*.

But here's the point. When later, after Bank of Michigan, I was on the run—seriously on the run, in a way that made everything we did in Weather look like a game—I knew I could not go to anyone in the aboveground network of people who had ever helped us. Helping Weather was one thing; helping the Marion Delgado Brigade, after the murder, another altogether. It was not—repeat, not—fashionable to help us after the robbery. So where I went was to McLeod, whom I had never actually met. I found him by tracking him through the two degrees of separation that he had put between himself and Weather. I won't tell you who they were; perhaps your father will. They helped me, I found McLeod in Mendocino. It was the right choice.

Mendocino in 1974. Probably no better place in the world to hide. Every resident had a hybridized plant somewhere, and if a stranger came up off of Route 1, phones started to clang all the way up to Fort Bragg. The first thing McLeod does is, he lays out a big sheet of white drawing paper from his kid's art set on the living room floor and graphs all the possible connections that could be made to each of the three "clean" identities I had on hand. There in the middle of the floor, on a winter's day in Mendocino with rain running down the windows, he chose Tess Sanders for me. The second thing he did was tell me he'd help me. And the third thing he did was tell me I had to turn in Vincent Dellesandro.

I remember his exact words. First watching me with that blank gaze he has when he's thinking. Then, in the total certainty of his decision: "And, furthermore, it's time to turn that good ole boy in, M. Dellesandro's no revolutionary. Get that lunatic off the street before he kills some other poor asshole."

I knew that was true. I had known it for days, days when the sound of his gun in the marble lobby of the Bank of Michigan branch had been echoing, again and again, in my head. So I told McLeod where he had gone. Three days later the FBI arrested Vincent Dellesandro in Louisiana, where he was hiding on a shrimp boat run by the brother of one of his childhood friends. And as if I had been waiting only for that, the life I was to live for the next quarter century—the life that ended on that day in June 1996—suddenly began.

McLeod hid me, there in the Mendocino Hills, right through that winter, while the FBI manhunt raged. He hid me through Vincent's trial, through the following year, when Vincent was killed during the Attica prison rebellion, all the way through to the following year, when the story had died out of the papers. He helped me change, plastic surgery in Mexico to take off a beauty mark; hair color, accent, details of underground life that made me think my survival, up to then, had indeed been as much incompetence on the part of the FBI as skill on ours, so careful was he as a professional criminal, so expert. He gave me new papers on Tess Sanders, papers so clean I could file taxes on them, which I did—in fact, I was using the same identity I used when I stepped off the *Evelyn II* in Monterey in 1996. And he gave me work: the next year when his second child was born, as his live-in au pair, which in any case was a job I'd taken for myself, caring for his first.

But always he bore in mind that by the time I came out to Mendocino, I had been living as a federal fugitive since the town house explosion in 1970, and I knew a great deal about living underground. How to use a disguise, how to clean a room, how to lose a tail, how to deal with some of the people that, inevitably, one meets in criminal circumstances. Above all, he knew that I knew how to handle fear, because it is fear, more than anything else, that makes criminals crash and burn. And finally, one day, he gave me ten kilos of weed to deliver to Washington, D.C., and when I returned, two weeks later, with $25,000 in cash, he gave me $5,000 to keep.

And now I want you to know something, Isabel. It's something that only McLeod knows, no one else. Not even your father. But if you are going to decide what to do, you need to know.

I want you to know that I may have been a self-styled revolutionary for some of my life and a marijuana smuggler for the rest, but that I have never broken any other law, ever. Not traffic, not tax. And when McLeod gave me that five thousand in fifty-dollar bills, I held it in my hand for less than a second before I gave it back. I gave it back, and I told him I'd read that the Ann Arbor police had a fund for the family of Hugh Krosney—the guard Joey killed. And I said that when each of Krosney's kids had their college paid, and graduate school, and Mrs. Krosney's nursing home had been paid for, and each of her future grandchildren had their inheritance arranged, then, and only then, could Mac pay me.

What I meant, of course, was that I never wanted to be paid, ever. Run weed? Sure, why not? This was clean, good product, grown in McLeod Seas of Green in California or Oregon or Costa Rica, or by his partner, Billy Cusimano, out east. No guns, no crime, no corrupt politicians. Just good, high-quality dope from a crew of unrepentant hippies. McLeod and Cusimano had a profit-sharing scheme for their employees. When Big Billy came out west sometimes, you thought you were looking at the Ben and Jerry of dope dealers.

McLeod did what I asked with the money. At least, most of it. The rest he put in the market, with his own. And, needless to say, no one could ever have predicted what would happen with that. By 1986 our position in Microsoft alone was more than enough to satisfy each and every demand I made for the Krosney family, and that was when I began to grow rich myself.

As for who the Krosneys thought was the source of the money that came their way, I don't guess we'll ever know.

But we may get a hint, if they show up at the parole hearing.

That day, however, not knowing how much money we were to make, and how easily, McLeod, his blue eyes on mine, took my five thousand back, then counted out another two-point-five.

"Employee matching plan, M. You get health insurance and retirement, too."

It was the beginning of a beautiful relationship.

5.

All through the eighties I ran weed for Mark McLeod and paid money to the Krosneys. I did runs east, posing, among many others, as a San Francisco lawyer's wife, following her husband to his new Wall Street job with the furniture (we bought an entire house from a department store in San Francisco); as a new Ph.D. going to take a teaching job at NYU (a forged job offer signed by Brademas and a lease on a West Village apartment in the glove compartment); and as a UPS cross-country truck driver (a straight job for which I took a tractor-trailer driving course advertised on late-night TV in the identity of a male).

But my great breakthrough came in 1985, when a run went bad. Mark's forger was arrested in Sausalito, and among his papers was the license I was running east on, as the male proprietor and driver of Bicoastal Movers. Our routine was to check in on a pay phone every two hundred miles or so, and my tipoff came as I approached Chicago. It was pure luck; I doubt if the DEA was more than a half hour away when I turned north. I abandoned the truck in Milwaukee, carrying thirty keys in two garbage bags, and caught a ferry to Muskegon. Then I bought a backpack, shoes, and a sleeping bag in an Army-Navy, and packed the full weight across the Upper Peninsula of Michigan on foot. And on the other coast, I chartered a Jay 29 and single-handed it to Cleveland.

See, it was easy: I grew up in Traverse City and had hiked the UP and sailed the Great Lakes all my childhood with my father and brother. I knew the woods and the water up there like today I know my own wardrobe. But man, was it innovative to McLeod. It was so successful that we bought a twenty-nine-foot Pearson and kept it in Saginaw Bay, and for several years that was my only route east. In the woods I was another nature child, hiking some of the last unspoiled woodland in North America; on the water I was a wealthy Cleveland lady who took her boat up north every spring and brought it back each summer.

Sailing became very big for us as, with the increasing strength of hybridized seed and the advances in forced CO_2 hydroponics, the value of bud soared. Very soon our cash supplies grew far too large to handle in America, and we bought the *Evelyn II*. For some years I did runs to the Islands under the guise of the Bermuda Races, twice every year. And McLeod, of course, took care of me very well, first arranging the anonymous contributions to the Krosney family, then, when that was done, paying absurd amounts of money into an account at Wells Fargo in the name of Tess Sanders and opening a retirement fund, all in Internet stocks, that did substantially well all through the nineties until MacLeod bailed into mutual funds, well enough so that, were it not for loyalty, I really no longer had to work at all.

We were big on loyalty. We always had been. If we hadn't been, none of this would have happened.

After all, Weather had split in 1976, filled with hostility and acrimony, and across this country were a couple dozen people who not only thought I was a criminal maniac but who—now surfaced, leading real lives—could have given the FBI more than they needed to find me. Tess Sanders, for example, had been created by a member of our Ann Arbor affinity group, Jed Lewis, and I very much doubted that Jed had forgotten that little fact—see what I mean about the statute of limitations? That makes Jed an accessory to Bank of Michigan as well as to the continuing crime of my existence, that I was living under that name. And that was Jed, who had been a friend. There were others who had never liked me, and never trusted me, even in Weather, and who only thought even less of me after B.O.M. None of them, ever, said a word either.

Explain that, Isabel, if you can.

Find me one other group of former friends, anywhere, who has never betrayed each other.

McLeod always said that if I hadn't betrayed Dellesandro, one of the old Weather people would have turned me in. But I knew that wasn't true. We had fucked up all kinds of things between us: we had too many drugs, too many fights, too much sex. If there was, in fact, anything I regretted from the underground—before Bank of Michigan, I mean—it was how horribly mean we had been to each other. That, and Teddy Gold, who had died in the town house explosion, and whom I had loved, the one thing in the world that can make me, hardened criminal that I am, cry, all these years later. But never, in all the years since Weather, had one of us turned another in to the law. Never had one of us talked out of line to a reporter, named the participants of a particular action, given away secrets that could have hurt someone. And here's something I can guarantee you: most of us will probably never talk to each other again in our lifetimes, but never will any of us do each other harm, either, and when the last of us dies, still no one but us will know which one of us took Dr. Leary out of jail. Behind all the bullshit, that much remains true.

Which is why, when Sharon Solarz was arrested during her attempt to negotiate a surrender in 1996, I had been concerned, and sorry, but I hadn't been scared.

Sharon, I knew, wouldn't betray me even if she could.

And when finally, that June afternoon when I came back from docking the *Evelyn II* in Monterey and McLeod told me that your father had gone on the run, I didn't have the slightest doubt about what I had to do. And why.

What I had to do was go to Ann Arbor.

Why I had to do it was because that's where Jason would come looking for me.

Don't get me wrong. I knew already what your father wanted from me, and I knew the answer was no.

But I also knew that I owed it to him to tell him myself.

Like I say: we were big on loyalty.

6.

McLeod's Big Sur house—where he moved from Mendocino in the early nineties—sits at the top of a hill just south of Nepenthe. His property comprises about ninety acres bordering the Ventana Wilderness to the north and east and crossing Highway 1 to the west. Were the highway not there, you could walk stark naked from his bathroom to the ocean, so private is it. As is, he gives the ocean beach over to surfers, letting them park on his land and hike down to the water, for which he is pretty celebrated in those parts.

Of course, the surfers also keep any strangers away from Deetjen's Cove, which is just how McLeod likes it.

His office, on the ground floor, overlooks the edge of the mountain, and from the windows, which define its western wall, the low fog I'd seen from the boat hid the sea under a cottony quilt above which shone a brilliant blue sky: Big Sur in June. The room itself, done in redwood and Turkish kilims, with a mahogany desk on which a computer showed a stock ticker and an E-Trade logo, was flooded with light, filled with a vast silence, a silence that, while I waited for McLeod to come in, seemed to me—as midday frequently does—antiseptic, to contain in its bright clarity middays from all through my life, all the way back to schooldays at home in Traverse City, my brother listening to Herman's Hermits and my mother vacuuming somewhere in the house's distance.

At fifty McLeod was a bald man, somewhat shorter than myself, quite slight, with a round face bisected by a pair of bifocals: black-rimmed, fashionable eyewear. He came into the room wearing running clothes, sweating profusely, and because he was sweating, patted my head rather than kissed me. As always his blue eyes held a kind of supplicating expression, an accident of their glisten: I doubt he had ever supplicated anything except grace, for he was a devout Buddhist. Then he sat down at the computer and did something with the mouse before turning back to me. It seemed he had a margin call and had bailed on Apple for the first time since '84.

I was surprised that Mac had to cover a margin. But I'd heard the McLeod philosophy of investment before, and now I heard it again.

"Doll, every penny either of us own is in this market—anyone who's not living on credit's a jerkoff. Know what? Last month was the fourteenth straight month in a row that we made more from the market than from the harvest. What say to that?"

I said that I'd stick to extralegal ways of making a living, if that was the alternative, thank you very much—a conversation we had had many times before. And in that comfortable way things go when you're spending time with Mac, we went on. The trip. The market. The wild news about Sharon. Being with McLeod, in his house, was the closest I had come to being at home in twenty-five years. Until he said what he said next, which was:

"And Jason?"

That surprised me. "Jason who?"

"Sinai, baby. Jason Sinai."

"Oh, Christ, Mac. What the fuck happened to Jason?"

And so he told me. An Albany paper connected him to Sharon. Jasey had gone on the run with his seven-year-old daughter. But something, somewhere, went real wrong, because they caught up to him in New York, and he abandoned the girl in a hotel room that very morning and took off alone.

"Jesus God." I was standing now, watching him with, literally, my jaw open. "Where was Jase living?"

"Upstate New York. Mim, you won't fucking believe this. He was living as a lawyer called James Grant, and you know who he represented? Big Billy C. It was Billy put him in touch with Sharon, of all the shitty goddamn bad luck."

"What is wrong with that fat idiot?"

"He didn't know who Jason was. Had no idea. No one knew, doll. And Jason must have had no idea Billy was connected to me, because there's no way he'd have handled a Brotherhood figure."

"James Grant, James Grant." Something was coming to me, slowly. "Julia Montgomery's husband? The actress? That's Jason?"

"Fucking A, Mimi."

"Good God. Jason Sinai married the daughter of a U.S. senator? How did he do that? Did you know?"

"Not a clue." McLeod sat across from me now in the twin chair to mine, a George Smith, and reached the cigarette out of my hand for a drag. "I admit I had some idea about Sharon, because she stayed in touch with Billy. But Jason? Not a fucking clue. I never even met Jason."

I thought about this for a moment. But, like I say, I already knew what I was going to do next. I had always known what I was going to do if Jason needed me to. So I didn't think that long.

Selling marijuana was not my job. McLeod had people for that. Still, when I told him what I wanted to do, he nodded slowly.

See, I knew that Mac distributed to the Midwest out of Ann Arbor. I knew that he had a man there who worked as a bartender and, out of his job, distributed all of the West Coast product. As always, it was a McLeod setup: the owner of the bar didn't know, the other staff didn't know, so there was no chance of a RICO investigation, even if the guy was ever caught.

What I asked Mac for was to let me take over the Ann Arbor job. I'd move his weight, stay around a few months, and when Billy C. harvested out east, I could come back with his bud, which was meant for California anyway.

Watching me, calculating, McLeod said, "Why Ann Arbor?"

"That's where Little J's going to be looking for me."

He absorbed that, mouth open. "That's what he's doing? Looking for you?"

"Yes."

"Why?"

I looked away now. I had never lied to McLeod, and I didn't want to start now. Then I looked back. "Don't ask me that, Mac."

"You can help him?"

"No. But until he finds me, he's not going to stop looking."

He didn't answer. He thought it out, though, his calculation showing in the focus of his eyes, staring at nothing. Then he said, "Alright. I'll make the call."

See, change came suddenly, the way I lived. Once I counted: I had walked out on six full lives in my time. Six sets of friends, six lovers, six homes, six names. Not counting my real one. Briefly, it occurred to me that McLeod was the last person in the world who called me by my real name, and if I lost him, I lost Amelia Wanda Lurie too. The thought opened up a tiny little tear in my stomach, and I stood up.

• • •

We sorted out the details. McLeod could have papers ready for me in three days. I asked him to pack a car. Paper a divorce. Dale, the owner of the Ann Arbor bar, was a friend of McLeod's; MacLeod's current guy would resign, and Mac would ask Dale to give me the job, get me back on my feet. I'd have two kids, one in college, one in the armed forces, a girl. My husband was an arc welder in the port. Asshole put a hand on his daughter. I have a two-hundred-yard stay-away order out on him. I'd have an American car, a Mercury Sable or a Ford Taurus, not too new. As for the weed, we'd do a backpack, just in case. An old one, like left over from college. That worked good: I'm running from my husband, don't want to give him a legal claim to find me by taking joint property, right? So I leave him the Samsonite and take my college backpack. Mac would get some Nouvelles Frontières stickers on it, or Eurailpass—find some old luggage at Goodwill and steam off the stickers. And I'd leave, right now, and stay in San Francisco, far from McLeod, until it was all ready.

Mac noted it all. With a nod, I turned to the door, and only stopped when McLeod spoke.

"Mimi?"

"Yes?"

"Do you understand why Sharon did it?"

My back was toward him, in the doorway, and I didn't turn. "Wanted to surface, you mean?"

"Yes."

I shrugged. "I guess I know what she was thinking about, at least."

"Think she's wrong?"

I answered guardedly. "I can't judge what Sharon did."

"Um-hmm. You know, I met Gillian Morrealle at a party a couple years ago. She said Jason and Sharon's status was totally different from yours. Said that the fact that Mimi had tipped off the state police where to find Dellesandro would mitigate heavily in her favor. With a negotiated surrender, she said Mimi could count on the minimum hit, ten to fifteen years, first parole eligibility at eight. Less if Gore follows Clinton: could hope for presidential clemency. Come out of jail legal at sixty. Get a fucking college degree in there."

"Mac?"

"Yes, doll?"

I still had not turned around. To be honest, I did not trust myself to.

"Let's not kid ourselves, okay? I'm already in jail. I've been there since April 1974, and I'm going to be there for the rest of my life. I can walk my ass off across this country, I'm still in jail. So I don't need anyone to give me absolution."

"Okay." He answered softly. And then, master of myself again, I turned around.

See, I knew exactly what your father was doing. I knew why he had abandoned you, and why he had run. I knew the moment I heard he had a daughter. And I knew because I had thought it all out, long before.

See? Isabel? I knew that your father had dumped you in a hotel bedroom so he could come looking for me.

And I knew that until I looked Jason in the eye and told him I wasn't going to do what he wanted, neither of us would really ever know it for sure.

And I don't need to explain to you of all people why, before I could do that, I had to look him in the eye.

7.

The next morning, at the Old Cigar Store in North Beach, a woman, good-looking and no longer young, sat at a window table over a cappuccino, smoking. She wore a light green silk blouse and a black skirt, both from Kmart, both bought for cash; black pumps; a faded jean jacket. Her hair was jet black, as were her eyes, and she held in her lap a weathered leather handbag. Next to her, on the floor, sat a vinyl American Standard suitcase, by no means new. On her nose rested a pair of Ray-Bans.

The Ray-Bans were out of character. But I have my vanity, too.

Outside the window, where she was vaguely watching, a Mercury Sable, maybe three years old, circled Washington Square, looking for parking. When a man in a suit, holding keys, left a building, the Sable slowed, trailing him down the street, ignoring the blasting of horns from the growing line of traffic behind it. The man in the suit finally climbed into a Toyota Land Cruiser, and the Sable waited for him to pull out, the cars behind him now no longer even honking. When the Sable had at last taken the parking space, and the driver exhibited her middle finger to the line of cars at last freed to pass, a young woman in heels, a skirt, and a leather jacket came out and, carefully locking the car and feeding its meter, came into the café.

Clearly the younger and the older woman were close friends, for they greeted each other with a kiss and a long hug. Then, busily, the young woman sat down, ordered a cappuccino, and got to work. She took a car registration and keys out of her bag, also an extra set of keys and a manila envelope, all the while talking in a flat California accent.

"Thank you so much for lending me the car, Cleo—I can't tell you how it helped. Did I keep you waiting? Here's your registration and extra keys, oh, and here's some papers I found in the apartment—important?"

The older woman transferred all these things into her purse, answering in a low-pitched voice with a slightly western twang. "My God, yes, darling. I was so scattered when I left the house, I left my papers there. Was the shithead at home when you went by?"

"Yes."

"How was he?"

"Drunk, doll. He was drunk. Now you listen, Cleo. Don't you think about that bastard any more. You just get into that car, drive safe, and do what you have to do, you hear? There's a full tank of gas, you don't have to stop before you're halfway through Nevada."

"Okay." The older woman smiled, perhaps bravely, because her lower lip was trembling. Then the two embraced again, and the older woman, after trying to pay for her coffee and not succeeding, stood up and left, leaving her suitcase too.

She opened the car and checked the trunk, where an old backpack with Eurail stickers lay. She put her jacket on the passenger seat with her handbag, and her shoes on the floor, as if she were, in fact, planning on driving through Nevada without stopping. Then she started the car, adjusted the seat and mirrors, and pulled out.

• • •

Once out of North Beach, I stopped and checked my papers. There was a social security card, bank card, driver's license, library card, a few other pieces. My name was Cleo Theophilus, Greek in origin, which was why McLeod told me on the phone, when we set up this meet at the Cigar Store, to make my hair black. I memorized my address and birth date, then started moving again, while I made a mental list of what I had to do. I needed to invent a family history, why my parents came from Greece, and when; where they lived, when they died, where I grew up. I needed grade schools, high schools, jobs, marriages, in-laws. And for all of those, I needed authenticating detail.

A new identity is like a novel, and like all novels, if they are to be good, you have to *need* to write them, not *want* to. With a sigh, I began to sketch out Cleo Theophilus's life, and by the time I was on the middle of the Golden Gate Bridge, I had begun to feel the whitewash of imagination over the present, perhaps the most seductive feeling I knew. The day was brilliant, that pure, thin northern California sun, all of the bay spread out to my right, the endless Pacific to the left. I was on the move, on the move, and for the first time since I'd come home, my spirits began to rise: to be on the move was lonely, but it was also the closest we ever came to being free. With a little flash I wondered if this was what Jason, wherever he was, was experiencing. Then, to chase away the thought, I turned on the radio, and I swear to you, Chrissie Hynde was singing, just like that:

All the love in the world for you girl
Thumbelina, in a great big scary world
All the love in the world for you girl
Take my hand, we'll make it through this world

Date: June 11, 2006
From: "Daddy" <littlej@cusimanorganics.com>
To: "Isabel Montgomery" <isabel@exmnster.uk>
CC: maillist: The_Committee
Subject: letter 17

You want to know how you walk out on your daughter.

Like this: you empty the Sportsac shoulder bag of her books and her stuffed animals.

Arrange them next to the bed.

Without looking at her.

Then you put some of your clothes in it.

Doesn't matter which clothes. All you need is the bag. Without a bag, you look strange, traveling.

Then you walk out the door.

Just like that.

Isabel. Everyone always wants to know how I left my seven-year-old-daughter alone in a hotel room. Everyone always wants to know the true, inside story of the Weather Underground, the first exclusive interview, the secret we've never told. They want the little thrill of terror and pleasure. How does it feel to be on the run, to be in an explosion, to be hunted by the police? How does it feel not to see your family for thirty years? How does it feel to lie, day in, day out? To live incognito? Not to be able to tell anyone the truth? To read of your father's death in the newspaper?

The world is full of people who think they can ask you to tell them about the worst moment in your existence. You are a criminal, a fugitive, an icon of an age gone by, you are public property.

Izzy. You, of course, you are the only one with a right to know, and you have never asked.

How do you abandon your daughter in a hotel room?

Like this: the freshly vacuumed carpet of the hallway, its synthetic pile all bending this way, then that, with the track of a vacuum cleaner, and far and away I hear the dulcet sound of a vacuum cleaner warping a childhood afternoon.

Like this: the elevator panel, a broken button for the second floor flickering at me with blank accusation, and for a moment I hang on the very borderline of feeling that accusation to be real, and intentional, and personal.

The denial of reality, as schizophrenics and acid lovers know, comes at a price. The symptoms of terror—tunnel vision, hypnagogic memory, distortion of vision, and paranoid delusion—years and years of practice are no good; each time they come, they are new. The tiled floor of the lobby, a chemical smell in my nose and mournfully, funereally, an orchestral version of "Harvest Moon" sounding faintly from hidden speakers. The hotel bar, a couple of men in suits with a woman between them, the bartender watching CNN, CNN being hosted by a woman with jagged black bangs, a background of desolate desert behind her, and the three people at the bar watching. Blackness beyond the bar's door to the street, a virtually uncontrollable urge to run: the police are waiting for me outside that door, everyone knows it, the people at the bar, the bartender, the woman on the screen reporting from a desert, they know it.

Outside, a moon I could not see angled silver light into the space between the buildings. A hooker in a leather minidress shifted from her perch next to the hotel bar to move down the deserted street. Air conditioners hummed from the windows above, and far away a police siren rose and faded.

I waited for the hooker to move away, the street shimmering, swimming before my eyes, my heart racing. And when she was gone, before pure panic could overtake me, I began to walk.

• • •

How do you abandon your daughter in a hotel room in downtown Manhattan?

In my case, badly. Stupidly. Dangerously.

I should have known a good, long, circuitous route to take, preferably through a large and crowded place, to where I was going, though it was only two blocks away. I should have had a partner watching my trajectory, ensuring no one was following, and failing that, I should have had a rehearsed itinerary, one of those I had figured out in the old days, one that crossed large spaces, doubled back, gave me the chance to check my tail and, should I find anyone, lose them. Most importantly, I should have been doing it all by day, in crowded streets, not at night when I was virtually the only figure to be seen. "Going downtown during the workday is like putting water through a filter." Mimi's rule. "You may get stuck, but if you don't, you're as clean as you'll ever be."

But to follow rules, you have to want to stay safe. The hollowness reamed through my body, the brute ache, the terror. And I knew it to be just the tip of the awfulness that was available to me. All of my being went into its denial. I had nothing left over to protect myself with. No energy to care about being safe. And so without the slightest thought for the safety of what I was doing, without ever looking back, I went toward the river, then turned north, then turned west, and had anyone been following me, they could have watched me as clear as in the light of day walking into the ornate lobby of an office building, where I signed the register in the name Daniel Sinai in front of the uniformed night guard who, once he had looked up the name, nodded me toward the elevators.

The Pine Street entrance of the Exchange Building. Daniel Sinai, tenant. Come to burn some midnight oil over a contract, a lease, a negotiation. The night guard went back to sleep and, not hurrying, I moved toward the elevators. Then my heart began to accelerate.

Not from worry, however. I had no doubt that my brother would still hold the lease on my father's law office, a two-room suite on the twenty-second floor that had once been my grandfather's. At least while my mother was alive, there was no chance of that office ever leaving the family.

That, as the elevator doors closed and the floor lifted, carrying me to a place I had not been for a quarter century, was not what made my heart pound.

2.

Here's a rule for you: when you are afraid, take the stairs. At least your beating heart can process the adrenaline in your blood. Left passive in the elevator, panic returned, not just an edge, this time, but the real thing: bad panic, so strong that I had to crouch down on the floor.

First it was physical, burning in my underarms and crotch, as if my skin had been massaged with pepper. Then it passed in a wave, leaving me dripping with sweat, and in its wake I felt a gravitational pull, like an ocean undertow, toward the hotel room where you still slept. All this happened in the moments of the elevator rising, that quickly, and yet it left me so weakened that I nearly could not get out when finally the doors opened on the twenty-second floor. I held the door until I was afraid the alarm would sound, and it was only that risk that made me, at last, step out of the elevator and walk, one step after another, down the hallway, my steps hollow against the green-marbled linoleum floor that had not, apparently, been changed, for it was as familiar to me as the very smell of the hall. Number 2232. At the door, another debilitating wave of panic came over me. I let my back go against the wall and, eyes clenched, lowered myself onto the floor, trying to visualize something, anything, that would organize my thoughts and make my panic recede.

Two-two-three-two, Exchange Building. A single-room office overlooking the Brooklyn docks. Sitting in the hallway, I could close my eyes and see the view. Once my grandfather, your great-grandfather, wrote deeds and supervised closings here. My father, your grandfather, joined the practice after his graduation from Fordham Law School in 1935. Sinai and Son: when I was a child, the clouded glass window of the office still held that name. In fact, it was not Sinai and Son for long: while my father was in Spain with the Lincoln Brigade, his father died, and when he came back, a twenty-five-year-old man with shrapnel scars up his left leg from the defense of Cape Tortuga, my father was no longer interested in property law.

His heroism in battle, however, was little celebrated in his own country, and likewise the law that my father now practiced did not impress the other lawyers in the Exchange Building. In the fifties, the building management moved to evict him. My mother, your grandmother, used to say that it was the single rejection that had really hurt Jack Sinai. Dies Committee blacklisting, rejection from the U.S. Army due to "premature anti-fascism," attacks by McCarthy and Hoover, death threats; my mother told Kai Bird for his biography of my father that the single thing she could remember depressing—as opposed to outraging—Jack Sinai had been the Exchange Building's attempt to evict him. He sued them, of course—disproving the adage about a lawyer who represents himself, necessarily, as virtually no lawyer would represent him—and in 1996, two years after my father's death, my brother Daniel now kept the lease out of pure spite.

The key had always been kept in a tiny hollow behind the door molding. When I at last was able to look for it, my heart sank to see that the molding had been changed to steel. Still, when I twisted my body, in its sitting position, to look more closely, I found the drywall hollowed out just where the wood used to be, and a Medeco key nestling inside. With a fingernail I pulled it out, letting it fall to the ground with a thin *ping*. Then I stood and opened the door onto the most perfectly preserved piece of the past I had ever seen.

3.

A Steel Age desk, massive, sat against the window; two smaller Wakefields, where the para and secretary had sat, against the wall. A black fan, its blades worn glossy by use, rested on top of a bank of black steel file cabinets. The windows had been replaced—they were double-glazed and aluminum—but the green venetian blinds lowered halfway over the glass were original, and the oak molding was too. With something near reverence I ran my hand over the wood, watching out at the lights of the Brooklyn Bridge, at the black of the river. The moon was over the West Side, and I could not see it, but the intensity of the light spoke of its size, lighting the whole of the cloudless sky. Far away the glitter of the Verrazano Narrows Bridge was faintly visible next to the ambient lights of Bay Ridge. As if in prayer I leaned my forehead against the glass and shut my eyes.

You want to know how I left you. By standing, for a very long time, thus, my eyes clenched shut against reality. I must tell you, Isabel, I have no memory of that time. Perhaps, eyes closed, I saw the view before me better than I had with my eyes open. Perhaps I was seeing the light glittering on the surface of the East River, the black water swollen with tide, inscrutable, lapping against the pilings of the Brooklyn Ferry. For so long, in fact, did I stand thus that again, far in my mind, I felt panic approach, and it was only when I felt that that I stood straight and opened my eyes, half expecting to see a hallucination in the place of the view, proof that I could not take the strain, that I should give up.

I would have welcomed that proof.

But once again, reality held.

I sat now, at the desk in the swivel chair I'd used to play in as a child, and put my hands on the surface of the desk where lay the draft of a *Nation* article my brother was working on. In the drawers, I knew, were the letters and deeds and records of a lifetime in New York, the office here, the house on Bedford Street, the Vineyard house over Menemsha Bay. Everything was here, preserved forever in the tiny office over the water, precious reminders of a glorious life, a life that would never be repeated. Only the smell was gone, the smell of my father's Bay Rum shaving lotion, and as I realized that, for me, suddenly the whole office became a tomb.

I rose and crossed the room to kneel in front of a squat black safe. The combination came immediately to mind, as did the workings of the ancient lock. I swung the door open and pulled out the sliding shelf on top. And here was my first surprise.

The papers were there, precisely where I had left them. March 8,

1970, my last time in New York: two days after the town house bombing I had traveled from the Midwest in the identity that I was to live in until 1974, just to hide this identity, Robert Russell. It was, I knew, the best identity I would ever build, and although I had no use for it in mind, although I had spent months building it, and although I was risking my liberty to be in New York at all, two days after the town house blast, while the rubble on West Eleventh Street was still smoldering, I had traveled east to hide it, here, in the one place I knew would never be touched by time. A social security card, a Wisconsin driver's license, and a passport—the big green kind they used to use—in the name of Robert Russell. Now they sat in the back of the safe, just where I had left them. That did not surprise me.

But below them was another set of IDs, and as I looked at them, I grew confused, so confused that I thought I had perhaps lost my mind. Here was another driver's license—also Robert Russell's, also Wisconsin—with a picture of myself wearing a black beard. The license was, however, current, renewed some eighteen months before. And here was another passport, not one of the big green ones from the seventies, but one of the little navy blue ones they used in the nineties. With confusion, I saw that this, too, was current—it had been taken out in 1995. The photograph on this one, clearer than the computer-generated license, was less convincing—it had clearly been taken before I'd had my nose fixed. The thought made my head swirl: the man in the picture was middle-aged, and yet I'd had my nose fixed twice, the second time in 1982, when I could still be described as young. The passport and driver's license shared the same address: Water Street in Racine, Wisconsin.

Dizzy with confusion, I looked back into the tray and found two more baffling items. The first was a stack of twenty-dollar bills, all old, tied with a rubber band. Later I would count a total of twenty-five thousand dollars. And there was a page torn from a perpetual calendar. Each day had a New York telephone number written next to it—a pay phone number, if this was in fact what it seemed to be. A yellow Post-it, clipped to the top, had in the same writing, the key.

> Ascend by one hour a day, starting 6 AM, ending midnight, in 12-day cycle, skipping the 6th and 7th of each month.

For a long time I stared at the documents, unable to understand. An identity I had created and hidden twenty-five years before had been updated with photos of myself. An impossibility.

Then I got it.

Peering closely at the pictures on the IDs, I saw that it was not me at all but my younger brother, Daniel.

Jesus Christ Almighty. I said the words out loud in the empty office. Daniel had been twelve when I went underground. I barely remembered the child.

How long had he been keeping a valid identity in the safe? And how had he known to do it?

Slowly, I saw that my forgotten little brother, in the forgotten little office, had for at least the last ten years kept up Robert Russell's identity. He must have grown a beard for the pictures, and dyed it black, for I distinctly remembered him as a redhead. And therefore the nose, which so resembled mine before it was fixed, an aquiline, Jewish nose.

Now why the fucking hell—I said it out loud—would he have done that?

And yet, even if speaking to myself about it would have helped, there wasn't time.

I checked my watch and found it to be nearly midnight on June 20. Starting my brother's time cycle, that made my first chance to call at six the next morning. Fair enough—in that case, I knew what to do. My plan had always been to contact my brother—this only made it easier. I rose now, packed the bills and the ID into your Sportsac shoulder bag, and left the office.

Now, at last, exiting onto Pine Street, I had the presence of mind to start following a trajectory.

4.

New York City. The financial district at two-thirty in the morning. Down the long canyon of Pine Street a garbage truck idled while a worker tossed bales of papers into it. In front of it, a limousine pulled into the intersection and passed, and I remember that instinctively, I stepped against the wall. When the limo was gone, I began to walk, watching the garbage man carefully. He did not turn, working his way steadily through a small mountain of corporate recycling. At the corner of Pine and Williams, where a delivery truck was turning north, I slowed, waiting for it to block the intersection, then ran across Williams Street under its cover, pulling on a baseball cap from my pocket as I reached the sidewalk. I jogged for a time at the side of the truck before, suddenly, coming to a halt. The truck passed and, walking slowly now, I crossed to Maiden Lane, doubled back to Cedar, then went north on Pearl, taking a long look at the empty street behind me.

The tunnel, we called it. At the beginning you are straight, and at the end you are underground. A long, clean passage away from everyone who knew you, unnoticed and unremarked. If it works right, absolutely nothing happens, and yet, at the other end, you are in another world. Your legal identity is changed. Your appearance is changed. And because there are no witnesses to either transformation, you are, now, literally, someone else.

The patterns were as simple as a three-point turn in a driving test. If there were two of you, you could walk a known trajectory—through a department store or public plaza—and have your tail watched. If you were solo, you could stop on the street, look in a store window, turn to look behind you, watch each face passing and pronounce its details to yourself. Change directions, walk, repeat. Each set of circumstances had been carefully choreographed by intensely smart, detail-oriented people, and the police were absolutely unable to follow us. That's why, Izzy, we thought we could rob a bank: everything else, from jailbreak to planting a bomb in the Pentagon, it had been so easy. We thought we could do anything.

Later, we had delighted in bringing friends through the tunnel, giving them directions to follow and, out of nowhere, appearing at their sides. It had been Thai and Arthur who had brought Emile de Antonio through the tunnel out in Sheepshead Bay, then choreographed all the twists and turns, the backtracking and switches, to bring a whole camera crew to their safe house near Los Angeles for the filming of *Underground*.

Now, at the top of Pearl, I walked quickly past Wolf's Deli and into the courtyard of the Mitchell-Lama housing development. I crossed the central courtyard and, at its edge, hid behind a corner and waited. For ten long minutes the courtyard was empty. Then I crossed back, still meeting no one. Walking slowly now, I took Fulton to Nassau, Nassau up past 5 Beekman and Pace. At Pace I descended the subway stairs, took the deserted underpass—a place literally impossible for any surveillance to hide—and climbed back up onto the Brooklyn Bridge.

Three o'clock. Immediately, on the walkway, in the night air, something struck me as wrong. At the top of the stairs I paused, trying to identify it, stomach sinking: despite my precautions, I found, I was not ready to face any serious threat of danger. That there could really be surveillance so wide that it could find me in New York—that implied a level of governmental interest that I would not have thought possible and, indeed, which I was not ready to acknowledge. Ready to run back down the stairs, I paused, trying to chase down the feeling of unease. And then I pinpointed it: the bridge was virtually silent; there was none of the ever-repeating Doppler of car tires against the metal mesh surface that characterized any trip even near the bridge as I remembered it. Gingerly I crossed to look at the roadway, and indeed it had been paved.

This, a mysterious and dangerous place, awash in the successive Doppler echoes of cars passing, was no-man's-land when I was a kid, a place so dangerous—like Coney Island at night, or Spanish Harlem—that even we, battle-hardened kids from the still largely Italian West Village, avoided it. Sometimes, on a dare, one or another would cross on a bicycle at night, more than once having to turn back on the uphill and race back, pursued by a gang from Brooklyn. Now, however, I understood the bridge to be safe—someone had told me so, part of Giuliani's cleanup of the city.

But who cared? What did I really have to be scared of now? There was resignation in my posture as I began to walk, carrying twenty-five thousand dollars up the arch of the bridge. For a few minutes I continued, anxiously watching over the river, a view I had not seen since 1970.

And then, as if by appointment, I turned and looked west to see the moon, full at last, resting on top of two massive, towering, columns of light. With real shock I stared at them, real confusion, as if I were hallucinating, or had been transported to another city. Only slowly did I realize that I was seeing buildings that had not existed the last time I was in New York, in the early spring of 1970. Only slowly did I realize that I was looking at the World Trade Towers for the first time in my life.

A literally incredible sight to someone who had never seen them before, transforming not just the view, but somehow the conception of the city. We did not know then, of course, how transforming the future reserved them to be. They were tremendously ugly, rectangular blocks of seventies nondesign. And they were shockingly beautiful, if for nothing else than for their sheer mass, towering over the ornate, suddenly quaint, turn-of-the-century Woolworth Building with its precious emphasis on the decorative, like guardians of a more innocent past.

For a long time, a great long time, I stared at those buildings, the moon moving slowly to bisect the southernmost tower. When I finally left, I walked backward, staring, and it was only when I reached the point that the Statue of Liberty became visible to the south around the eastern edge of the Battery that I turned and found myself looking at the Verrazano-Narrows Bridge, far away across the water, and I remembered crossing this bridge with my own father in 1960 on the way to Washington for the civil rights demonstration.

My brother, with his ID and money, had come to help me as surely as if he were there, holding my hand. And now, as if an ancient oracle had spoken, my father, now that he was dead and gone, came to my rescue and guided me over that bridge and into what I had next to do as surely as he had, a lifetime ago, driven me across in his Dodge Dart.

5.

Brooklyn. Three-thirty in the morning. Cadman Plaza, the green of the trees around the park lost in the black of night, but still casting a carpet of shadow in the moonlight. I had been the only person on the bridge, the only person at all, and if that didn't prove that I was not being followed, nothing would. My mind now was empty, flat: the next few hours, I had planned them out years ago, and now all that I needed to do was follow the plan. What was important, now, was to stay untraceable, or rather, to calculate when and how I was traceable and use it.

At High Street, I took the A train into Brooklyn, riding with a few Latin American workers heading for the early shift at the airports, in cowboy boots and jeans and hats, a tough uniform for gentle people. I knew the train well—in high school we would travel out this way again and again, Coney Island, Owl's Head, Borough Park, Bay Ridge, strange, often violent places: I had had a taste for the gutter from a very early age. But, you see, the level of violence then was so low-tech, I could participate in it too: playing on an even field with Brooklyn blacks and Italians, crossing paths with Guardian Angels and JDL kids in their tiny little yarmulkes. There were no guns and no one ever got seriously hurt. And later, when the time came to fight seriously, I knew how.

At Howard Beach I got off, stepping out and directly across the platform to the shadows of the wall. Along with the Latin Americans, for whom a shuttle was waiting, two kids had also gotten out, way down the other end of the platform, but they were too busy shouldering their backpacks to notice me. I watched them descending the stairs and climbing onto the waiting airport bus, and when that was gone, I went down myself and began to walk along Conduit Road.

God, I was hungry. The little streets next to the road held an occasional open bodega, but I did not want to be seen by anybody. And so I walked. Walked my heart out. I remembered John Sanford's line about his years on the blacklist, his passport confiscated: "You can walk your ass off but you're still in jail." Then, after a time, with each step a flash of you came into my mind, your face tilted upward, your nut-brown hair flowing back, and your lips pursed. For a time I watched it, consumed in the pain it conjured. Then, to the contrary, I began to worry about losing it. But it never left me, and in time I came to accept that in some way you were accompanying me while I walked, walked and breathed, walked with my steps hitting the concrete the way they had as a kid, hollow and lonely at night in Brooklyn.

And at last, when a distant sun was just beginning to color the sooty day gray, I found myself before the chain-link fence of Kennedy Airport.

I found and took the long-term parking shuttle, now, and got off at the TWA terminal. Inside I ate breakfast at a McDonald's, with distaste but with appetite. Then I bought a calling card at a newsstand and went over to a bank of pay phones, my brother's perpetual calendar page in my hand. The phone rang twice. And to my surprise, a woman's voice answered.

"Don't hang up. My name is Maggie Calaway."

I paused. Then, slowly, I answered. "Where's Daniel?"

"He's in jail. In Canada. I'm his wife."

Even more confused, I paused. But the woman went on. "You were reported to have fled to Canada in the *New York Times*. When we read about it, we thought it was probably a red herring. Was it?"

This time I answered, hesitantly. "How did you know?"

"I know someone who used to be . . . with you. She suggested Daniel drive up to Canada and get himself arrested. She also suggested we keep the identity updated and the money and all in your father's safe. You found it, right? She showed us how to do all that. I'm telling you all this so you'll trust me. Is it working?"

She had a low voice with a Boston accent, and seemed to be injecting an ironic lilt, almost as if making fun of me, into the question.

"Yes. It's working."

"Good. Our friend suggested Daniel go up to Canada as if he were going to meet you. Suspiciously, and stupidly. It worked: they arrested him in Montreal, and they're holding him for questioning. They still think you're there, but I doubt they'll keep thinking that for long."

I didn't know what to say, Isabel. Why would my brother be taking this kind of risk for me?

"You all are risking trouble."

"And you? What are you risking?"

I hesitated. "Maggie, I'm the guilty one."

"Are you now." She answered immediately. "That's not usually a dis-recommendation to lawyers. My husband—your brother—and I are both lawyers."

"Neither of you have privilege."

"Nor are either of us cowards."

It was as if we were having a fight. "What does that *mean?*"

"Nothing. Nothing." Her voice had changed now, as if soothing a child. "You know, I did a death penalty defense in Michigan a couple years ago?"

"Did you now?" I was, Isabel, utterly at sea.

"I did. I took it on for the University of Michigan Law School Death Penalty Project. Daley Stewart? Guy convicted of killing his girlfriend? You remember the case?"

"Sure."

"We lost. But, you know, I got to know the arresting officer pretty well. Being friends with me did *not* fit his profile, let me tell you. Vietnam vet, undercover with the FBI on the U of M campus. And still, we got to know each other. Wonderful guy. Had me to dinner with his family one Saturday."

"How nice." My heart was jumping out of my chest. Could she conceivably, conceivably, be talking about Johnny Osborne?

"Isn't it? He's the head of the FBI field office in Traverse City. John Osborne."

Iz. There was a long, long silence while, word by word, I absorbed what she had just told me. A long silence. Then I said:

"When was this?"

"Couple years ago." She spoke blithely, cheerfully, as if to counterweigh the enormity of the message hidden in what she was saying. "You know, he's this big Republican, Vietnam vet, right? But staunchly against the death penalty. And after he saw my work, he . . . well, he took me into his confidence about another injustice. An old, old injustice. Something that happened in the seventies."

There was silence on her end now, and I left it there for a long, long time, struggling to understand. Then I said, simply:

"He told you?"

"He told me."

"Did you tell my brother?"

"I told your brother."

"And that's why he left the IDs."

"We'd have done more, if we could."

It was an amazingly powerful thing, Izzy. An amazingly powerful thing, this . . . this beneficence from a total stranger. Finally I said, "Maggie, can you help me?"

"That's the idea, Jason. That's exactly the idea."

"I'm bringing you yet more trouble."

"What is it?"

"My daughter. Her name is Isabel. We call her Izzy. She's a lovely girl."

"Where is she?"

"At the Marriott Hotel on Wall Street. Room 504. She's alone. She won't wake up till eight. When she does, she'll be terrified. Can you go to her? Do you have kids?"

"Yes. I have a baby-sitter with my kids. I'll catch a cab right this second."

I was speaking quickly now. "I doubt you can avoid being followed. All that matters is that you get in before the police. Tell Daniel I'll need to get a court order to keep my daughter from her mother. Tell him to take her up to the house on Martha's Vineyard, because Massachusetts law will give me at least a stay of custody against my ex-wife. Ted Kennedy hates my ex-father-in-law, that should be worth something. Also—"

She interrupted me. "Jason. I'm a partner at Frankfurt, Garbus, Klein and Selz. I'll tie the thing up every which way but Sunday."

I was crying now, but so softly that when your aunt Maggie helped me to reconstruct this conversation, just last week, she still didn't know it. Still, I managed to tell her about your allergies, what you liked to eat, and how important it was to keep you from the television. "I'll need a few weeks."

"Go. What's your plan?"

"I'm going to find Mimi Lurie."

"You know how?"

"I think so."

"Go then. We'll keep your girl. Tell us when we can help."

Still crying, I hung up. Left the terminal. Caught the bus back to Howard Beach—the crowded bus now filled with the departing night shift, and arriving passengers, where no one would notice me—and then the A train, settling in for the long, silent, sinister ride through the morning back to New York. Got off at the Port Authority. By then it was nine-thirty in the morning, and I had slept only an hour in the past seventy-two. Which is why, once I had located the 10 A.M. bus to Denver, bought a ticket, and climbed into the evil, stale, antiseptic atmosphere, I fell into an immediate, total, defenseless sleep. Or better perhaps, a defensive sleep. For it kept me from even imagining the scene that was taking place at the Wall Street Mariott, where by then Maggie Calaway had arrived, accompanied by no less than Martin Garbus himself. She had with her a court order granting her temporary custody of her niece, a court order that protected them entirely from the two dozen armed Rapid Response Force police who stormed the hotel, minutes behind her, having—we found out later—had her under surveillance continuously since I went on the run.

Later, your aunt Maggie told me, remembering the scene, it occurred to her that it was Garbus who confronted the police with the court order. She, to her amusement, was not being a lawyer then, but a mother. Sitting on the unmade bed where a terrified, crying little girl was sitting in her nightclothes, shaking uncontrollably, having woken to find herself abandoned by her father in a hotel room, surrounded by police.

You want to know how I walked out on you? Just like you do anything dangerous. You plan for as long as you can, then you throw yourself on the mercy of events. You count on nothing but foresight, and you watch to see what is your luck. You expect help from nobody, and you take any help you can get. You try to manage your mind. Close it down. Focus your perceptions on the immediate. Put off pain, manage panic. Later there will be time to feel both in all the blossoming and flourishing of their horror.

Or have I got it wrong, Izzy? Is it that you don't care how I walked out on you, you only want to know why?

Oh, well, why. Why is also the same as why you do anything unthinkable. You do it when there's no other choice.

Date: June 12, 2006

From: "Benjamin Schulberg"
<benny@cusimanorganics.com>

To: "Isabel Montgomery" <isabel@exmnster.uk>

CC: maillist: The_Committee

Subject: letter 18

I find it kind of amusing that your father and Mimi were both writing all weekend. Myself, I have a life that takes up my weekends and a job to go to on Monday. It's taken me a couple hours to catch up with this story. It's nearly Tuesday already, and I'm just getting to work. So if this is less than perfectly crafted, Ms. Isabel, you'll have to excuse me, okay?

Now, one thing that's bugged the many observers and critics of this little drama is that by the end of June, that summer, virtually every player in this story was in Michigan, including me. At the time, that even let loose some talk of conspiracy, which will do no one any good if it comes up at the parole board. So let me explain something right off the bat. Mimi Lurie had her reasons for going to Ann Arbor, like she said. That of course meant that your father had reason to go there too. Rebeccah Osborne was already in school there, as is natural for a girl from Traverse City. Jed Lewis, too, had been in Ann Arbor as an undergraduate, graduate, and now as a professor. So in fact, the only real unlikely thing was that I, Benjamin, a New Yorker who has been to Europe more often than to any of those weirdo states between Jersey and California, should end up in Michigan.

To understand how this happened, you have to figure that one of the real prime places the story of your father was getting attention was, of course, Ann Arbor, because Jason Sinai was seen there as something of a native son.

I knew all about it. Because in the day or two after your father's flight, all I could do—and all I in fact did—was watch the Web and see what was being written, and where. And when those dozen or so times a day I ran a Nexis on Jason Sinai, the tiny little daily paper from the University of Michigan often turned out to have the most interesting stuff—a sad commentary on our national media, considering that the rag was run by a dozen stoned undergraduates.

When I exposed Jim Grant's identity in the *Albany Times*—and the story was picked up nationwide—it was, in Ann Arbor, a time of indignation. The next morning's *Michigan Daily* ran an editorial asking why we cannot forgive a crime twenty-two years old when we forgave a president for concealing from the American Congress and people alike a secret campaign of bombing and terror in Laos and Cambodia, Nixon's secret war of 1970. "If we're prosecuting war criminals," the article went on, "let's get them all. Lieutenant Calley's still out there somewhere, Fred Hampton's murderers too, Henry Kissinger's in New York. But if we're *pardoning* war criminals, then let's *pardon* them all, and Sharon Solarz, Jason Sinai, and Mimi Lurie are just the right place to start."

When it became known that your father had gone on the run, it was a time of jubilation in Ann Arbor—all the more so because it was summer, Hash Bash season, and there were pot smokers from far and wide on campus, most too young too have any idea what it meant that Jason had abandoned his seven-year-old daughter in a New York hotel room. A local group of high school students that had formed in Seattle lockup during the anti-WTO protest celebrated by posting all over campus excerpts from an article in *New Left Notes* from August 1969:

> Look At It: America, 1969: The war goes on, despite the jive double-talk about troop withdrawals and peace talks. Black people continue to be murdered by agents of the fat cats who run this country, if not in one way, then in another by the pigs or the courts, by the boss or the welfare department. Working people face higher taxes, inflation, speed-ups, and the sure knowledge—if it hasn't happened already—that their sons may be shipped off to Vietnam and shipped home

> in a box. And the young people all over the country go to prisons that are called schools, are trained for jobs that don't exist, or serve no one's real interest but the boss's, and, to top it all off, get told that Vietnam is the place to defend their "freedom."
>
> None of this is very new. The cities have been falling apart, the schools have been bullshit, the jobs have been rotten and unfulfilling for a long time.
>
> What's new is that today not quite so many people are confused, and a lot more people are angry: angry about the fact that the promises we have heard since first grade are all jive; angry that, when you get down to it, this system is nothing but the total economic and military put-down of the oppressed people of the world.

And the local T-shirt company began selling T-shirts with FBI Ten Most Wanted posters from the seventies on them, a fact that became dramatically known to Mimi Lurie when a girl walked into the Del Rio—where she was now installed as a bartender—wearing Mimi's twenty-year-old face on her own twenty-year-old breasts.

That there could be any connection between the middle-aged lady serving her a drink, though, and the sixties icon she sported on her T-shirt—that, I think, was too far-fetched to occur to anyone.

Only a day or two later did the *Daily*'s editorial page express a dissenting view, one that called for Jason Sinai to face the charges against him and let them be decided in court. With Jason's family pedigree, the article pointed out—son of Jack Sinai, brother of Daniel Sinai, a professor of law, Columbia University, brother-in-law of Maggie Calaway, and, if that wasn't enough, his parents were the adoptive parents of Klara Singer, who worked in Clinton's Commerce Department—the editorial did not see him lacking either Beltway connections or representation. Nor did it miss the fact that Jason Sinai had abandoned his daughter—the author of this editorial gave that prominent play. She also gave prominent play to the fact that were it not for the overturn of Mitchell's 1970 wiretap, Jason Sinai—as well as all the extant members of the so-called Weather Underground—would all be in jail anyway.

Finally, and most importantly, it disclosed that its author was the daughter of the director of the FBI field office, in Traverse City, that had originally been tasked with investigating the Bank of Michigan robbery. The article was signed Rebeccah Osborne, and her father, I found out in short order using PACER, was called John.

As it happened, Rebeccah Osborne, Mimi Lurie, and I were all to meet the next day.

Of course, we would not know who Mimi was, any more than the girl wearing her picture on her T-shirt did.

This is how it happened.

2.

After your daddy went on the run, I had spent a couple of the most frustrating days of my life in Albany.

When his flight to Canada turned out to be an elaborate and highly successful setup of the police, I published a front-page article on the real identity of James Grant, an article that was picked up all over the country or, in those papers that had done their own reporting, quoted extensively. That was good, and for a few moments there, it looked like my editor might actually address a sentence to me that did not contain any obscenities. Until, that is, he got into his third drink at our celebratory Shandon Star office party, and I overheard him tell the J School graduate that "fucking Benny Schulberg turned out to be right on the fucking money, for once."

Sure, I was hurt by the sentiment. But more than that, I was shocked by the language in so august a figure of authority.

Anyway, I was riding high for a moment or two there—as evidenced by the fact that Harmon even invited me to the Star, as the invitations to his drinks parties were pretty capricious, one of his little ways of keeping the staff divided. But when you, Isabel, were discovered in a hotel in downtown New York, the tables were turned. Now all the big papers gave the story to big metro reporters, and I was relegated to recycling their on-the-scene reporting in the *Albany Times,* which declined to pay my expenses to go 150 miles down 87 to New York City. A legal affairs stringer in Massachusetts had then taken over the story of Maggie Calaway's maneuvering to keep you from your mother—God forbid I should get any travel money, which could have run into the low three figures.

The only things that left me with were, firstly, the satisfaction of having been used by a person or persons unknown—Montgomery, I assumed—to expose Jason Sinai, and secondly, the exclusive story on Julia Montgomery's drug addiction and child abuse. I didn't need to ask my editor how he felt about running that. For one thing, he had been kissing Bobby Montgomery's ass for so long now I doubted he'd remember how to stop. For another, the Julia Montgomery story had the singular inconvenience of adding moral ambiguity to the Jason Sinai story, which the *Times,* in the finest contemporary standards of American journalism, hated to do.

So I sat on what I knew about Julia Montgomery, promising myself that my time would come.

Still, I did not give up. When my editor tried to reassign me, I put in for all my vacation owing—never having taken any at all, I had six weeks coming—and requested permission, hastily granted—as if my editor couldn't believe his luck—to spend them at my desk.

I then spent a single day moving out of my apartment and into a Super 8 Motel—it had weekly rates that groups of Mexican men were taking good advantage of—happily abandoning my security deposit and last month's rent to my landlord, his due, I felt, for dealing with the refrigerator. My possessions, which were few, I had put into storage, and my bills and unanswered correspondence, which filled two cardboard boxes, I recycled. That settled, I went back to my cubicle at the *Times* and set about making Kevin Cornelius of the Albany FBI field station regret ever having had the idea of using a journalist to leak news. I called Kevin every day, often several times, to check in on his progress in tracking Jason Sinai. The trail, however, had ended at Clayton. Finally, in exasperation, Cornelius admitted that they were powerless to catch a practiced, well-disciplined fugitive. America, he said, just wasn't built to find a person who was determined enough to get lost. "Could be anywhere, Ben."

No, he couldn't, I thought to myself. If he were just anywhere, he would have taken his daughter.

I didn't tell Cornelius that. For one thing, I doubted that Cornelius would understand.

To me, though, it was clear as the big blue midwestern sky. If Jim Grant had wanted to go hide with his daughter, he would have done so. Changing identities, hiding somewhere: this is what Jason Sinai was good at. Probably, in fact, he had been making preparations to do so well before Sharon Solarz was arrested. He must have known there was no way he was going to win his custody suit. He was, after all, a lawyer.

But, and this was the thing, he *didn't* go hide. I thought about this for a great long time. He *didn't* take his daughter and go hide. What he did was much more complicated. What he did was, he conducted a delicate and risky series of switches, got to New York, and contrived to get his daughter to the safekeeping of his brother. Then he ran off, alone.

That changed everything.

Why had he done this? I thought about that a long time, sitting in the baking heat of the courtyard outside the *Times*, smoking cigarettes. Why would Mr. Grant—I still could not think of him as Jim, never mind as Sinai—have gone through so much trouble to get his daughter to his brother, when he could just as easily have taken her with him? The apparent answer to that—reported by the *New York Times*—was that Sinai's sister-in-law, the constitutional lawyer Margaret Calaway, had removed Isabel Sinai to the commonwealth of Massachusetts, filed for custody on behalf of her husband Daniel, Jason's brother, and successfully obtained a temporary injunction against Ambassador Montgomery, who had come from London to take his granddaughter immediately upon receiving news of Jason's flight. This, however, simply did not satisfy me, and even as I followed the legal battle between Calaway and Montgomery, which twice held the front Metro page of the *New York Times*, not because of Jason but because of Margaret Calaway's involvement, I still didn't buy it.

For one thing, I realized that the combined might of Daniel Sinai,

Calaway's law firm, and the friendly Teddy Kennedy was only going to delay—not prevent—Montgomery's eventual custody of Isabel Sinai. You can't take a child away from her mother like that, even when the mother is not connected up the wazoo. And Jason, I knew, knew that also. It was a temporary measure.

And for another thing, I knew that Jason was not a man who left his daughter easily: an idiot could have seen that, and while in 1996 I was something of an idiot about my own life, I wasn't about other people's.

No, the only conclusion was that Jason had found a very good, very temporary solution to the issue of his daughter's custody, the only way to keep his daughter from his ex-wife without making her a fugitive too. But it was only a temporary measure. So what did he have in mind?

See, you know, because Mimi just told you so, what your father was doing. You know, and now I know, that he was preparing to go find Mimi Lurie. In June 1996, however, there was no way I could know that.

And still, I could know something. A day of nearly constant telephoning, as well as using up virtually every favor owed to me by anyone with any faintly liberal credentials, finally got me a short off-the-record telephone call with Daniel Sinai, speaking from his house in Martha's Vineyard, where he had gone to join his wife, two children, and you, his niece, directly upon being released from the Canadian jail. Sinai, a soft-spoken man with a slightly patrician accent, began the conversation by telling me he had nothing to say. It was an opening that made me, uncharacteristically, feel defeated, and I let dead air hang on the line until Sinai spoke again.

"Just what is it you want, Mr. Schulberg?"

"Well . . . what is it you think your brother's doing, Dr. Sinai?"

"I haven't spoken to my brother in twenty-six years. How am I supposed to know what he's doing?"

A reporter's reflex to give an interviewee the chance to lie made me ask, "You haven't spoken to him since he went on the run?"

Sinai spoke carefully, accenting the first word. "I have not."

That meant someone had. But I found myself still feeling bad. "Well, what do you think he's doing?"

"I have no idea."

"How long do you think you can hang on to your niece?"

"However long the law says, Mr. Schulberg. Until I can return her to my brother, I hope."

"I see." I suddenly felt fed up. It was one thing when a right-wing government source clammed up on you; another altogether when someone you admired treated you like the enemy. "Well, Dr. Sinai, you've been very informative. Thank you."

"Mr. Schulberg?"

I put the phone back to my ear, and waited.

"This is off the record. Agreed?"

"Okay."

Now his voice shifted. "I don't know what my brother's doing. I probably know less about him than you do, if you want to know the truth. The last time I saw him, I was twelve. But I'm guessing the same thing that occurs to me about him has already occurred to you."

"And that is?"

"That . . ." Daniel Sinai hesitated. "That nothing my brother's doing makes any sense if he's guilty."

I took a moment to absorb this. Then I answered slowly, with equal honesty. "No. I mean, I knew there was something I didn't understand. I hadn't quite put the question that way."

"Well, think about it. If he's guilty, he should have absconded with his daughter. Changed his name, moved away. Clearly my brother knows how to do that. And I can tell you, also off the record, that he has the means. The only logical reason to leave Isabel with us, temporarily, is that it buys him time."

"Okay. For what?"

Your uncle answered without hesitation. "To exculpate himself of charges stemming from the Bank of Michigan robbery."

I took a long moment to absorb that. "To prove himself innocent? And how could he do that?"

There was a silence now, and for a moment, I had a strong intuition that your uncle knew the answer to this question. That, in other words, what he said next was a lie. "Mr. Schulberg, if I knew that, I'd be out helping him now."

I thought about that for a long time. Then I began the process of getting a call through to Gillian Morrealle, Sharon Solarz's lawyer.

• • •

When I finally did get through, Morrealle informed me that she had nothing to say, would only speak off the record, and that only because of our common friendship with Jay Cohen at the *North American Review* out in Los Angeles. Then she proceeded to answer my questions with a lawyer's care. Sharon Solarz had been arraigned, had pleaded not guilty, had been remanded without bail to Bedford Hills Correctional Facility pending extradition to Michigan. Morrealle was now preparing to represent Sharon at her Michigan arraignment, which would be in Traverse City in the next day or two. Sharon's morale was good; she had of course met old friends at Bedford Hills in Kathy Boudin and Judy Clark; as an accessory to a cop killing she was being treated with respect in the prison; she was already becoming active in the AIDS education program that Boudin and Clark had built up. No: Sharon had specifically instructed Morrealle to go to trial on a not guilty plea; she wanted to see the issues tried in court. No: she had given no interviews; she had turned down *60 Minutes* and the *New York Times* and was not considering any other interviewers, including Mr. Schulberg. No, she could not suggest anyone else for me to talk to.

"Mr. Schulberg? Let me tell you something. You don't have a snowball's chance in hell of getting anyone who knew Sharon to talk to you. You know why? Because Sharon's prosecution is a travesty of justice, and everyone with any sense knows you won't write that."

That, at last, was too much for me. "Ms. Morrealle? Let me tell *you* something. I would write it, if I thought there were a snowball's chance in hell of it being true. Since no one in your little coterie of supposed defenders of the Bill of Rights has enough faith in our free press to go on the record with me, of course, I don't have any way of determining that. And seeing none of you heroic lefty freedom fighters will tell me anything, your moral indignation plays with me like just another damn lawyer's ploy."

And, of course, I thought as I hung up the phone, there's the small problem that even if someone *would* speak to me, and even if I *did* write the article, what with our free press being such a Mickey Mouse operation and all, there's the minor problem that no one would publish it.

• • •

By the Saturday after your daddy's flight, I was nowhere closer to knowing how to pursue this story than I had been when your daddy had taken off. I woke at six, as I did every morning, not by intent but by insomnia. And as I did every morning, I came straight to the office to turn on my computer and search Nexis for regional newspaper coverage on Jason Sinai's flight.

I could have done the search back at the hotel on my laptop, but that meant taking the three half-filled coffee containers, the ashtray, and the pile of newspapers off my laptop, which was in the passenger seat of my car.

That's why I was in the office when I found Rebeccah Osborne's *Michigan Daily* editorial.

Reading it, suddenly something crystallized for me.

And this is what it was. I already knew that if there were some way for Jason Sinai to exculpate himself of guilt in the Bank of Michigan robbery, then he would be able to reclaim his daughter.

Now I realized that if there was some evidence that he could find and produce to so exculpate himself—to prove himself innocent—wouldn't it be logical to think that the original investigating officer from the FBI might have some idea what that evidence might be?

I launched Netscape, did a MapQuest search, then went to Travelocity.

I could drive to LaGuardia, fly to Detroit, and drive to Traverse City in about nine hours.

Or I could leave right that moment, drive through Niagara Falls and Canada, to Port Huron, and to Traverse City in about twelve.

The last thing I did before shutting down my computer, pulling out the packed suitcase I kept under my desk, and leaving for Canada was look up the address of the Traverse City Resident Agency whose daughter had written the *Michigan Daily* editorial, and write down the name and number of its Senior Agent.

John Osborne. From my car on the way to the airport, I called the Traverse City FBI office, found that Osborne was not in, and talked the duty officer into calling Osborne at home and having him call me back on my cell. It took perhaps five minutes until my cell rang, which surprised me. Osborne, a man with a soft voice who let a couple ponderous seconds pass before replying to any one of my questions, told me he was going down to Ann Arbor for the weekend but could meet me there for a quick coffee the next day, Saturday afternoon.

"You're there on Jason Sinai business, Mr. Osborne?" I was writing the name of a café down while driving with my knee and talking on my cell phone.

Pause. "No, sir. I'm going to see my daughter."

The *Michigan Daily* editorial writer. I hung up now and settled in for the long drive. Feeling, for the first time since this story started, that I had actually done something right, although, for the life of me, I couldn't say what that was.

Date: June 13, 2006
From: "Daddy" <littlej@cusimanorganics.com>
To: "Isabel Montgomery" <isabel@exmnster.uk>
CC: maillist: The_Committee
Subject: letter 19

Well, Benny, I'm very sorry to make you stay up past your bedtime. I mean, with only a human life at stake.

Izzy, try to ignore his nonsense, will you? Think of him as a means, not an end. We need him right now, but we can leave him on the sidewalk and drive right away when we're done, okay?

As for me, what I remember most distinctly from those days is waking that afternoon on the bus to Denver, with big images of dreams still subjacent to my consciousness, realer than the real and filled with menace.

The enigma of awakening. That little interstice where all the preverbal mystery of existence can be experienced again. There was a swirl of pink, filling my still closed eyes, the thin color of sun through the blood in my eyelids, the heat of the sun against my skin. For as long as I could, I held myself there, in that country of swimming pink light, in the limpness of my body, in the unawareness of where I could be. And when I could hold memory at bay no longer, I opened my eyes.

I opened my eyes and watched assemble the view of a parking lot, liquid with midday sun, deserted but for a man and a girl walking their long shadows toward a truck stop restaurant, the man sweating, the girl in shorts and a tank top. In their wake the air above the hot tarmac shimmered. Total silence filled the scene but for the thrum of big engines beating under me.

Where was I? A stale and antiseptic smell impinged on my consciousness, insistently, as if it were a clue. With a physical effort I sought to bring it into focus, to name its familiarity, to identify the emotion I carried. When I at last succeeded, it was in fact not enigmatic but as simple as can be. "I am on a bus. It must now be afternoon. I am on a bus."

Then it all came back.

Izzy. I used to be able to sleep anywhere, and wake so happily, when I was young. Now sleep is a brittle physical state, a different consciousness as difficult to attain when you want it as it is, when it's unwelcome, impossible to escape. I forced myself to repeat, like a mantra, that I was on a bus, on a bus, on a bus, on a bus. And with each repetition emptiness washed through me—a feeling so bleak, so hopeless, that in a man approaching fifty it can be dignified with the name of despair.

How many days had passed since I blew a joint with Billy in his Sea of Green? Four? Five? How fragile Jim Grant turned out to be, falling apart in three days, four, the very first time he was challenged. Not for the first, but for perhaps the eighth time in my life, I had seen how fragile that whole collection of papers and lies that compose an identity turn out to be, tumbling apart the instant the right pressure is applied. And yet, how unexpected had been the vectors of forces that lined up to take Jim apart! Any one of them I could have weathered; perhaps any two. First Julia, and her lawyers. Then Sharon's stupid capture. I had always been ready to run with you, Isabel, I had always known this could happen. And now, on the bus, I admitted to myself that the moment Ben Schulberg showed up and began poking around, I had known it was time.

I had been Jim Grant for twenty years, since the summer of 1976, bicentennial year, the year of Carter's election. I had been Jim Grant almost as long as I had been myself; certainly through the most important parts of my adult life: college, law school, fatherhood, and divorce. And given that between 1970 and 1976, I was not Jason Sinai but a series of other, fleeting, ever-changing identities, I had been Jim Grant longer than I had been myself. Sitting, face against the bus window, looking at an overheated parking lot, now deserted, I realized that everything that had meant anything profound to me as an adult was born and built as Jim Grant.

And now it was gone.

• • •

I am Jason Sinai. For the first time in twenty years, I pronounced the name of my birth to myself; for the first time in twenty years I let it slip past a little mental firewall that kept it out of my memory. How strange it was: even after twenty years, Jason was immediately present to my mind, intimately familiar. How easily I had let myself be separated from my entire past—my family, my parents. At first it was youth, wasn't it?—youth, and the potency of my beliefs. And then came Bank of Michigan, and something stronger than my beliefs interposed itself; something that made it impossible for me ever to go home, the way Jeff, and Billy, and Bernardine had moved back to the real world, slowly, their consciences clean, even proud of much they had done. Something that made me abandon, with plain determination and grim realism, any thought of ever going home again.

And what would happen, now, to Jason Sinai? Sitting in the bus, the thought came to me like a song of mourning. All of the safety nets had belonged to Jim; Jason had nothing. No law license, no house, no friends, no life. No daughter. No daughter.

It was coming now, like a swimmer surfacing, gasping for air, and with all the twenty years of mental discipline, I tried to escape the truth that had swum into my awareness, the truth that had been sitting there, just below my sleep, when I awoke. But it was everywhere, the bus engine throbbing loss; the carbon-monoxide bouquet of interstate anonymity; the depthless well of mourning that constituted my being. I had lost my daughter. And at the thought, instantly, I decided to surrender.

But what was surrender? Surrender meant nothing for me but hard time in maximum-security lockup, a state prison in Michigan; Ionia, or Standish. There is no daughter in state lockup. At best there is the harsh neon-lit visiting room where rapists and murderers sit nearby, some in shackles. Such a room had awaited me all the time I was Jim Grant. Now Jim Grant no longer existed, and I doubted seriously that Jason Sinai, in jail, would be able to claim paternity of his daughter.

And if I could, what good would it do me, when no court on God's green earth would order Jim Grant's divorced wife to bring my child there? What good would it do me when, at fifty-six, I would be released, if I was released, and you would be seventeen? What happens to aged vanguardists of a failed revolution, without income, without insurance? How do they live? I'd have to find work, and what might that be? Could I teach? Teachers, I knew, had to swear they had never been arrested. And who would hire a teacher at nearly sixty? Only the marginal would be available to me: clerking somewhere, driving a cab, working at the counter of a Wendy's. And of the possibilities of freedom I had always so thoughtlessly enjoyed—an empty beach, a private piece of woods—not one would remain. Even state land would become closed to me, as I grew older and more infirm, wouldn't it?

I had, I thought, more in common with Julia than I'd have thought: she had outlived her time in front of the camera, and I my place in American politics.

And you—where would you find the time in your life to visit this person I would become: you with your youth and health, you with your mother's money and a world of expanding possibilities?

I had always known where this would end. And all this thinking, all this thinking, I had done it before. I had done it in bed, nights; I had done it on long drives; I had done it standing by the window of my office in Saugerties, staring down at the empty streets. I knew the answer, and knowing it, I said it, once again, aloud. *Al tegid lilah,* Little J. Never say night.

I opened my eyes again, now, and began to think.

2.

So where was I? Slowly, as I pieced together the events of the night before, reality reassembled itself: this was a truck stop on I-80 to Chicago; I was on a bus; the bus had stopped for a break. Judging by the time, we must be in Michigan. And judging by that same time, Jim Grant by now existed no longer, and Jason Sinai was the object of a manhunt that involved law enforcement from U.S. marshals to the FBI.

That I was probably still being sought in Canada, not America, was only some help.

Slowly, gingerly, I pulled my mind back from its grief, detaching it piece by piece, like the tentacles of a starfish from an undersea rock. When I could, I rose, reached my Sportsac shoulder bag from the small luggage shelf above, and climbed heavily out of the bus.

A wet heat hung over the tarmac like a shroud, endless Doppler whines radiating from the highway with the sound of complaint. On stiff legs, I forced myself inside the truck stop, promising myself a cup of coffee before anything else. But on the way to the restaurant I passed a bank of newspaper machines, and from the front page of the *Detroit Free Press* I saw both Jason Sinai and Jim Grant's faces watching me impassively.

Ducking my face toward the ground, I changed course toward the bathroom and went into a stall.

Here I locked the door, sat on the closed toilet with my bag in my lap, pulled my legs up, and buried my face in my knees.

Like this, I sat for an hour.

A good hour, to let the bus leave, to let the population of the truck-stop restaurants change.

An hour. Repeating to myself, over and over.

Let me do what I have to.

Then I can go to hell.

Izzy, have you have ever been in danger? On a boat, while traveling, on a city street late at night? Only if you have had an experience of real, sustained danger, danger so unrelenting that you cannot avoid confronting it, will you understand the change that occurred to me that hour, hiding in a truck-stop bathroom on the I-80 through Michigan.

I had come, at last, to the place you go to if you can be focused, rather than scattered, by risk. Whether decisions are right or wrong, here, you act on them quickly, before they can become too obscured by doubt. I know that's hard to understand, but it's true. Perhaps it's because when you're in danger, even a wrong decision carried out with determination is better than vacillation. Fear, you see, is the great friend of vacillation, and vacillation is where mistakes are made—mistakes that, here, can be fatal.

Those who are experienced in danger, those who are practiced in risk, know that you cannot stop yourself from anticipating catastrophic failure, that it might even be the most likely outcome, and that it's foolish to try to pretend it's not there. Nonetheless, in the presence of the possibility of imminent disaster, the only sensible thing to do is to keep acting, one decision after the other after the other. Each decision that leads to the next is a tiny triumph. That's why there's not only fear here, though there's lots of that. Every second of liberty is also a tiny triumph, a tiny dose of intoxication. It's why people become criminals and why most criminals are gamblers, and it kept me, like I say, focused on what I was doing. Against that focus, however, was all the force of grief. Fear, I could use, but grief had to be repressed: fear could be a conscious tool, but grief had to stay where it was without being seen.

First I stood up and peed, lengthily, and with relief. Then, sitting again, I withdrew from my bag a laundry kit and carefully took out some Grecian Formula hair dye and a black toupee, a small black mustache in a plastic case, an electric razor, a mirror, and a number of little tubes and combs.

Now, I don't particularly want to teach you the tricks of the trade, but I will tell you this: if you want to buy stuff to disguise yourself, no matter whether you're going to leave it in a closet for months, do it at Halloween—no one will bat an eye. Sitting in the bathroom stall, knees pressed together to hold my impedimenta, I stripped off my shirt and began working carefully with the kit that I kept replenished each Halloween. First, I used the Grecian Formula to turn the red hair on my head black. Then I shaved carefully and by feel with a disposable razor, shaving cream, and witch hazel—that way I didn't need to leave the privacy of the stall for running water. I put on the mustache and the toupee with adhesive. With a pair of barber's scissors and the mirror, I trimmed the toupee and mustache. Finally, I put on a pair of horn-rimmed glasses with a very slight prescription—so slight that it did not much impair my vision, but still avoided the telltale glare of flat glass on fake lenses.

When finally I held the little mirror away from my face, I was shocked to see a handsome Jewish man staring back. It was the Jewish part that shocked me—it had been a very long time since I acknowledged my tenuous relationship with my parents' religion. As for the handsomeness—I have warned you before that I am not without vanity—it saddened me. I did not like to admit how much better I looked with more hair. Perhaps, I told myself, it was just the color.

I put my shirt back on and cleaned up, then waited for the bathroom to be—or to sound—empty. When at last I thought it was, I left the stall, then the bathroom, and walked directly out into the parking lot. Repressing my now imperious need for coffee, which was making my head ache, and carrying my bag, I crossed the lot to the service road leading away from the highway. Without looking back, I stepped down its verge toward the low skyline of suburban sprawl, soon finding myself in a residential neighborhood of small clapboard homes.

The streets here were empty: a blue-collar bedroom community on a weekday—at least, I thought it was a weekday—air conditioners letting a dull hum into the air. For a time I walked, nearly thoughtlessly, watching the trim lawns and modest houses, feeling the lassitude of heat in the suburbs. Finally, at a public park where a couple children played listlessly in front of their mothers, I sat under a tree and waited the couple last hours until nightfall, feeling my caffeine-deprivation headache rise to new heights.

When it was at last dark, I rose and retraced my steps toward the highway, or where I thought the highway should be. This time, my route must have been different, for after several blocks of lit houses in black streets, I came to a gas station and convenience store, both built of cinder block, sitting under a pool of neon light from a high streetlamp. Cicadas had started sounding, so slowly I had not noticed it, but now I became conscious of their ululating scream, like Arab women in mourning, and with it came a sudden sense of panic. There was a video camera mounted on the lamp, pointed to catch the entrance doors of both shops. I crossed a little patch of oil-stained tarmac behind the grocery store to point my back toward the camera and then, shoulders hunched slightly, walked into the store.

Coffee, here, came in large and extra large. I took two of the latter. I knew I had to eat, and although it broke some of the firmest principles of my life with you, I finally took a bag of Doritos from a shelf and bought those too. Munching the Doritos and sipping coffee thirstily, I walked back out into a din of crickets and went on through the streets of little houses. A soul-destroying place to live, I thought, and as the coffee quieted my headache, somewhere distant, for the first time since leaving you, I felt a grief bigger than my own, the grief of people forced to live lives of work and consumerism in houses like this.

When, after a mile or so, I found the entrance ramp to the highway, strong halogen streetlamps cast a thick curtain of luminescence—a shower of light that emitted an electric buzz and held a swarm of insects at its top—through the summer-warm air.

I did not enter the highway but stood just outside the border of the light. The first car that came was a Taurus, and as it approached I stepped fully into the light, thumb up, wrist toward the car. It swerved slightly, then accelerated down the ramp, a woman at the wheel looking steadfastly ahead. A full fifteen minutes passed without another car passing, then a battered Tercel driven by a single man came up. This time I stepped into the light more fully, showing my face, and held a hand up. The car pulled up while its driver, a boy in his twenties, leaned over to unroll the passenger window.

"Can you give me a ride, man?" I leaned onto the window and showed my whole face, which held anxiety. "My car died. I left it at the gas station up there."

"Where to?" The *r* was French. His face, not recently shaved, was framed by dirty-blond hair, and he wore a denim shirt over a faded orange T-shirt.

"I'm going to Chicago."

"Chicago? *Merde*."

"Wherever, man. As far as you're going is fine."

The boy looked me up and down, appraisingly. "O-kay. *Venez*."

I climbed in and slammed shut the door, defining thereby a microclimate filled with the warmth of my body and the smell of tobacco. A pack of Canadian Export A's sat on the well under the handbrake. The kid pulled out and the car sank down the ramp into the zone of bright, yellowish streetlamp, merging into fast traffic while accelerating at the limit of its little engine. Now the interior of the car was lit, and I felt sweat come out on my face.

"J'ai cru qu'on fait plus de stop aux États-Unis."

The kid was speaking to himself, I knew. Still, I asked: "Sorry?"

"No 'itchikeeng anymore. In America, I thought."

I watched the cigarette pack, feeling a horrible desire rising in me. I looked down at it, then back up. The kid was watching me now.

"Listen, man. Can you take me into Chicago?"

The kid laughed. "I go to Joliet. I already come from Quebec. You make me drive all night."

"Yes." It was, I thought to myself, like getting in a stranger's car in New York and asking to be driven to Boston. Without thinking, I reached ten twenties out of my pocket. "I'll pay gas and food and this on top." I glanced at him, then back to the road.

"What ees your problem?"

I tried to enunciate clearly. "I'm in trouble with the police. Marijuana. Do you understand?"

"*Oui*. And een Chicago, it ees better?"

"In Chicago I have friends. They'll help me get a lawyer"

He watched for another instant, then turned back to the road, smiling. "*Allon-zy donc*."

Relief flooding through me, I reached a cigarette out of the box. "And I'll buy more cigarettes too."

"O-kay, man." It came out, this time, in an imitation American accent, as if the kid were making fun of me. And I lit the cigarette, drawing the deep richness into the back of my throat, sitting back in my chair. Feeling, in the interior of the car, the slightly sweaty warmth of my savior. Thinking, as the nicotine swirled into my bloodstream, numbing my lips, cooling my hands, that it was always like this.

It was always like this. Total strangers would help, for no reason whatever. Some of us had been very public figures in SDS, sometimes addressing crowds of thousands of people, and when we were underground, we would be recognized wherever we went, in restaurants, in bars. Recognized, and after the moment of recognition, ignored. And later, when the police came—and the police came early and often, with warrants, with subpoenas, and with a whole boatload of COINTEL-PRO tricks—not one person, not a single, solitary person, ever told them a thing.

All of us, for years after, when on left and right alike we had been condemned—on the right for adventurism, on the left for destroying the movement—we would all remember the hundreds and hundreds of total strangers who, at enormous risk, helped us. People who lent houses, gave money; doctors who saw us; kids who gave us rides, and cars, and apartments.

How hated were we? Sure: There were those like Gitlin, who hated us on political grounds, and those who hated us on personal grounds, for our arrogance, for our plain meanness. But apart from these, I have never been convinced we were widely hated at all.

Except for how much some of us came to hate ourselves.

And we were lucky. Endlessly lucky, as I had been tonight.

And so as a stranger started to drive me hundreds of miles out of my way to Chicago, as the sweetness of nicotine spread through my blood-stream, I remembered something: luck is never surprising, always inevitable.

Perhaps that is because you only see your luck when, as few people ever do, you put yourself in a position truly to need it.

Date: June 13, 2006
From: "Amelia Wanda Lurie"
<mimi@cusimanorganics.com>
To: "Isabel Montgomery" <isabel@exmnster.uk>
CC: maillist: The_Committee
Subject: letter 20

Little J. I must have been somewhere in Utah, on the 80 East, before I stopped inventing Cleo Theophilus's identity, and let my mind go where for so long I had kept it away, to thinking about your father.

Jason Sinai. There were so damn many Js in SDS, not just Jeff Jones and JJ but all manner of Joannas, Jaffes, Johns, Jeans, Justins, Jennifers. First person to call your father Little J, that was JJ, and when he did, your father's face fell. Years later I found out why—Jack Sinai and Jason, in the big extended family that gathered in the Sinai's house on Bedford Street: Big J and Little J.

Little J. I've tried a thousand times to see him, crossing the Brooklyn Bridge that midnight after leaving you, a man who had moments before abandoned his daughter in a hotel room, and like that, he finds himself watching across the black water at the Verrazano Narrows Bridge, the same view he had seen with his father in 1962.

Little J. I've tried a thousand times to see him, waking on that bus to Chicago, that June day of 1996.

I see him in a room on the Cape, sprawled naked on white sheets, the long autumn sun crossing the wooden wall, lowering, lowering, until it sweeps over his face: his thick red bangs, his forehead, his eyebrows. In houses upstate, lent to us, rented, or stolen. Apartments in the Mission, Hyde Park, Williamsburg, the cheap neighborhoods of cities across the country. Always off-season, the time when the radical chic, not needing their pricey country houses, could lend us them in return for a daring dinner party story, a thrill up their spines, and that without interrupting their summer. Stay as long as you want, but be out by Thanksgiving, because the kids are off school and it's the last time we can get out of the city till Christmas. Cars and trains, buses. Tents. A precious collection of mornings, waking in places where we had been safe enough, provisionally, to sleep, to fuck, to hold each other in the protection of the dark.

When you are a fugitive, it is in the day that the regrets, the terrors, the awful memories come. "Whatever gets you through the day/It's O-kay, Okay—" We rewrote the words to the song, our first year on the move, and I remember wondering how night could ever be a threat to anyone. Night, with the amazing chances it offers to hide, is always the respite. Mornings, only the innocent—like Jason—wake unafraid.

That is why it is so hard for me to imagine how your father woke, that day on the bus to Denver after leaving you in New York, the swirling of blood-pink before his eyes. I can't, or I won't, accept that as a man your father no longer wakes as he did as a boy, no longer wakes happy, no longer wakes hopeful. That, in my opinion, is the greatest casualty of his marriage to Julia, and I will give you any odds that it only became the case after Julia became an addict. I will bet you anything that those magical first years, as your father realized how solidly James Grant was holding, as your father floated on the safety net of the Montgomery fortune, as life unfolded to him with magical ease, I will bet you that he woke happy and rolled toward Julia's beautiful naked body as he once rolled toward mine. And I will bet you that it was only after you came along and Julia, a line of coke at a time, started abusing first herself, then herself and Jason, and finally her daughter too, that at long last peace began to drain from your father's nights.

For this, I will never forgive your mother. Not only for taking hope from your father, but for taking its possibility, its very possibility, away from me.

For as I came to understand your father's part of this story—and I have had ten years to learn it in its every detail and imagine its every thought—I realized that for all the time that I lived as Tess Sanders, for the entire central period of my life, the belief that happiness might be possible, not just for me but for others, was founded on your father's way of waking into happiness, each morning, his ability to face the day with hope. Later, when your father was often described as foolish, even naive, how it must have galled him to have those things for you to read, someday, yourself. Let me tell you something, Isabel. To be an optimist like your father is not naive, nor is it an error. Only the naive would think so.

I, who lost my naïveté the day my father put a gun in his mouth on the dunes at Point Betsie; I, who have lived without the slightest fantasy ever since, know that optimism is the highest of spiritual developments, and I would trade my soul for it, if I had a goddamn soul.

Shit. I keep writing exactly what I promised I wouldn't. Promised myself, that is. I promised myself I would just tell you what happened. Here's what happened in June 1996, Isabel Sinai: I drove east from San Francisco. On the 80. I got the story every hour, on the hour, on NPR as I headed east, not sleeping, living on coffee. In the evenings *All Things Considered* gave background, interviews, human interest. And in between broadcasts I could hear, rather than just imagine, the conversations that were taking place, that day, in hundreds, even thousands of ex-Movement houses, telephones, e-mails.

See, people love to see us fall. I can't complain about it, because we asked for it. With all our proclamations, communiqués, declarations. Each time we set a bomb, it was nothing if not a dare. Daring the law to find us, daring other lefties to follow us, daring both ends of the spectrum, we were in nothing so successful as getting them both to hate us. Now, looking back, I see that each time we were a little further away from the people we thought we were communicating with.

Now, looking back, I wonder what we thought was going happen to us after the war was over. I ask myself, did we actually think that we were going to head a revolutionary government, a kind of collective American Castro, and make of our fallen comrades the collective American Ché? When the Mitchell Justice Department so violated the Constitution that most of us became unprosecutable, I remember watching with awe as one by one, people began to surface and return to normal lives. For me, even without Bank of Michigan, I don't think I'd have been able to. I think I'd just have been too embarrassed.

You want to know what we thought was going to happen? The best answer I can give, it's that basically, I don't remember. The best answer I can give is, when you are engaged in a project like, say, trying to lead the second American revolution, wipe out war and imperialism, and render justice to the oppressed black minority—just to pick a wild example—you don't think that way. You can't. The way you think is: What Castro accomplished seemed impossible. What Mao accomplished seemed impossible. And what Ho Chi Minh *is* accomplishing—and at the time, it *was* the actual present—*is* impossible. He was fighting off the United States of America, and in the end would give two million lives against our 58,000, and would win.

Did we think we were going to lead a revolution? I don't know. Did you ever think that a handful of suicidal fundamentalist maniacs with box cutters would be able to collapse two of the tallest buildings in the world, kill three thousand people in the center of New York, bring the country's economy to its knees, cause hundreds of thousands of people to lose their livelihood, redraw the map of Asia, and launch a cycle of world war that, today, five years later, is still raging?

Maybe you did. I didn't.

So I don't know what we thought we were doing. I just can't say anymore. What we didn't imagine, however—and as I say, I'm not complaining—was how notorious we would become. Not only at the time, but afterward. That we would take on the aura of an American myth: the underground sixties radical. Or that the last few of us who refused to surface would be such big news when we were found.

Want to know what I think? If you ask me, we came to partake of the American myth of the maverick, the last wild horses, roaming free across a western frontier. We were the last mavericks, the last ones who refused to admit that it was over, that it was all over, that everything we believed in had either been forgotten, discredited, or packaged by corporations and sold for a profit. And certainly we didn't guess how fervently our ex-peers—thousands of people who made up the Movement—would hope for us to fail.

Here's the rule, Isabel. With criminals, people root for them secretly, secretly hope they will evade the police, even while they publicly moralize against them. With us, they root for us publicly, and secretly, deeply, profoundly, they hope we will fail. The thousands of conversations that I knew were taking place among ex-Movement people while the manhunt for Jason was on, I guarantee you that not one of them ever expressed the hope that he be caught. They talked about the ridiculous scale of the manhunt for a man who had lived as a model citizen for the past twenty-five years and who was only tangentially involved in the crime in the first place; they talked about the disproportionate punishment of criminal and political defendants; they talked about how desperate a man must be to abandon his daughter, and by all accounts, Jason was a model father too.

And behind it all, I knew that these thousands and thousands of people were looking at each other in the deepest satisfaction, and saying to each other, Sinai's gone nuts. Just like Abbie Hoffman, Eldridge Cleaver, David Horowitz, even Ira Einhorn. Yet another icon of the sixties had abandoned his principles, had proved that it was all a delusion, all a childish fantasy. And in their hearts they are comforted, reaffirmed, to know that it was a dream that the machine could be stopped, that a society could be fair, that the planet could be saved and people could be free—a dream of children, and now the very last holdouts have made fools of themselves, have ruined their lives and abandoned their principles, whether by inventing a ridiculous pair of trousers like Eldridge Cleaver or by committing suicide like Abbie Hoffman or by becoming a neo-conservative like Ronald Radosh.

Or by abandoning their daughter in a hotel room.

See, now we can get on with the real work of going to jobs we hate, of raising children who hate us, of finding and defending our place in the status quo, the grim, competitive, bitter status quo, which is a relief, because it is frightening to step out of the status quo; it is a relief because even the quiet desperation of daily toil in corporations is less frightening—in fact, nothing is more frightening—than the possibility of freedom.

Never mind that Jason, Sharon, and I, we're not icons of anything.

Never mind that for hundreds of thousands of people the revolution never stopped. Never mind that in fundamental ways, real ways, and irreversible ways, our lives were transformed, and each one of us and our children feel the benefits of that transformation, every time one of our daughters graduates from medical school, every time one of our sons cooks dinner for his family, every time a public school class studies Martin Luther King and Rosa Parks, every time a black woman marries a white man, every time a court stops a corporation from emitting pollutants. If the Committee will look the other way for a moment—and even if they won't—I'll show you a quote. Ready? It's from an interview with Chomsky, and don't tell anyone I snuck this in.

> The movement against the war in Vietnam had long-lasting, I hope permanent, effects in raising the general level of insight and understanding among the general public. . . . Despite the intense efforts undertaken in the 1970s to reverse this general cultural progress and enlightenment, much of it remains. . . . The accomplishments, which were very real, can be credited largely to young people, most of them nameless and forgotten, who devoted themselves to organizing, education, civil disobedience, and resistance.

I felt it so intensely, driving east after I heard on NPR what was happening to Jason. I felt so intensely the gloating of a certain portion of my generation, the whole country over.

And I felt something else, even more intensely. I felt the endless strangeness of the fact that in the whole of the United States of America, there were only two people who understood how fantastically, enormously, not crazy Jason Sinai was.

So I thought, in any case. In fact, besides me and Jason, there turned out to be two others: your aunt Maggie and your uncle Daniel.

Like them, I understood that everything he was doing, your father, he was doing to find me.

Was he going to succeed? I didn't know.

Know something, Isabel? That was a kind of peaceful feeling, not knowing.

Because if he did find me, then I was going to have to decide what to do.

Did I want him to find me?

How can I answer that? No, it was the last thing in the world I wanted.

And yet with everything I had ever believed in my life, I knew that he must.

There was only one way I could help your father find me, Isabel. I like to think that had I been able to do more, I would have tried. I like to think that I went to Ann Arbor, which was the worst place in the world for me to go, in order to make it just that little bit easier for him to find me.

I like to think that there was nothing I could do but wait, and wonder whether Jason was inventive enough, and persistent enough, to put the trail to McLeod together, the single trail that could connect Mimi Lurie with me.

Meanwhile, fittingly enough, I would go back to where it all started and wait.

Don't say that was nothing different, Isabel. Do not tell me I had been waiting for Little J since 1974.

It is not true. I had been waiting for him much, much longer than that. All the way back to the time I first saw him, in a dormitory dining hall at the University of Michigan, in 1968.

And I was still waiting for him on June 21, 1996, as what was to be a historic summer heat wave swept in over the Huron River Valley; I drove into Ann Arbor on the 94, crossed town and campus, my head literally swimming with the uncanniness of the experience, as if I had never left but been there my whole miserable life.

Which, in a way, I had.

In a way, after all, nothing had changed. In my head, I was still a young woman bringing dope to the people. In my head I was just the same person as a quarter century ago when I first came into the Del Rio. The only thing that had aged at all was my body.

Which, Isabel, is both a depressing and a heartening thing to say, at forty-five years old, depending on what it is you want from your life.

Date: June 13, 2006
From: "Daddy" <littlej@cusimanorganics.com>
To: "Isabel Montgomery" <isabel@exminster.uk>
CC: maillist: The_Committee
Subject: letter 21

Run, hide, and think. The rules were simple enough. I had had identities blow up on me again and again. Everyone had. And when they did, the rules of what to do, like most of the things in criminal life, were so simple as to be obvious.

Run: intelligently, instinctively, or from panic, but always somewhere you had never been before and always alone. Don't go home again. Don't go anywhere you have ever been again. Run, and in one direction only: away.

Hide. As soon as you can, hide to rest, to change, to recover, but mostly, hide to think. And when you think, try to clear your mind of everything except what was ahead of you. No regret, no remorse, no confusion, and no fear.

There would be time for all that later. Time to experience each and every one of the distinct kinds of pain that were available to you: mourning for lives and neighbors lost, fear of an utterly unknown future, shame of failure; time to think of all that and leisure to wallow in its multifaceted pain. But now, think only of what you had to do to stay alive, and free, so that when the time came, you could regret all that had happened, all the mistakes, all the stupidity, all the bad luck that put you in the position where your life was whittled down to three lousy actions to preserve your freedom a few moments, hours, days longer: running, hiding, and thinking.

Simple, and so hard to follow; it makes you wonder how any criminals ever get away with anything at all.

• • •

The highway to Chicago. The French kid, his wide face appearing briefly in oncoming headlights, skin oily and eyes long, then disappearing again as for long stretches of black road, no one passed.

We stopped once at a truck stop, where the kid ate enormously and I paid. I also bought a carton of Marlboros while the kid got gas. Then the night again, where he disappeared behind the wheel again, the lights of the occasional passing car the only proof that I was still even there, and I, in darkness, sat open-eyed, although there was nothing to see. Just the few yards ahead of headlighted air, bug-infested and hot, and the flashing white line of the road west.

The kid let me out near Grant Park at four, the heat of the night only slightly more bearable than the day. Through the doorway I offered him the carton of cigarettes and the money I had promised. In exchange, however, I took the half-full pack of Export A's from the dashboard. I slammed the door and walked north, waving at the car as it passed and watching it go all the way to the curve to Navy Pier. In the ambient noise of the city at night, the lake could not be heard, but the lights of Lake Shore Drive, lying flat on slowly shifting water, allowed me to imagine the little lap and hiss of the tiny shore waves landing on rock beach. When the kid and his car were out of sight, I crossed Michigan Avenue, suddenly and at a slight run, then slowed back to a walk and, holding my bag close to the side of the buildings, walked south. As soon as I could—which was very soon—I then turned right into the alleyway behind the Congress Plaza Hotel, and then right again.

Now, in the loading dock of the hotel, or more precisely, a little bricked courtyard in front of the loading dock's office door, I dropped my bag. Then I sat on it. And then I lowered myself flat onto the ground, head on the bag, and stared up the thin canyon of brick—the brick backside of these marbled buildings—up to the sky.

Now I had already run and hidden, and it was time to think.

My biggest concern was video surveillance—that scared me much more than a manhunt. They'd be watching the many video cameras in many transportation hubs all over the country. In some places face recognition software could already be in place, comparing thousands of faces to a computer-aged image of myself, and I wasn't sure what protection a disguise afforded. I thought about that, then decided to stop thinking about it: it was out of my control.

As for the manhunt, besides an FBI task force that could involve hundreds of agents, besides U.S. marshals, and besides bounty hunters, local police all over the country would have received photos of me. Never mind the newspaper, which made virtually every person I passed a potential captor. The best possible thing to do was to avoid public places.

And that was the problem: I needed to be at the train station, which was precisely the kind of place that would be under the highest surveillance.

The only answer was to be there during the rush hour. I needed to be disguised, be smart, and be lucky.

So now I had thought. I knew what I would do when the sun rose. And beyond that, it was impossible to figure out in its details. Beyond details, in fact, I knew virtually everything. I knew, in fact, what I was going to do for the days or weeks ahead until this was over. Where I was going, and how: this was unknown, but an unknown considerably softened by my brother's having saved me the arduous tasks of finding ID and money—it reduced the tasks ahead from weeks to days. Why my brother had done this, and on whose advice—as well as how he had done it, and what it meant to me that he had done it—were unclear. But as for what I was doing, this was crystal clear to me. I had thought about it for years.

There were perhaps two hours till sunrise. Lying, now, staring at the sky I could not see, I searched for details that required planning, and found none.

And that was why, for the first time since I had left you, thirty-six hours before, I could no longer keep myself from thinking about you.

• • •

It was as if an unknown clock had been counting the hours since I left you, the longest time in your life I had spent away from you. Where were you? I knew precisely: Maggie Calaway would have taken you promptly up to Martha's Vineyard. Bob Montgomery was already on a plane to New York, surely, but you were in the commonwealth of Massachusetts, asleep in a bed above Menemsha Bay.

Which room? I found my mind's eye wandering, now, through my father's Vineyard house, built in the fifties when he represented the New Bedford Carpenter's Union in their strike against Mallory Shipyards. Perhaps you were in my own childhood bed, the little iron bed that looked out over the horse pasture, mowed trim and clearly lit by the same big moon that now drifted above me in Chicago. You'd met your uncle by now, and your cousins. And then, with a shot of adrenaline that ran from my kidneys to my scalp, I realized that by now you had probably met your grandmother.

I didn't want to, but I couldn't help myself. I saw you, in the living room with its low Eames couch and its Wakefield furnishing, with your grandmother, now a woman in her eighties, my mother whom I had not seen in twenty-six years. What would you make of her? What would you make of these people who claimed to be your family? Would they be able to communicate anything to you that would make it make sense? Was it possible for you to come to trust them? In the best of circumstances, I knew, no matter how kind these people were, it was nonetheless terrifying to you. In the best of circumstances, I knew, no matter how good a job they did, they were nonetheless forging a scar in your consciousness that would never go away.

There in that alleyway, the worry gnawed me, gored me, till I had to stand and pace, small groans coming out of my throat. How would I possibly make that scar heal? How could I possibly turn the battering I had given you into muscle? How would I possibly teach you to turn that experience of abandon into strength? I would need to be with you, every day, for years and years; through tantrum and rebellion, through drugs and boyfriends, I would need to show you, daily, hourly, the extent of my love. Without that, that scar would close over a part of your heart; would filter reality for you for the rest of your life, would infect love, work, joy, and would make of your adulthood the great, central challenge to heal it, taking the great energy that you should have given instead to love, to work.

I sat, and even through the wall of nicotine in me, for I was smoking cigarette after cigarette now, regret seared; remorse for all the scars I had dealt you, for all the places I had let fear and horror into your heart; for all the ways I had wounded you, and I ached.

It was a long time coming, the time when I at last found the will to swear, to swear that I would find a way to cure you. It was a long time coming, and I swore it not on my death but on my life: I swore that I would ache my whole life long unless I found a way to cure you of what I had done to you.

By then the sun was rising, and I rose on stiff legs and walked back into the street.

2.

At a phone booth, using the 800 operator, I found the schedule for trains to Milwaukee. During rush hour, the busiest train would be the nine o'clock. By seven, the streets filling with downtown workers, I felt safe enough to walk across town until I hit the river, then head up toward the station. I had two hours to kill.

Now, walking next to the river, the temperature rising toward the triple figures, where it would rest all day, it all seemed preordained. Jim Grant's identity had been a very solid set of papers, one I had been preparing for years, preparing with the greatest possible care, as the identity that I would, if I had to, spend the rest of my life in. At the base of the identity was a dead baby, killed in a car crash in Bakersfield, California, in 1959. Two things made the identity extraordinary. First was the deaths of both of that baby's parents in a second car crash in 1967. Now Jim Grant was an orphan, with no family to explain away. Second was a complete set of school transcripts through high school graduation in 1976. For this forgery, I owed a resourceful secretary at the Bakersfield Community Board, a woman who had not only typed up the transcripts but made sure they were added to each year of stored files all the way back to first grade. She had known she was helping a fugitive and trusting her had been a real risk. When, a few years later, I heard about her death by drowning—surfing off the coast of Big Sur—I felt real loss. Then I felt something else.

Now there was no witness at all to Jim Grant's falsity.

After Bank of Michigan, as if it had all been preordained, I went out to Bakersfield under a transitional identity. From a motel room, I got copies of Jim Grant's high school transcripts and applied to five colleges. While I waited for answers, I got a job at a local print shop and began to familiarize myself with the place of Jim's birth. And, even more importantly, I began the process of becoming seven years younger.

Most of it was easy. I cut my hair shorter, I learned the music that eighteen-year-olds listened to, I stayed in shape. When a collision with a wall during a pickup basketball game broke my nose, I took advantage of the situation to have it fixed, an operation that considerably changed my appearance, much more than I would have thought. Suddenly, if it weren't for the brown eyes, I could be Irish.

April 1975 was the first time I was required to file taxes under my new name. It was also the month that college acceptances came out.

The IRS refunded me $3,500 in overpaid federal taxes.

The University of Chicago offered Jim Grant, an orphan from Bakersfield, California, with a nearly perfect GPA and glowing references, a work-study scholarship.

I had been in Chicago twice: once in 1968 for the Democratic National Convention, once in 1969 for the Days of Rage. Both times I had been arrested. Apart from those arrests, I knew no one in the city, not a soul.

And so, in the summer of 1975, with the dreamlike feeling of revisiting the past, I became a nineteen-year-old college freshman named James Marshal Grant from Bakersfield, California.

I started classes at the university, taking step after step into the insane imposture that was to become my life, and step after step, I found I had not been caught.

• • •

You will ask me where Mimi Lurie was during all this. The answer is, I don't know. The cutoff between us was absolute, never to be negotiated. I had no idea of her plans, her name, her intentions, her whereabouts. Nor did I ever intend to find out, ever.

You will ask me how I forgot her so quickly.

Isabel, I swear to you, it was as if she were dead. There was grieving, and it was intense. But so absolute was the fact before me—the fact that I would never see Mimi Lurie again—that after its course was run, the mourning ended, exactly as if she were dead. We both knew it. It was not negotiable: we no longer counted. All that mattered was that we never meet again.

And then, there was another fact.

There was the fact that after my first year in Chicago, in the Indian summer of 1976—the purest, most poignant autumn of my life—under the crystalline sun over the University of Chicago campus, I met your mother.

Julia Frances Montgomery, at nineteen. Watching out a restaurant window as the square in front of Union Station filled, smoking from the pack of Export A's, I could see her, moving through the campus of the U of C in an oversize plaid shirt and jeans.

How do I describe your mother to you? She was like a perfectly ripe piece of fruit, warmed by the sun, glowing with vitality, nearly exquisite.

It has been, for years, very hard for me to think about those days. It's hard for me to remember the girl, then, who was going to become the woman who would be your mother. Everything that was going to happen later was in her then, but none of it was bad. We drank, but drinking was a celebration, a thing that enhanced everything we did rather than, as it came to for her, ruining everything she touched. We smoked dope, but it took us deeper into the now, the complex, exciting, hilarious now, that wonderland we were exploring, day after day, together. We shared a taste for the gutter, but the gutter was such a different place, so much less dangerous, so much more fun.

It was 1976. I had always looked younger than my years, and by virtue of dressing carefully down passed easily for a hard-lived nineteen. Your mother at nineteen, on the other hand, passed easily for twenty-six, how old I in fact was. She had grown up in her father's town house on Washington Square, a full turn-of-the-century town house looking directly at the park. She had been through two Senate campaigns with her father, a charismatic, beautiful daughter who knew how to play to cameras and interviewers, as if by instinct. She had tremendous native talent, and combined high ambition with the energy to work. She'd studied—after school, weekends, and summers—voice, tap, figure skating, and acting. By the time she graduated Dalton, she'd sung twice on Broadway and appeared in a half-dozen films, some in acting roles, some in dancing.

Do you know all this? Has your mother told you? I cannot tell you, Isabel, how talented she was. She did not dance; rather, she let choreography be personified by her body, and as for dramatic roles, she inhabited her characters so completely, so thoroughly, that the lines of her own identity seemed simply to disappear. She had known all her life she would be an actor. College had been her father's one demand, and the University of Chicago had the merit of being near the Steppenwolf Theater, where she was determined to work and where in fact she did, appearing in ensemble with Gary Sinise, Joan Allen, John Malkovich. It was watching her in a Steppenwolf *Cherry Orchard* that I fell in love. Blond, with nearly translucent skin; brown-eyed with depthless irony behind her pupils. Slim, with a grace that takes generations of ease to produce; angular of feature and sharp of wit in a way that, by contrast, comes from nowhere.

I admit that later it did occur to me, it was made clear to me, that there were other advantages to marrying Julia Montgomery than the fact that I was in love with her. I admit that, Isabel. Later, it became clear that a marriage to Julia Montgomery was a very practical thing for me to do. It allowed me to become a lawyer, to establish a life, to work, for many years to come. But I absolutely deny that there was any calculation to it. That was all luck, that being married to your mother was so good for me. At the time, there was no thought of anything but love. She erased, for me, the years between 1970 and 1976. She allowed me, very literally, to do it all over again. This time there was no fumbling through first sex, no reexamination of monogamy, no politics, and no sharing. This time, there was just intense, focused love, and the chance to make up for all the things I had, for all those years, missed.

And on this point, I would like you to be very clear. In my life as Jim Grant I had two lovers, and I told both of them who I was before I got into their beds. The second was Molly, and I hadn't the slightest doubt that she would keep my secret. The first, however, was the single greatest risk of my life, and when I told your mother that I was Jason Sinai, I was ready to go back on the run.

Do you see? I was in love.

It was 1976. That summer, for the first time since 1970, I came east, staying in Bob Montgomery's huge Oneonta Park house in the Catskills. It was easy to like my future father-in-law, a Bobby Kennedy protégé, and, the war over, even my contempt for his liberalism seemed possible to overlook. And of course, because Bob was, that summer, nearly constantly campaigning, we had the run of the summer house. Which is how your grandfather met me, coming home one night from upstate unexpectedly and finding me asleep in his daughter's childhood bed.

You have to remember, Isabel, that once your grandfather and I loved each other. True, in 1996 Bob Montgomery was hiring the highest-powered, most right-wing lawyers in the state to take you away from me. But in the summer of 1976, when he found me asleep in his daughter's bed, a different set of responses prevailed. Call it a sign of the times. He knew, anyway, that his control over us was practically nonexistent, and his best way of reeling us in was to give us our heads. So to speak. Perhaps he thought I wouldn't outlast the summer. What he found was that Julia and I stayed together right through college, and that four years later we were back in the Catskills, this time for our wedding.

My wedding present from my father-in-law was a new social security number.

• • •

It was the night before the wedding when your grandfather asked me to walk out on the lawn with him, in the middle of what passed, in those days, for a bachelor party. On the edge of his property in Oneonta Park, looking out at the Blackheads he stood silently, while I tried to guess what kind of speech was coming. What he said, however, was something very different from what I ever could have guessed.

It may seem obvious to you. When you marry a senator's daughter, an FBI background check is run on you. In fact, when you date a senator's daughter, it's FBI business. For four full years, your grandfather had known who I was.

The other thing he knew, however, the FBI hadn't told him.

He knew that I could cost him everything. Not just his career, but his daughter, too.

Because neither your grandfather nor your mother had the slightest doubt that if I went on the run again, Julia was going to run with me.

Can you understand? Now, since 9-11 and the War on Terrorism, we aren't part of the "counterculture" anymore, we're "internal terrorists." But that wasn't the case in 1976. With the war just a year over, then; with the insults against the Constitution from the Nixon years still so fresh; with COINTELPRO still being revealed, it was a very different thing, then. Everyone who was still underground had the same experience of being recognized, again and again, by strangers who never thought to call the police; of meeting old friends who kept our secrets; even of taking new friends into our secret. All of our families and known friends were constantly subject to interrogation, surveillance, and never did a single soul turn a single one of us in. In context, what Bobby Montgomery did was not only understandable, it was sensible. When the first FBI check produced grounds for reinvestigation, Bobby Montgomery thought for a great long time about what to do.

Then he called in a favor.

The same kind of favor he would later call in for your mother, to ensure that her arrests and rehabilitations were never recorded.

Jim Grant's identity was expunged in every federal and state record, his social security was redone, and he passed his FBI background check.

What had I thought was going to happen? Uptown, in Jersey, in the Rondout Valley of the Catskills, across the Midwest, in California; all the Weather members who had been underground were surfacing, whether they had, while underground, been part of the Revolutionary Committee or, like me, been expelled from the organization. I had no contact with any of them: the B.O.M. robbery had alienated me from every contact, every old ally. I, Sharon Solarz, and Mimi Lurie, none of us knew where each other was, except that we all three lived in a different legal dimension from our old Weather comrades. For us, there was no possibility of surfacing; for us there was no possible legal way out. One by one the others came aboveground, protected by the gross illegality of the government's evidence gathering, unprosecutable. One by one they settled their problems and launched aboveground lives as parents, educators, lawyers, activists. Others—Judy Clark, Kathy Boudin, David Gilbert—stayed under, graduating into the May 19th Movement, the Black Liberation Army, ending up finally jailed in a robbery gone wrong. And still others were then in jail. But of us all, only three were still fugitives, actively wanted as accessories to murder for the Bank of Michigan robbery, and I was one.

So what had I expected? Not much, is my impression. I expected to have a run for my money as Jim Grant, and I expected, eventually, to get caught. Until then I planned to do the thing that the war had stolen from me. I worked at college with a vengeance, an energy channeled from all the frustration of my career in Weather, an abandon fueled by my awareness that each day of liberty, of productivity, could be my last. Do you know, Isabel, how well you can do at college if you go as an adult? To say that youth is wasted on the young is, I assure you, an incredible understatement. With the focus of an adult I did brilliantly.

And instead of getting caught, in the spring of 1980, Julia and I were married under cherry blossoms in Oneonta Park. That fall I started law school at Yale, where your mother was to do an MFA in theater, and for the first time since 1970 I was at last safe.

In 1982 Julia Montgomery, having already earned a great deal of money on the stage and before the camera, inherited from her paternal grandfather and set up the Montgomery Foundation.

And in 1984, when Jim Grant passed the New York State Bar, and he and his glamorous wife moved to Woodstock, I became the Montgomery Foundation's only full-time employee, practicing public interest law out of Saugerties and lending my glamorous wife's splendid home the added celebrity of my radical chic.

The only difficulties were physical: my ever-hastening baldness, normal for a man of Jason Sinai's age, premature for Jim Grant. And attending properly to Jim Grant's prostate was a calculated risk, a necessary one after I read in an *In These Times* interview that my father was under treatment for prostate cancer: Jason Sinai's prostate was seven years older than Jim Grant's, and a history of prostate cancer was a positive indication for a PSA test.

But it was as if from the moment I came to Chicago, an angel had put his finger on me and guided me through everything, all the danger, all the hardship, all the lost opportunities and limitations of the life I had decided to lead, and kept guiding me, year after year.

The only thing was, that angel, he forgot to bring Julia along.

And now the whole trip was ending. Right here in Chicago. For a moment I looked out the window of the restaurant as if expecting to see that whole diorama of the seventies still out on the streets: Puerto Ricans in wide-brimmed hats, blacks in Afros, white kids with stringy long hair and oversize plaid shirts and denim, smooth dealers gliding in with loose joints, bare-stomached women in halter tops and hip-huggers, someone playing the Jackson Five on a transistor. . . . Instead, walking in and out of Union Station, I saw young women looking like movie stars sipping cappuccinos, young men in Donna Karan with shaved heads and Armani sunglasses, each one of them so smooth that if Brad Pitt and Gwyneth Paltrow walked by, no one would have batted an eye because you couldn't tell anymore who was the movie star and who was the high school senior from

Winnetka. Sitting there, that morning, the hot summer sun coming up, waiting, I felt incredulity that it had come to this, and not for the first, but for the thousandth time, I asked myself if there was no other way out.

But what way was there? I didn't know what made Julia an addict—I had my theories, naturally—but I did know that addicts aren't good mothers. They tend to leave their kids in front of the TV while they get high. They tend to take their kids to all manner of sleazeballs' houses instead of the library or a playground. They tend, instead of teaching their kids to read, to pass out on the couch with their mouths open and their chests moving shallowly, as if content with only the minimal amount of air. I moved out, with you, after the police found you in Julia's convertible Saab, alone, on Route 212, with Julia scoring an eightball from a high school kid in his parents' house, and you with what later would turn into a black eye, for it came out that she had hit you when you objected to being left alone in the car. And she divorced me a year later, from London, where her father had taken her to clean up as soon as I left. At first Bob was my ally against her, or rather against her addiction. Then that changed.

For a time we had a truce: Bob could destroy me, but I could destroy Bob—a man who had concealed the identity of a known political fugitive throughout two terms in the U.S. Senate was not, repeat, not, going to become ambassador to England.

When Sharon was arrested, everything changed.

Now, it did not need to be Bob Montgomery who was going to expose me. Ben Schulberg would. As soon as Ben Schulberg realized how strange it was that I refused to defend Sharon, I knew it was all over.

Within two days the tender care of twenty years had fallen apart, and I knew it was time to do the thing I had most feared over the last twenty-five years.

Isabel. Had I not had you, I would simply have disappeared. You changed everything, for everyone. Your right to be Isabel, to be protected from your mother, and still not to become a fugitive: it was absolute.

That day in Chicago, steeling myself to leave my seat in a restaurant and walk out into Union Station, I wished that I had never done anything in the world, that I had never had any kind of a past, except as your father, and that there was nothing I ever had to do again but take care of you.

But I had, and now I had no choice.

3.

By 8:45 the entrance to Union Station was thick with people, a line of taxis perhaps fifteen long dropping off and picking up in front, buses arriving down the street on both sides, sidewalks full of commuters from the suburban trains both coming out and going in. There was of course no way to be sure what surveillance there was, but there was no obvious sign. I left the restaurant now and bought an "I Love Chicago" sweatshirt and a White Sox baseball cap at a little tourist storefront, then wandered into the crowd in front of the station and into the entrance.

The seconds of my transaction to buy the ticket, crossing the interior of the station, boarding the train, were as if in time lapse. As if I were watching each event pass seconds after it had in fact happened, and that from a slight distance. Whereas everything I'd done since leaving New York had been with a nearly suicidal abandon, unable to care if I were caught or not, now I found myself caring nearly too much. With the caring, with the fear, came its inverse, tiny bursts of excitement in my stomach. I recognized the feeling as that which came in the center of an action; stealing guns, planting a bomb: each second free opened a vista of another second, and another, and another, until you found yourself, despite all, believing in the possibility of success, and that that belief feels so good it hurts.

There were police in two sets of three toward the center of the hall; I kept to the side by crossing first to a newsagent for a paper, then to a Starbucks. When I started a trajectory toward my gate, I tried to visualize their focus, predicting what in the crowd might attract it—two businessmen laughing, a beautiful woman—and keeping away. An impossible task, I knew, though I also knew that there was the movement of a policeman's optic muscle between freedom and failure for me, and that every tiny advantage I could give myself could make all the difference. And in fact my luck held, because I was sunk in my seat behind the paper before I noticed that my picture—bearded and surprisingly bald—was again on the front page under the headline: "Sixties Radical Fugitive Thought to Be in the U.S.," and the subhead, "FBI Thinks Flight to Canada Was a Ruse."

Date: June 14, 2006

From: "Benjamin Schulberg"
<Benny@cusimanorganics.com>

To: "Isabel Montgomery" <isabel@exmnster.uk>

CC: maillist: The_Committee

Subject: letter 22

As for me, the drive to Ann Arbor took somewhat longer than I had anticipated. In retrospect, this probably had something to do with the speeding ticket I was given somewhere just south of Niagara Falls. That is, the ticket itself didn't take that long, but the fact that the police records turned up my car as unregistered, as well as the couple dozen unpaid tickets stemming from that registration . . . that took quite a while to straighten out, and in fact required following the police into a town called North Tanawanda—Mohican, I believe, for "speed trap"—and calling my editor, and then going to the local MVB, paying all the unpaid tickets—over a thousand dollars, with penalties—and getting my new registration. The entire process was rendered all the more humiliating by the fact that I had to be grateful for not having the car confiscated outright, and furthermore I now owed not only my career and livelihood but my very freedom to my effete, officious, and phony editor.

The upshot was that I spent a night in a motel in Canada, a room with cinder-block walls that resembled nothing so much as the hole in a maximum-security prison, an impression much strengthened by what sounded like a gang bang in the next room. In the morning, up bright and early by ten o'clock, easy, I had all the time in the world to get to Michigan—or would have, had I not found that every item of clothing in my always-ready suitcase had been worn on my last business trip, a month before, and I had apparently neglected to wash them. The smell struck me, interestingly, as very familiar, and after reflection I was able to place it as not unlike that of a bagel and lox left in a refrigerator for an indeterminate time during which the electric supply to the refrigerator may or may not have been cut off due to nonpayment of bills. The next few hours were spent in a charming Laundromat, then I had to rent another hotel room for a shower—a hundred and twenty bucks for a shower, North Tanawanda's meaning turning out to include, in some linguistic innovation peculiar to Mohican, "hapless tourist ripoff"—and in the end I arrived in Ann Arbor with minutes to spare. Minutes that I spent finding State Street by a process of pure chance—necessarily, since I could not bring myself to ask directions—and, at last, the café where John Osborne was waiting.

Immediately on entering the café, I saw a large man of about fifty with thick brown hair and a long face sitting over a table by the window. The little café table seemed dwarfed under his arms. He wore khakis and a blue denim shirt showing sweat under the arms. I'm not sure how I knew it was Osborne, a guess really, but a good one because as I approached, he rose, courteous and curious, and shook my hand; then we sat and regarded one another in silence while I decided on a soft start to the conversation. He seemed, despite his size, gentle.

"So, you have a daughter at the U of M, Mr. Osborne?"

Pause. He did not ask me to use first names—not very midwestern of you, Osborne, I thought to myself. "Yes, sir. A senior. Going on to Quantico next."

"Quantico?" I was surprised. "To work?"

"For a few years. Until she begins her training."

"Wow. You must be proud."

Pause. "Yes, sir."

There was something strangely distant in the response. I tried again. "Do you come down to visit a lot?"

Pause, and I sensed a struggle in which a surprisingly moving pride suddenly won: this large man, I saw, loved to talk about his daughter. "We do. It's hard for her to get upstate with her work. She's always insisted on having a job, even though we tell her she doesn't need to. She's our one and only, so there's enough to go around. But she says we can save our money for someone who needs it. Has a three-point-nine;

Dean's List every semester here, and three evenings a week and Sunday afternoons, she waits tables at a diner downtown. My wife's picking her up now—they'll be here in a half hour or so. That enough human interest for you?"

The last sentence was unexpected. Now, in this man's kind face, I also saw wryness. But I didn't feel that confrontation was what I needed, so I carried on as if I hadn't noticed.

"I was just thinking, coming to town here must be a blast from the past for you. I mean, you were here in the days, no?"

"Well, yes." Pause. "I was on campus from '65 to '68 as a student. Then again from '70 to '71, but that was undercover. Yes, you could say I have a lot of nostalgia for Ann Arbor. But you know, a lot of people in Michigan feel the same way."

"So you must have known the folk in Weather, then?"

"Well . . . not the ones who went underground. I only started on FBI work in the end of '70, after they were gone."

I experienced a moment of dissociation, hearing Weather referred to so factually, and nonjudgmentally, a historical event rather than a question of culture.

"Never encountered Sinai or Lurie?"

"Not to speak of, no. I mean, I might have seen Sinai talking somewhere. But nothing past that."

Osborne shifted, and I caught the edge of a light leather holster inside his open collar.

"Then you were in Vietnam from—"

"Sixty-three to '65."

"Two tours of duty?"

Pause. "One and a half. I came back on a medical evacuation."

I pushed one more time. "Injured?"

Pause. Then, in a tone that showed this was his last answer, he said simply: "I took a bullet at Songbe. Phuoc Long Province. I got a medical discharge in December 1965, and came back to go to college."

I answered quickly, changing the terrain. "That would have been quite an adjustment, coming back."

Pause. "You could say. Convinced me to go into FBI work."

"And undercover."

"And undercover."

"What convinced you?" I couldn't resist asking. There were no more than three answers to this question, all of them bullshit, and which one this man subscribed to would be telling.

More telling than I expected, because it was a new answer altogether. "Where you fell on the question of Vietnam, Mr. Schulberg, didn't depend on what you believed."

"No?" I watched him now with new attention.

"No. People tell you that, I advise you to ignore them. Where you fell on the question of Vietnam depended on the company you kept, nothing more, nothing less. Your friends went, your neighbors went, your family went—then you went too."

"That's it? No politics, ethics, beliefs?"

"No, sir. Good people fell on both sides of the question of Vietnam. That's the side I was on, and I'm not about to apologize for it now."

I absorbed that. "And today?"

Osborne answered evenly, saying, I realized, something that sounded very simple, but which required a very complicated process to get to.

"Today, the question's over, so it doesn't matter anymore. Time only goes one way, Mr. Schulberg, and it happens to be in the direction away from the war in Vietnam, thank God."

Pause, and I, sensing that time was going only one way, shifted the conversation slightly.

"I would have imagined that Jason Sinai was big business for you all just now."

"Well, of course the Traverse City station's following what's going on. The manhunt is national, though—we don't see any particular reason Sinai should return here."

"Do you know what he's doing?"

"Sure. That's no mystery."

I said nothing, and after a moment the man went on. "He's saving his freedom, Mr. Schulberg. That's what he's been doing for the past twenty-five years; it's what he's doing now."

"Saving his freedom by abandoning his daughter?"

"Yes, sir."

"You don't find that hard to believe?"

Pause. "No, sir. Lots of revolutionaries have children. You're talking about people who've abandoned their families, their professions, their lives, for what they believe. Jason Sinai, his father died while he was underground, and Sinai never even contacted his family. His father *died* while he was underground. That didn't make him surface. Now he has to lose his daughter. That won't make him surface either."

Osborne shrugged, as if he wished he could change the fact of life he'd just told me. The shrug, I felt, which was the only occurrence of this gesture in the whole conversation, was curious. Then I tried again.

"I see a difference between an eighteen-year-old who's prepared to leave his parents and a thirty-nine-year-old abandoning his only daughter."

"Forty-six, Mr. Schulberg. Jim Grant was thirty-nine. Jason Sinai's forty-six. But I take your point." Osborne thought for a time. Then he went on, in what seemed to me a very considered tone. "I myself can't understand how someone could abandon their child for what they believe. I'd certainly sell out everything I believe for my daughter. Someone who could do that—that seems to me a very dangerous thing."

Osborne paused for thought now, a long pause that I didn't interrupt.

"However, these are dangerous kinds of people. I'll tell you, Mr. Schulberg, if there's one thing I've learned from the work I've done, it's that there's nothing more dangerous than someone who believes in what they're doing. Most of us who went to Vietnam—no way we were cold warriors. No way we were going out of some kind of patriotic fervor. We were going to share the danger that our friends and neighbors couldn't escape, and I doubt you'll find one in ten who thought beyond their duty. But folk like Sinai—it's real different, Mr. Schulberg. They were true believers, and that's why I was prepared to take an undercover assignment against them. You know that when twenty FBI agents came to Jeff Jones's door to arrest him after fifteen years underground, fifteen years of terrorist activity, they found him inside with a four-year-old child? What's the difference between that and the Branch Davidians going to war with children inside their compound? To my way of thinking, I've been fighting the same kind of threat all my life."

I couldn't let this pass. "You don't see a difference between the radical left during a brutal, undeclared war and the radical right during the most democratic period in American history?"

"No, sir. I see true believers who don't think that American democracy is good enough for them. Don't forget, Mr. Schulberg, it was Democrats who got us into Vietnam, and Republicans who got us out. So where's the failure of democracy there?"

"Well, the war *was* unconstitutional, Mr. Osborne."

"And millions of people told the government that without becoming federal fugitives. Jason Sinai, David Koresh, what's the difference? Let me tell you, Mr. Schulberg: one thinks he's saving the Constitution from the government, the other that he's saving the government from the Constitution."

"One holes up, armed, in a compound, and starts shooting at the FBI, that's one difference. When the FBI came after Jeff Jones, he surrendered."

"Question of circumstances. Who was it that said, 'If it takes fascism to stop the war, then let's have fascism?' And don't forget that Sinai, Lurie, and Solarz—like Boudin, Gilbert, and Clark—are accessories to murder of policemen."

Quickly, I answered. "Let's not confuse Weather and what happened after Weather."

And now Osborne nodded. "I knew you were going to say that. But all these people were in Weather. You know, and I know, that if they hadn't killed themselves, the town house bombers were going to take action against human targets. Excuse me."

To my disappointment, now Osborne rose to greet two women as they approached the table, one a trim middle-aged woman with salt-and-pepper hair, the other a tall young woman in shorts and a tank top. The younger one gave me the sudden impression of a swan, but aware of her father's gaze on me, I was careful not to stare. John Osborne greeted both with a kiss, then turned to me, who had by now risen too.

"My wife, Marianne. And my daughter Rebeccah. I'm afraid I'm going to have to excuse myself now, Mr. Schulberg."

The introductions gave me the chance to reach my hand out to the daughter.

"Oh, hi. I enjoyed your piece on Jason Sinai." I could see the line of her ribs just above the low neckline of her T-shirt. Her hand, when she shook mine, thanking me, clearly without the faintest idea who I was, was slim and dry.

"Well, I hate to ask too much, but I'd sure like to continue this conversation, Mr. Osborne." I reached over to shake his hand. "Can I stay in touch?"

"Well . . ." Osborne, clearly, had the disinclination of country folk to say no. "I'll be back to Traverse City tomorrow afternoon."

"Maybe I could come by on Monday?"

He answered hesitantly. "If you like. I don't have much more to say."

I told him I'd come by in any case, then watched curiously as the family walked out.

It wasn't the first time that I had been shocked by how reasonable, educated, and thoughtful people on the right could be. I'd noticed the fact before: conservatives of a certain kind could, if not agree, at least understand people on the left, whereas leftists generally feel they have a monopoly on the truth. But it was an unusually strong experience of that shock. Then I brought my mind back to my real work.

Was this, then, trail's end? Was there nothing to learn in Michigan?

I would, I decided, stay around till Monday—take a look around Ann Arbor, where Sinai had, after all, started his radical career. On Monday I'd go up to Traverse City and try one more time to get something out of Osborne. If that failed, well then, I'd go home.

Though somehow I didn't see myself going back to Albany, all of a sudden.

2.

Ann Arbor itself, I'm sorry to say, was a big disappointment. I'm not sure quite what I was expecting. Hippies, maybe, or an antiwar demonstration. What I did find failed to live up to its onetime status as epicenter of the youth movement. An orderly, pretty town, filled with restaurants and friendly midwesterners. Those who looked something other than out of

Leave It to Beaver did so by virtue of being pierced in more places than I would have thought possible—and these were only the places I could see—while on campus, either summer school was in session or there was a casting call for a new installment of *Girls Gone Wild*, for the concentration of tall blond women with perfect legs showing out of short shorts defied belief.

Sitting on the steps of a vast library, I half closed my eyes and tried to imagine what this had looked like when John Osborne, Jason Sinai, and Mimi Lurie had all been on campus. What would there have been? Most kids would have been dressed in, say, jeans and T-shirts; the girls in tank tops or Indian cotton prints, the boys often shirtless. There'd also have been well-dressed, clean-cut young men going in and out of the ROTC building, although by Jason's time even these would have been growing out their hair and sideburns. With them might have been women in not-too-short minidresses and bouffant hairstyles—the silent majority, Agnew had called these ones. Then there'd have been freaks: white kids with Afros or long straight hair, purple people, hippies, yippies. There'd have been Black Panthers in leather and black berets. Girls in colored silk, hip-huggers, sandals. There'd have been booths set up: people selling *Rat* or *Liberation*, or *New Left Notes*. There'd have been dope: kids sitting cross-legged in small groups, passing a joint. There'd have been guitars. I opened my eyes again on the quiet, hot August day on campus and watched a Campus Ministry of Christ booth being set up.

Finally, terminally bored, I registered in a Days Inn, had dinner in an Italian restaurant, and that evening wandered downtown, looking for a jazz bar I'd seen advertised in a local paper. Even in the evening, the town seemed sunk in a heat-induced lassitude, air so hot that it rippled above the sidewalk. For a time I wandered, unable to find the bar. And as if finding the damn place was the whole reason I had come to this town, frustration began to mount in me.

I was aware that I was losing focus, but I just didn't know what else to do. There was no manhunt after Jason that I could follow. The battle for his daughter was being fought in New York City. There was just no *entrance* into the story, I thought with sudden clarity. For days, all I had been doing was looking for a way back in, like a crack addict trying to regain his original high. And yet I was morally certain a story was there.

Bitterly, I felt how close I'd been to it, sitting in Saugerties with Jim Grant. Walking aimlessly, smoking endlessly, a deep weight defined itself in my chest. I had been right there, right on top of this story, and I'd let it slip away. Now what? I was supposed to forget it and let my pompous, smug editor reassign me elsewhere?

For a long time I wandered through the hot night, lost in these thoughts. And as the sense of my rootlessness grew, so did a depression. At last, more by chance than design, I found myself in front of the Del Rio, the bar I'd seen advertised, and a small and not laudable decision to get drunk crystallized in me.

When I entered the bar, I found that most of the town had had, apparently, that same idea. Still, it seemed a pretty good crowd—no one seemed about to break out into the Michigan fight song, or tell me to have a good day, or call me by my first name, if for no other reason than because they were all paying serious attention to the band. I elbowed my way through the crowds to the corner of the bar, then waited a long time for the bartender, a middle-aged woman with black hair, to make her way over. When she did, I ordered a double scotch and soda. It was busy enough that I drank it quickly, hoping to catch the bartender again while she worked my end of the bar. Although the strategy seemed to annoy her—she seemed, in fact, easily annoyed, as if she rather resented that she had to serve drinks in the first place—it was successful enough to leave me drinking my second double when she moved off down the bar and I turned to the band.

A bald man, with a fringe of white hair, on an electric keyboard, a three-piece backup, all deeply into a long improvisation on a bluesy theme. And the crowd was not bad either: slowly, feeling the booze arriving in my brain in little increments of relaxation, I observed that it was an unusually pleasant-looking group of people, all clearly here for the music, for there was virtually no talking going on. To my great surprise I had even begun to enjoy myself—so much so that as the band wound down the song and announced a short break over the sudden surge of applause, I felt real disappointment.

The clapping died down and was replaced by a wave of conversation, which threw me again into loneliness. Time, I thought with disappointment, to leave: I didn't feel like being the only person drinking alone in a college-town bar. And perhaps I would have left had I not suddenly recognized a long-necked woman sitting at a table with a man I couldn't see. The man's arm was around her bare shoulders, and she was evidently listening, then laughing.

It was, of course, Osborne's daughter.

Now I had a chance to look at her at length, and what I had suspected at the café turned out to be truer than I cared to admit. Her head, a highly oval-shaped object, was facing down at an angle while she listened to the man with her, and sat at the end of a neck that, it seemed to me, was so long that it literally curved up to balance it. Her hair, back in a tight ponytail, was blond, and seemed to have a life of its own, so perfectly did it hang over her neck. The skin of her neck was of a paleness that was nearly translucent and blended into bare shoulders that sloped under her neck, showing one bra strap under her sleeveless silk shirt, which was white. Farther down the neckline, visible in contour under the shirt, her breasts sank heavily.

I felt my breath literally catch. Then I stood and stepped to the right to try to see her through the crowd. Now I could see the flat of her stomach and the slim jeaned legs, crossed, ending at leather sandals over bare feet.

I must have been staring, for she suddenly looked up, meeting my eyes directly, holding my gaze across the crowded room with a puzzled expression, as if trying to think if she knew me. And I, suddenly entirely at sea, found myself crossing the room.

3.

Now, as to my initial appraisal of Rebeccah's attractions, closer inspection showed that I had, if anything, underestimated them. They were, I felt strongly, unusual, as if the classic American handsomeness of her father had been mixed with some rogue gene that screwed with the symmetry, the regularity of her features just enough to change her from pretty to beautiful. The man she was with, on the other hand, was so handsome, so clean-cut, and—when he stood up—turned out to be so broad-shouldered that I did not think he could appreciate the beauty of this woman. In fact, I was morally certain he could not.

Whether I was right or wrong to approach the daughter of my interviewee, that's a more difficult question, and has to do with the dubious ethics of my chosen profession. But as to my method of starting a conversation with her, I don't think I was that off. When you are as beautiful as Rebeccah, you tend to see a lot of different kinds of introductions, and certainly mine stood out. Come to think of it, you probably are as beautiful as Rebeccah, and know exactly what I mean.

Approaching her, I reintroduced myself, reminding her that we had met with her father that afternoon. She in turn introduced me to the man she was with. I disliked him immediately and with intensity. He, after a look at my face—admittedly unshaven, and probably showing both fatigue and drunkenness—seemed barely able to conceal amusement, and decided to go to the bathroom. At which point I, uninvited, sat in his chair.

"I had a great talk with your dad this afternoon."

"Did you?" Rebeccah regarded me with curiosity. "What about?"

"Didn't he tell you?"

"No. Why should he?"

"I don't know. I thought it was interesting."

"I'm sure he did too. I'm sure he found it interesting all thirty-five times he's spoken to reporters about Jason Sinai this week." At this, she delivered me a wide-mouthed, white-toothed smile.

I watched her, rendered temporarily speechless by the smile. The waitress came, and I ordered another drink, wondering how drunk I was. And perhaps my next move was in fact an indicator of inebriation. I turned to her solemnly and let my voice drop nearly to a whisper, so she had to incline her ear toward me to hear. "I'm not a reporter, man. See, I was with him underground in the sixties. Jason, I mean. We blew up the Haymarket together. Brought the war home to the honky moneyfucking pig, man."

At that the wondering ovals of her eyes suddenly, in a flash, collapsed into dancing ellipses, and her mouth split into a smile.

"Bullshit. You're no older than me." Her voice had then, as it has now, the inflectionless clarity of a midwestern accent.

"Am so." I put it in a five-year-old's inflection. "What are you, a junior?"

"Senior."

"See? I'm a real working person."

"Oh, yeah? Working at what—besides being a pain in the ass."

"Right now? Not much. Well, okay, I admit it, I *am* a reporter. *Albany Times.*"

"Is that right?" She was still smiling. "Where's Albany?"

I didn't answer that. "See, that's why I came to see your father."

"Uh-huh." The clean-cut man was coming back, and Rebeccah gave me her wide smile again. "So nice to talk to you."

"Um-hmm." I stood, smiling agreeably at the man. For a moment, the thought of sticking my tongue out seemed an actual possibility. Then, just before leaving, I leaned down to Rebeccah and spoke quietly into her ear. "You're aware that you're out with a total bozo, aren't you?"

With which words I left her, and returned to the bar and the business of getting blind drunk.

Fortunately, the crowd was by now too thick for me to continue observing her.

Although, looking at her or not, I'm not sure I can say that she ever really left the focus of my inner eye again, that evening or in the weeks to come.

4.

One difference between Rebeccah Osborne and me has to do with how we each woke up Monday morning. For my part, I had a splitting headache and a mouth so evilly dry that I thought seriously about dehydration. Also, I was filled with remorse. Rebeccah, on the other hand—as she was later to tell me—woke as she always did, luxuriantly in her sun-flooded bedroom on East Ann Street, stretched out in the full length of her bed, and thought curiously about her day. I, covering my head with a pillow, felt my aloneness keenly, and wondered how hard it could possibly be to pick up a woman, no matter what woman, somewhere in this town. Rebeccah, as the night before reassembled itself, felt on balance glad she had sent her date back home—he was too damned handsome to go to bed with too quick, if at all. I, when I finally got out of bed, swung my legs to the ground, buried my face in my hands, and coughed for perhaps thirty seconds, clearing my lungs for the first cigarette of the day. Rebeccah, in contrast, was by then already out doing her daily four miles along the Huron River.

Fortunately, being hung over wasn't an altogether unknown experience to me, and therefore didn't keep me from doing what I had to, which was to take a mouthful of aspirins, drink a dozen or so cups of coffee from room service, smoke a few eye-opening cigarettes while padding around the room in my bare feet, and finally drink half a single of vodka from the minibar. Then I left immediately for Traverse City, a five-hour drive.

Long enough to allow me to piece together all I could from the night before, which was not much. I wasn't quite sure what Rebeccah and I had talked about during our conversation, but I was fairly convinced she had not given me her address, her phone number, or an invitation for dinner. Still, there was something tugging at me about her, and although I certainly tried to shrug it off, it didn't seem to want to go away.

I arrived at the Traverse City FBI office just before lunch—so closely before, in fact, that Osborne had already left. Apparently he had left word that he was expecting me—it made me worry that we'd been meant to eat together, and I'd forgotten—because they seated me not in the waiting room but in the little lunch area, where I could drink weak coffee and eat from a vending machine. What I couldn't do, however, was smoke, and as the lunch hour ticked by, that became a more and more imperative need. In the end I asked for, and received, permission to make my way through a little communications room with a back door open to a little rear parking lot, and stood at the door smoking, while I listened to radio reports coming in from the field in the room behind me.

All that came of the waiting, however, was being there to overhear Osborne radio in that I was to be told he was being kept away by a murder investigation, and discouraged from returning. And whether simply by his voice or by a more obscure association centering around the rejection, I remembered what had been evading me earlier: Osborne had said his daughter worked in a diner in town.

Back in Ann Arbor that evening, without ever quite pronouncing to myself what I was up to, I liberated—or expropriated—a yellow pages from a phone booth and, guided by the Restaurants section, began a leisurely tour of the town. It was not until an hour later that I reached the first of the two entries under *F* and turned up outside a tiny corner diner close to the bar I had been in last night. The place was crowded, but nonetheless, through the window I could see Rebeccah working behind the counter.

For a time I sat and watched her through the car window: in a sleeveless T-shirt again, her strong shoulders steady as she took two overloaded plates from one end of the counter, next to the cook, and carried them smoothly, the weight on her hips, to a table. Her hair was up again, this time under a baseball cap, and while the oval of her head was so pronounced as to be nearly absurd, the length of her neck and slope of her shoulders obviated any suggestion of ungainliness. She was, I thought again, like a well-muscled swan, a combination of grace and strength that at the moment struck me as virtually impossible. It was, I thought to myself, a beauty so particular that no one in the world could possibly appreciate it to the degree that I did. And that, I know now, is a typical attribute of great feminine beauty: to make young men feel that only they are good enough, or sensitive enough, or in love enough, to understand.

At length I got out of my car and walked hesitantly into the little diner, without any clear idea of what I was doing. Inside, the noise was that of a party. There was an empty seat at the counter, which I took. Then I waited, watching as Rebeccah moved surely and definitely up and down the small restaurant—clearly she was the only waitress, and clearly she knew what she was doing. She did notice that a new customer was in—on one trip, passing by with more of the diner's signature overladen oval plates, she dropped a menu in front of me and asked if I wanted coffee. She did not, however, seem to notice who I was, which gave me the leisure to study her face in search of what it held, exactly, that made her so different from the superabundance of sun-bronzed, blond, pretty college girls that filled this, like any campus town. It was, I finally decided, that although her bearing was so American—the blond hair, the well-exercised body, the white teeth—there was also a somehow un-American, nearly Slavic cast to her face: the brown eyes, the slightly crooked smile.

Still without noticing who I was, Rebeccah took my order, and I continued my inspection while I ate, slowly. So slowly, in fact, that by the time I'd finished, the dinner rush was over, and the crowd in the little diner had thinned considerably. Now Rebeccah was much more involved in clearing tables than serving customers, and her pace slowed, enough that she actually poured herself a cup of coffee, standing with her back to my inspection. It was an appreciative inspection. Still, I cut it off finally by speaking to her, conversationally, as if continuing a discussion that had been going on all evening.

"So. You lose the bozo?"

"Which bozo?" She answered without turning.

"The one you were with last night."

"Oh. Yeah." She turned now and put her coffee on the counter in front of me, inspecting my face carefully. "I thought you looked familiar, but I couldn't quite . . . remember you."

"Um-hmm." Holding my coffee cup in two hands, I gazed directly at her, feeling my stomach turn. And as I felt that, I also felt a sense of abandon. "So did you?"

"Did I what?"

"Lose the bozo."

She answered with a smile of her white teeth. "You know, you were so right. Till you pointed it out, I just didn't get it. I thought he was a Rhodes scholar, about to get a law degree, and squash team captain. Good-looking, too. Then you showed up and cleared it all up for me. What a bozo."

I narrowed my eyes.

"Always glad to help."

She widened her smile. "Um-hmm. See my dad today?"

"Nope. He blew me off."

"Boy. Maybe he doesn't know where Albany is either."

I let my face show suspicion by deepening my frown and squinting. "Well, I doubt that's it. I think there's more to it than that. Much more."

And now, at last, before my gravity, Rebeccah stopped smiling, as if something serious were going on. "Is that right? Like what?"

"Like, outside a few undergraduates writing earnestly for the college paper, no one gives a fuck about Jason Sinai."

It was my turn to smile now, widely and innocently, and Rebeccah's to frown.

"Well, you sure seem to." Her concentration now was steady, and her big lips had settled into seriousness.

Not wanting to say what was on my mind, I shrugged, and Rebeccah, in response to a call from the cook, moved down the counter. As she did so, I suddenly remembered Osborne's shrug from the day before.

In a moment, however, she was back with a plate of food, which she set in front of me and began to eat from, still standing behind the counter. She spoke with nearly complete uninterest. "So what are you doing here? I mean, your paper must think there's a story to send you here."

The question—a good one—made my stomach sink. And for lack of a better answer, I told her the truth. "Kind of. If you want to know the absolute truth, I'm using my vacation for this. And paying my own expenses. My editor thinks my talents would be better used covering the local 4H show."

"You mean, you're so obsessed by this story, you're doing it on your own dime." She seemed actually impressed by this—to me—depressing admission.

"Um-hmm." Buoyed by her interest, I lit a cigarette. Then, noting her expression—she stared at me blankly, a forkful of food hanging in the air—I put it out again. With a nod, she let the fork finish its voyage to her mouth.

"Oh. Why?"

"There's a story here."

"And that is?"

"Well." Now I dropped my voice and leaned forward on my elbows. "See, I think there's still a vast underground out there, waiting to bring a revolution against capitalism. I think Sinai's going to strike, and strike soon. And this time, they're going to go all the way."

Whispering, I smelled perfume.

"I see," she whispered back while chewing, and now I smelled tamari. "So you're a wacko."

"Not at all." Leaning back, I laughed now, and saw that she was laughing too. "Hey, I'll tell you all about it. Come have a drink when you're done."

"No way. But thanks."

"But why?"

"Why? It's Monday night. I have work to do tomorrow morning. The only place I'm going is home."

"Where's that? I'll come over tomorrow with my Doors collection. You got a bong?"

Now she laughed outright. "No thanks. I work tomorrow."

"Well, when are you free?"

For a moment, she studied me. Then she said: "We can have coffee Wednesday afternoon, if you're sticking around that long."

"Oh, I am, I am. Where and when?"

And as I listened to Rebeccah Osborne's directions to a coffee shop next to campus, I wondered what the hell I was going to do in Ann Arbor till Wednesday afternoon.

Date: June 15, 2006
From: "Daddy" <littlej@cusimanorganics.com>
To: "Isabel Montgomery" <isabel@exmnster.uk>
CC: maillist: The_Committee
Subject: letter 23

And while Benny was stalking Rebeccah at her place of employ, I was sitting on the train to Milwaukee, staring at myself over a quarter century's distance.

The picture on the front page of the *Times* showed eight young men and women gathered around a car, the car out of the fifties, the men and women out of the sixties. The caption called it an SDS protest in Ann Arbor in 1968, and in fact the car was leading a column of young people down what looked like State Street under trees dressed in late summer foliage. It would have been, I realized, the days leading up to the Democratic Convention.

In the shifting light of a moving train to Milwaukee, I peered close into the picture's depth of field and identified Sharon Solarz, Diana Oughton, Bill Ayers, myself, Milton Taube, and Mimi Lurie. One by one, looking for some hint of what these young people in this grainy electronic halftone may have been thinking. Clearly, they had no idea they were being photographed. Sharon Solarz was focusing at distance and bending her neck to address her speech way upward to Skip Taube, who towered above her. Just looking at her crooked smile, I could hear the sardonic lilt of her voice. Mimi was drawing pensively on a cigarette, looking at Bill in black Ray-Bans; Bill speaking to Diana, who listened, frowning downward. I, myself, wore a wide, open-mouthed smile and eyes squinting into the sun.

The second picture carried in the paper was of Jim Grant, and I could not remember where it was from. This one I glanced at only quickly: Jim Grant had never much liked looking at himself, with his nose job and his balding head. It was if his image of himself was still the handsome Jewish face of Jason Sinai, and seeing it changed had always been something to be avoided. Neither photograph, in any case, could be connected to the black-haired, mustachioed man sitting on the Milwaukee commuter.

The train drew into the Milwaukee station at 10:30. I left in the small stream of travelers, emerging into a bright summer day, swimming with heat.

I walked for a while now, drank some coffee, browsed in a bookstore, and bought a new pair of shoes. This last purchase was totally unnecessary. Still, I found it strangely comforting, the very normalcy of the transaction, and I found it intelligent to be carrying a shopping bag with such an everyday item as a pair of new shoes in it—what cop would suspect a shoe shopper of being a fugitive? Still, for the following hour, walking downtown, I described the perimeter of a rectangle twice, crossing River Street for the short sides and reversing direction down the opposing sidewalk for the longs, and drank seltzers in two bars. Like that I looked for the shape of a tail: a person changing direction in response to my movement, a familiar shirt, any kind of order in the random pattern of movement around me. There was nothing I could see, though, and so at last, toward midafternoon, I made my way to the middle of the block, where a bouncer sat at the door of a small bar that a red neon sign in the window announced as the Old Town Café.

Inside, the room was surprisingly deep, with tables extending back to a small stage, on which a band was setting up. The tables were half full, a mixed crowd in age as well as color. At the long bar, the faces were mostly black, and the attitudes were of easy familiarity with the young woman, wearing a halter top, serving them. All the way down the bar a man sat alone over the sports section of the *Milwaukee Journal Sentinel*.

I ordered a beer as I came in, motioning down the bar with my head, then made my way down to the man sitting alone. Closer, you could see how tall he was, and how handsome: a full head of black hair over a strong Irish face, weathering well. When the barmaid had brought the beer and gone away with my money, I took a pull, watching the man. Then I reached over in front of him and helped myself to one of his cigarettes.

The man looked up, briefly, then down to his paper again, evidently to finish a paragraph, which gave me time to light the cigarette. When he was ready, he looked up again, more slowly this time, and studied me.

"Now, what the fuck might you think you're doing, asshole?"

I held his gaze, smoking.

Only then did he let some expression into his face. The expression was interest.

"Well, well. What are you doing here?"

"That all you have to say?"

"No." Donal James held out his hand. "Hey. Nice to see you. What the fuck are you doing here?"

I didn't answer, and after a moment, Donal went on.

"Jase, I have social touch with a couple people. That's it. I mean—" I seemed now to have caught up with his surprise. "You need some money, man? Or anything else? No problem. But you didn't come all the way here just for that. Did you?"

I shook my head. "Wanted to ask you some questions."

"I can't imagine what. But listen." Now Donal took keys out of his pocket, and a pen, and wrote an address on the edge of his paper, tearing the number off with his left thumb and forefinger. "You don't want to be out and about. Go up to my place. Last call's two-thirty; I'll see you then."

I took it, feeling frustration. "Can't you get away from here?"

"No. There'll be a crowd for the music tonight. I can't pay two bouncers on the volume I get. So I have to do the inside myself."

I nodded now while I read the address, which was over on Mechanic Street. "Okay. Thanks, man."

"See you later, boy."

Donal James's was a three-story brownstone in a neighborhood of the same, perhaps once a factory worker's neighborhood, possibly constructed by a mill or a sweat shop and leased to its workers, now housing little bistros on corners and a few upmarket groceries. Donal's place had clearly been his parents': it had well-kept linoleum on the kitchen floor and was furnished with vintage pieces from the fifties and sixties, none of them showing refinishing or restoration.

I found the kitchen and hunted through the refrigerator, which had a brown paper bag of apples on one shelf, and the little pantry, in which I found a half-finished bottle of honey. In the freezer was a bottle of Finlandia. I washed two of the apples in the sink, found a knife, and cut them, then ate them, standing at the counter, dipping the slices in the honey. I opened the freezer and drank some vodka from the bottle. Then I carried the bottle through the archway with varnished bull's-eye molding, through the little dining room, and into the living room.

This was a hexagonal room, its point made of bay windows over the street. The ceilings were low, and the furnishings looked as if they might have been brought from Ireland at the beginning of the century. Through the window lace, streetlamps threw a gentle luminescence over the carpet. I lay gingerly on a couch, put the vodka on the floor beside me, supine for the first time since I left you in a New York hotel room, and fell asleep.

2.

When I woke up Donal was sitting on the couch, long legs crossed and reclining, so that I saw his face over one black, Cuban-heeled boot.

"What you doing there?" I spoke from where I lay.

"Checking you out."

"And?"

"Looking good, baby."

"Hair's not real."

"Fuck hair. The important thing is, you didn't get fat. You work out?"

"Uh-huh. You?"

"Nah. Never needed to. Cholesterol's okay, never put on weight."

"Quit smoking, and you may find that changing."

"So I hear." He stood up now. "Go back to sleep. We'll talk in the morning."

But I sat up. "You going to bed?"

"Nope."

"Let's talk now."

"Oke. Want a drink?"

"Sure." Donal left the room, and I followed, picking up the vodka from the floor.

At the kitchen table, the black summer night swimming in the alleyway outside, we talked, not about what I needed, but about what had happened since last we met. Donal had surfaced in '79 and served a negotiated two in New York for charges stemming from Columbia—days before coming back to Milwaukee to take care of his aging parents. He'd inherited the house from his father, and mortgaged it to buy the bar—when he got kicked out of Columbia over the occupation of Bryant Hall, he had lost a full scholarship, which would have made him the first member of his family to get a college degree, and while underground he'd worked in enough bars to learn the business well.

"Want to hear something funny?" A shaded lamp lit the kitchen table, and in the fall of its light he showed a missing tooth in his smile, which seemed to me a fond smile. "I just paid off the damn mortgage. Fifteen years. That makes it exactly fifteen years since I got out of the slammer."

"Congratulations." I watched him, remembering something I had heard. "That why you sold film rights?"

Donal's eyes narrowed. "How do you know that?"

I shrugged. "Heard it from an entertainment lawyer, once. Said most of the major folk from SDS and Weather had sold life rights to a producer. That true?"

Donal shrugged. "Not only me. Why should someone else make the money from our lives?"

I shrugged again. "You see anyone?"

"Sure. Not particularly Weather people, though. Bernardine and Billy. Each of their kids worked at the bar the summer they turned eighteen. Jeff and his family come out for Thanksgiving, I go east each spring. Oh, shit, Stew and Judy out in Seattle, Cathy in New York. I go see Dave Gilbert a couple times a year. Klonsky, Mike James, lots of people, man. There was an SDS reunion in '94. You should have seen the number of children out there."

"None yours?"

He shrugged. "Mine live out west with their mothers."

"How many?"

"Kids or mothers? Four and two."

Donal didn't ask me about whom from the old days I saw—he knew the answer. But he did, now, ask me his original question again.

"But none of these people, I don't think, are what you want from me."

"No."

"So what do you want?"

Now I watched him, wondering not so much what to tell him, but how to phrase my question. Finally I said, "To ask an historical question."

"Shoot."

"After Bank of Michigan, Sharon came to you for help."

His eyes narrowed. "How do you know?"

"Because of the name she lived under until she was married. It was in the paper when she was arrested. Coyle. That was you when you went under in '70. I figure you must have married her out of her first identity to give her a new name. Then she went somewhere else, and after a couple years, you did an uncontested divorce that left her with the name."

He whistled. "How'd you figure that out?"

"Just logic. Am I right?"

He watched me for a moment. "Let's say you are. Then what?

I nodded. "Want to hear something funny? Jim Grant's seven years younger than me. I've been thirty-nine for the past seven years. So I have a thirty-nine-year-old's memory."

"Very funny."

I sat up. "I'm not kidding. I went to college again. When I was twenty-six. Four straight years."

He whistled again. "Shit. Lay a bunch of freshman women?"

I shrugged and sat back. "Just one. Married her."

With a smile, he brought the conversation back. "So Sharon came to me, so what?"

"Did Mimi come too?"

"Why?"

"I'm not telling you why," I answered evenly.

"I realize that. I mean, why would she have come to me?"

We watched each other, me thinking that, really, it was amazing the way this man had grown handsomer as he aged.

"You know my answer."

"Say it."

"They both knew you had transitional identities available. You know, papers to live under while building a more solid set."

"Yeah." Donal snorted. "Neither of them had any fucking right to ask me a thing. I wasn't with you for B of M. I wasn't even on the damn revolutionary committee. I was the fuck out of it, and you knew it."

I answered readily. "We're talking about twenty-five years ago. Nothing happened to you because of Mimi or Sharon. No one knows they came to you but me. I'm sorry they did it."

Now Donal deflated, emptying his lungs, dropping his shoulders from the ready response of someone used to fighting.

"And you, boy? Why didn't you come to me?"

Was that, I wondered, what had really offended him? "I had a waiting identity. I didn't need to involve you."

"Okay." Donal lit a cigarette, watching with interest as I did the same. "So Mimi came to see me. I gave her some papers. I doubt they lasted her very long. I never saw her again."

"Right." I spoke carefully now. "But Mimi didn't only ask you for ID. She asked you for a name. The name of the dude from the Brotherhood of Eternal Love. The one who gave you the money for Dr. Leary's breakout."

Donal answered without expression, he was that surprised. "And you know that because?"

"Because Mimi always thought that way." I stood up now and walked to the window, where a thin sun was beginning to light the little tenement backyards. In Donal's, I saw, were tomato plants, which made me feel, suddenly, very old. Before my eyes was a memory of the two of them, descending the stairs in the house Sharon Stern had in Seattle, flushed and stoned and smiling, with Donal's hand in hers. I was nineteen then. Really nineteen. And now, a quarter century later, my face burned. I spoke without turning.

"Mimi's like you, Donal. She liked being underground. The rest of us, we were half in mourning for our families, always scared, always wishing we were normal again. Mimi, the whole thing gave her a bounce. Like being good-looking. And you. You liked being underground, you liked being famous, you liked the way people looked at you when they recognized you. You and Mimi, man. You loved breaking the law."

"Didn't seem to bother you none. Breaking the law. You did your share."

And I had. I did my share of fucking, too, I was thinking. I spoke, however, with intellectual rather than emotional heat.

"There's a big difference. I was a revolutionary criminal. You two, you were criminal revolutionaries. Mimi wasn't going to take some suburban matron's identity. Or become a small-town lawyer. Mimi wanted to go see if she could run smoke out of South America for the Brotherhood of Eternal Love. That was her idea of a lifestyle."

I sat again. "She'd been looking for them for years, but she'd saved the one real connection she had. You. You were the connection. When Leary was arrested and the Brotherhood decided to reach out to Weather to get him out of jail, they used a distributor they had in New York. The distributor sold to a Panther called Douglas Lowe. Lowe drank at the West End, where you bartended. You made the connection between Lowe and Weather, and someone from Weather got to meet the Brotherhood."

Donal looked amused. "Who from Weather?"

"Ah. That's the question. Who from Weather? Because when Mimi came to you after B of M, you gave her a transitional identity and sent her to see whoever it was from Weather that met the Brotherhood."

"And why would you want to know that?"

"Because compartmentalization of information dictated that he be the only connection with the Brotherhood. And so, if you tell me who he is, I can go to him and find out who the Brotherhood contact was. And if I can find the Brotherhood contact, in turn, well, I'm thinking I can find Mimi Lurie."

Donal whistled. "So you want to find Mimi Lurie."

"I do."

"And why?"

"That's my business."

"I see."

I could see the calculation behind the blue of his eye. Patiently, I watched him conclude that he did not have the datapoints to know what his old friend was doing. Finally, Donal exhaled.

"Jase, you always were a lucky bastard. You know that?"

"I didn't figure this out through luck, Donal."

"I know that. I mean, you're lucky that the one person who can answer your question is me. Because I'm the only one who'd trust you with information that makes me accessory to murder."

"Donal. Christ sake. They could take my left arm off, you know that."

Donal lowered his voice. "The Brotherhood dude made us submit a list of names of Weather people. I took the name to the Panther, Doug Lowe, and he had some way of getting it out to the Brotherhood dude. I don't know if Doug ever met the Brotherhood dude, but I never did. Then the Brotherhood dude gave Doug Lowe the name of the guy he was prepared to meet. They set up a meeting, and from then on every contact between Weather and the Brotherhood took place through him."

Donal paused, watching me, as if still, all these years after, the discipline of those days made it hard for him to break security and tell me a secret he was supposed to have kept forever. "The one he picked from Weather was one of yours. Jed Lewis. In Ann Arbor. This is why: before Jed got into Weather, he did the Hash Bash with Billy Cusimano, right? Then Big Bill moved out to Mendocino and began planting the seed professionally, right? At which time, he must have hooked up with the Brotherhood of Eternal Love. So Billy vouched for Jed Lewis, and that was good enough for the Brotherhood dude."

Jed Lewis. I thought. "Jesus, Jeddy never told me about this? We were tight, man. We were part of an affinity group."

"Right, go figure. Now, Jed put together the personnel for the Leary thing, notably Mimi. And that was the end of that. Except, after B of M, in 1974, Mimi came and asked me the exact same question as you. After B of M, she wanted to find out who the Brotherhood dude was."

"And you sent her to Jed."

"No. What I did was, I went to Jed for her. And Jed made some phone calls. Then he gave me a sealed envelope, which I gave to Mimi."

I interrupted. "Still sealed?"

"Still sealed. And Mimi took it, and took off, and that, my friend, was where the revolution ended for me."

I thought about that. "So Jed's the only one who knows where Mimi went after B of M?"

"Only Jed, pal."

"And where's Jed now?"

Donal hesitated for some time, now, watching me. Then he spoke, pronouncing the words slowly.

"Still in A-squared. Only now he's a professor. University of Michigan. Department of American Studies."

Watching his eyes intently watching mine, I nodded.

Donal washed the clothes I was wearing while I showered and redid my mustache and toupee. We talked while the clothes dried, then we went out for breakfast in a Jeep Cherokee, a brand-new one, clearly Donal's pride and joy. After breakfast, we went on downtown, where Donal parked in a lot next to the Marriott. In a couple stores—Kenneth Cole, Banana Republic—I bought a new wardrobe. Outside Banana Republic, on the—by now crowded—sidewalk, we stopped, and I put out my hand.

Donal looked surprised. "Where you going?"

"Train station."

"Train? What the fuck for?"

"Got to go do my thing, Donal."

"Sure, but why the train?"

I was confused. "You think I should take a taxi?"

"No, man. I think you should drive." With a wide sweep of his arm, he slapped the keys to the Cherokee, attached to a little transponder, into my palm. Then he took out his wallet for the registration. "Leave it somewhere sensible when you're done. Backseat sleeps two. There's a half a J in the ashtray."

Holding the keys, I looked at him in some wonder, and Donal shrugged.

"You want to tell me what you're doing, I'll come with you. You want to tell me?"

I shook my head.

"Okay then, brother. And hey—"

He paused portentously, as if waiting for me to give him a sign I was listening, which I did with a nod.

"Let's be careful out there."

And then I was standing alone on a sidewalk in Milwaukee, watching Donal disappear into the crowd, his black jeans and shirt blending into the businessmen's suits around him, beginning to pull my mind from where it had been and focus it on the fact that after a quarter century I was going back to Ann Arbor.

PART THREE

Hush little baby
Don't you cry
When we get to Tucson
You'll see why
We left the snowstorms
And the thunder and rain
For the desert sun
We're gonna be born again
What's important
In this world?
A little boy
A little girl.

—Chrissie Hynde,
"Thumbelina"

Date: June 15, 2006
From: "Rebeccah" <beck@cusimanorganics.com>
To: "Isabel Montgomery" <isabel@exmnster.uk>
CC: maillist: The_Committee
Subject: letter 24

So now it is my turn to take up the thread of this story.

I'm not so sure what I have to add. None of this is anything I talk about happily. And now, ten years later, as you know, my role in this whole story is still secret.

Secret. That's a word I know a lot about, Iz, my girl. Secrecy is my profession. One more secret, you could say, doesn't hurt.

Okay, it hasn't hurt. And now it may even help.

But if that's the case, then why on earth are they making me put my whole role in this whole thing on-line, for all the future to read?

It was a weekend meeting, earlier this summer, with what Ben calls "the Committee" when it was decided—an expanded meeting of the Committee, out at Michelle Fitzgerald's beach house on Long Island. Basically, everyone who had the slightest chance of helping with the parole board was there, which meant everyone and his brother was there, and let me tell you, everyone and his brother had an opinion. When toward the end of the weekend I was told that I was to be a writer of this little history of the summer of 1996, I protested vigorously. I am a Johnny-come-lately to this story, I had no stake in the politics, I was then, and am now, a Republican.

To which it was pointed out to me—rather dryly—by Jason that, A, if it weren't for me this story would never have happened, and B, the very fact that I was not a perpetrator but a victim of the events of the summer of 1996 only makes me more convincing in my role in explaining them to you, Isabel Montgomery Grant, who is being asked to change her life and the lives of people she loves for us.

Anyhow, it was all a total waste of time arguing because, as you will find out if you join our little party in Michigan later this month, there's no discussion with these guys. The reason they all got involved in their little drama of the sixties in the first place is because they are such powerful personalities, each of them in their own way, and why they bothered with bombs is a mystery when they could probably have ended the war in Vietnam by force of character alone. Peer-pressure Lyndon Johnson into dropping acid. Browbeat McNamara into a criticism–self-criticism session. Argue the McBundys into a semicomatose state.

They'd have probably given in just to shut them up.

God knows I did.

So, as my daughter would say, "whatever." It's a perfect June day in 2006, and instead of sitting in traffic on the West Side Highway trying to get out of town, as every other self-respecting New Yorker is doing, I'm staring out a window at the sunstruck green of what passes for my garden and typing away on my laptop, and the way things are looking, I'm going to be spending the next few days doing that. But here's the deal: if I'm going to tell my story, I'm going to tell the part I care most about first, and believe it or not, this part is not about Jason but about someone else I first met in the summer of 1996, and who was to become a very important person to me indeed.

So picture with me, if you will, a summer afternoon in a college town in the Midwest. Ann Arbor, late June of 1996. Streets of little lawns and houses divided into student apartments; kids skateboarding; an occasional snatch of music, or a conversation, as if the whole town were an outdoors dorm.

Joseph Brodsky once gave the commencement speech at the U of M, and in it he said that you can judge your success as an adult by how fondly you remember Ann Arbor. By that standard, my adult life promised great things. This was my last summer in Ann Arbor, and already a patina of nostalgia was over everything I saw, the dear, familiar streets, the happy stops in my routine, the diner, the library, the Honors Office in Angell Hall. Even Dr. L's office—Jed Lewis, my senior thesis adviser, now a member of the distinguished body we call the Committee—was a place where I savored the minutes, the last long, engaging discussions with his head framed by the light of the window, the picture-perfect views of campus. That summer I was writing my senior thesis in American studies, on the siege of Khe Sanh, to be exact. It was the last requirement for my degree, and I had delayed it to the summer in order to spend May, after classes ended, interviewing participants, largely friends of my father, who had lived through Khe Sanh and were prepared—unlike the friends, I may add, of Jason—to tell their story. Now it seemed I could not work slowly enough, the pages piling up on my desk with effortless ease, the summer spinning toward its end with all the speed that happiness lends to time. In August I would move to Virginia and begin training to become an FBI agent. From that, there would be no turning back: the agency would be sending me to law school at Georgetown, and when I finished, I would be one highly qualified criminologist. The change loomed: inevitable, exciting, unwelcome. It was, I knew, the last summer of my childhood, and every moment was precious to me.

In this rich time, the advent of a person who gave every appearance of becoming an admirer did not make much of an impression on me.

Not at first.

There was no reason for it to: you work at a restaurant in a college town, you are a sitting duck for men to fall in love with you. Any college town is filled with tortured, good-looking young men, each seeming more interesting than the last. Once you've hung out with a couple of them, though, you find that everything so interesting about them is just some phase they're going through, and that sooner or later they're going to reveal themselves as what they in fact are: boys. I had long ago sworn not to meet any more boys at the diner. And then there was Robert Bruner, who really was captain of the squash team and a Rhodes scholar, and who really was no longer a boy, having finished law school and a year at Oxford, and who really was moving to Washington in August, just when I was moving to Virginia, and had driven down from Traverse City to take me out every night I had free for the past month. Rob had been a senior in high school when I was a freshman; was back from England just for a month, and when Ben showed up, I was very close to taking him to bed.

Altogether, Ben appeared to me rather like a guy at a party who no one wanted to talk to. There was nothing wrong with him: he was probably very nice. It's just that no one knew him, and no one really wanted to get to know him—the party had been going on too long before he got there. So I don't think I thought about him even once between the Sunday night he came to the diner and the Wednesday when I was supposed to meet him for coffee. And in fact, I'm a bit ashamed to say, when I remembered, on Wednesday, that I was due to meet him in five minutes, I thought seriously about not going. There was just no *room* for him in my summer, my summer that was hurtling through space and time to autumn, every moment of which I needed to taste, to hold, and to miss its passing.

But I couldn't stand him up. He knew where I worked, after all. And so Wednesday afternoon I entered the sudden dark of Drake's, a coffee shop next to campus—not the modern cappuccino joint my father had taken Ben to, but a dark little place from the fifties that I adored—and, once my eyes had adjusted to the light, saw the guy sitting alone at a booth. That wasn't hard: no one came to Drake's anymore. Outside, within a three-block radius, there were seventeen or eighteen beautiful light-flooded, air-conditioned cafés, each serving spectacular coffee, biscotti, and panini, in contrast to the watery brew the rude waitresses poured here from big vats, big vats that added to the ambient temperature of about one-oh-one . . . in fact, the summer of 1996 was the end of Drake's existence. No one understood my fondness for this place, and when that day I sat down in front of Ben, he, sweating profusely, expressed some opinions in this regard. I nodded, bored.

"Uh-huh. Lots of people feel that way."

"Doesn't stop you, though?"

An inauspicious start to the conversation, I thought, resisting the urge to look at my watch and changing the subject as quickly as I could. "Not at all. I commune with the ghosts of the fifties. So, have you seen my father again?"

He answered quickly, agreeably, although there was something in his eye that made me think he had caught my boredom. "Yeah, we caught a Tigers game last night. Tonight we're playing poker. He asked me to call him Dad, isn't that sweet? And you?"

"Nope." He was an interesting, if not exactly agreeable-looking, person: badly shaven, with full, expressive lips and black eyes. "He's coming to town tomorrow. For the night."

"Oh." His full lips smiled happily and, somehow, easily. "Great. What time?"

"What time what?"

"Dinner. What can I bring?"

I smiled now too—really, he was too ridiculous. "Nothing. Including yourself. You are so uninvited, I can't tell you."

"But why, Beck? Dad and I are probably going to be meeting to shoot some stick after dinner, anyways."

Beck. Only my parents call me Beck. "He doesn't want to see *you*. Why do you think he's ducking your calls?"

"Boy." His smile faded, as if he were really hurt, and yet his black eyes remained steadily trained on mine, observant, expressive. "I'm not angry, you know. Just very, very hurt. Now look."

"Uh-huh."

He looked around the place, no doubt observing that the single waitress, a blond adolescent girl, was ignoring us, and lit a cigarette with his outsize hands. Then he leaned forward to me. "It's ridiculous to call Sharon Solarz and Jason Sinai murderers. Sharon and Jason drove the getaway car. They were twenty-four and never dreamed ex–Special Forces Vincent Dellesandro would use his gun."

Apparently we were on to a new part of the conversation: he was referring to the *Michigan Daily* editorial I'd written the week before, in which I argued that Solarz should serve the maximum term possible for the Bank of Michigan robbery. Okay. I can adapt, I was thinking, and I gave him a stern look.

"Oh, nonsense. A guard with a wife and two children was killed at B of M, and in this country, we punish murderers equally, whether they're the perpetrator or the accessory. Anything else is an excuse. A liberal, paranoid, nonsensical excuse."

While I talked, I watched his mouth, of which the wide lips, which were very red, seemed to be forming words of response even before I finished. And in fact he hardly let me finish.

"I agree, it's no excuse. But that's not the point. Four students were killed by the National Guard at Kent State—four *Americans* on *state* ground exercising the constitutional right to free speech, by the National *Guard*. But no one was punished for that."

"So what? That excuses the murder, in cold blood, of a bank guard?"

"No, no, of course not. The question is, why are some murders legal if all of them are wrong?"

I was thinking, what a jerk, and perhaps I let some of that tone into my voice. "Listen, democracy's imperfect, we all know that. Don't give me a bunch of garbage about Vietnam. My father was nearly killed in Vietnam, and anything he did there he was required to do by the United States Army and its commander in chief. You call soldiers murderers? That's ridiculous. I know dozens and dozens of vets, and they're just like anyone else in this country, only they were called on to kill, and they did it. As for those kids in the National Guard who screwed up at Kent State, you think they're proud of it? There was a civil war in this country: what's amazing is that there were so few screwups and so few casualties."

And now, to my dismay, he smiled, and I realized that I had just been baited. Quietly now, in a calm, very reasonable tone, as if speaking to a child, he answered. "Well, that's my point. Jason Sinai's mistakes had a context. He's not proud of his past either, I'm guessing. But the context is a meaningful part of his punishment. When Clinton pardoned the Puerto Rican terrorists from the FALN, that had a context in the bombing of Vieques—same thing when Clinton let Sylvia Baraldini go to apologize for his air force cutting down an Italian ski lift. I mean, Sylvia Baraldini was convicted in the Brinks robbery, just like Kathy Boudin. But Clinton needed to appease the Italians, and so she got out, while Boudin stays in. Even Ford's pardon of your hero Nixon had a context. I mean, you don't believe in the pardoning of criminal misconduct on the part of government officials, do you? But I think we all agree that there was no point in sending Nixon to jail. Please let me finish."

This last part was in response to my trying to interrupt. When I stopped—trying to interrupt, that is, although I was more than a little outraged—he went on, enunciating clearly.

"When those . . . those *children* robbed the Bank of Michigan, the context was that it seemed to a great many reasonable people in this country that a real, genuine coup was going on, a coup against the Constitution by the Nixon White House. Such gross illegality was going on at the highest levels of our government that the president had to resign over it to avoid being impeached. This country was at war with itself. I'm not saying they were right to rob the bank. They were, in fact, wrong. That's a given. But that war's never ended, it's just gotten deeper and more bitter."

This time, when he finished, I thought before I answered. "So we were at war. Great. Then the murder of that cop was a war crime, a crime against humanity."

He nodded now, letting a thick shock of brown bangs fall over one eye, then brushing it back. Pleased with himself. "That's exactly what I think. Our law doesn't account for war crimes. South Africa has a Truth and Reconciliation Council; Argentina has the same. For God's sakes, after World War II we even reconstructed our enemies' countries. But Nixon only ended the war in Vietnam—the war *over* Vietnam's still going on. Clinton and Gingrich are fighting it today, Gore and W are going to fight it next election! Nothing in our constitutional law encompasses the idea of reconciliation: we are a country adamantly opposed to ourselves."

"Listen." I sat back now, and nodded. "I understand what you're saying. It's interesting, it's perceptive, it's maybe even true. But to go from there to defending Jason Sinai and his crew is a leap you're not going to get anyone to make."

He too lowered his tone. "I'm not defending him. If Sinai's complicit in manslaughter, he should be convicted. Then he should be pardoned in the name of national reconciliation. We don't call soldiers murderers, fine. But William Calley served *three years* for murdering a village full of women and children at My Lai. All I ask is that we pardon someone who made a mistake in the context of what we now understand was a patriotic duty to fight against the war in Vietnam. Calley served three years? Between Kathy Boudin, David Gilbert, and Judy Clark—I'm speaking only about accessories, now, the helpers, not the shooters—you know how much time's been served for the Brinks Robbery? *Sixty years*. Hard state time in maximum-security prisons, and no one expects any paroles to be handed out, ever. What should Solarz and Sinai get for driving the getaway car in a misguided robbery gone wrong? What should Mimi Lurie get for participating in it? How about double Calley's sentence? Would you be happy with that, counselor? How about six years apiece?"

2.

Now apparently Ben had been foolish to think that his smoking would go unnoticed, because it was during this last speech that a man came out of the kitchen and suggested that we leave, immediately. But such was the heat of our discussion that neither of us really paid any attention. We walked together out of the café back into the light of the afternoon, me holding my books to my chest—I was wearing a tank top and a short cotton skirt—and he fell into step beside me, his head exactly at the level of mine. For a time we argued on. And only after some time did the conversation fall to a more normal decibel level.

"So, what's your dad think of this Jason Sinai thing?"

"Thinks it's a pain in the ass. I think," I answered absently, because something was beginning to disturb me.

"They gonna catch him?"

"If Sinai's stupid enough to come to Michigan, they are."

"Uh-huh. Not that they have any great track record, of course."

"Yeah, yeah." I was unwilling to go on in this vein; strangely unwilling. "Hey, mind if I don't defend the whole FBI this afternoon?"

He didn't answer, walking next to me with his big hands clasped behind his back and his head bent down toward the pavement. Finally, I asked, "And you? What do you think?"

"I don't know. They didn't even know who Jim Grant was till I figured it out."

"Then why did you help the FBI out?"

He looked at me now, surprised. "Because I'm a reporter. And he's a criminal."

"A criminal you sympathize with."

"Hey, don't simplify. I'm just talking. I don't sympathize with anybody."

We were at the door of the diner where I worked now, so I stopped and turned to face him. We were almost exactly the same height. And I still felt disturbed—enough so that I was willing to put an end to this relationship before it started. I spoke without the hint of a smile.

"You know, Ben, you don't fool me with all your East Coast liberal bullshit. This isn't about the war in Vietnam, for God's sake. It's about a bank robbery, a shooting, and a dead cop. A quarter century of evading the law. Oh, and then that finicky legal issue about being an accessory to a crime carrying all the weight of being the primary perpetrator. I'm just a country girl, I guess, 'cause it's all so simple to me. You can romanticize the left all you want. It's still a bunch of damn criminals."

He answered me with the same seriousness. "Think so? Me, I think the left can use a little romance, after the beating they've taken the last twenty years. But I'll tell you what. I'll give you the cosmopolitan, liberal, Jew perspective on it tonight, over dinner."

"No, you won't." We were standing face-to-face, talking quickly, now.

"And why not?"

"Because I work tonight."

"After work then."

"After work I have a date."

"I see. The bozo?"

"The bozo."

"Okay, then, we're on. You cancel the bozo, and I'll defend Jason Sinai, Mimi Lurie, and Sharon Solarz against the charge of accessory to murder. And I'll throw in Kathy Boudin, David Gilbert, and Susan Rosenberg too."

And suddenly the root of my discomfort crystallized for me. The problem was, do you know how many people in 1996 had any idea who Susan Rosenberg was? Robert Bruner didn't. None of my friends did. In fact, outside Jed Lewis and my parents, I doubted there was a single person I knew who did.

But this guy—this funny-looking guy with his full lips and big hands, staring straight across a few inches of space into my eyes—he did.

I answered more slowly this time. "No. Tonight's out. And my dad's in town tomorrow. Friday night. I get off work at ten. I'll meet you at the Del Rio. Now tell me, where are you staying?"

He answered without a beat. "Me? Good God, you move fast, Beck. Gimme an hour, I'll run out and get a waterbed, a Lionel Richie CD, and a gram of cocaine."

I put on a patient voice, now—the kind you use for children. "You do that, Ben. I, meanwhile, will go to work, and then out with Robert Bruner."

"And meet me after up at my hotel? The bottle of Grand Marnier's a given, don't worry."

This time, to my slight surprise, I found myself poking him in the chest with my forefinger. "Friday. And don't let me see you before then. Is that clear?"

For a moment we watched each other. And then, with what I can only describe as a grin, he turned on a heel and walked away.

3.

So, as for Ben, I don't know what he did for the next few days. I admit, at the time, I was kind of conscious of him, at a distance, waiting to see me again. I didn't give it much thought. My attitude was, maybe he'd disappear, which would simplify my life.

As for me, when later that night I met Rob—the squash team Rhodes scholar bozo—for drinks, I found myself pretty attentive. I watched him carefully over the little table in the Del: his amazingly handsome face with its evening shadow over the jaw; his strong neck with its tanned, warm skin; his beautiful hands gesturing as he spoke, with passion, about the job he was going to take in the Justice Department. I watched him and thought about the fact that we had known each other most of our lives, he a few years ahead of me in school, our parents friends. It was when he came back from Oxford in the early spring that, for him, I'd become something other than a local girl. Watching him, I tried to remember when that change had occurred, and whether he knew, then, that I was also about to become an FBI agent with every reason to expect her career to take her high up into the administration, a powerful wife for a Washington insider lawyer. When we stood to go, I looked at the pure solidity of his chest and shoulders, just like my father, and when, on the sidewalk outside my house in the summer night he kissed me, I felt that strength as if pierced right through my breast to a spot in my back just below my shoulder blades. I gently stepped back, and for a moment, although I did not know it, a great deal of my life balanced. Then I said good night, quickly, and walked into my house alone. Not pronouncing to myself why I had just done what I had just done.

Of secondary importance to me, but much more, I suppose, central to our business at hand, was the next evening, which I spent with my Dad.

Daddy, as is usual when he has business downstate, stayed with me, and as usual, I cooked for him—my father does not like restaurants, he likes to be in a house, and preferably a house where he's had the chance to check the security himself, as—I suppose—befits a man who has arrested dozens and dozens and dozens of people throughout the state of Michigan.

He's a good eater, being enormous and active, and I get a kick out of cooking for him. I suppose, Iz, you've realized already that I adore my father about as much as possible. As for Daddy, I think he got a kick out of being cooked for, as Mommy had stopped doing much cooking since being named to the appellate bench: she was by that summer Judge Osborne and got home too late to cook. Whereas my dad ran what had to be one of the sleepier FBI stations in the country, and hadn't really worked through dinner since Vincent Loonsfoot went on his little spree up north.

So I did not tell my dad that I had been arguing politics with the exact same reporter whose calls he was ducking. That gave me a little twinge: I do not lie to my parents—my mom, for example, knew I was thinking of going to bed with Rob. I personally thought then—and think now—that because I was adopted and our relationship transcends genetics, my tie to my parents had always been infused with the choice of friendship, rather than the obligation of family.

So I was not in the habit of lying to my father. But I thought that if he knew that a reporter who was dogging him was also chumming up to his daughter with clearly sexual intent, he might run the guy right out of the state, and I did not want Ben run out of state. So I swallowed my sense of dishonesty and asked Dad if he had known Jason Sinai when he was at school—"at school" being a euphemism for the time he spent undercover, infiltrating the SDS, after his return from Vietnam.

And when he answered, I had the feeling that the subject wasn't far from his thoughts, which when you think of it wasn't so far-fetched. I mean, he never told me what business he was on when he came to town, but I suppose I could have guessed that a manhunt for fugitives wanted for a Michigan crime might have involved the station chief of a Michigan FBI office, could I not? He gave the question one of his long thinks while chewing—I had barbecued vegetables out on the porch, because my father is vegetarian since Vietnam—and then answered in his slow, slightly drawly voice.

"You hear the report on them the other night?"

"Um-hmm." The local public radio station had done a long piece on the Bank of Michigan robbery, and I had heard it twice: once on local radio, the second when *All Things Considered* picked it up.

"Huh." He bit, chewed, and watched me through these blue eyes of his, which, more than anything else, reveal that you're not talking to some country-dirt cop. "I never met Sinai, though I saw him around campus. He was too big to speak to us little folk. Those guys, they had a social hierarchy like the military."

Chew. Think. I could see that he was thinking, so I waited, and after a time, he went on in a different tone.

"You know who I did know, Beck? I knew Mimi Lurie."

"Really? When you were undercover?"

"No. I had to avoid her, then. That's the weird part. I knew her when I was a kid. Her parents had a cabin up by Point Betsie; summers, they'd be at church with us."

"Huh?" I had stopped eating and was watching my father with real surprise. "You knew Martin Luria?"

"Yes, ma'am."

"Daddy, for God's sake. Why didn't you ever tell me that before?"

"Never came up. What's so special about him?"

"Well, that he was a Soviet spy, for one thing."

He shrugged. "So they said. Martin Luria—Mimi changed it to Lurie after he killed himself. Poor bastard. He was red, that's for sure. Was he a spy? I don't know that, Beck. I do know that your granddaddy hated Commies as much as J. Edgar Hoover, and he still made us all go to Luria's funeral."

My fork was still hanging in the air. "My granddaddy made you go to the funeral of a known Communist?"

Pause, but not, this time, to chew: he paused to look out the window, not attentively as when he's heard a noise, but absently.

"Communist, Communist. All communism said to someone like Lurie was that the rich in this world are too few and the poor too many." Now he looked at me again. "You know, we were the only people there beside the immediate family and the FBI agents taking pictures of the immediate family. My daddy, when the funeral was over, he shook hands with all the Lurias, and then with all the agents. They worked for him, after all."

"And how were the Lurias?"

"Oh, God, I don't remember. I used to think Mimi's brother was great, sharp as a damn hawk, this kid. Had these eyes like he was Chinese. Always wondered what happened to him."

And that, I can tell you, was my father all over. Works undercover infiltrating the SDS—after returning from Vietnam with bullets up his left thigh and through half his stomach—then becomes a career FBI agent, but feels awful over the red-baiting that came before he was even out of high school. See, Martin Luria had been pretty famous up north: a physicist, a Los Alamos Red, and he'd killed himself by the beach at Point Betsie after losing his teaching job to the blacklist. Listening, I realized that my fork was still poised in the air. "What happened to him?"

Daddy looked confused. "He killed himself. You know that."

"No. The son. Mimi's brother."

"Oh, him. Well, he was in grad school when I was here. Did archaeology. Totally nonpolitical. Supposed to be some kind of genius. Then, I don't know. Someone told me once he went to Turkey, for God's sake, to work on a dig. Apparently, if you're an archaeologist, Turkey's the place to go. He never came back. I never heard of him again. . . ."

I waited, and when he didn't go on, kicked him under the table.

"But?"

"But . . ." My father filled his big chest with a sigh, then leaned back and crossed his legs. "You remember that case last year? That arms dealer they arrested in Phoenix? His conviction got overturned because the AUSA—the assistant U.S. attorney—was having an affair with the perp's daughter?"

"I remember you went to Washington over that. Never knew why."

"Well . . . this is between us, right?"

"Right."

"Why was because the guy—Rosenthal, he was called—some of his transactions were papered through a Saginaw holding company, which got me a week in Washington helping out. But while I was there, I got to see the whole file. And I saw that when the daughter took flight to Europe, we got Interpol to watch her. She ended up taking a job for this Italian businessman, a guy who did a lot of business importing antiquities from Turkey. And, Beck, I saw a picture of this guy, and you could have knocked me down with a feather if I wasn't looking at Peter Luria."

"Did you follow up?" My mouth was open, watching my father. See, this is why you go into criminal work. It is so *interesting*.

"No way. European art market? You get involved in that kind of thing, it's hello investigation, good-bye five years. Besides, there were no grounds for investigation: we weren't looking for extradition, and there was no reason he couldn't hire her. No, I let it go."

"Huh." I started eating again, watching my father. "So when you going to catch Sinai?"

"God, I don't know." He uncrossed his legs now and put his face in his hands, which surprised me quite a bit. Then he looked up. "Truth to tell, Beck, I don't have a lot of heart for this hunt."

I thought about this. The thing was, I didn't ask him a lot about Vietnam. In fact, my mother and I avoided subjects that were close to Vietnam—he had seen and done a lot of horrific things, and very nearly died. As it was, his injury had left him on lifelong hormone replacement therapy, and if you can't figure out what kind of an injury it was from that, then you'll just never know. It wasn't the Jake Barnes injury—thank God for my mother—but the equivalent of a vasectomy, performed by machine-gun fire and without anesthetic. Still, I thought I could maybe ask a little more about Sinai.

"Okay. Why not?"

"Oh, God." He had returned to his food now and was eating steadily. "See, they got a change of venue for the Solarz trial, they're moving it up to Traverse City, and already, the bugs coming out of the woodwork, man, it's intense. Up to Roby's, you'd think it was 1965, the way these bastards are talking."

Roby's was the bar Daddy went to up in Traverse City. "I fought that damn war once, Beck, that's the truth. It was not fun, and I do not want to do it again. And I don't have a lot of heart for any gung-ho manhunt. Sharon Solarz? She's spent the last twenty-five years in jail, you ask me. Living underground is no life at all. I mean"—his plate completely empty now, he put his big hands on the table—"I got to watch every public school to see kids aren't into their daddy's arsenals to shoot up their cafeterias; I got crackheads blowing each other's heads off to get high another sixty seconds; I got whacked-out white militias sealing off farms with barbed wire and buying satellite surveillance of synagogues from Russian companies; and I've got a population of depressed Michiganders who feel ripped off blind by the government and see no reason at all not to turn to crime. I do *not* need a trial of a twenty-two-year-old crime in my jurisdiction, and I do *not* need a bunch of liquored-up vets getting out their MIA black flags over this."

"Daddy, take it easy." Like I always do, I reached over and rubbed my hand on his heart, thinking about the 250 pounds that little thing pumps blood to, and how once it stopped pumping for just a few seconds and nearly killed him. "I hear you. Let's just have some dessert now."

We did have some dessert. Then we watched the news, and played some cards. And finally, toward eleven o'clock or so, I made up the couch for my father—it was the one piece of furniture in my house that hadn't come, used, from Treasure Mart, because he needed a full seven feet to sleep on—and went into my own room. And as always, when my father slept over, it was with particular delectation that I changed into my nightgown and climbed into bed, particular comfort, and a particular sense of safety. If you come to Michigan later this month and meet him, I think you'll see why: to have this man sleeping in your house is to know that whatever happens during the night, terrorists, war, or natural disaster—whatever morning might bring after he leaves, during this night, everything is going to be all right.

Something, in other words, not far from how you felt, in June of 1996, before he abandoned you in the Wall Street Marriott, about your father too.

Date: June 17, 2006
From: "Benjamin Schulberg"
<benny@cusimanorganics.com>
To: "Isabel Montgomery" <isabel@exmnster.uk>
CC: maillist: The_Committee
Subject: letter 25

So, that is all very interesting, Beck's account of those days in Ann Arbor. Very interesting. And worrisome, if you want to know the truth. I mean, her claim that she did not in fact find me the single most seductive man she had ever met in her life, for example. It casts a certain doubt over everything else she has to say. But let it pass.

As for me, if you want to know what I did for the days in between Wednesday and Friday, the answer is absolutely nothing.

Nothing productive, that is.

The heat over town was so intense, so enervating, that I never wanted to leave either my hotel or my car. The only real business I had was with Beck's father, up in Traverse City—or, as they put it in Michigan, up *to* Traverse City—but by now I'd faced up to the fact that he was not going to see me. Just for the hell of it, I kept the pressure on by telephoning his secretary pretty frequently. He was unavailable all day on Tuesday, and on Wednesday failed to return any of my calls. Journalists are supposed to be inured to this kind of thing. Not me: some alcoholic bum in a county jail refuses me an interview, I take it personally. Not very polite of you, Osborne, was my feeling, and in fact I was spending quite a bit of time writing cutting letters to him about it, focusing largely on his obligations as a federal employee to the citizenry, and also mentioning the First Amendment frequently, but in the fight between my indignation and my laziness, I did no more than compose them in my head.

What did I do? I lay around my hotel a lot. I smoked. I drank at a sports bar up near campus, though never, I assure you, before breakfast. I used my mobile Nexis connection on my notebook computer, looking for something, anything, anywhere, that might indicate that someone knew something about where Sinai had gotten to. I called everyone I've ever known in either journalism, law enforcement, or any criminal activity whatsoever. Jay Cohen, out in Los Angeles, who knows as much about people who do things secretly, and illegally, as anyone else in the country, laughed at me.

"You want to find Jason Sinai? Easy. Just sit back and relax, Benjamino. He'll show up. When and where he wants to."

Thanks a lot, Jay. You asshole.

Thanks to the town's many and excellent used bookstores and the fact that my entire life had become a totally useless waste of time, I read, cover to cover, Judy and Stewart Albert's collection *The Sixties Papers,* Stanley Karnow's *Vietnam,* and Ron Jacobs's *The Way the Wind Blew*.

Mostly, however, what I did was I avoided Rebeccah's neighborhood altogether.

See, that was a careful professional calculation. I did not want a source to think of me as some pathetic loser who was hanging around a totally irrelevant town in the Midwest pretending to work because he couldn't think of anything else to do with his vacation.

I certainly did not want her to think of me as some useless geek who was using up his whole vacation and spending his own money on a wild goose chase.

Finally, I did not care to have her thinking of me as a ridiculous bozo who had become convinced that she was his only chance.

His only chance, I mean, of course, to find Jason Sinai.

Because, whatever else may have been going on, and I admit that something else was going on, the fact remained that I knew, with moral certainty, that the way to find Jason Sinai was to hang around Ann Arbor. No, I don't know why I was convinced. I never know why I'm convinced of anything. Yes, I believed on a logical level that Rebeccah's father, sooner or later, was going to become involved in the manhunt. And yes, I knew that Sharon Solarz would soon be extradited back to Michigan, and I could go to her arraignment, and see who else was there, and all that kind of reporter's crap. But that wasn't really it. It was on another level that I *knew* it. I knew it as if the whole shape of what was about to happen, what was on the very verge of exploding, was just waiting for me to discover it. I didn't know what I was going to find, but I knew it was there, and that has been how every good story in my career has worked.

Now, in the interests of my credibility with you, I will admit freely that I had another hunch about Rebeccah. I admit that I had come to suspect that my acquaintance with her was likely to end up with me taking someone hostage somewhere on a rooftop until she agreed to marry me.

But that was easier to explain than my conviction that unlike every other reporter covering this story, I and only I was in the right place, at the right time. That somewhere, somehow, the tiny clue that was going to break this story wide open was going to happen here, and if I could only be around for it, I would be the one to get it.

Call it desperation.

Now let me settle the one big question you will have right away. If I had to choose between using Rebeccah to get to her dad to get my story, and taking Rebeccah to bed, did I know which I would choose?

Yes, I did.

Fuck fugitives. Fuck issues. Fuck Vietnam.

At last Friday night came around, and I—now with Kai Bird's *Color of Truth,* William O'Neill's *Coming Apart,* and Fredric Jameson's *Sixties without Apology* under my belt, was back at the Del, standing at the bar, leaning over an ashtray, drinking beer and bourbon, feeling like I was twelve.

Good Christ, I had it bad. What was I going to say to her? Was she going to stand me up? Did she like me? Was that a zit on my chin? It was as if everything in between high school and now had all been a dream—the college degree from Stanford, the Porter Fellowship at Yale, the three years of beat reporting in Albany—all a dream, and I was an adolescent sitting at a bar in a college town, drinking Dutch courage, feeling terrified.

In short, I was a dead man. I had met the girl two, three times, and she was like a smell in the back of my throat to me, a sense so interiorized, so inward, that I felt I had known her not three, four days, spoken to her on two occasions, but that she was as familiar to me as my own family. I woke, I swear to you, every night since I first saw her, early in the morning hours, with an image of her oval face in my mind. It had been so strange to me, that week. Doing nothing in the middle of nowhere, being all alone, all day long, and yet somewhere in this town she was walking around, and talking, and eating, and sleeping. I'd never, in all of my life, felt anything like what I was feeling now. I never, ever wanted to feel it again.

Jesus, Isabel, I don't know why I'm even telling you this. Except that for me, in the story of the summer of 1996, believe it or not, your father was only a little part of it all. Rebeccah Osborne was the rest.

And then at last, it was Friday night, the minute hand of my watch inching toward ten, and I was back at the Del Rio, sitting at the bar, watching the bartender—the good-looking rude older one again—work the mobbed bar, Keith Jarrett on the stereo. And I had had a couple of beers and a couple of scotch and sodas and a half dozen cigarettes and was wondering whether to look at my watch again or just lower my forehead to the wooden surface of the bar and howl when at last I felt a presence next to me and looked up to see her in jeans and a black silk shirt, standing, looking at me with a grave expression that made my heart first squeeze in my chest, then sit still for a long moment, and then, at last, shoot a jet of pure adrenaline into the center of my being.

2.

"So, Schulberg. You look like you've been sitting here since last we met. Drinking,"

To my surprise, I heard myself speaking. "Not at all. Early to bed, healthy eating, exercise." I paused while the bartender brought her an Elm City, slammed a new drink down on the bar in front of me, and walked away. "Good deeds, religious observance, chastity, charity, piety, patriotism. This bartender does not like me."

Rebeccah looked at the bartender, then back.

"Cleo? Why on earth would she not like you?"

"Not sure. But I do get that vibe."

"Oh, well, so you're a paranoid. That goes with your particular kind of liberalism, doesn't it?"

She had settled onto her stool now, and to speak through the noise, she had to lean quite close to me, which I appreciated. "My father always says, 'You're given a face till you're forty; after that, you have to make your own. You ask me, that woman's done a good job."

"You know her?"

"Yeah, everyone who works downtown in the restaurants knows each other."

She sipped her beer. And I, ignoring her look of distaste, with which I felt quite familiar by now, I lit a cigarette and started talking.

"So, Osborne, I've been thinking it over, and my feeling is, these little sombitches, playing at being revolutionaries with Mommy and Daddy's money. Fuck 'em. It's not just that they were turning the boys our president sent to Vietnam into devils, it's that they risked life and limb all over this land. Their death trip, their stupid orgies, their glorification of Manson. And in the Bank of Michigan, they killed a father of three. I want to see Solarz jailed, and Sinai and Lurie caught. Lurie's dad was a Commie spy, too. And, let's face it, Sinai's a J-E-double-ew."

"Oh, cut it out." But she couldn't help laughing. "Just cut it out. Okay?"

"'Kay." I sipped my beer, watching her over the rim. "How was your dad's visit?"

"Good. You ever catch up with him?"

"Naw, gave up. I know when I'm not wanted."

She laughed again. "I doubt that."

"Ah, you mean I'm not not wanted. That's a relief."

"I don't mean that at all. I mean I doubt you know."

"You ask him about those days at all?"

"A little. He never talks about it that willingly." Then she stopped to think. "How much do you know about my dad?"

"Well, there's the public record. And I asked him a few questions when we met. I know he worked undercover on campus here."

"Uh-huh." She watched me for a second. Then she said, "I don't think those are anyone's proudest memories. Chasing a bunch of college students across country and not being able to catch 'em. You know, I have a professor who was caught by my dad? Jed Lewis, head of the American Studies Department. He's directing my senior thesis. He told me he had to practically walk into the FBI station to get arrested."

"What was he, Weather?"

"Um-hmm. Not a major member, and he left early. But he was wanted on explosives charges, and served time. Some coincidence. Now he's directing my thesis about the siege of Khe Sanh."

"I bet your dad says that no one had ever developed any criminology to capture internal revolutionaries, those days. Hadn't been any since the American Revolution itself. I bet he says they had fixed that deficit by the time the FALN came along."

"No." That seemed, unlike most of what I had to say, to make sense to her, and she nodded. "My dad isn't so interested in Jason Sinai. I think he wishes Sinai would just go underground again."

"Really? Why's that?"

"Oh, he's a lot like you. Feels that the war *in* Vietnam is over, and the war *over* Vietnam should be too."

"Yeah." I nodded, appreciating the tone of the conversation, and she went on.

"Besides, Dad and Mimi Lurie were childhood friends. Isn't that strange?"

3.

So there it was. I remember turning from Rebeccah as if she had said something tasteless, then taking a big hit from my drink to cover my dismay. It was like a bad dream: the absolute center of the ethical dilemma before me rearing its head so early.

I did not—I did *not*—want to be in the position of using this woman for the story.

And yet, on the other hand, it wasn't me who had lied to Osborne, but he who had lied to me. Because *he* had told *me*, as clear as day, when we met for coffee, that he had never met Mimi Lurie.

All this took perhaps ten seconds.

I turned back and said nothing.

But Rebeccah didn't have any reason to think that my hesitation was anything other than the time it took to drink a sip of my drink. She went on readily. "My dad's family had a summer house up in Point Betsie, where the Lurias lived. Way the hell up north."

"Wow." I smiled now, and what I said, you have to admit, could have been meant to change the subject. I certainly meant to change the subject. I think. "Good story, Beck."

"Uh-huh. I asked my mom about it this morning, on the phone. She told me that every year the Luria family would take my dad with them on a camping trip. Martin Luria, he was friends with this Detroit beer baron, Carl Linder—there's lots of Germans in Michigan. Linder had like a three-thousand-acre estate up by Rose City, virgin forest. They say Linder's father bootlegged Canadian whisky from there; bought up the land to protect his trade from Lake Erie. Anyway, when my dad was growing up, summers, the Osbornes and the Lurias would all go and camp there. The locals say that Mimi used it as a hideout, later, when she was underground. That's probably a myth."

I stopped her at that. "Is it possibly true?"

"Sure. Vincent Loonsfoot evaded capture up on the UP for, what, thirty days? Thick woods up there. Someone who knows the territory? Could stay at large a very long time."

In my defense, I have to say that I was edging her off the subject. "What did he think of her once she became a revolutionary?"

She snorted. "I don't think he thought of her as a revolutionary. A spoiled-brat hysteric, more likely."

Drinks arrived, and I insisted on paying. Then I got off her father altogether: "So I gather you agree with him."

"About Mimi Lurie? Sure I do. I'd say just about everyone in the world does, with the exception of you."

"Well . . ." I hesitated and drank half my drink. Then I asked her, "Do you have a pretty good idea of what it was like to be alive in, say, 1969?"

She eyed me a little, almost as if I were setting a trap for her. "What's that mean?"

"I mean . . ." So maybe I was a little drunk. I had been sitting in a hotel room reading about the sixties for a week. Maybe, in fact, I was half crazed. I leaned forward and spoke seriously through the noise of the bar. "Well, what I don't mean is what it was like to drop mescaline and listen to the Moody Blues while having sex at a Summer of Love be-in or any of that shit. I mean, what it was like to be, say, eighteen and facing the draft to Vietnam. Having friends being killed. And watching Johnson on TV. Now wait."

I held up a hand to stop her. "I've been thinking about this quite a bit this week. And I don't mean, like, '63, when your dad volunteered. I mean, '67, when there's already a Vietnam Vets against the war movement. And you're eighteen, right? Johnson is lying to you, and that's a fact, not an opinion. Everyone knows it. And he's such an ugly bastard, this jowly Texas gladhander; he's so transparently phony, you're thinking, how the fucking hell did this guy get to be president, and what the fucking hell is the presidency worth if some total jackass like this can do it? Remember, you're thinking like an eighteen-year-old. Chances are, in fact, you're stoned on that weak dope they had back then, and the whole world looks like a cartoon anyway. And there's this virtual civil war going on, with police and hard hats beating up demonstrators, and all manner of real, horrible violence. If you had been to just one demonstration that flared up, then you know what the sound of wood hitting a skull is, you know in a very personal way what it feels like when the state comes down on its citizenry. And remember, the state isn't treating you like a kid, except of course it won't let you vote. It's sending you to war, it's getting your friends killed, and when hundreds and hundreds of thousands of people say to it, Stop, it's implacable. The state? It's beating you up and putting you in jail, and it doesn't listen to any explanations."

I stopped now, and she, to my relief, answered calmly. "Okay. I know what you mean. I've talked to Professor Lewis about this. And in fact, what he said was quite a lot like what vets say. When the state steps in between what you want and what's actually happening to you at the most basic level—like, you want to be home soaking in Epsom salts but you're being beaten up and dragged into a Black Maria, or you want to be out getting your deer in the woods but instead you're being forced to go down a booby-trapped Vietcong tunnel with a knife in your teeth—it's a devastating experience. People never get over it."

I nodded, grateful to her for what she'd just said. So grateful, in fact, Isabel, that I went on and spoke for quite a while more.

It's that, Isabel, as smart as Beck is—as smart as you are—to a certain degree, understanding your father is not only about facts. It's also about context. It's about understanding that it's 1969, and it doesn't matter which side of the war you're on, on either side, you see every day that the state is causing citizens' deaths. You may support it, you may not, but it is a chilling part of your life. And there's been so much violence: it's so close you can touch it, that mass violence had swept through the South, violence of white Americans against black.

And then what the fuck happens? What happens next? Not only does the war not end; not only is there no accommodation from government; but by Christ, Nixon is elected! Nixon! It's like a nightmare. He brings with him this entire history of anticommunism and COINTELPRO and this vile, antidemocratic red-baiting. And then, one, two, three, there's the bombing of Cambodia, there's Kent State, there's Jackson State. And you're *right* there, right there waiting to go to Vietnam, or watching your friends go, and seeing this fucking all-out slaughter going on, day after day after day.

I said all this to Beck, more or less like I'm saying it to you. Just imagine the choice, on one hand, between this jowly, unhealthy, vile, lying son of a bitch Nixon with his horrid little sidekicks, and on the other hand, this vast movement throughout the country where people are not just getting laid, and getting high, and listening to fine music, and having fun, but to boot, they're right! Remember, this is the war that Martin Luther King called "that abominable, evil, unjust war in Vietnam." What they're saying is so obviously true, you can't believe everyone doesn't know it! The cold war is a damn excuse for an imperialist incursion that's killing millions of foreigners while making billions for American defense contractors. Blacks are being systematically colonized throughout the whole country. Sexual repression and materialistic ambition is the name of the game, and the schools—the schools, with these caricatures of buzz-cut gym teachers and home ec classes taught by ladies in perms—these bogus schools.

And in the middle of this whole thing, what happens? Do you have any idea what happens? Nixon bombs Cambodia. Don't forget, Isabel, not all of the articles of impeachment brought by the U.S. Congress against Nixon were for Watergate. One was for illegally bombing Cambodia: a prosecutable crime if Ford hadn't pardoned him. Nixon bombs Cambodia! And the National Guard kills four Americans in, of all places, Ohio, while they're protesting. And just imagine now: all this being true, I come up and I say to you, Hey, Izzy, this is it, man. Each time we get freer—each step of the way we get more happy, and less tied down, and get better music; each time we open up the universities, and get better drugs, and have more sex—each step of the way, the state comes down harder, and now they are not only killing brothers, man, but white students too. So listen up there, Iz, I think, in a very reasonable and calm way, that it's time to blow something up. You with me or without me?

This is, more or less, what I said to Beck, that night in the Del Rio. And when I finished, she had finished her second beer now, and motioned for another, and her eyes were glistening a little, not just with drunkenness, I felt, but with engagement, and happiness.

"With you all the way. All the way, there, Benjamin. In fact, I feel the same right now. That's the problem. I got a cut rate, phony neo-liberal cracker from Arkansas in the White House, cronying around with his big-business friends, illegally selling arms to the Bosnian Muslims, aiding and abetting in globalization that's playing dice with the economy and sending our environment right to hell, making interns perform sex acts in the Oval Office, and corrupting all the principles of fairness and democracy at every step. Know what I'm going to do? Get some fertilizer and some oil and blow up a federal building."

It had been nice while it lasted. "That's bullshit," I told her, "and you know it. That's like saying that Nazis and partisans were equivalent because they both used machine guns. Or even, say, fundamentalist Muslims and Palestinian intifadistas are the same because they both use bombs. I hate that comparison."

"Nonsense. You're twisting the entire question."

"I'm not. The most basic, most fundamental descriptive statement you can make about Weather and Timothy McVeigh is not that one was right and the other was wrong. And I don't mean the obvious fact that Weather, as far as we know today, didn't kill and McVeigh did. In any case, Weather has all the moral responsibility for encouraging the lefties that did kill, up in Madison and in Michigan and Boston."

Rebeccah was trying to interrupt, but I went on. "The fact is, Weather was making a last-ditch protest against a government that refused to obey the Constitution, and McVeigh was protesting a government *for* obeying the Constitution. Right? All Weather was saying was that this government has to follow what the Constitution says. It has *not* to declare war without Congress. It has *to* protect the Bill of Rights. It has *not* to take up arms against its citizenry when that citizenry avails itself of First Amendment principles. It has *not* to turn the apparatus of the intelligence establishment against its own populace. It has *not* to turn the legislating of our country over to the military-industrial complex. It has *not* to conduct a foreign policy in secret, and then attempt to squash the First Amendment when the press reveals that policy. Period."

She answered so quickly that she practically was pinching the corners of her mouth together to pronounce the words. "Okay. I understand. But the fact remains, the criticism of the radical edge of the antiwar movement isn't from the right. It's from the left. You go speak to Todd Gitlin, Rusty Eisenberg, virtually anyone who was really involved in SDS, and they'll tell you that after Weather took over the national convention of SDS, they put the New Left to death. They'll tell you that they were involved in a movement that could have transformed our entire country, and a gang of thugs—shortsighted thugs on an ego trip and a death trip—ruined everything."

I stared at her. "How do you know this?

"I've met all those guys. Jed Lewis is always having them out here as guest lecturers, and he always invites me to dinner with them."

"That doesn't make sense. Aren't you the enemy?"

"Ben, for Christ sake. It's 1996."

She was watching me quizzically as she said that. But I shook my head. "I don't see that. I don't see any of the divisions of the war healed."

"That's because you only speak to people when they're on the record.

You probably don't even know any vets. You know what this one friend of my father told me? Had done three tours of duty in Vietnam, high ranking in CID, told me the one thing he reproached the Weather Underground with was that they didn't use 'command detonated explosives.' Said that would have been much safer to bystanders than the bombs they did use, which were controlled by timers."

"Aren't you rather contradicting yourself?"

She answered with decision. "Yes. Yes, I am. But so what? My father has his balls blown off in Vietnam, and he can see the other side of the question. Shouldn't we be able to also? Now, tell me something about yourself."

"Like what?"

"Like . . ." She had turned in her seat now to face me, forming a kind of little island of intimacy in the crowded bar, defined by our knees, which were touching. "Where you're from. Where you went to school. Have you ever been convicted of a sex crime. You know, general stuff, like who the fuck you actually are?"

4.

What did I tell her? Well, I told her a lot, and it's all going to stay just where it was then: in the sudden intimacy between us. I told her about my family, my parents, my childhood. I told her about college in Stanford and my famous fellowship at Yale. I told her about my job. And then, under close questioning, I told her about things more personal, things I'm not going to tell you. About Dawn Mahoney, for example. About my ambitions. Maybe I even told her about my novel in progress, I don't know. I was, after all, drunk. What I didn't tell her, however, was the thing most on my mind.

You see, Isabel, people my age, when I was a kid, they didn't see politics the way I did. They had come of age in an incredibly strong economy, had the highest of expectations, and couldn't care less who was president. But it was in the middle of the strongest stock market in history, when money was literally flowing in the streets of cities like New York, that John Keane wrote in the *TLS* that three-quarters of the humans in the world didn't have enough money to buy a book, most people had never, ever made a telephone call, and despite the fact that the World Wide Web was driving the whole world's economy, less than 1 percent of the entire population of the world had ever even been on the Internet at all.

In other words, everything that was true when your father got involved in radical politics as a boy was only truer in 1996, only it had been made worse by globalization. And no one cared! No one, among my peers, cared—or at least very few.

To meet someone like Rebeccah, someone who had come to this kind of political consciousness, who knew as much as she knew . . . I think, Isabel, that Rebeccah's awareness, her interest, and her curiosity, they were more attractive than her breasts under the thin silk of her black shirt that night, and that means they were very attractive, very very attractive indeed.

We closed the bar that night, and because of Rebeccah working in the diner, we were allowed to stay after the bouncer locked the door and Cleo, the mean bartender, gave us a couple of beers for last call. And when they finally told us it was time to leave, we walked out into the empty street, not just me but the pair of us a bit unsteady on our feet.

A wet little wind was blowing, chasing litter up the deserted street, lamps reflecting off the sheen of the sidewalks, like a stage. She led me down across First and, to my surprise, up a little stone culvert to the old train tracks that cut through the west side of town. Up here, out of the streetlight, a high sky of dirty clouds could be seen to be blowing across an inky sky, the clouds visible mostly by the appearance and disappearance of a waning moon. We each took a track and walked, for a time, in the silence of the wind. At last she spoke.

"You know what I think?

"That you should probably drink a whole lot less if you want to be able to balance on train tracks?"

"No." She stepped over and nudged me off my track, then stepped up and, with one hand on my shoulder, balanced along. "About Sinai."

"Oh." My shoulder felt suddenly tense, and she must have felt that too because, to my endless regret, she stepped off the track, walking now with it between us. "No. What?"

She was quiet for a minute. Then she said the following: "I can't help but notice that he's exactly like my father."

I turned to watch her in profile. "In what possible way?"

"In that . . . both of them, the most heroic things they did in their lives? Facing death? Risking everything for what they believed? Killing people, planting bombs?"

She stopped talking, looking down as she walked, and after another moment of watching her, I said: "Yes?"

And now she looked up, smiling. "They both did them for the wrong causes."

Walking next to this woman on the train tracks under a sky of scudding clouds, three-thirty in the morning in the spring of my twenty-seventh year. I nearly skipped, so alive did I feel. Such a big night it was, so filled with gusty breezes, the clouds running so fast, like, it seemed to me, the stream of time itself above my head, and next to me, this perceptive, original being.

We walked in silence off the tracks and through the empty, silent, lilac-scented streets to her house. In front, I stopped and watched her, a cigarette in my mouth, hands in my pocket. For a moment, nothing happened. Then I was just about to turn when she spoke.

"You know something, Ben?"

"Um-hmm?"

"I can't even imagine kissing someone who smells so precisely like an ashtray."

"No?"

"Nope. Just can't imagine it."

Now she walked up the flagstone path to her apartment, and I turned away up the street, still smoking.

But, not to put too fine a point on it, when Rebeccah Osborne woke up the next morning—or later that morning—to go on her daily run, she would have encountered, sitting at the end of the little flagstone path, a half-full pack of Marlboro Reds, and she must have understood what it meant, because she called me later that day at the Days Inn and talked to me for a long time, about nothing.

Date: June 18, 2006
From: "Daddy" <littlej@cusimanorganics.com>
To: "Isabel Montgomery" <isabel@exmnster.uk>
CC: maillist: The_Committee
Subject: letter 26

A field of brown dirt, acres large and surrounded by a barbed-wire fence. A low, flat concrete structure, ringed by plastic boxes and wooden pallets. A metal fence, next to which lean a few huge tractor tires, followed by a border of rusting Merck shipping containers, so far from the sea. Then, green lawns, and a double-spired red-brick church appears, ministering to the little neighborhood of frame houses slowly developing on the edge of the industrial expanse. A half-disassembled Mustang in a driveway. A neat lawn sporting a cast-iron jockey. And now green trees swaying high over the houses, nearly surreal in their luminescent glow: a swimming, cartoonish caricature of summer, motionless in the windless day, backlit by a high, hot, blazing sky. Driving into Dexter, Michigan, in a rented Ford Taurus, I realized, as if for the first time, that it was midsummer. A dry, hot, Michigan midsummer afternoon. And at the thought, all of my senses—sight, smell, hearing—swooned in unison, and I thought, I've seen this day before.

I had left Milwaukee northward in Donal's car a week earlier. This enabled me to cross the Michigan state line midwater on the ferry from Sheboygan, Wisconsin, to Manistee, Michigan. Like that, I could both break my trail and approach Ann Arbor from the north, the last direction anyone would be expecting. That, I knew, was how Mimi would have done it.

That, I knew, was how Mimi would have done it, and if I knew anything about this kind of traveling, it was because I had done so much of it with Mimi Lurie during the four years we were underground together, the five years between the town house explosion and the Bank of Michigan robbery.

Mimi Lurie. On the upper stern deck of the ferry across Lake Michigan, watching for surveillance among the passengers milling on the deck, I saw her as I always saw her, her gray eyes alive, shifting left and right as she took stock of her surroundings, her lower lip between her perfectly white, perfectly even teeth, calculating.

I had known her for two full years even before the town house, I had known her intimately, and never had I seen her as alive as when we had come to be full-time fugitives, constantly on the move, constantly afraid. Plane and train schedules, buses, directions: she absorbed them instantly, retained them precisely, as if enjoying some kind of genetic predisposition to schedules. Each move—to or from an action, a meeting, a safe house; across state lines; through a government office—was a puzzle to her, and she teased it and worried it until, when she made her move, it was so convoluted, so carefully fabricated, that it could only appear, in its utter randomness, to be innocent.

Mimi. The Wisconsin shoreline disappeared into a blue haze at the end of the trail of wake, the two blues of sky and water—approaching, approaching, and then effacing the distant shadow of green, land. I moved to the bow, now watching for the first green glimpse of the Upper Peninsula of Michigan, and I no longer thought of pursuers, or sanitizing my trail, or safety, but of Mimi. For if Mimi was an inventive, resourceful fugitive, always thinking ahead, never was she better than in the great northern woods of Michigan, where she had first learned to live by her own resources. In fact, everything Jim Grant had so famously known about the Catskills—and Jim Grant had three times led the New York State Police through the Blackheads, Mink Hollow, and Devil's Tombstone to search for missing hikers—Jason Sinai had originally learned from Mimi Lurie, here, in the Michigan woods.

Even taking this ferry, here, today. It was thanks to Mimi that I knew that to travel across water made detection much, much harder, for, as Mimi was fond of quoting, "water is a constantly moving and changeable thing." It does not hold a trail, it does not carry scent, and its passage can be arranged through dozens of local, virtually untraceable means. The last advantage was worth, perhaps, more than the others all put together. Water gave you an unparalleled chance to look if someone was following.

That was a chance you had to take advantage of whenever you could.

Earlier that day, in Sheboygan, Wisconsin, under a noonday sun, I had pulled abruptly into the ferry terminal, put the Jeep Cherokee in line, then climbed right out and onto my hood and stared backward. The view was perfect: anyone pulling in here had to come to an immediate stop, and a car deciding to drive on would be sure to show some hesitation. As for the people around me, I was unconcerned with what they thought: there could be any number of reasons why a man would do what I was doing: standing on top of a car, a salute over my eyes against the sun. Say, looking for my wife. "She's coming up from our place in Oak Park with the kids and the dog; me from downtown. Figured we'd stay in touch by cell, but damn battery's out again—I cannot remember to recharge that thing. Hell if I know whether she's already crossed or not." I rehearsed the explanation to one of the other white middle-aged males in line standing next to their Explorer, or Suburban, or Jimmy. My company was Donnelley, the massive midwestern web printer—web in the old sense. We were up to our cabin in the woods in Point Betsie. I rehearsed it, but I didn't say it: as long as no one was paying me any attention, there was no reason to interact.

But no one asked, despite the geniality with which I gazed, casually, around at my fellow passengers. And no one was following. On the boat, I bought a Heineken and drank it, watching the wake west: Lake Michigan at two o'clock on a late June afternoon, pleasure boats moving at random pattern behind them; a tanker going in to Chicago; a regatta at distance to the right. As the Wisconsin shoreline disappeared, I examined the other passengers, slowly, carefully sectioning off quadrants of the deck and looking at faces. No one moved in a way that might be anything other than the random milling of boat passengers. No one looked at me with a casual glance that was not casual. No one looked first at me, then at someone else. That didn't mean that Wisconsin police hadn't followed me to the shoreline and called ahead, nor did it mean that the ferry's bridge was not in touch with the police: the disadvantage of a ferry was that everyone knew where it was going. But that, too, had its advantages: if someone were waiting on the Michigan coast to start running a surveillance pattern, the weak point of their operation would be the start.

And I was watching.

I wore khaki shorts and a black T-shirt with a pocket, neither bought with Donal at Banana Republic but afterward, at a Gap. I wore my hairpiece, under a Cubs cap, but the phony mustache had been replaced with a real one, grown in and dyed black and part of an emerging goatee. I wore sunglasses, a camping model with side panels protecting from peripheral glare, and the picture was completed by, visible through the back window of the Cherokee, a backpack and sleeping bag, a tent and binoculars, a canteen, a fishing pole, a camping shovel, a packable tackle box, and sticking out the back window, a molded plastic kayak. I had bought it all from an advertisement I'd seen in a Laundromat bulletin board in Racine, when I'd gone to get my passport.

If anyone had asked, at home in Chicago I was a pressman in the Donnelley plant, the one down by the convention center. That was easy—I'd worked a web press out in California in 1973, just after the Pine Street factory had been busted, when like everyone, I was rebuilding my thing from the ground up. And if I met anyone who worked for Donnelley—unlikely, but I'd be sure to ask first—I did the same job, but at Edwards Brothers in Ann Arbor, and if they knew people at Edwards, I was new, just moved up from Pennsylvania. Just to be safe, on the way to the ferry, I'd gone to Madison and stopped at a cybercafé; done a search on web printing and come up with the on-line version of *Production Weekly* from Ziff Davis, in which I'd been able to familiarize myself with the issues a pressman would be apt to discuss nowadays: on-demand printing, computer-generated plates.

I had another reason to get on the Internet. After reading *Production Weekly* on-line, I went to www.uofm.edu and did a search at the University of Michigan faculty directory. Then I went to Hotmail, opened a new account in the name of Paul Potter—a name anyone my age recognizes as a onetime president of SDS—and sent a single e-mail to jedlewis@uofm.edu. When that was done, I continued east to the ferry, slowly, convolutedly, stopping often and always looking back.

• • •

By the time I came to the ferry and stood up on my hood, watching the cars pull up, shading my eyes against the high sun with a salute, I'd been sleeping out of the back of Donal's Cherokee for four days, making a slow way from Milwaukee north to Racine, over to Madison, slowly putting my character together, pausing at the little intersections of inspiration and luck to add details to my emerging identity. It had been inspiration to stop at every Laundromat I passed to see if there was a neighborhood bulletin board, luck to find the grunged-out car mechanic selling his father's old stuff. The mechanic's father had been a serious camper, served in Korea, died the year before of bone cancer. The mechanic didn't give away much about whether he had liked his father or not, just waited while I looked quickly through the things, spread out in the living room of his father's small house, his mother sitting, back to us, in the kitchen. I went back to the Laundromat, washed the sleeping bag in the industrial capacity machine. Waiting, I read in a local paper where the cost of paper, a big industry here, was rising due to a new environmental initiative passed by Wisconsin's left-leaning legislature. Seemed midwestern printers were going as far as the Scottish Highlands, where years of forest planning was starting to yield the first harvests of spruce, for paper.

That was a good day, three solid pieces falling into place.

Other days were not so good. South of Grayling on the 75, a state trooper pulled up next to me, looked up at me with attention, spoke to his partner, and looked back for a long moment. I looked down at the cop, nodded, then back at the road. When after a full thirty seconds—horrible seconds, each one longer than the one before; familiar seconds, nearly identical to those Mimi Lurie spent on the Troy, during the Coast Guard search—they were still next to me, I looked back and with an interrogative expression motioned my head to the verge, mouthing, "Should I pull over?" The cop shook his head, and only then did the cruiser pull ahead of me and into the distance.

Worry grasped at me for a long time after that. I left the highway at the next exit and drove north on two-lane roads, reading a map next to me on the seat. In the Big Rapids State Park I registered, put my car next to a trailhead, and hiked into the woods. Then I left the trail and doubled back, making a bivouac fifty yards uphill from the trailhead and watching my car through the binoculars. If there were anything like a nationwide search for me they would, I knew, include the state parks registry—the local federal marshal's office would be sure to check the park ranger's log, since the vast northern woods were made for criminals. I watched for two days, lying there virtually without moving but to wriggle my sleeping bag over my body during the nights. I'd brought no food, so I didn't eat; I had luckily had a fresh thermos of black coffee in the car, which I drank in tiny sips, carefully keeping a caffeine headache at bay. For two days no one came. Still, I spent another two days carefully picking my way downstate again on local roads, circling back through parking lots, side streets, to look for anyone who might be following.

Was any of it necessary? Perhaps I had shaken off a pursuer; perhaps there was no one there to elude. The ID was good; the news reported me consistently as missing, the issue kept alive by the steady progress of Sharon Solarz's arraignment in Ann Arbor. But each occasion of caution mathematically steepened the probability curve of my getting caught, and if so far that curve was, happily, an abstraction, the time could come when mathematics became very real indeed.

More important, maybe, was that if I were going to succeed in what I had in mind to do, I felt I owed it to Mimi to travel not just clean, but very clean.

On the boat, I watched Wisconsin disappear into a blue haze at the end of the trail of wake, the two blues of sky and water approaching, approaching, and then effacing the distant shadow of green land.

When the green disappeared entirely, I walked to the front of the boat, peering into the distance until in a precise reverse process, Michigan appeared.

Saginaw. Altogether, it was two days for me to cross the state of Michigan, watching behind, and when I was convinced I was clean, I drove into town and rented a U-Haul Storage shed, one of twenty-five garages built into the ground floor of a largely deserted warehouse, up the 75 behind a multi-acre generating facility. The clerk, an Indian or Pakistani boy, clearly filling in for his father, was eating a curry while he worked with an *Eight Is Enough* rerun on a black-and-white TV. That was why he neglected to check my driver's license when I placed it—admittedly at an inconvenient angle—on the counter. I quickly pocketed the card lest the boy remember and wrote an invented name on the contract. This, I took as a big—big—piece of luck.

In the storage garage I neatly packed the Korean vet's belongings and with regret parked Donal's Cherokee—I did not want to part with it, but the Pakistani or Indian boy's error, which left no paper trail to Robert Russell, made it an unmissable chance to break the chain between me and Donal. Inside the storage garage, by the light of a bare, low-wattage bulb, I found the clothes I'd bought with Donal where I'd carefully packed them on the inside of the zip-up cover holding the spare wheel. I dressed now in black jeans, a blue denim shirt, and Timberland boots, and packed the rest of the clothes into a small leather bag. I took also my toiletries and makeup. Then I locked the storage garage, pocketed the key, and walked the side of the road back into town.

In a motel room, that night, local TV advertised a secured credit card to credit risks. "Foreclosure? Bankruptcy? Bad or no credit? Visit the Credit Doctor." Immediately following the thirty-second spot, it was repeated in Spanish. In the morning I secured a card with two thousand of the dollars my brother had given me, paying an annual charge for the card of three hundred dollars. The Credit Doctor also offered loans as low as fifty dollars, on a hundred percent interest, provided the borrower was ready to have the Doctor electronically receive payment directly from the borrower's employer. I found a Rent a Buggy franchise next and rented a 1991 Ford Taurus. On the floor, under the seat—I was hiding my makeup there, having slit the carpet with a single-edge razor blade—I found a card from an auto repossession company.

And so it was in a 1991 Ford Taurus that I approached Dexter, Michigan, some thirty miles west of Ann Arbor, through Michigan countryside of a nearly surreal green, a swimming, cartoonish caricature of summer, shimmering in the windless day. And so it was I thought, I've seen this day before, and my senses swooned in unison, sight, smell, hearing. I've seen this light dropping from a high Michigan sky of pastel blue; I've smelled this dry heat, tinged with balsam from the great softwood forests to the north; I've heard the vast ululation of silence through these fields of green; and I've tasted this sense that nothing is real, nothing is real.

And at the thought such a wave of familiarity poured through me, for of course, such a sentiment was an old, old one, felt by a near child, a college student, who first came to Dexter with Jed Lewis nearly thirty years before.

Date: June 19, 2006
From: "Jed Lewis" <jeddy@cusimanorganics.com>
To: "Isabel Montgomery" <isabel@exmnster.uk>
CC: maillist: The_Committee
Subject: letter 27

Paul Potter. Paul Potter, with a Hotmail address.

A surprising e-mail, to put it mildly.

In 1965 Paul Potter was the president of SDS and the author of a speech delivered at an early march on Washington that I can still quote by heart. I should be able to: standing in front of the Washington Monument on April 17, 1965, Paul Potter convinced me in three statements, echoing across a sea of people, that everything in my life had to change.

First he said:

> The further we explore the reality of what this country is doing and planning in Vietnam the more we are driven toward the conclusion . . . that the United States may well be the greatest threat to peace in the world today. That is a terrible and bitter insight for people who grew up as we did.

Then he said:

> I do not believe that the President or Mr. Rusk or Mr. McNamara or even McGeorge Bundy are particularly evil men. If asked to throw napalm on the back of a ten-year-old child they would shrink in horror. But their decisions have led to mutilation and death of thousands and thousands of people. What kind of a system is it that allows good men to make those kinds of decisions?

And finally, in the calm and humble passion of his delivery:

> I believe that the administration is serious about expanding the war in Asia. The question is whether the people here are as serious about ending it. Maybe we, like the President, are insulated from the consequences of our own decision. Maybe we have yet really to listen to the screams of a burning child and decide that *we cannot go back to whatever it is we did before today until that war has ended*.

Paul didn't mean to convince me to do what I did for the fifteen years after I heard that speech. I went much beyond anything he ever did, including participating in the illegal and immoral dismantling of his SDS, including engaging in multiple fistfights with multiple policemen, including planting numerous bombs at numerous targets, including being arrested again and again, including meeting with my country's enemies on foreign shores, including plotting the illegal overthrow of my government. But he never stopped being my dear friend, not even the years I was underground, and when he died in 1984 of cancer, a larger part of my happiness than I cared to admit died too.

His was the first death of a friend between 1970, when the town house blew up, and 1984, and as it turned out, the first of the slow series of deaths of friends—from cancer, from accident, and from suicide—that all of us experience on the other side of fifty.

In retrospect it strikes me as fitting.

Paul ended my innocence about life in 1965, and some twenty years later he ended my innocence, too, about death.

When, therefore, in April 1996, I got an e-mail from Paul Potter, barring the improbable existence of an Internet Service Provider from the Great Beyond, I felt strongly that it must be from someone else. You see, I am a highly trained academic. My mind leaps to these insights.

Like a gazelle.

For a time I contemplated the e-mail on my university-issue Mac in my Angell Hall office—my extremely good corner office, overlooking campus and guarded by a secretary, as befit the chair of the Honors Program, which I was in 1996—not bad for a person who had been on academic probation from 1970 to 1980, while on the FBI's most-wanted list.

> Well, I remember it's Brendan's birthday coming up. What are you going to get him? Not shoes again? How about a barrel of those big pickles I loved when I was a kid?

I looked at this e-mail for a long time.

Then I erased the letter and left the office. In a moment, I came back and set the computer's hard drive to defragment—naggingly, I'd reflected before I'd left the building that the erase command only trashed the name; the file remained on the hard drive until it was reformatted, or—which also worked—defragmented.

I crossed the campus in noonday sun, a man of fifty whose age showed neither in his hair, which was full, nor in his carriage, which was straight, nor in his clothes, which—during summer semester anyway—were virtually the same jeans and T-shirt I'd have worn on this same campus thirty years before, but in his face, where wrinkles radiated out from the corners of his eyes, and his stomach, which had grown. My son, Brendan, had a birthday on July 1, which was a few days away, a Monday. But why would I get him shoes? I walked across campus, down Liberty into Sam's Shoes, where I wandered, looking: Stride Rite, Timberland, Sebago, Dexter.

Dexter.

From nowhere, like a soap bubble rising and bursting, I saw big German pickles served out of a tub in a dark bar. It was somewhere I'd been with Jason, somewhere not far. We had driven there. It had been summer. And the town it had been in had been . . . Dexter.

Now it came back to me in a detailed memory. It was during the building of the I-94 overpass, and we'd gone right into the Army Corps of Engineers field office to requisition dynamite. Nan, who had in this action as in most done all the intelligence out of a secretarial job for a related company, had gotten it all: letterhead, paperwork, company routine—all the way down to floor plans of the field office's entrance, allowing us to walk in, wearing jeans and hard hats and carrying rolled-up blueprints, talking casually, and go directly to the right office. Nan had gotten it all, and so solidly, so competently, that we hardly felt afraid handing in the forged requisition form.

Nan, myself, Jason, and Mimi: this was the Ann Arbor "affinity group," later "cell." Mimi planned, Nan executed. Nan was a mole, they used to say, but Mimi was a field officer. Nor was it lost on your father and me that we were rank and file. Waiting for the Army Corps office to fill the order, we'd done what troops do everywhere: stood in a bar, drank too much, a bravado to show each other how unscared we were. Mimi watched into the window of the office from a parked car with binoculars, and when she saw that the explosives had been pulled and packed in four little wooden boxes, she'd walked into the bar, ignoring us, and ordered a Stroh's. If she had ordered Bud, we would have walked out and split up to the two parked cars, your father waiting for Mimi to join him, me waiting for Nan. As was, Little J and I finished our beers, went out and picked up the dynamite, and drove it straight from Dexter across the country to Oregon, knowing that crossing the other way, to Michigan, was dynamite that had been stolen out there. That, too, was a Mimi invention: the risks of transporting explosives, she said, were less than the risks of being traced ex post facto by a chemical signature found at the site of the explosion. That's why, insofar as the FBI ever traced any of our explosives, they never found the suppliers—at least, not within two thousand miles of the explosion itself.

Okay. Now I knew who had e-mailed me, and what he wanted. That is, I knew Jason Sinai wanted me to meet him on July 1, a Monday, Brendie's seventeenth birthday, at the bar that served big German pickles out of a tub in Dexter, Michigan.

Not a small thing to ask the chair of the Honors Program, holder of an endowed chair in the humanities at the U of M, ex officio of the Guggenheim Nominating Committee, and MacArthur Fellow. Not a small thing to ask him to meet a fugitive, wanted on charges of murder and kidnapping, the subject of a nationwide manhunt.

On July 1, a Monday, the first thing I did was wish my seventeen-year-old son—whom I had to wake for the purpose—a happy birthday, and present him with his present: a book of practice SAT tests. Then I went through two of them with him: Brendan Lewis had spent far too much of the previous year stoned to be sure of getting into the U of M, where baby boomers' kids competing for admission—not to mention the private-school kids from New York—had made even in-state entrance questionable except for the strongest students. This took the better part of the morning, but finally when I finished battling the boy through the two tests, I also gave him a 1976 Stratocaster I'd battled even harder for on eBay. I accompanied it with a short commentary, of course, on what, for him, passed for music. Brenden listened with forbearance—my son's musical interest tended toward the Beastie Boys, intersecting with mine only once at Jimi Hendrix. While Nan, smiling, watched the boy holding the guitar in awe, I watched Nan, and while I watched, I debated whether to tell her what I was doing. By the time Brendan took off to show his girlfriend the guitar, I had made my decision, against.

Not that she would have been scared. In the days, Nancy McGinn had been a far more prominent member of Weather than I, had planned and executed some of the most daring actions, and now, as an adult, was still ahead of me, as a doctor and—since Brendan had grown up—a frequent traveler for Médecins sans Frontières.

Nan, in fact, probably could have planned what I was about to do better than I. Still, something decided me in favor of secrecy. A lot was at stake in meeting Jason Sinai, more than enough to outweigh the demands of communal interest in favor of the demands of compartmentalization. I was quite sure that Nan would agree.

So without telling my wife what I was doing, I dressed in my bike clothes and, carrying my helmet, left the house.

The bike allowed me to cross from Awixa Road to Highland Drive, through the Arboretum, out by the hospital, and against traffic all the way across town to Main Street, where I wheeled it inside the Avis office. Already Nan would have been unhappy with me: I'd *washed* rather than *cleaned*—washed away the chance of being followed rather than analyzed it and identified any possible followers. She, who had with Mimi evolved a virtual religion around how to detect a tail, would not have approved one bit.

Against that, however, was my absolute surety that I was under surveillance. I absolutely could not believe that the FBI would not be watching me if they were looking for Jason. They would have to be deeply stupid not to, and I was no longer convinced that they were that stupid. Sometimes, even, I found myself supporting them. Waco, for example. And if they were following me, then a washing, quick and dirty, as I had just done, was appropriate: I didn't need to identify people I was already assuming were there.

In the Avis garage I carefully packed my bike into the trunk of a Dodge Intrepid, which I had arranged to have rented for me by the departmental secretary on a university account, in case my credit card records were subpoenaed. Then, sheltered by the open trunk, I took a pair of jeans out of my bag, slipped them on over my bike shorts, tucked in my T-shirt, put on a baseball cap, and slammed the trunk shut. Finally I pulled onto Main Street and out to the Huron River Drive toward Dexter, noting with satisfaction the empty road behind me.

Reflecting that I would likely not recognize Jase.

Wondering what Jase had in mind, coming to Michigan, finding me.

Never once, however, questioning what I was doing, now, putting my entire life of the past twenty-five years in jeopardy, risking my family and safety, to see my old comrade when my comrade was wanted by the law.

Date: June 19, 2006
From: "Daddy" <littlej@cusimanorganics.com>
To: "Isabel Montgomery" <isabel@exmnster.uk>
CC: maillist: The_Committee
Subject: letter 28

Did I think Jed was going to show?

On balance, I think not. I was open, though, to the possibility that he would. And in any case, that afternoon of July 1, I found myself attracted by the very starkness of the possibilities.

Life, I was thinking, hardly ever gets as clear as it as now.

Dexter, Michigan. A booth at the back of the Sportsman bar. The bar darkened against the afternoon sun, all mahogany, all smoke, all the murkiness of a place where light was totally unnecessary to the business of men drinking seriously, all just the way it was twenty-five years ago and more. The only nod to the present was the races from Saratoga on high-definition satellite TV. Other than that, the horrors of the present were as if still a quarter century away.

Life, I was thinking, sitting in the furthermost booth in the dark bar, drinking more beer than I had drunk in the past twenty years all together, watching the windows casting through the half-closed venetian blinds, narrow bars of light against the smoky air—life hardly ever gets as clear as this.

Three choices. If Jed showed, then I stood a chance of coming closer to what I was looking for. If the police came, then the run was over, and I had lost everything. And if no one came? *Don't waste time trying to answer questions you don't have the data for*. Mimi's voice, sounding the old rule, as if reverberating within my skull.

My job, for the instant, was to wait. As so often in these things, waiting was the hardest job.

I, Jason Sinai, in a bar. A handsome, determined man, handsomer than even my disguise alone would have made me, due to the fact that people look their best when they are facing danger. Their skin flushes, their features set, their eyes hold their steadiest gaze. Perhaps they look their worst—pale, drawn—when they're scared, but surely they're at their best when they're being brave.

There are two consolations in facing real danger—which few of us ever do—as opposed to running from imagined danger—which happens all the time.

The first is how good it makes you look.

The second is how free it makes you feel.

I, Jason Sinai, alone in a bar. A bar I had last been in during an operation to procure dynamite, in 1969. We'd used the dynamite in four different bombings, and never was any connection made with the I-94 construction in Dexter, Michigan, never, to this day. Now I was back in that bar after twenty-six years, and for the first time it occurred to me that, these twenty-six years later, I had not only escaped capture for the robbery of the explosive, for the bombing itself, but I had somehow remained free. And for the first time since leaving you, a deep sensation of that freedom passed through me.

Isabel. Should I try to describe that day in the Sportsman's bar, Dexter, Michigan?

Let me put it this way. Buddhists say enlightenment is preceded by four glimpses of freedom. I had long felt that two such glimpses had come my way, both years ago while I was fugitive.

Once, I felt I had glimpsed freedom as an ideal for which I was fighting—freedom from a whole system of repressive rules, of course, but a freedom deeper than that: the freedom that comes, as the Port Huron Statement put it, from seeking what might be unattainable but what was a liberation, in its very pursuit, from the unimaginable.

Another time I felt I had glimpsed freedom as what I was living as I crisscrossed the country under phony names: freedom from the expectations that defined me; freedom from the oppressive; above all, freedom from the constant awareness of an unwitting network of police, computers, tax collectors, doctors, schools. To be unknown. To be anonymous. Together, they meant to be autonomous, in a way that few people ever experienced in their lives.

Both experiences had been greatly potent, so much so that it became a question I was always asking myself, in the long, searching, torturous exercises we called "self-criticism sessions," in the soul-searching kind of conversation we used to have, whether I was more fundamentally motivated by a selfish wish to feel free than a revolutionary principle. For there was, at the heart of the experience, something in being a fugitive I valued more than any other experience of my life. A fundamental freedom, one that I had never been able entirely to define. Was it the chance no longer to be yourself? Was it having no responsibility? I wasn't sure.

And thinking of that, now, in a bar in Dexter, Michigan, I experienced what I now think of as my third glimpse of freedom.

It was the first time I was here, with Jed, that I had first committed myself irrevocably to ending what I had been becoming and to becoming who I was, in fact, to become. Jed was older than me, had been in SDS while I had been in high school, and in his person I had first seen the possibility of transforming myself. They were still so clear to me, then, the inexorable dullness of the years that came before, living in my parents' vast West Village town house. The big Sinai family gathering for Passover, for Rosh Hashanah, in the same rooms where I could still remember watching the Army-McCarthy hearings on my parents' first black-and-white television. The Sinais, Singers, and Levits: a collection of vested American interests and middle-class ambitions that gathered a few times a year in my father's rambling house; a collection of hypocrisies too varied for me to catalog, and yet which I knew, at sixteen, at seventeen, at eighteen, were more than I could bear.

There in that bar in Dexter, Michigan, where I had been twenty-five years before, drinking beer after years of abstinence, I remembered how I had seen myself, the product of a liberal arts education, carrying the expectations of postwar America. Twelve years of private school education, an education specifically arranged by Old Left New Yorkers virtually indistinguishable from my own parents, Little Red Schoolhouse, Elizabeth Irwin. And all the while my parents and their self-congratulatory friends built their schools, and did their jobs, and had their parties and meetings and arguments; all the while they carried their candles in midnight vigils, voted for Kennedy, Humphrey, McCarthy, the big machine churned on.

Why couldn't they see it? To me, it was so obvious, and I was only a high school student. Their pacifism and their complacency, their money and their houses and country houses, the steady rise in their fortunes through the farce of the war against Hitler, the Holocaust he carried out with virtual impunity, the cold war evil of America's compromised process of de-Nazification. And all the while they got richer, had children, collected honors, and argued their arguments in the pages of the *Nation,* all the while, McCarthy rose, the Rosenbergs were killed, Mississippi happened, and the war in Southeast Asia grew, and grew, and grew.

Sitting there, drinking, waiting for Jed, I could remember the exact feel of it, the texture of evenings in the Bank Street house, smoking dope in my room, door locked against my brother, while outside in the garden my parents and their friends drifted in one of their endless arguments, Israel, Castro, Czechoslovakia. SNCC, Marcuse, Mills, Mailer. Phil Ochs and Lenny Bruce. My father had fought in Spain. My father still limped, in 1969, from shrapnel taken at the defense of Cape Tortuga. And now what was he if not a *liberal,* a comfortable New Yorker arguing in the backyard of his town house while that red-hating, imperialist, warmongering pig Johnson and his henchmen rained liquid fire on Southeast Asia. I was thirteen when JFK was killed, and even then I'd known that the world had tragically, horribly, lost a murderous, dangerous phony. Why hadn't my father known? *Liberal*. It was the worst insult I could think of.

I, Jason Sinai, your father. Forty-six years old. In a bar in Dexter, remembering with drunken clarity the rage that had animated me a quarter century ago when I was barely older than you are now, and the freedom I'd glimpsed, one day, in this same bar. It was that I couldn't stand the roles available to me. I couldn't stand it: doctor, lawyer, professor, politician. Living and dying in the compromises of my parents. Nothing that was available to me in my parents' expectations could offer me a way out. I could make more money, I could have greater exposure. I couldn't, however, be any more involved than they were, nor could I be any less of a phony.

Unless I got out.

And as my mind cycled into that train of thought, that familiar train of thought that I had followed all those years ago, I remembered, not for the first time, but more strongly than I had before, what it had felt like, the very first day I came to Ann Arbor in 1968, when I'd walked into the SDS offices on Hill Street—before I even went to my dorm room—and met Billy Ayers and Diana Oughton.

Now, in 1996, I was not sure I could even stand to be in the same room as Billy, and Diana, of course, was dead. For so long had I felt such horror at having been a part of Weather—regret at the risks we had taken, remorse at how mean we had been to each other, and foolishness at what we had done to the left—that the real experience, the original experience, had become lost to me.

Sitting at the bar in Dexter, drinking too much and waiting for Jed to show or not to show, it came back to me with shocking clarity, those fall days of 1968 when I first came to Ann Arbor, and first went to the SDS headquarters on Hill Street, and first realized that all the while I, in New York, was figuring out for myself what liars the Kennedys were, these guys already knew it. All the while I, an adolescent smoking dope in my room, was figuring out why my parents' long history of leftism that started in Spain had become a compromise, a lie, these guys already knew it, and not only did they know it, they had argued it, analyzed it, written it, and were, most importantly, acting on it.

Not for the first time, but with a clarity fueled by alcohol and the absolute bizarreness of the fact that I was back in Dexter, a place I had never thought to visit again as long as I lived, I remembered the clean, serious awareness I had experienced, standing at this bar with Jed while we waited for Mimi's signal. Pretending not to be scared. Aware that we were taking steps from which there was no coming back, no coming back. And in the glow of Jed's eyes, I knew that Jed was feeling it too.

These people. I saw them suddenly neither as I had come to see them over the quarter century of my adulthood—as arrogant, violent, deluded young children of privilege, stealing SDS and cheating their friends—nor as I thought of them now, as middle-aged people with only a hint of the beauty that had once been theirs, but as I saw them then: big-hearted, articulate, brave, beautiful. Billy Ayers, Kathy Boudin, Ellen Radcliff, Bernardine Dohrn. Suddenly I could vividly see each and every one of them, their names, their aliases, the actions they were in. Cathlyn Wilkerson, David Miller, Nancy Ruth, Paul Millstone, Marsha Cole, Richard Rudd, Lou Cohen. Michael McGinn, Sharon Gresh, Judith Freed, Ann Delaney. Their names flooded into my consciousness, names of people I had not thought about in years and years. Teddy Gold and Terry Robbins. David Gilbert. They had, to a one, been older than me, upperclassmen when I was a freshman, the ones who had gone before. After the town house bombing, and the decision was taken to go underground, Mimi and I had been two of the very last to be picked to join them. The ones left behind, the ones who had not been picked, they were devastated. But the ones who were picked, the ones who made the cut, we had been free.

I had been waiting too long, I knew. I had been drinking too much: after years of not drinking, the beer was buzzing in my ears, and my vision had the clarity of real drunkenness. And yet it was there, sitting in this bar in Dexter, that for the first time in twenty years and more I remembered what it was we had fought for, what it was we had risked our lives and even worse, made fools of ourselves for. It was for this feeling: this feeling of clarity, of courage, of strength—of freedom.

Life, I thought in words that pronounced themselves with clarion clarity, hardly ever gets this clear. There were three choices. I would be okay, or I would not be okay, or nothing would change. Jed would show up, or I would be arrested, or I would go on looking. There was simply nothing else that could happen, and therefore nothing to imagine, nothing to plan, and above all, nothing to fear. And for long seconds, as I sat, I glimpsed, for the third time in my life, what it was to be free, not because of an ideal or a hope, but because there were simply no more choices.

And in the middle of that feeling, the door opened in the front of the bar and out of the square of blinding sun framed in the open doorway a silhouetted figure entered, stopped, observed, then crossed the room toward me slowly. I, blinking against the light, watched as my eyes adjusted again to the darkness and the figure revealed itself as a middle-aged man who once had been my friend and comrade in freedom.

2.

"Are you the person I'm looking for?"

It had not occurred to me that Jed would not recognize me, but of course he didn't. Nor did it occur to me that there would be so little affection in his manner. It should have: Weather was a competitive organization, and Jed and I had competed for status, for assignments, and for women. These were old wounds, and they did not appear to be healed now. Looking up from my seat at the man in front of me, a portly, somehow outsize middle-aged man who bore some distant, nearly imaginary resemblance to a kid I had known, I nodded. "I am."

"Mind giving me some proof?"

"Not at all."

Jed had evidently thought about this, for he asked two questions relating to specific crimes, one committed by him, one committed by me, neither of which I intend to describe to you now. When I'd answered correctly, he sat down.

"You're in a great deal of shit, aren't you?"

I nodded again, and this time I smiled. "Hi, Jed, how are you these twenty-five years? Nice to see you, old friend."

Lewis actually grimaced. In a false voice, he answered: "Fine, thanks. Great to see you, too. What do you want?"

But I went on. "You look awful. Fat and fifty."

"You probably do too, under that disguise. What the fuck do you want, Little J? I don't have time for this."

"I want to know where Mimi Lurie is."

Jed shrugged, unimpressed. "Why, you planning on turning her in?"

This time, I didn't answer. Finally, Jed ran his hands over his face. "I'm sorry. I'm sorry I said that."

"That's okay." I answered in a softer voice now. "Why you coming on so strong, Jeddy? Seems to me our differences have aged a lot quicker than what we had in common."

"Okay, okay. I'm sorry. I just don't know what you want from me. You know the risk I'm running to be here. For Christ sake, Little J." He looked up again now in a fresh access of anger. "I'm the chair of the Honors Program. Do you know how hard I worked to get to this? Do you know how many people would love to see me get screwed for failing to report a known fugitive?"

"Yes, I do know." I answered without any hesitation, I assure you. "I know exactly the risk you're taking, and I know exactly how many people there are in your horrid profession who'd like to see you lose your job. Okay?"

"So why are you making me run this risk?"

"Give me a chance, I'll tell you. Listen: you came here, I assume you felt you were clean?"

"Sure of it."

"Then let's have a couple drinks, okay? I been living out of the back of a car for the past week. And I don't have that many friends right now."

And so we talked. For a great long time, we talked. Talked like I had never, in all of my time as Jim Grant, talked with anyone. You know what it was like, Izzy? It was like singing. Open-throated, full-chested singing. For the first time since 1974, I talked openly with someone who knew who I was, who knew where I came from, and from whom I had nothing to hide.

Maybe for Jeddy, too, it was a pleasure. Gradually he relaxed, and then he began drinking beer, and then—with me—bourbon, and after a while we took turns walking out and smoking one of a few joints that Jed had brought with him. We did it purposefully, with the same abandon with which we'd gotten together and dropped acid when we were on the run: an act of faith, to lose control, to risk everything, and feel the faith that we'd come out okay on the other side. Like we used to say: "We're not free unless we act free. And free people get high."

And I remember saying to him, at one point during what turned into an afternoon and evening of serious drinking, something like this:

"Jesus, you know, all those years of being Jim Grant, man. I was so *focused*. All the time, I was like . . . like when you're stoned, and you have to cook dinner, and you get analysis paralysis? And the thing looks impossibly complicated to you, you know, you've got all the details blown out of proportion, and you see the clock moving, and you can't decide what's the first step, and you're overanalyzing each thing? Should I get the water boiling for the beans first, or start sautéing the onions, or put on the rice, and fuck—do we have garlic? That kind of thing?"

"Sure." Laughing, Jed looked like himself now. "Sure I know. Happens to me twice a week, still."

"Yeah. So you take a page from the Buddha, right? You think, here I am, I'm cutting this fucking carrot, and all the hell I'm going to do is cut this fucking carrot. Then I'm going to do something else. Right?"

"Right."

"That's how Jim Grant was. So focused: first on school, then on marriage, then on work, then on . . . on fatherhood." I paused for a moment, focus lost, looking into the distance. Then I shook my head. "And I never thought about anything that happened before '76. Before B of M. I mean, I *was* Jim Grant, through and through. And I hated everything I'd ever been before. And now . . . now that I'm myself again, now that I'm on the run again, you know what? It's all coming back to me. Jeddy, we fucked up so bad."

He was still smiling, as if he'd heard it all before. "I know we did. But we did a lot right, too. Never ratted anyone out. And we took the whole thing at its word, didn't we? Didn't we? I mean, forget the domestic shit. What about the international contacts? Make an identity strong enough for a passport, get the money together, travel behind the Iron Curtain, right? It's not easy, it's hard, and we did it, time and again. I've seen the FBI FOIA yields. They don't know the half of what we did. No—you can't say we didn't go all the way."

"Uh-huh." I put my head in my hands a second, and shut my eyes. "I read a couple interviews over the years with Billy and Bernardine. Saw them on TV once. They sound proud of themselves."

"Well, maybe they are." Jed's voice was gentle now. "And maybe some of that's just show. And maybe optimism is not just a personality trait, but something you earn. They have plenty to be proud of, you know. The best work of their lives been since 1980, not before. That's true for nearly every one of us."

"But how do you live with it? How do you live with the past like that? Aren't you just too ashamed?"

"Little J. Don't get carried away. Do you know, when I lecture about SDS, once or twice a year, they have to give me Rackham Auditorium? When I get people in to speak about the Mobilization, sometimes we have to get a chemistry lecture hall—one of the big premed amphitheaters with closed-circuit TV for the overflow? Okay, proud, I don't know. But not ashamed either. Not when you see the number of people who respond to us. Not when you see the number of kids who want to hear us talk—I mean young kids, J, freshmen, sophomores, kids who were born in the late seventies."

I was watching him, now, my mouth slightly open. "So? What's it mean?"

"It means two things, Jasey." Jed looked away, licking his lips, and for a moment I saw what he must look like when he lectures, saying something he's thought out to the last degree of clarity. "Firstly, there is a thirst in this country for a meaningful political involvement. These kids, they are . . . impoverished. They long for a way to engage the system. That's one."

Now he thought again, and this time he spoke more slowly. "And it means that no matter how wrong we may have been, the government was equally wrong to mass all the force of its law and its police against the antiwar movement. After all, they killed us. We never killed them. At least, Weather didn't. And that, in turn, means that no thinking person can ever remember how wrong we were without also remembering that the government, with all its power, was even more wrong."

Jeddy was quiet now, eyes absent. Then he focused again, as if just having reached a conclusion in an internal argument, and nodded. "No more, no less. Don't you forget it, J. We may have fucked everything in the world up, but not as bad as they did."

And it was only then, after that long afternoon drinking, and in that same quiet, scholarly voice, that Jed Lewis asked me:

"So why do you want to find Mimi?"

I didn't answer immediately. And then, in fact, I didn't answer at all. I just shook my head and looked at the table. "You wouldn't believe me if I told you."

"Okay. Then why me? What makes you think I can help?"

Still looking down. "I don't. I think you can find the guy who contacted you on behalf of the Brotherhood to give us money to go get Dr. Leary out of jail in San Luis Obispo."

"I see." Jed was staring at me now. "And how would that help?"

"Because after B of M you gave his name to Mimi, by way of Donal James. In a sealed envelope."

Jed considered that. "I guess you won't tell me how you know that, will you?"

"No."

"I see. And why, Jase? Why would I help you now, after all these years?"

Patiently, as if explaining a self-evident fact to a child, I told him: "See, Mimi's the only person who can get me my daughter back."

Date: June 20, 2006
From: "Jed Lewis" <jeddy@cusimanorganics.com>
To: "Isabel Montgomery" <isabel@exmnster.uk>
CC: maillist: The_Committee
Subject: letter 29

Night. On Miller Road two little lanes of tarmac cut through fields of midsummer corn, chest high. The headlights of the rental car were out of balance and cast an odd oblong of light off the side of the road. I drove with my left elbow up on the open window, my head, resting on my knuckles, pounding from my afternoon of drinking with your father. Driving back to town.

I've tried hard to remember what I was thinking about, that ride home. I distinctly remember stopping for coffee and aspirins at a gas station, parking my car, and finding myself, minutes later, standing under a buzzing streetlamp, staring at the oil-stained tarmac, lost in thought.

It had been a long time since I'd last stood thus in such a place, a country gas station, at night.

It had been a long time since I had last spent an afternoon drinking with a friend.

It had been a long time since I'd last thought so long about a decision.

I like to think I was worrying about your father. What your father was up to. How he thought Mimi could get his daughter back for him. I like to think I was feeling how desperate your father must be, a man his age, on the run, losing everything. Or that I was wishing that things had turned out differently.

I tell myself I was, as will happen as forty draws into the distant past and sixty into the immediate future, musing on the simple materiality of time, the quarter century of it that had passed since last I'd sat in the bar in Dexter. Perhaps I was simply letting it wash through me, through and through me, the feel of that time.

But I suppose I have to admit, to you, that the process that went on in my mind during that drive home, that drunken drive during which I had to bite my lip and shake my head to keep myself focused on the road, was just fear, and not for your father, but for myself. I was afraid of what your father had asked me to do, far more afraid than I had been of going to Dexter. Dexter, that had been dangerous, but it was a journey through space. What was ahead of me now, it was a journey through time. Back to the time before I was what I had become. Back to a time when all that I was, and so depended on being, now were things for which I had come to feel a deeply private, heartfelt contempt.

And yet I got back to town and went about the tasks ahead of me without any hesitation, as if I had planned them all out before, which should say something in my defense. I remember, without another thought, parking by Angell Hall and going in to my computer, where, despite the fact that the screen was shimmering in front of my eyes, I successfully retrieved a telephone number of a man I hadn't spoken to in twenty years—I'm not going to tell you how. And I remember coming out again into the summer night and realizing that I was far too drunk to drive. For a time I sat on the stairs of Angell Hall, searching for the energy to walk to a public telephone. Nor, I must tell you, did that take long. It just took a single vivid memory of Jason Sinai, talking to me, to make a little puff of adrenaline bloom in my stomach, and I was up and walking again, fairly steadily, downtown.

Later—much later, when Rebeccah and Ben and I reconstructed that night—the kids didn't believe it was pure coincidence that I decided to make my call from the public phone at the Del. It was sentimental, I admit that. And it was stupid—I didn't need to be drinking anymore. Call me sentimental and stupid, but the fact is, after midnight I walked into the virtually empty Del Rio and sat down at the bar, a few empty seats away, as it turned out, from my student Rebeccah Osborne and a young man sitting next to her who would soon be introduced to me as Benjamin Schulberg.

According to Ben—I don't remember it myself, which I think you'll find understandable by the time I get to the end of my part in this story—there was something distinctly odd in the way the bartender approached me. It seems that in the two or three nights in a row that Rebeccah and Ben had met at the Del, even Rebeccah had come to share Ben's conviction that the bartender didn't much like him. Now, as they watched her approach me, both of them felt strongly that something even stranger was going on. She served me a beer and a shot of bourbon without a word, shook her head emphatically when I asked her if she could give me a few dollars in quarters, then returned to the far end of the bar and showed me her back. That was when I turned to find Rebeccah and Ben staring at me with interest.

"Hi, Dr. Lewis. How are you?" This was Rebeccah speaking.

"Rebeccah." It took me a moment to place her, in this context, looking like a woman—she was wearing lipstick and drinking a martini—rather than a girl, as I usually saw her, in jeans and carrying a book bag. "How are you?"

"Fine. Uh, Dr. Lewis, are you okay?"

I wasn't sure if she was referring to my inebriation, which turned out to be more evident than I thought, or the baffling encounter I'd just had with the bartender. In the end, I decided to assume the latter. "Well, kind of. I needed some quarters for the telephone. The request would appear to have offended the bartender."

"Well, Cleo's a little touchy, I guess. Let me run over to the Diner and get you some. How many?"

I asked her for twenty dollars' worth, which, if it surprised her, she didn't show. Rebeccah left the bar after introducing me to Ben, ran across the street to the restaurant, while Ben and I made small talk. When Rebeccah returned, I took the roll of quarters she'd brought and made my way to the pay phone.

As to the conversation that occurred, I guess Mimi has already told you the name of the person I was calling. His telephone rang, some two thousand miles away on the coast of California. And when I introduced myself by the name of Duane Compton, a name Mac McLeod had not heard in twenty-six years since handing me ten thousand dollars for the rescue from San Luis Obispo of Timothy Leary, there was a pause.

"Wow, Mr. Compton. Nice to hear from you, man."

I laughed. "I doubt it. Would you like to call me back?"

"No need, no need. What can I do for you?"

Now there was a silence. Then I laughed again, but this time nervously. "Well, how sure are you about this telephone line?"

"Very sure."

"Okay." I felt reluctant, but Mac should know. "Um, look. A guy I used to know has got it in mind to find an old girlfriend. He thinks that this girlfriend, I might have pointed her in your direction in '74. And that you might have stayed in touch with her since then."

"I see." He answered readily, unsurprised, which surprised me. "And what if she doesn't want to be in touch with him?"

"Well, that's what I wanted to ask you. I mean, I'm thoroughly convinced that my friend will not, um, importune her, you know? I mean, I was pretty skeptical myself. Didn't want to get involved, and all. And to be honest, there's no love lost between me and this guy, so if I believe him, he can be believed. You know? But I spent the afternoon with him, and I really put him through his paces, and . . . Look. There's a lot at stake for him. He just wants to talk. I trust him. I don't like him, but I trust him. And I think that my friend and his ex-girlfriend need to trust each other right now."

A pause, and across the country, I could feel McLeod calculating. Then: "I don't buy it. There's nothing for them to trust each other about. They all face the same decision, same problem. I don't see that they can help each other."

"That's not actually the question, helping each other. My friend has a child."

"Ah." This was a point that evidently struck home. Mac answered slowly. "And how does that change matters?"

"It may not change them at all, who knows? But, well, my friend thinks that his ex-girlfriend can help with the child. And I thought, if there's a kid at stake, that would make it up to her to decide, don't you think?"

"Maybe." He conceded the point. Then, suddenly focused, he sounded more familiar. "Can I reach you at this number?"

"When?"

"Within the hour."

"Okay. I'll wait."

In the Del I hung up and, tiredly, stepped back to the bar. Watching the strangely hostile bartender, I picked up my beer and was going to settle in for the wait when I remembered Rebeccah Osborne and her boyfriend, both of whom were staring at me with that kind of curious hopefulness students display when you meet them socially. Reluctantly, I moved down the bar to them and asked the unfriendly bartender for a round of drinks.

But before the round arrived, the telephone rang behind the bar and she answered it, then turned her back altogether and bent over to listen, leaving us without drinks. Nor was it a quick call, and after the bartender ignoring us some more, I said, "Listen. I've got to wait for a call on the pay phone. I'm going to move to that table there."

They nodded politely, clearly showing the disappointment on their faces, and I hesitated. Then I found myself talking again. "So, if you're up to it, why not join me? Seeing the bartender won't serve us, let's get the waiter to bring us some drinks over at the table."

And so spontaneous, so untroubled, was their pleasure at the suggestion that out of all the bullshit of this day, I remembered why I had started teaching in the first place and began to feel, as we made our way over to the little table by the telephone, that perhaps things were going to go back to normal; that everything was going to be the way it was before Little J e-mailed me, after all.

Date: June 20, 2006

From: "Daddy" <littlej@cusimanorganics.com>

To: "Isabel Montgomery" <isabel@exmnster.uk>

CC: maillist: The_Committee

Subject: letter 30

When I left Jed, I went back to my motel, the single motel left in Dexter—a five-story brick rooming house on the main drag, offering day and night rates.

I took no care for security. As far as I was concerned, the entire town of Dexter could know that two middle-aged men had gone on a bender at the single bar in town—wasn't the first time, won't be the last.

But no one asked me anything, looked at me, worried me: this was central Michigan, and here the right to privacy was worth, if not fighting for, at least shaving your head and getting a swastika tattooed on your chest for. Once inside, I meant to sleep off the five, six drinks and couple of joints Jed and I had consumed. Instead I found myself, after a short time lying on the bed in the dark, going back out and across the street to the liquor store to get a pint of bourbon. Then I lay down again, but instead of sleeping, sipped from the mouth of the bottle and went back through the conversation I had just had with my old brother in arms.

God, but it had shocked me, how mad Jed still was. Now, I thought that perhaps it shouldn't have. The last months, before B of M, when Weather had been a group of fugitives looking for a new role in the counterculture, horrific animosity had surfaced between us. Years of competition that had been held in check by group discipline suddenly showed; years of resentment, of jealousy.

And still, we had found the way to talk, and as we talked, through four, five drinks, it had started to seem like those differences were less important, after all, than the things that once had united us.

I rose unsteadily and walked to the window. In a house across the street someone was playing the piano. I could only see the hands on the keyboard, moving with an agility that spoke of a piece of considerable tempo and complexity. Up until my fifteenth birthday I had played the piano, hours spent at the Bechstein in the big living room of my parents' house. They had thought, of course, I was going to be a musician, but at fifteen I had given it up, a decision that had cost real pain, and real guilt. Now, dimly, in the stoned and drunk swirl of my mind, I felt a hint of how responsible that guilt had been for what I was later to do; just dimly a hint, and no sooner had I glimpsed that insight than it whirled away again. But watching the hands play, pause, practice, and then play again, I thought of all the lives that could have been mine other than what I in fact was, and a searing regret went through me.

And I knew the thought was a drunken indulgence. Watching the hands move under the light of a lamp, I knew that I was too old for that kind of regret. What you have to do is navigate this life, not another one, not a life you wish you had or a life you see in the window of a room across the street, but this life. And beyond doing that right, there's nothing to think about, so clearly true is it that all lives are all equally apt, no matter what their actual circumstances, for the commission of right and wrong and for the achievement of brief glimpses of freedom that may or may not precede enlightenment.

And this life? This life, this life. Perhaps Jed had woken in me all the things that I had once hoped to be, and hoped to do. But Jed had children, too. What did it matter what I was? I was nothing, anymore, except a father. I was nothing except the person who had a chance—a slim chance—of making you better than myself. And nothing I did with my life had any meaning beyond what it meant to you.

Like Oedipus said at Colonus: it's now, when I am nothing, that I become a man.

Standing at that window, my forehead against the glass pane the only thing keeping me upright in my drunkenness, I wondered if ever my father had thought like this, about me, and as I wondered, I ached. My father. My daughter. And me, reduced to nothing and became everything in a by-the-hour hotel room in a tiny town in Dexter.

So I was thinking, and while I thought, as I was to learn later, the long electronic loop from the Del Rio Bar to California and back again completed its course. In time, while Jed Lewis and Rebeccah Osborne and Ben Schulberg sat drinking shots and beers at the back table next to the telephone, in time the bartender at the Del Rio hung up the phone, and moments later, the pay phone next to where they sat began to ring.

And moments later, again, in my hotel room in Dexter, the phone rang, and through the endless tunnel of my drunkenness I made my way from the window to pick it up, and as if from miles and miles away heard Jed Lewis say:

"She says she'll see you. In October of 1973, this weekend."

October 1973. This weekend. With the care of the utterly drunk, I wrote that down. Then, leaving until tomorrow the job of figuring out where we were in October of 1973, and how I was going to get there again by the weekend, I let myself go backward onto the bed, asleep before I finished falling.

Date: June 21, 2006
From: "Amelia Wanda Lurie" <mimi@cusimanorganics.com>
To: "Isabel Montgomery" <isabel@exmnster.uk>
CC: maillist: The_Committee
Subject: letter 31

October 1973. We lived, from October to December of 1973, in a cabin at the end of a disused logging road on some three thousand acres of privately held northern Michigan forest.

It was a place where I had spent some of the happiest times of my life.

The Linder estate. The nearest neighbors were miles of thick woodland away. To the south, the Au Sable ran to Lake Huron. To the north I-75 crossed the Mackinac bridge and up to Ontario. One hundred and eighty degrees of the compass held escape routes ending in water.

Even then, I knew how important that coastline was.

Even then, I knew what bootleggers and Indians had known before me about the Upper Peninsula of Michigan.

October 1973. Pronouncing the words to McLeod over the telephone from the Del Rio, I felt as if I were telling someone the secret I had never told before. And watching Jeddy Lewis receiving a phone call on the pay phone—a call I was certain was McLeod relaying my message to Jeddy, who would relay it to Little J, I felt as if I had just made an appointment to travel not through space, but through time.

But then, how much stranger could I conceivably feel, after seeing Jeddy and Rebeccah sitting together in the first place?

Strange? My dear, there are no words to explain how strange it was, that summer.

• • •

I had to let them stay in the bar after last call—local restaurant etiquette required that. And they did want to stay, ordering two shots of bourbon apiece and two pitchers of Stroh's to drink while the waiter and I cleaned up the bar. Really, I shouldn't have served them: the two kids were lit already, and Jeddy, Jeddy looked like he'd been drinking all day. While they drank, I cleaned up, not looking, trying not to listen. Seeing Jeddy—recognizing that this middle-aged professor *was* Jeddy—had been surreal enough. But it was like a nightmare come true when I overheard that Rebeccah and her boyfriend were quizzing Jed about Sharon Solarz in the days. I heard Jasey's name in their conversation. I heard my own.

It took them forever to leave.

I see us all that night, in an Edward Hopper tableau through the window from the street. The three of them drinking their last calls at a table while the waiter upended chairs and mopped around them. And me, at the bar, a green-shaded light illuminating the cash-register drawer as I counted the night's take.

I doubt that my count was that accurate.

Because what I was seeing was not the money in the drawer but another scene altogether. What I was seeing was afternoon light falling through the kitchen window of the Linder cabin in October 1973, a shaft of thick autumn light falling through dusty air and splashing, like water, onto the wooden floor.

It was a place where I had been very happy, perhaps the happiest I had ever been. And yet this night, in Ann Arbor, closing the Del Rio after last call, it seemed that all I could clearly capture from the two months we spent there was that single view of the light falling in the kitchen window onto the floor.

That light, that precisely defined shaft of light, so thick I had felt I could reach out and hold it in my hand. The light of the great northern woods in autumn, the woods in which I had grown up. And the silence in the cabin while Little J slept, a silence itself so multilayered with the the endless inventiveness of mourning, there was everything in it.

The silence of a suburban house at noon.

The silence of the beach at Point Betsie, on the dunes of which my father died.

• • •

The Del Rio in 1996, and I came back to the present as the waiter ushered Jed Lewis and the two kids out, then called good night himself. And I, at last alone, I lowered my head to the top of the cash register. My eyes tight shut to the present, traveling deep into the memory of that morning in 1973, lying on the floor of the cabin, listening to the low moan raised by the blustering wind moving through the woods outside the cabin, watching the light through the window.

Every locale that had ever meant anything to me was in that light. I was in my childhood room, in the iron frame bed, upstairs at Point Betsie. I was about to rise by the window, look out to the little sandy road to the beach, through the turning woods of trees bowing their reddening crowns this way, then that. I would descend the dark stairs with their smooth wood surfaces, sit at the Wakefield table my mother had bought when we'd moved to Michigan in the fifties, drink hot chocolate, poured into chipped white tin cups from the white tin jug, sitting with my father. I was a little girl, a little girl in a lost time, before it was all taken away.

But even then, in October 1973, it had already all been taken away. Our Point Betsie house with its chipped white enamel tin cups, our dear little house on the dirt road, lying in the slanting sun from the water, had long been sold, and not only was my father gone but also my mother, my mother. It was not 1958, or 1962, or even 1965—all of those times were gone now. As I watched the shaft of light falling through the window of the Linder cabin, illuminating the dust in the air and making it move with the complexity of a ballet, there was already an abyss between all those things and what I was now: a woman who had made her face and her name synonymous with outlaw life, a woman who had gone so far there was no coming back. And in place of all those things I missed, in this depthless, anonymous well of silence and light, of wind and memory, in this little cabin in the woods, there was just this one thing: this black-haired head asleep on my naked shoulder.

October 1973. I saw myself lying there, cradling Jason's sleeping head, in the shocked, thoughtless clarity of the newly awakened. In this sun so thick with the color of memory. In this wind moaning with the woods-carried scent of autumn. This black-haired head and no more and I, Mimi Lurie, fugitive and criminal, lying there in October 1973, had understood that I was learning with new poignancy, new and profound poignancy, exactly how much I had come to need this black-haired head.

In the Del Rio in July 1996, under the light of the green-shaded lamp above the register, I came to myself. Quietly I took the night's cash and zipped it closed into the vinyl bank bag. I shut the light, I left the bar, stepping out into the heat of the early morning. An hour after last call, two hours to sunrise.

What could I expect? Sharon's arraignment had been all over the news for days. Kids had even protested in support of Sharon outside the jail where she was being held, pending trial, and the Washtenaw County Police Benevolent Association had organized a counter-demonstration. Listening to Jeddy talk to the two kids, I told myself, I was crazy to come back to Ann Arbor. But then, what choice did I have?

Carrying the deposit bag as I had been taught—under one arm, held by the other—I walked up to Main Street, deserted at 3:30 in the morning, then over to the Bank of Michigan branch on the corner of Huron Street. This was not the branch of the robbery—they'd closed that branch, which had been in the Briarwoods Mall, years before. Still, other nights, I had at least wryly observed the strangeness of it all. Tonight, with the sunlight of twenty-three years ago before my eye, I hardly noticed what I was doing.

October 1973. Early in the month, a long and meticulous operation had concluded with the bombing of the Capitol Building in Washington. Placing the bomb had been the single most dangerous thing we had ever done, and still, when it failed to go off, Little J and I had returned from the safe house we'd rented in Baltimore to the Capitol and dropped another small explosive devise in to ignite the bigger one. This one worked, and in the extreme heat of the manhunt that followed, we judged it reasonable to sever all links with the collective, for a time, and go off on our own.

I took him north. I knew the cabin—had hiked the holdings extensively with my father. My father had been, in fact, instrumental in convincing the current generation of the Linders to deed the land to the Nature Conservancy. The last time I had been there before 1973 was 1962, when old Boris Linder had lent the place to my father and we had gone with Dougy Osborne and Johnny—and my brother Peter—to camp out for a week. It was one of the last times any of us were to be together: over the next six years my father killed himself and my brother disappeared. As for Johnny Osborne, our childhood friendship, already stretched thin, snapped when he enlisted to Vietnam. Two years later, my mother died. And then old Mr. Linder died, and by 1973 his grandchildren, who now owned the land, had long forgotten the cabin was even there.

It was probable, in fact, that no one at all had been in the cabin between 1964, when the Luria family had our last happy vacation, and 1973. It was probable, in fact, that no one had been there since.

Now, walking slowly back from the bank past the Del Rio again, I wondered if J would remember how to get to the cabin.

For a moment, the thought made me intensely anxious.

Then I thought, well, if he didn't, then he wouldn't see me: there was no reason for us to meet, anyway. Just Little J being Little J, wanting to torture himself, and me, with things that could not be changed.

He had never been able to accept defeat. It was what made him a good activist, and I had no doubt that it made him a great lawyer.

Probably, I thought with an ache in my belly, it also made him a good father.

There was, however, nothing I could do for him.

I knew that, and I hoped that beyond the sentimentality of wanting to see me, he knew that too.

I walked slowly, heading across the deserted town to the little apartment I had rented on Hill Street, close to where the SDS offices had been.

There was no hurry: I was unlikely to sleep this night. And in fact, as I approached campus I turned suddenly past the Rackham Building, past the old observatory and over to the medical school parking lot above the Arboretum. On the stairs leading down to the Arb I sat and the night, the hot June night with its symphony of cicadas, rose around me.

October 1973. We'd traveled north from Washington separately. For three days I'd waited for him, camping out in the woods and coming to the diner in Rose City every day at four, as we'd arranged. Each day I grew more and more nervous. But it was not a fugitive's nervousness; it was fueled by something other than fear for our physical safety.

In fact, the manhunt did not worry me. As always, the FBI had been our unwitting ally by working every influence they had to restrict national coverage, seeking to minimize the publicity Weather actions generated. They did this successfully: most of our actions were only reported regionally. The downside of that, for us, was reaching fewer people with an awareness of what we had done. The upside was that the national manhunt for us was not widely known, and its intensification after such a visible action did little to hamper our movements.

I was not frightened. I knew that our identities—as well as our craft in evading pursuit—were more than just good. And in 1973, with a nation of young folk on the move, one girl more or less in bell-bottom jeans worn nearly through at the ass, traveling by bus and thumb with a backpack: I attracted only the most cursory attention. It was not the danger of being caught by the FBI that worried me. It was the danger of being caught by my comrades in my desire to be alone—absolutely alone—with Jason Sinai.

For in fact, the manhunt that followed the bombing of the Capitol building was more an excuse to flee together than a reason—an excuse for being alone. The Weather Bureau, with their militant ban on couples, was a greater threat to us right now than the FBI.

Not that either of us admitted it. From the beginning, we had tacitly kept the depth of our attachment secret, and neither of us had ever been subject to pressure to break up what would have seemed, to the Bureau, a bourgeois monogamy. And yet, when we realized we had a plausible explanation for leaving the collective for a time, together, without discussing it, we'd both put the steps in action to make it happen.

Later—much later, when we were discussing these things openly—your father would even say that was why he went back to the Capitol a second time, the most dangerous thing he'd ever done, as a Weather member or otherwise.

See, if the bomb hadn't been detonated, he and I would have had no reason to run away.

On the third day, when I came in he was there, a handsome young man with a head of loose, curly hair, dyed black, in jeans and a T-shirt, a pack of Winstons in the breast pocket, chatting with the waitress. On the floor, behind him, was a backpack. I'd had my own coffee, watching jealously from down the counter, not acknowledging him. Then I'd walked back out of town to the campsite and prepared to leave. In time he'd followed, and together, traveling by my skills with compass and topo map, we'd made our way out of state forest and into the great northern estate of the Linder family, heading for the cabin I knew from vacationing there, as a girl, with my father.

Christ. Sitting on the top step of the wooden flight of steps leading down into the Arboretum, I remembered that morning on the trail, hiking in to the cabin with Jasey. A golden late summer sun, as thick as honey, poured through the maple and oak leaf, the leaves themselves amplifying, rather than shadowing, the light with their spectrum of greens and reds. A silence as infinite as the sky was upon us, interrupted only by the breath of the wind through the woods, the wind that, if you stopped to listen, played out all the distances around you: huge sighs of rustling leaves across huge distances. And the light, the light: the light that seemed to combine in one shocking flash all the autumns of my life—of school years starting and Thanksgivings passing—with the unknown promise of this particular autumn, this autumn that promised nothing but the freedom of a new stage in my fugitive life, my life as a fugitive with Jason.

I rose now and went down the wooden steps to the Arboretum, watching the waning moon come out of clouds overhead and cast a silvery obscurity over the treetops. To go back north. To be alone with Jason in the great north woods of my childhood. I'd known for twenty-two years that Jason wanted to see me, and I had known from the moment I heard about his flight what he was going to ask me to do. That wasn't the problem. It was something more.

It was that Jason's actual success in making contact with me was the final proof that my life, as it had been, was no longer tenable. This careful construction of Tess's identity, shielding me not only from the police but from my old allies and, in particular, from Jason: it was ending now, in Ann Arbor, where it had all started, and once again I was going to have to face the unknown of the future and, even worse, its promise.

2.

We met in 1968, freshman year at the University of Michigan. I was a work-study student, and the work I'd been assigned was at the cafeteria in East Quad: I was an efficient, neat person, good in a kitchen, not a hippie yet, nor an urban revolutionary—in any case, if you don't know it, let me tell you that in those days, it was revolutionary girls, using the skills taught to us by our fifties moms in our clean kitchens, who kept the revolutionary boys warm, fed, and at least somewhat clean.

My work-study job started when dinner was finished: to clear the tables of salt and pepper shakers, collecting them on a big tray and then taking them back to the kitchen to refill, as well as any odd crockery or silverware left by careless students. Behind me, another work-study student wiped the tables clean. By the time I began, the cafeteria was meant to be empty, but there was always a group left at one table, emptying the coffee urn, cup after cup, and talking. Jason was one of them.

A thin guy, wiry, strong in black T-shirts with a pack of Winstons in the breast pocket, jeans, work shoes, curly black hair cascading onto his shoulders, a strong face with an aquiline nose, a brown-eyed man. Now, when the *Michigan Daily* was running pictures of Jason Sinai from the sixties, I saw a child, a child young enough to be my son, and I asked myself how I had ever thought this child sexy. Then he was beautiful to me, an animated, intense person, with a body always poised for fight.

Or, I knew now, for flight.

The group that sat talking with him, East Quad hippies, were a gang of guys who dressed like him, except one was black. The black guy went on to become a press secretary for Christopher Dodd—often I wondered if Dodd knew that his secretary's political education had started in East Quad, listening to dark, intense Jason Sinai talk sedition. For what he was there for, no pretense was made. He was there as a representative of a far-left faction—the Action Faction—of the University of Michigan SDS; he was recruiting members; and what he had in mind for them to do, already in the fall of 1968, a month after the Democratic National Convention in Chicago, was against the law.

Later, I was to know exactly how few of the people Jason recruited actually became functioning members of the Weather Underground. In fact, the one person he convinced, those nights in the East Quad dormitory cafeteria, was the one person he was not talking to: the girl cleaning the tables, ignored by them, as they talked. Nor did he really convince me. He didn't need to: I had come to the same conclusions as he—and the several hundred-odd members of what was soon to be named Weatherman—on my own.

I was born in Ann Arbor. You know, by now, who my father was, Martin Luria, a physicist at the university, himself born in Germany, exiled to America before Hitler, not as a Jew but as a Communist, inducted into the Manhattan project, and then tenured at Michigan until, just after my birth in 1951, blacklisted by McCarthy. He committed suicide in 1966, on the beach in upstate Michigan, leaving his wife his insurance to bring us up, me and my older brother Peter. My mother survived to see Peter vanish: he disappeared on a dig in Turkey while doing an archaeology Ph.D.; and me be admitted to the university. Then she died of a stroke. I buried her during the summer after my high school graduation, alone: even if I did not really believe my brother was dead, I did not know where he was. On some level I understood that he did not intend to be found. Then I moved to Ann Arbor. When I got there, I legally amended the spelling of my last name. "Luria" was too known a name in Michigan.

Nights after my mother died. Home from my work-study job, in Betsy Barbour, the all-girl's dorm on the hill: my mother had insisted I live there, one of the last things she did before she died. For so long had I feared this death, the loss of this last tie, that at first I hardly felt it, a numbing sensation. Then, nights, in Betsy Barbour, it had begun to ache. Sometimes I thought that loving my mother had been the greatest, the only, success of my life. Now, when there was no longer anyone to love, I could no longer recapture the reality my mother had had for me. I knew only that I had adored her. I had adored every inch of the little clapboard house in Point Betsie, filled with Teutonic kitsch and the smell of cabbage. I had loved to touch her, hold her hand, kiss her cheek, put my slim, strong body against hers on the sofa, thigh to thigh, shoulder to shoulder, and my mother, forbearing, had given in to her daughter's constant demand for intimacy. Then she was gone, like a blanket falling off the bed at night, leaving my thigh, my shoulder, cold.

Not even the house was left: I had had to sell it at once to cover death duties and pay my tuition. I did have enough left over to put its contents in storage until the eighties, when the FBI tracked it down and confiscated it, nearly following the paper trail of the storage rental to me, forcing me into Canada for six long months. As for my brother, a few years later I traveled to . . . well, to another country to be trained in the use of a new blasting cap, and on the way home, looked for him in Turkey, where he had disappeared from the Cornell-Harvard dig at Sardis. There was not the slightest trace—Peter Luria had disappeared from the face of the earth. But by then, so had Mimi Lurie, hadn't she?

So in the autumn of 1968, Betsy Barbour, with its oak-paneled hallways, its lamplit lounges, had become the only home I had; the dining hall my hearth; and the little room I shared with two girls from Dearborn my only privacy. Nights, I listened to Dana and Haley's whispered secrets fade into even breaths and the silence of five hundred girls sleeping under one big roof. The big Michigan sky first quilted over with fall cloud and silver moon, then grayed with high storms and chilling air and began to snow. At first, a vast numbness had sheltered me.

Then I began to ache.

The house in Point Betsie yielded four years' tuition for me and a good portion of my room and board. My brother's half, as far as I know, still sits under his name in Washtenaw Savings and Loan, if Washtenaw Savings and Loan survived the S&L crash. Freshman year passed, 1968 to 1969; classes in the day, the East Quad cafeteria at night, listening to Jason meeting with an ever-shifting group of recruits. At the end of the winter semester, the Point Betsie Boat Club, where my father had sailed a little skiff, offered me three thousand dollars, a collection made after my mother's death. That was a surprise: the club, like most of Point Betsie, was as Republican as Henry Ford. It made more sense when I found out that the collection had been organized by Douglas Osborne, Johnny's dad. Three thousand dollars meant, I slowly realized, that I needed not work for the entire summer. It meant, I realized, that I could volunteer full-time to help in the SDS office.

That was not what Doug Osborne had meant to make of me.

I stood five-nine, a tall, slim, well-made girl, with waist and breasts of an adolescent but a woman's hips under tight jeans. I was blond, gray-eyed, perfectly pretty but for the imperfection of my sloping shoulders and long neck, which made me, instead, beautiful. Now, looking at the picture the *Michigan Daily* ran—for they ran as many photos of me as of Jason—I understood, which I hadn't really, then, how beautiful I was, my breasts bare under the cotton of an Indian embroidered shirt, my hips full in my jeans. In May, when school let out, the People's Park uprising happened in Berkeley, and I became the corresponding secretary for the Ann Arbor SDS. It happened so naturally. Jason, Nan, Jeddy—articulate, passionate people, like I had met around my parents' dinner table for years—they welcomed me into the Ann Arbor office and made me at home. We were motivated, oddly, I saw now, by the same naive optimism that had animated my father, before the blacklist, at least. But it was, so unexpectedly, the same naive optimism that would animate Johnny Osborne when, to my shock, I heard that he'd enlisted and was going to Vietnam. A belief in his own possibilities; a belief in the country's boundless capacity. It was, I saw now, an equal but opposite measure of the postwar American optimism—same as had caused educated, liberal men to undertake the war in Vietnam; same as had allowed our government to plant a flag on the moon. Now it was making us think we could end the war and reinvent our society.

In June, *New Left Notes* published "You Don't Need a Weatherman," the primary accusation that the New Left as we had known it, the antiwar movement as we had known it, had failed to stop the escalation of the war as well as the intensification of governmental repression. This was true, and many people listened. And when, later in June, SDS split into Progressive Labor on one hand, and Revolutionary Youth Movement on the other, I naturally went with RYM, the same group as Jason and his friends. When, over the rest of the summer, RYM split again, a small group going on to start planning the Days of Rage in Chicago, I went too.

Trotsky or Lenin or Mao, Sweeney or Baron, Marcuse or Mills, everyone had their own analysis much as they had their own taste in music. To lead in this environment the most immediate challenge was to discern whether people see beyond our attachment to our own analytic framework. If so, they were potential for cadre; if not, they were part of the well of people on which a vanguard depended: support staff, sources of money, covers, protection, alibis. That is not a pejorative: if you number those people, around Weather, in the low hundreds, you still have to measure on one hand the number who betrayed our trust in any serious way.

In mid-August Bobby Seale was arrested in Berkeley.

A week later, I traveled, with Jason and a group of others, through Canada and Niagara Falls to Woodstock.

Richie Havens in his raw voice boomed out across the crowd: "It's a long, hard road to Freedom," and his words rolled out over the thousands and thousands of roaring voices, into the canopy of dripping sky.

Neither J nor I went back to school in September, although only I—mindful of the little money I had left—bothered officially to drop out. J let his father pay the full, out-of-state semester's tuition.

In September four members of the Ann Arbor collective formed an affinity group, me, Little J, Jeddy, and Nan, and took forty sticks of dynamite out of the I-94 overpass construction in Dexter, Michigan, then traded it for an equal amount stolen from a construction project in Oregon.

On October 7, the Oregon dynamite was used to blow up the Haymarket Police Statue in Chicago and launch the Days of Rage.

Jason and I both spent the first days of the National Moratorium against the War in jail in Chicago. Then, on November 15, we joined a full million people at the National Mobilization to End the War.

One day later, the My Lai massacre was revealed, and two weeks later, Fred Hampton and Mark Clark, Black Panther leaders, both of whom I knew, one of whom—Hampton—I loved, were killed, in their sleep, by Chicago Police.

Nashville Skyline came out. *Butch Cassidy* came out.

Nixon's attorney general, Richard Kleindienst, suggested that demonstrators should be put in "detention camps."

In December, Weather held the Flint War Council.

I traveled to it with Diana Oughton.

Three months later Diana was dead in the town house bombing, and of our affinity group all four of us were chosen by the central leadership—the Weather Bureau—to go underground.

Later, much later, I learned that Little J and I were very nearly left out, due to being the youngest members of a Weather Collective anywhere.

In the end, it was the fact that both of us had Communist parents that saved us.

And so, the myth of Martin Luria's communism—and it has been proven by now that it was a myth—came to rescue his daughter, long after his death, and got me the thing that I wanted more than anything I had ever wanted in my life, that is, to belong.

3.

Five A.M., July 2, 1996. I had descended the wooden stairs from the parking lot to the Arboretum; walked into the park, directed myself to the railroad bridge over the Huron River and sat, on the edge, to watch the black surface of the river, on which I could now see a silver trail of half moon.

I, Amelia Wanda Lurie. Most people my age have grown up most of their lives knowing that since Vietnam has passed into history and they have gone on to do the things they were going to do, most of these people, they've never really forgotten that somewhere out there, Mimi Lurie and Jason Sinai still live underground. We've become icons, rather than people. We're not the only ones. Just last month the *New Yorker* gave a full page to an Avedon portrait of Bernardine Dohrn from 1969, and it's 2006 now. Do you know what a full page in the *New Yorker* costs?

But it's me, alone, who came for most people to symbolize never giving up. Lots of people don't like me, lots believe all sorts of horrible things about me. How I killed the left in America, how I ruined the antiwar movement, how I played into the hands of the FBI—and indirectly, of corporate interests—in the cooption, commercialization, and parodization of the antiwar movement. True, or not true, for most people I'm something other than a person, a symbol. Someone who did something much more important than themselves. It's hard, to be an icon rather than a person.

And I was different from your father—different, in fact, from all of us. The others—they all came, eventually, to live much the lives we would have lived anyway. Parents, teachers, lawyers, activists. Some came closer than others to what they would have been had they not given ten years of their lives to clandestine activism—especially those with money and connections. Others paid a price: became high school teachers instead of university professors, lobbyists rather than elected officials. In this your father too was lucky: he was able to do much of what he wanted to do with his life, even though he had to do it under a different name.

But I, I never wanted a normal life, not in any real way. I had, your father used to say, a taste for something like the gutter. Bars, dark in the morning, next to a Great Lake port. Working people, people who lived with physical danger; criminal people, who lived under the threat of capture. And as is often the case for those who live outside the law, I came to know my adopted dimension of American life better than the one into which I was born. I knew the places left untouched by the present. Depressed towns—Congers on the Hudson, Derby on the Housatonic, Ogallala. The wrong side of cities like Denver, or Philadelphia, or St. Louis. Places where the cars were still models I recognized, the telephones worked with a rotary dial, and the brands of things were the brands from the America where I had been aboveground.

Desolate places had another advantage: in sparsely used bars and shuttered streets, in cheap hotels and lousy restaurants, you might be in danger but you were never surprised.

Nights, in my opinion, should be lit either by the moon in places where no one ever went or, failing that, by the neon of a place where no one was wanted.

The places we had: so many rented houses, they had all blended into one place where, like children playing a game of hide-and-seek, we were briefly safe. A bathroom with a stained sink, an aerosol can of air freshener, a plastic dish of dirty soap, mouthwash of uncertain provenance, a bent-bristle toothbrush, a copy of *Rat*, an empty toilet paper roll. Carpets: in my memory I have a vision of endless vistas of synthetic, stained carpets, patterned carpets, plain carpets, carpets with thick pile, and carpets worn practically to nothing. I see thinly painted drywall with water stains and mold, cheap light fixtures with insect stains, linoleum kitchen floors filthy beyond cleaning, veneered dining tables, sticky from countless dinners, sloppily cleaned, cheerless decorations—an embroidered platitude, a dog at a card table—lighting cheerless rooms.

And yet each of the kitsch houses was a little refuge of light and heat against the night, filled with safety, with security. In each a fire could be lit and a cigarette smoked, a joint, a beer; in each bacon and eggs could be fried at the electric stove; in each were friends, united in danger, heartening and familiar; in each we, the brave, could sit and talk in safety far into the night. Safety? The safety, we found, was more solid then we might have thought. There came a point when you couldn't hide anymore, and you couldn't protect yourself anymore, so you might as well relax. You might as well smoke a joint in one of those endless rented houses and let whatever danger lurked out there come and get you, and when you did, night after night in house after house you woke to sun through the stained curtains and knew you were free.

Sometimes it seemed to me that the whole thing was a vast riff on safety and freedom; that again and again I had been playing cat and mouse with dangers that existed for me only to prove, morning after morning, the possibility of safety. TAZs—temporary autonomous zones—Hakim Bey calls them now: these little bubbles of light and warmth in dark landscapes across the country, little places where for a night, for a few nights, you were not a fugitive and not a criminal but rather free, free behind a lit window and curtain, safe. This is exactly what we were: we were autonomous, and we were temporary. But that we were temporary was not a disrecommendation, it was an asset, because the drama of risk and safety could be played out again and again, the way a smoker courts withdrawal for the sweet safety of nicotine again, an endless game of cat and mouse with terror. Freedom, I came to understand, was only sweet in that it was transient. When it became the norm of life, then it became meaningless.

No one ever found us. And it came to inform the rest of our lives, the knowledge that one could be hidden, and one could be safe.

Until the day, of course, when nothing was safe.

The day when nothing was ever safe again.

I, Amelia Wanda Lurie, at five in the morning, sitting on a train bridge across the Huron, in the middle of Ann Arbor's Arboretum. Not an icon, not a hero of the sixties, but a tired woman of nearly forty-five, watching water pass under me, and thinking about October 1973.

Thinking now, as I had before, that October 1973 had been my last chance. By then I had been living as a fugitive for three years, and yet, I found in those weeks in the cabin with Jason, I had not yet become a criminal. I was still a college student gone awry, and everything was still possible for me: I could still keep a house, finish college, get a job. It could be a good job, too: a job that helped people, a job devoted to a cause. I wanted that. I wanted it very much, that October in northern Michigan. And as if we had been waiting for just such an opportunity, our lives fell into a domestic pattern nearly immediately, a deeply satisfying one.

We stayed until the first snows drove us out: two full months. For two months we lived in total seclusion in the little cabin, cooking tinned food from an occasional trip to town, catching fish and finding local mushrooms, and once, when Jason found a gut-shot deer dying in the woods, a few weeks of venison. I baked from my mother's recipes, breads so rich and varied that we could have lived on that alone. Jason pulled trout after trout out of the lake, which had once been stocked but not fished in years. We read: old Mr. Linder had left a copy of *Buddenbrooks,* and I read each evening to Jason, translating the German fluently, if sometimes approximately. We made love on our sleeping bags by the stove. We slept, bodies as close as we could be without becoming one.

That was when I taught Jason what my father had taught me about the woods. How to keep the cardinal directions in mind, how to travel by topo map and compass, how to read a trail for animal spoor and tracks. I taught him the recognizable declensions of sun and moon, which allowed an approximation of the time as well as direction, and a few key stars. I taught him what mushrooms could be eaten, how to build fires, how to find water, what the noises were at night, and on one memorable occasion, how to deal with an angry black bear.

A logging road, disused for decades, led out of the little clearing of the cabin and northeast for some miles, probably following an old Indian trail, itself probably originating as a deer path. Where it ended, bootleggers had cut it to the coast to meet boats carrying Canadian whisky; that path too was still discernible, these years later. That was where Jason, who had grown up in the city, developed what was to become a lifelong running habit, running those trails miles and miles through the woods.

Watching him through the kitchen window one day, returning from his run, his thin, muscled body glistening with sweat, I had realized that I had never been so happy in my life.

4.

October 1973. The season's clock ticked, a degree colder each day. We knew we could not survive a winter in the Linder cabin. But what were we going back to? Days, the questions were held at bay by the business of living, the hard work of surviving in the woods. Nights, by the fire, there was nothing to do but think.

Little J. Struggling with loyalty to a group of people he no longer felt a tie to, with commitment to causes that he no longer felt he could affect. I can see him, your father at twenty-three, standing by the window of the cabin, shaking his head. "The time for Weather is past. At this point we're just giving them an excuse to crack down on the left."

And me? My voice, echoing through time, a fatal weight carried in every word. "But that's just the point. Their crackdown has taken on a life of its own. COINTELPRO is becoming the mainstream law of the land. Watergate's proved that, Jasey—the FBI can do whatever it wants to dissenters, whatever it wants, and if they won't do it, then the president can collect a few thugs instead. People aren't going to put up with this forever."

"Aren't they?" He seemed tired, which frightened me more than if he had been angry. "What's going to change them?"

"Stop it, Jasey."

"No, I mean it, Mim." He turned now, lit a cigarette from his breast pocket, and leaned against the sink. "You can't get a country awash in a wartime economy to take any serious notice of its government's destructive role in the world, or of its own disenfranchised underclass. Never going to happen. Yeah, yeah: you can get them to try to stop the war—when they run out of blacks and have to start drafting white folk, that is. But even then, we've proved—proved, Mimi—that the government is completely impervious to popular protest. The higher the level of protest, the higher the level of repression."

Patiently, I explained the obvious. "So we give up? What then? How long do you think the third world's going to stand being raped by us? How long you think it's going to be before they find a way to slaughter innocents here, just like we slaughter innocents there?"

"Mimi." He crouched in front of me now, and while he talked, I looked into the black pupils of his eyes, as if hidden back there somewhere were a magic door, and if only I could find it, I could find the way out of our own logic. "There isn't going to be a revolution. We did what we did. It's time to move on."

"Jason. We're already committed to Sharon's operation."

"I don't want to do it. It's not even a Weather action."

"But I have to do it. It's just a little thing."

"And after?"

"Jasey. After, we surface. It'll be our last job."

On an early December morning, as the first flakes of snow started to fall from a low gray sky, we packed our few belongings for the hike out. Cleaning the cabin's tiny kitchen for the last time, watching the lowering sky, I felt tears in my eyes. And in that moment, I think, everything could have changed, then, before it was too late. Had not Jason approached me from behind, linking his hands across my stomach, and speaking softly.

"Okay. Mim. I'll come along a few steps. It's our last job. Okay?"

What did I feel? I held my breath. Then I let it out. "Okay."

"What's the first move?"

"Let's go find a place to live near Ann Arbor. I'll contact Sharon. We'll start planning for the spring."

"Why spring?"

There were three answers to that question. I gave him two. "Sharon's got a trainee position at a Bank of Michigan branch in the Briarwood Mall. We're going to give her the time to become a teller. And then, in the spring we can get away through the Upper Peninsula, after the snow melts. Vincent's a careful planner."

"Vincent?"

"Dellesandro. He's Sharon's contact."

"What do we do until spring?"

"Establish identities. Work with Weather. Try to convince them to join us."

"Okay. But one condition."

"What's that?"

I felt his thin arms tighten around me. "We go back to Weather as a couple. No collective living, no group sex. Just us. If they don't like it, we leave."

I turned in his arms, now, and let my face into the crook of his neck, into the pulse-warm skin of his neck.

What I said, my voice muffled in his neck, was: "Yes, Jasey. That's a deal."

But what I was thinking, as I held onto him before leaving the cabin for the last time, was how much easier that would make the months ahead. Because I had, by this point, no doubt whatsoever that I was pregnant. In fact, I was three months pregnant, with a child due to be born in June.

Which was the third reason why the Bank of Michigan robbery had to wait until spring.

Dawn. July 2, 1996, sitting above the Huron River on a railway bridge, my head was in my hands now. Not seeing either the water running below nor the snow falling on that day twenty-three years before as we put on our packs and began the hike out to the Greyhound depot in Rose City.

Just seeing blackness, pressing the heels of my hands against my eyes, like a child.

And then, of course, I rose.

Not being a child.

Being an adult who had long ago gotten used to facing the truth. Stood, and walked across the bridge back to the path out of the Arb.

If I was to be in the Linder cabin by the following weekend, I had a lot to do.

Date: June 21, 2006
From: **"Benjamin Schulberg"**
<benny@cusimanorganics.com>
To: **"Isabel Montgomery" <isabel@exmnster.uk>**
CC: maillist: The_Committee
Subject: letter 32

I feel a little guilty, being the one to tell you this part of the story. See, there are ways in which I have nothing in common with the others in what, I'm told, your mother likes to call "the Committee."

Obviously, I am responsible for everything that happened to your father in the summer of 1996, including that he abandoned you in a hotel room. Don't think that the rest of the Committee often lets me forget that. Still, that's not what I mean.

I mean that of all of us, including you, I am the only one for whom the summer of 1996 was unequivocally a happy time. It was, for one thing, the time of my life when I made my career a national rather than a regional one.

And that it was the time of my life in which I fell in love with Rebeccah Osborne.

Isabel, I don't how you remember that summer, if you remember it at all. I don't know if you remember it as a time of terror and dislocation, or if you've come to see it in another sense. After all, even given that you are so much younger, you must have figured out by now that you are not unique, that there are other children who had experiences much like your own, children of radicals, red-diaper babies.

Not knowing how you remember that summer—not knowing, in fact, even how you are reacting to this—I have no choice but just to tell you what happened, and how it happened.

And so, here is the truth of what happened, starting from that Tuesday morning of July 2, 1996, after Mimi Luric closed the Del Rio Bar and went to walk in the Arboretum.

When we left the Del after closing, Rebeccah and I walked Dr. Lewis home all the way across town to Awixa Drive, because he was, not to put too fine a point on it, loaded. More loaded, I thought, than made sense for a man who had had, with us, perhaps three or four drinks, which made me think he had been drinking in the afternoon—not to mention that he had a certain vagueness about him that strongly suggested marijuana. So loaded, in fact, that it was not until we got to his house that he remembered that he had left his car next to Angell Hall, and Rebeccah and I had to take his car keys and promise to park his car over by Rebeccah's and bring it to him the next morning.

Not that either of us were in any shape to drive, either, but from the Del to Rebeccah's house was only a few blocks. When we left Professor Lewis at his front door, swaying somewhat, he collected himself enough to say to us frankly, "I haven't done a very good job as an authority figure tonight, have I?"

Rebeccah answered pleasantly, with that wide smile of hers. "Sure you have, Dr. Lewis."

I, perhaps mistakenly, took exception to that, on the grounds of journalistic accuracy, and pointed out that he had certainly not shown his authority in the matter of holding his liquor. I suppose I shouldn't have been surprised that he found that comment less amusing than Rebeccah and I did. Still, he smiled while he watched us trying to repress our mirth—Rebeccah actually crossed her arms over her stomach and bent double. We were loaded too, after all.

"Thanks a lot. It's been a very strange day for me. One day, I'll tell you about it."

That was a promise he was to make good on, although not until years later, when we started putting this account together for you.

• • •

As for me, I got a little hint as to how strange Professor Lewis's day had been when I took his car keys from him. They were to an Avis rental.

"Why would this guy have rented a car?" I wondered to Rebeccah on the way back across town. In fact, I guess I wondered it several times, because I was still wondering as she—less drunk than I, or so she claimed—drove it through the deserted, predawn streets to her house.

"Hey, the fuck do I know? Maybe he's having a secret affair." Frowning with the effort to drive normally—she was, as I had assured her when she'd insisted on driving, equally drunk as I—she answered irritably, but I didn't buy that. Ex-hippies don't have secret affairs, they have open marriages, and I muttered as much to Rebeccah, but not loudly enough or clearly enough for her to hear, I think, as my head was thrown back on the seat and I was feeling too splendid to care.

I cared even less when we got out of the car outside her house, and she started up the flagstone path with, it seemed to me, the expectation that I would follow. But no: halfway up she turned to face me, and in the night air we regarded each other for a moment.

"So, do I still smell like an ashtray?"

She answered by stepping toward me, so close that I could feel the warmth of her body against mine, and, with her left cheek next to my right, sniffing profoundly. Then she stepped back, so that her eyes were inches away from mine.

"Nope. You smell like a piece of nicotine gum."

For a moment, we watched each other. On the slight slope of the path, she was a hair taller than I, and behind her head I saw over the roofs of the low houses and up to the sky. Then she said:

"You know, the bozo who heads the squash team and has a job waiting for him in the Justice Department?"

Not daring to speak, I nodded.

"The one with the chiseled cheekbones and Paul Newman's body?"

Nod.

"I mean, like, Cool Hand Luke Newman? Like, Cool Hand Luke who's planning to be a U.S. senator after he makes his first couple mil, and wants to marry me?"

This time I didn't even nod, and she smiled.

"He's history."

"Is that right?" The words may well have come out in a falsetto.

"Um-hmm." Her lips against mine were dry, slightly chapped, soft in a way that seemed an insight into not her physicality, but her personality. Then they were gone.

"I get off work tomorrow at ten."

This time my voice was hoarse. "Yeah? What time do you start?"

Surprised. "Five. Why?"

I looked at my watch. "That gives us more than twelve hours to make love."

Which were the last words I got in before she disappeared up the path and behind her front door, and I was walking home through the infinite, kind, midwestern night.

2.

How long had it been since I last felt good? That, if you'll forgive me, Isabel, is what I was thinking about on the way back to my hotel, that night. My memory felt so corrupt, so littered with things I did not want to think about. But that night, under a sky of smudgy clouds, walking through a hot midwestern night in a pretty college town, if I could dance, I would have.

On Wednesday morning, I called my editor and put in for the balance of vacation I had owing me, which amounted to nearly a month. The reaction I got was not so good. It involved, to my way of thinking, the words *fuck* and *fired* far more than behooved an august figure such as he. We ended the conversation with the understanding that the latter word would become applicable to me on Monday morning if I was not at my—and here, the former word came back into play in its adjectival form, morphologically identical to the gerund—desk by nine A.M.

Upon which, with mutual expressions of goodwill, we hung up.

It must have been right around then—that morning, while I stretched out on my hotel bed and fondly considered the various options my editor had left open to me, some of them requiring a physical dexterity I doubted that I possessed—that, for her part, Mimi Lurie was calling the owner of the Del Rio and telling him an emergency required her to take off for a while. And it was roughly the same time that, for his part, your father was leaving Dexter toward the north. It was also the day that Sharon Solarz was transported to Michigan, because the papers that morning showed her being led into jail in Ann Arbor, and a banner headline showed that a state judge had ordered a change of venue for her trial, which would be in Traverse City, due to the court's concern about demonstrations and counterdemonstrations in Ann Arbor.

None of that is what I remember that day for. In fact, I don't remember the day at all, just the night, when I met Rebeccah at the Del after work.

Here, too, when I think back, there turned out in retrospect to be a hint that all was not as it seemed. This was contained in the surprising fact that the black-haired bartender who hated me was absent, the bald owner with the white fringe of hair having taken her place. When he came to serve us, Rebeccah turned out to be on good terms with him too, making me wonder, not for the first time, why a young Republican like her seemed to be on such chummy terms with every sixties burnout in Ann Arbor. He explained to her that the black-haired bartender who hated me, Cleo, had been called away for a few days on an emergency. The significance of that, of course, was lost on us. When he left, I turned to Rebeccah.

"Tell me, why is a young Republican like you so chummy with every sixties burnout in Ann Arbor?"

"Hey, Schulberg?"

"Yes, Osborne."

"Shut up. Or do you want me to call the squash-team bozo back?"

The answer to that question was, no, I did not.

And that was only all the more true when, later that night, after I had walked her back to her house on East Ann Street, instead of leaving me on her flagstone path, she led me into the front door, through her neat little apartment, and into her bedroom, where, first turning me around, examining me gravely, as if for hidden defects, she put her hands on my chest and pushed me through what seemed like miles of high, thin air onto her bed.

• • •

An event that was, apparently, nearly as momentous for Rebeccah as for me, because Thursday she actually took the entire day off from her senior thesis—an exception to her puritan work ethic that I was not to see repeated ever again. Of course, it also was the Fourth of July.

I spent the day watching the muscles of her back and neck from the stern seat of a canoe, which we rented to paddle on the Huron; the evening watching those muscles from a variety of angles as she cooked me dinner in her kitchen, and the night conducting a closer examination of their intricate, complex strength, in her bed, while the Fourth of July fireworks boomed in the distance. When she slept, she did so with her right arm across my chest, allowing me the chance to continue my inspection over the rounded muscle of her shoulder, all the while using the pad of my fingers to understand more precisely the fantastically tender skin on the back of her neck, extending, with an infinitely subtle set of gradations, into her back.

This, it was clear to me, should last forever. This, I was perfectly convinced, mattered more than anything ever had, or ever would. Truth, justice, history, fuck that noise.

Friday morning, my run came to an end. When I woke, I found her dressed and packing an overnight bag.

Leaning up in bed on my elbow and starting a piece of nicotine gum, I asked brightly, "So, we're going away?"

"I am. You're not."

"Aw, that's not fair."

She sat on the side of the bed. "Sorry, buddy. I'm going home for the weekend."

My stomach sank, thinking of the solitude of the weekend ahead of me. Then it sank again, thinking of my editor's deadline. I wasn't, however, going to share either of those thoughts with her—I may have been falling in love, but I had my pride, and I had no intention of telling my adored object that I was going to spend the weekend sadly moping in a hotel room, waiting for her, then on Monday morning lose my job. But then my spirits rose again when she spoke.

"I was thinking, my parents have a cabin in Point Betsie. If you want, we could meet there on Sunday and spend a few days. I was kind of planning to go up there anyway for a little time alone—finish my senior thesis."

She said it offhandedly, but I had a sudden feeling that she cared about my reply. So I said: "I don't think so, Osborne. No thanks."

"Oh, okay." She wasn't looking at me.

"See, I'll be spending Saturday stalking your parents' place, hoping for a glimpse of you. Where'd you say they live? Mind if I take them hostage?"

Now she laughed and came to sit next to me. "I've been meaning to mention that. I told my dad I've been seeing you."

I nodded. "Smart move, Beck. Should I start running now or do I have time to get dressed?"

"Um, my dad *did* seem to feel there's a possibility that you're using me to get to him."

"Yeah? Has your dad seen you naked lately?"

"Not in a while, no. But I think I won't tell him you're meeting me in Point Betsie."

"So you're suggesting I'm actually enough of a loser to want to sneak up to your father's own country house, although he detests me, and secretly screw his daughter there?"

"Um-hmm."

"Okay. How do I get there?"

After she left, I went back to my hotel and called my editor. This time, while his language was more or less the same, the message was somewhat modified. No, I told him, I had not gotten any further on the Sinai story. Yes, I told him, the trail seemed to have gone cold. No, I did not see that Maggie Calaway had won a temporary custody order from a Massachusetts judge of Isabel Montgomery-Grant pending investigation into Julia Montgomery's current status as a drug addict. I didn't see, I had to tell him, because I hadn't yet seen the newspaper, which was embarrassing, given that I'm a reporter. Nor had I noticed that Sharon Solarz's venue had been moved to Traverse City before he told me; however, I did not tell him this. Instead, thinking quickly, I told him I was going up to northern Michigan on Sunday to be sure to be there for Sharon's arraignment on Monday morning.

I didn't tell him that I would be visiting at the house of the FBI field station chief there for the purposes of conducting a liaison with his daughter, although perhaps I should have. If I had, it may have mitigated the length, if not the content, of the speech he then gave me, the gist of which was that if I could remediate my ignorance about a story that I had myself broken, I could hope to stay over and cover the court appearance, but that if my expenses ran over twenty-five dollars a day I could pay them myself.

Here, again, the word *fuck* entered his diction twice, first—interestingly—in its adverbial form modifying the transitive verb pay, and the second time as an adjective modifying the plural noun *expenses*, as in: "fucking pay your own fucking expenses." It seemed to me that the language should have differentiated the adverb: *fuckingly*. The third and final instance of that word, however, seemed to have no grammatical relevance whatever, unless it could be considered a salutation of some sort, or a peroration, as it preceded him slamming down the telephone.

That day, as I sat in my hotel room reacquainting myself with the Solarz story, I wondered what Rebeccah would make of this. On balance, I thought, it was easier to tell her that I'd be driving over to Traverse City to cover the arraignment than to tell her that I had quit my job and ruined my career so I could avoid having to leave Ann Arbor. In any event, when she called me late that Friday night, her voice thick with sleepy desire, she was fine with it. In fact, it seemed she had decided that I should come up and meet her at the Point Betsie cabin on Saturday, as she didn't think that it would be good for her health to wait for Sunday.

"You've done something to my hormones, Schulberg."

Saturday morning, I started the drive up to Point Betsie.

Which was how it came about that I, too, joined what must seem to you to be a general exodus of people involved in this story to northern Michigan on the weekend of July 5, 1996.

3.

Point Betsie, when I arrived there on Saturday afternoon, was a collection of cabins that sat in thick woods around a little peninsular extrusion of coastline into Lake Michigan. From the wide front windows of Rebeccah's parents' house, none of the other cabins were visible, just an endless expanse of blue water rippling under an offshore breeze. Reflected from the water, the sun came into the house from two angles, making absolute the difference between inside and out, light and shadow. The windows open, the muffled clanging of a buoy bell drifted in.

While Rebeccah opened the house, I wandered through: kitchen of dark wood, simple cabinetry, ordered and bare; bedrooms neatly put away; an office containing a computer and a radio setup, government-issued, no doubt. Upstairs, Rebeccah's bedroom looked out over the water through narrow windows.

Without talking, we pushed the two iron frame beds together and lay down, feeling the breeze through the window, listening to the distant sound of the buoy bell. The air, like the light, autumnal, northern and chill, although it was early July. Rebeccah took her shirt off and leaned over me, offering her throat to my lips as she moved her body weight onto mine. When she sat up to open my shirt, I ran my hands over the inverted curve of her waist, over her ribs, and onto her breasts. She looked up, drawing in her breath, and the sun fell from the narrow windows exactly over her throat. And I was raising my hand to that when a noise sounded from downstairs that could only be a knuckle against a wooden screen door.

With a sigh Rebeccah came back to herself and, after leaning down for a long kiss, rose off me. She slipped on her T-shirt and made her way out and down the stairs. And I, after a moment, heard the following discussion.

"Hey there, Becky. Your daddy here?" It was a man's voice; and a well-known man, for he had clearly, by the sound of his voice, let himself into the cabin.

"Hey, Timmy. No, he's down to the city. What's up?"

"Oh, I was out this way. Thought I'd get these to him rather than have them sent downstate. No big deal."

"What is it? Photos?" Rebeccah's curiosity struck me as polite, as if she were hoping he'd leave. At least, I hoped that's what she was hoping.

"Um-hmmm, yep. Check it out. Satellite pictures. You can buy them from a Russian company. Quicker'n getting 'em through government channels. Your dad's been getting pics of the Linder estate done every other day."

"Is that right?" A pause, perhaps while she looked. "That's the cabin, right? Cool. What's that?"

"By the cabin? Bears, I'm guessing. No cars have been up that road—we'd have known, 'cause your daddy has Fish and Game monitoring. There's two."

Another pause. Then: "Well, I'll get these driven over to your old man, I guess. You talk to him, tell him I stopped by, will you?"

"Sure will." The screen door slammed, and Rebeccah came back upstairs. This time I heard her dialing a rotary telephone and reporting the conversation to her father. Then she came back into the room, took her shirt back off, and swung her legs over me again.

A lot of other things happened that weekend. We had dinner out in the sandy garden next to the water. We made love again, hidden by the dark in the sand dunes, while a quarter moon crossed the sky. We spent Sunday sailing Rebeccah's father's Hobie Cat out of the little yacht club at Point Betsie. And Sunday afternoon, something big happened to me. It happened fast, as these things will, but once it had happened there was no going back.

We had come in from sailing, and showered together, and while Beck was in the bathroom, I went downstairs to mix a drink. Which I was doing when Beck appeared, in a towel, her skin a flat tone in the light through the kitchen window.

"What's this, Schulberg?

I knew, right away, something high-stakes was happening. "Scotch and soda. Want one?"

"I do not."

There was a silence.

"Fuck, Beck. What is it you do want?"

She answered right away. "A sane, healthy, kind father for my children."

"Isn't that looking pretty far ahead?"

She looked away now out the window, and I watched her shoulder blades, shadowed in the long light, while the buoy clanged far out on the water. When she turned, she said softly but clearly:

"This is our first fight, or our last? It's up to you."

We watched each other a moment now, while I tasted the peaty scotch in the back of my throat.

"What about healthy and kind?"

"What?"

"Healthy. And kind. Father. But not necessarily sane."

"That'll do."

So we went upstairs after our first of many, many fights. Without a drink.

Sunday night, we swam in the light of the waning moon, then climbed upstairs together and, in the chill of night, like little children hiding, climbed under the blankets. We slept, arms and legs wrapped together, breath moving and falling in and out of synchronization and syncopation.

Early Monday morning, before dawn, I woke as suddenly as if a floodlight had been turned on, eyes wide open in the dark. And, as if continuing a discussion rather than waking her in the middle of the night, I said: "Rebeccah. You saw people up at the Linder estate."

"Ben?" She sat up. "Are you awake?"

"Uh-huh."

"You're talking in your sleep, right?"

"Uh-uh. In the pictures. The guy brought for your dad. You didn't see bears, you saw people."

"Jesus. Ummm . . . no. Timmy said it must be bears. Says the only road in is monitored, and no traffic's been reported on it."

"Uh-huh. And why is your dad monitoring the road?"

"Ben?" I felt her head shift on the pillow. "Guess he doesn't want any cars on it."

I considered that. Then I said: "And if someone hiked in?"

She laughed sleepily. "They get there on foot, they're unlikely to do any damage. My dad won't care. Mind if I go back to sleep now, you wacko?"

I did mind, and I told her so.

What I didn't tell her was why.

I mean, I minded losing her company.

But mostly I minded the fact that once she was asleep, there was nothing for me to do but lie there in the dark, thinking, thinking, and feeling my heart pound with entirely unwelcome certainty.

Date: June 22, 2006
From: Multiple Users
To: "Isabel Montgomery" <isabel@exmnster.uk>
CC: maillist: The_Committee
Subject: letter 33

Time: 10:29:54
User: Amelia Wanda Lurie

How did it all happen? It's so hard to put together now. As if, at the end, everything accelerated, beyond my ability to differentiate event from event, toward its conclusion. As if, after meandering along for the past twenty years, the pace of our lives suddenly grew urgent as our paths veered to collide.

In fact, it is a trick of memory that makes it seem so. In fact, events continued at exactly the same pace, the two of us drifting slowly—almost accidentally—toward each other.

Little J. Jason Sinai. Your father. I can see him, that night in his hotel in Dexter—I can see him more clearly than just as if I were there: I can see him as if I were him. I can see him getting off the telephone with Jeddy; I can see him writing down the words "October 1973"; I can see him falling promptly into a sleep so black, so total, and so dreamless that when he woke, in the morning, for a moment he wondered if he had had a stroke.

October 1973. With all the pain of age that he had for so long been holding at bay, your father swung his legs out of bed and began his trip to October 1973.

A trip through time that started through space. To Rose City by bus, changing in Flint and Saginaw, each time cleaning his tail carefully, in Flint through a Woolworth's, in Saginaw through the bus depot itself. In Flint he bought a new sleeping bag, a backpack, some Montrail trail-running shoes: this time, in this season, he felt the role of a suburban Detroit yuppie attracted less notice than anything else. In Saginaw, on the other hand, he switched personae diametrically, and bought a set of camouflage in an Army-Navy store and a complete set of angling gear. For each he invented a narrative: in Flint he was in sales at a company that made hospital accounting software; in Saginaw a machinist—and, incidentally, shop steward in Local One-oh-nine—at a tool and die factory in Kalamazoo.

In Rose City he filled the backpack with food at the little Superette in town, just across from the diner where he and I had met in October 1973.

None of this surprised anyone: to see a man dressed for war preparing to hike in to state land in Michigan raised not an eyebrow.

Time: 11:29:04
User: Jason Sinai

A woman, however, would have, which was why Mimi took another route in. She drove her Mercury all the way to Alpena, nearly the northernmost point of the continental state, and sold it at a used-car lot. Then she walked into town, as if she knew the place. She shopped at the little grocery store for supplies and carried them in three brown paper bags to a white clapboard house. A young woman sat on the porch with two children in a muddy yard, next to a rusting dishwasher to which was tethered a puppy.

The woman seemed entirely indifferent to Mimi's arrival, as did the children and puppy. The thin man inside, however, sitting in shorts and a T-shirt in front of the TV, took notice, rising to turn off the TV and then sit back on the couch, attentively. Mimi spent a few moments giving him some marijuana—rental for a room in the house, evidently, because when it was done she went upstairs, unlocked a door to a room, and inside, extracted a full pack from a closet from which she changed into well-used hiking boots, shorts, and a plaid shirt. She left the house through the back door, crossing an expanse of stubby grass to the tree line, and stepped out of view into the forest before taking out a compass and a topo map and, crouching, figuring her direction. This she did quickly enough to show her familiarity with the territory—she neither needed to read the magnetic deviation from the map nor had to take bearings from it. Then she shouldered her pack and, holding the compass, pushed deeper into the woods.

Time: 12:01:51
User: Amelia Wanda Lurie

When your father left Rose City by the North State Forest trailhead, the little parking area was deserted. There had been rain during the week, and a couple yards in, he stopped carefully to examine a mud puddle. The mud was thick and drying and held old and new deer tracks and what could have been a coyote or large dog, but no shoes. Looking up and as far as he was able, he counted three mushrooms growing in the middle of the trail. Gingerly, he stepped into the woods and around the mud puddle. Then, still moving slowly and carefully, he made his way through the woods for perhaps two hundred yards, until he came back down to the trail and began to walk.

Time: 12:07:58
User: Jason Sinai

Mimi bushwhacked southwest from the little house in Alpena, following her compass, until she broke through onto state land and the DEC trail. Then she pocketed her compass and, examining the trail for signs of recent use, as I had done at the trailhead far to the south, moved along carefully for a time.

Unlike me, what she found was not reassuring. The mushrooms along the path, all sprung up since a recent rain, had virtually to a one been pulled, torn, and dropped. Farther down the trail a flat rock had also been turned, and on examination, four white marks showed on its side, as if scratched by nails. She stopped to consider this. Then, cautiously, she went on.

The answer came soon. Straightening out, the trail crossed a stand of new pine, growing so thickly that it became a precise corridor through eye-level walls of green. In this corridor, in front of her, a black bear, perhaps three hundred pounds, ambled on all fours, stopping to turn rocks or taste mushrooms. Mimi stopped short and watched the bear as long as she could, until it rounded a turn. Then she went forward again, stamping her feet and whistling. As she approached the turn, she felt a high singing in her head, a high aria of danger, and closer yet, dizziness seemed to swirl behind her eyes. When she rounded the turn, however, the trail stood empty, the bear clearly having slipped into the woods. Feeling watched, she walked on.

After seeing the bear, Mimi found herself with a sense of being irretrievably deep into the forest, at the mercy of the trail. It was an unusual feeling for her: like me, Mimi feels afraid when there are people by, and safe when she's alone. Now, however, she felt as if the forest had tricked her, trapped her, and in fact there was no turning back: already the afternoon was enough advanced that she could no longer be out of the forest before nightfall. The thought caused her unaccountable fear. Not the energizing, challenging physical fear, the kind that can be a source of energy, but a debilitating and intellectual one, a force that drains. She walked against it as long as she could, for several hours certainly, and indeed was able to push herself to the little clearing that houses the junction of the state trail and the old logging road south. Here, beyond a barbed-wire fence and a small crowd of No Trespassing signs, the road runs into the Linder estate. Only then did she sit and rest, and when she did so, she realized that she was scared of her destination, not of the forest. The forest, to the contrary, was the ultimate hiding place. The forest, to a fugitive who knows how to use it, is the next best thing to being at home behind locked doors.

Early evening, and the sun, cooling perceptibly, cast long light into the little clearing. Her breathing calmed, and silence rose around her, and for a moment there was a pause, in which she could hear a breath of wind making its way lazily through the treetops to the south, moving eastward. It shifted and came toward her, carrying with it colder air from the shadowed depth of the forest, growing in volume as it curled over her, heading north. Then, like an audience stopping clapping slowly, it faded, and the air heated again in the resounding silence under the dome of sky.

Time: 13:06:05
User: Mimi Lurie

Just before sundown, your father emerged from a long stand of primary growth to a rocky vantage on the cusp of a bowl between two short ranges. The valley was heavy with darkness as the sun disappeared behind the hills. The sky, however, was still bright, as if borrowing the light from another day in another part of the world.

To one side, here, a little clearing sat next to the tree line, and in it he quickly built a fire ring, then gathered wood from the forest floor. When he had finished, the light was nearly gone, but he managed to put out a ground cloth for his sleeping bag and pitch a rainfly made out of a tarp. Then he lit a fire and warmed a can of beans. He ate hungrily, sitting by the little light, drinking from a plastic bottle of water, finishing his dinner with a Snickers bar that, he hoped, would kill his appetite until morning. Then he extinguished the fire.

A waning half-moon was up, throwing patches of silver into the woods around him. With the fire gone, the distances rose, carrying noises from miles off: a woodpecker, a deer, perhaps a squirrel chattering at danger. The eerily distorted cry of owls rose, warping through the trees and over the little hills, nearly electronic in its spookiness. With a piece of climbing cord Jason hung his backpack ten foot above the ground, then tied off the cord, leaving it swinging softly in the darkness. He felt his way back to the sleeping bag now, and climbed in.

Time: 13:31:21
User: Jason Sinai

Mimi in the morning, wrapped in her sleeping bag, opened her eyes suddenly, feeling afraid. In the chill dawn a mist hung over the forest, shortening distance and muffling sounds. For a time she tried to pierce the muffled silence with her ears. Then in fluid movements she rose, packed her sleeping bag, retrieved her backpack from its hanging place, shouldered it, and moved directly back onto the trail without peeing or having breakfast. In a few feet she found her answer: a thin, delicately curled spoor, still steaming—perhaps coyote, perhaps wolf: an animal had been watching her sleep.

For a time she walked thoughtlessly, feeling the familiar weight of the pack, the welcome exertion of her legs. For a time, she managed to forget what she was doing here, in these woods of her childhood. The sun came up, warming the air, and intensely she felt the distances around her. She crossed a stream and stopped, using a tiny butane stove and a tin cup from her backpack, boiled water, then mixed in instant oatmeal. A whippoorwill was singing, and without realizing, she began to supply words to the song. *It's really real, Betsy. It's really really real, Bet-sy.* Finished eating, she washed out the tin cup carefully in the running stream, watching the sun reflected in the silvery little rocks at the bottom, the water brilliantly clear and purely cold. Crouching, she dipped her hand into the water, holding it until her bones ached. The words to the bird's song had come to her from her father, her father who was always playing with his adopted language, who'd invented the birdsong's words years in the past. *It's really real, Bet-sy, it's really really real.* To her surprise, she found herself crying. *It's really real, Betsy.* But why hadn't it seemed real? The years passing, one after the other. *They were really really real.* The irrevocable things that had happened, each one making her a different person than she had ever wanted to be. God, she had loved him. She had loved him. She had loved him. Like her hand ached in the cold water, she had loved him, that thoughtful man with his frail body and whitening hair making play with words all the while he was implacably being destroyed by men working for the government, deliberately, his work, his home, his life being removed, one by one. What had he ever done other than try to be decent? Even his famous communism had been nothing but decency, the idea that the gross inequities of the world must have some redress, that there must be a better way. America had saved him from the Nazis, for Christ sake, by VE Day he had put every penny—every single penny—he owned into war bonds. But decency, mere decency, it turned out not to be a right but a privilege, didn't it? Decency, it turns out, you can die just for it and nothing more: not for justice, not for patriotism, not for truth, just for the chance to be a little fucking decent, that too was only for the rich in America.

For a long time, Mimi Lurie watched her tears fall onto the surface of the stream and be carried away while in the ice cold water her hand ached, and ached, and ached. The whippoorwill, as if shunning her too, moved off farther from perch to perch, its song—*It's really real, really real, Bet-sy*—tracking its passage as it grew fainter and fainter. Then she stood and, cherishing her bloodless hand, began to walk again.

Time: 14:42:34
User: Mimi Lurie

Your father crossed onto the Linder estate from the south, and began following the old logging road in. The dusk thickened, like a syrupy substance poured into the space between the trees. He walked until he could no longer be sure he was on the trail. Then with real reluctance he finally gave into the imminence of night and made a camp, using the last few minutes of night to gather twigs for a tiny fire. That was unfortunate, because it gave him only the barest of light to open a can of chickpeas and one of sardines, which he washed down with water he'd taken from a stream that afternoon. Then, again, he climbed into his sleeping bag and lay awake, staring at the moon, which was no longer discernibly a half, while still days away from a quarter.

Tomorrow he would reach the Linder cabin. Tomorrow. Tomorrow the question would be decided.

Time: 15:01:33
User: Jason Sinai

Saturday morning at ten o'clock Mimi looked up from the mantra of her boot steps on the trail to see the blue of Linder Pond. Gingerly she stepped around it, watching the big midsummer tadpoles flick away frenetically. At the south edge of the pond lay a field of high grass, at the edge of which she saw emerge the roof of the cabin.

She lay down on the trail and watched for a long time. Then, leaving her pack next to the pond, she made her way to the front door and swung it open on its rusted hinge.

Two of the four windows had lost their glass. The wooden floor had sagged in at the middle, and the doors of the cabinets in the little kitchen all hung askew with the slope of the walls.

Piles of leaves were collected in the corners. A nest had been made, and long deserted, on a rafter, and a decomposed raccoon lay against the wall, under it a leather-bound Goethe, chewed nearly beyond recognition by sharp animal teeth.

The door swung shut on the breeze. With careful step she circled the room. When the door opened she turned and saw, first a shaft of thick, nearly autumnal midsummer light falling into the cabin, defining a corridor of swirling dust particles as it fell and splashing onto the wooden floor, and second, standing in the doorway, holding a shovel, a middle-aged man with, in his unshaven, wondering face, what was left of Jason Sinai, that is, me.

"Don't clean up. We won't be here long enough to bother."

Those were her first words, and she said them in response to my first movement, when I broke the stare we held each other in and moved to scoop up the raccoon's decomposed body with a rusted shovel I had just found on the other side of the lake from where I had watched her come in. A half hour before, when I had arrived, I had noticed the dead raccoon also. When she spoke, I paused in mid-action, listening without looking at her. Then I continued, deliberately, to shovel up the body and carry it outside.

Time: 15:07:12
User: Mimi Lurie

I found him standing, leaning his forehead onto the shovel handle, outside in the tall grass where he'd buried the raccoon. The sun, falling unimpeded through miles and miles of blue sky, showed him in cinematic composition. Now, watching him, I saw more of the child I'd known in the middle-aged man. His body had, of course, thickened, but so had his muscles grown. His hair, under his baseball cap, was black—dyed, I assumed—and thinned. And a fine set of wrinkles spilled down his face from his eyes. None of that mattered, however, when he looked up, and showed in his brown eyes that in no essential way had he changed at all. It was a surprise—a noticeable one, apparently, because he now spoke.

"What?"

I hesitated. "I'm just surprised."

"How little difference the time makes, right?"

"How'd you know?"

He shrugged and looked away, and while he did, a line of poetry came back to me: *But across the open countryside/The grass is waving its good-bye/To someone waving his good-bye to us.*

Time: 15:12:12
User: Jason Sinai

When I could, I answered her question. "I've seen Jeddy, and I've seen Donal James. I noticed it with them. The age is like a disguise."

"That's not the case with everyone." Her voice sounded faint in my ears, in the distances of the field around the cabin.

"We always did think we were better than everyone else, didn't we?" I spoke, leaning on my shovel, looking at her with helplessness.

Now it was her turn to shrug. "Time's been on our side on that one."

"Has it?"

"You tell me, Jasey. Name the neo-con from Weather. Who ratted who out? Who went corporate?"

I squinted at her now. "Is that a fact?"

"As far as I know, it is."

"You see someone, then."

She answered carefully, and I remembered how she was when skirting something she couldn't say. "I don't. I read the papers. I've seen some people act like jerks, but I haven't seen one of us ever, in any profound way, betray anyone."

By way of response I turned back to the hole I was digging. For a moment I worked, until my shovel hit something hard. Then I leaned down into the grass for a time, then rose again, holding a thin tin box.

"Remember this?"

Wonderingly, she reached out for the box I was proffering, and opened it to reveal, wrapped in cellophane, five carefully rolled joints and a pack of matches from the West End Bar, in New York.

"Jesus, Jasey. I thought you were burying the raccoon."

I was smiling. "Twenty-three years. Think this'll still get us off?"

"I don't know."

"Um-hmm. I sealed it tight." I reached across the distance between us, not looking at her, and took the box back. "Did you bring any soap?"

"Yeah. In my pack. By the pond."

"So, I'm going to take a bath in the pond. If you'll lend me some soap. Then I'm going to go clean up the cabin, no matter what you say. See, I have nowhere else to go."

"And me?" She spoke to my back as I began to walk to the water.

"You, if you'll hang out, I'll make you some dinner." I spoke without looking back. "Believe it or not, I packed in a bottle of wine. Then we can find out if that dope's any good."

Time: 15:31:19

User: Mimi Lurie

I stood, watching him walk away.

Thinking, so that's how you meet Jason, is it?

Clean up in a lake, cook dinner, drink a bottle of wine, and blow a joint?

As if nothing has changed, and nothing has happened, and you can take up the conversation just where you left it, twenty-two years before.

Moving slowly, now, I followed him over the uncut meadows to the edge of the lake.

Date: June 22, 2006
From: "Benjamin Schulberg" <benny@cusimanorganics.com>
To: "Isabel Montgomery" <isabel@exmnster.uk>
CC: maillist: The_Committee
Subject: letter 34

Sharon Solarz, in person, was a handsome woman with thick black hair and a face that had aged hard, bringing out a certain pugnacity that would not, in my opinion, sit well with a jury.

In the Traverse City courthouse, she stood while Gillian Morrealle entered a not guilty plea to the judge and the judge remanded her without bail to await a trial date some six weeks forward. Afterward, Sharon was escorted out, handcuffed, and Gillian went out to face the reporters on the courthouse steps. I, alone among the reporters, made my way over to Rebeccah's dad.

It was, when you think about it, a pretty comical situation. But of course, I wasn't feeling very funny. To the contrary, of course, I was pissed. The time when Osborne had a choice about talking to me was long past, and I had been planning to make that clear to him. In the event, he seemed to know it already, because he watched me approach with an impassive face, then shook my hand without surprise and, as if we had an appointment, walked with me out of the courthouse, away from the press, and down the street to his car.

In town, the day was hot. The weather forecast had called for a storm, and although there was no sign of it in the endless sky of blue, perhaps the heat did have an ominous quality. We didn't talk about much of anything: what was happening between his daughter and me made it impossible, of course, to venture outside of our most impersonal business. For his part, while he clearly knew that his daughter's affective life was not within his control, I felt that he still wasn't able entirely to conceal his dislike of me.

I didn't take it personally. In fact, I didn't think about it at all. All I wanted to do was to stand there and look at him. To look at him and try to understand what in the world he could conceivably be up to. Of course, since we were walking side by side, and the guy was huge, and my neck therefore wasn't capable of the angle required to look up at his face, that was impossible. So instead I subjected the region about the level of his underarm to my interrogation, and waited for later to stare at him.

I got my chance, finally, to meet his eye when we reached his car and he stopped by the driver's door, clearly showing that this was as good as it was going to get for me. So I took a breath and, speaking very carefully, pronounced the following words into the space between us.

"Mr. Osborne, I need to ask you some questions. They're on the record, and they have consequences. I think you have to answer them."

As soon as I'd spoken, I panicked briefly. Why was I the only journalist here? But he nodded, as serious as I, and I went on confessing my confusion, really, rather than accusing.

"It doesn't make sense that Sinai abandoned his daughter to save himself, and you knew that when we first met."

I saw calculation, but no surprise, behind his eyes as he considered that. Then he answered quietly:

"Yes. It doesn't make sense. And I knew that."

"The only thing that makes sense is that Jason Sinai has been searching for something or someone that could exculpate him."

Again, he considered that. "Granted."

Now I thought for a time, looking away, trying to choose my words.

"Could . . . could Mimi Lurie exculpate Jason Sinai?"

This time he answered readily, with a nod, as if I'd just settled something for him.

"I want to go off the record."

That surprised me quite seriously. But I nodded, and he went on, this time in a surprisingly gentle voice. As if, suddenly, trying to help me.

"Sure she could. Exculpate him. But think it out, Mr. Schulberg.

First he'd have to find her and convince her to testify. And second, she'd have to surrender herself."

I was totally lost. And because we were off the record, I told him so. "How does that work?"

He licked his lips. When he spoke, he lowered his voice. "Think it out. Think it out. Only one was in the bank with Dellesandro. That was Sharon. We know that because we know Sharon had gone through a training program and gotten a job as a teller. She could only do that under her own name, to get through the bank's vetting process, right? Background check and such like. So where were Jason and Mimi?"

Watching up at him, thinking, I repeated the question to myself, utterly at sea. "In the car, of course. That's the charge against them."

"Exactly. In the car, the famous getaway car. So, Sharon left the bank, carrying one bag of money, and left Dellesandro inside the bank. He kept guard for two, three minutes until the car pulled up. Then he left. It was in that time that the shooting occurred."

I nodded. "The shooting occurred while Dellesandro was alone. So what? They're all still accessories."

He answered in a flat voice, then watched my reaction. "Why did Sharon leave Dellesandro alone?"

What my reaction was, was to stare at him for a long time, trying to hide the mental effort I was making from showing in my eyes. "You tell me."

"Mr. Schulberg, I don't know. I wasn't there. But I do know that if there were two people out in that car, it shouldn't have been necessary for Sharon Solarz to walk outside to call the driver. Do you follow me? One of the two should have been at the wheel of the car. The other should have been either in the bank, or keeping watch outside, ready to signal the driver to bring the car out. Instead, what happens? Sharon Solarz walks out of the bank, leaving Dellesandro alone. Why? Why did she do that?"

"Is there doubt? About who was in the car?"

Now, for the first time, Beck's father let annoyance into his voice. "It's not that there's doubt. It's that there's no *witness*, Mr. Schulberg. You should know this."

I nodded, my stomach plummeting. "I should know it."

He stared at me for a moment, now, as if my ready admission had impressed him. Then he went on in a softer voice. "No one else noticed it either, if it's any comfort. But think it out now. If Mimi was in the car alone, then she could testify to that. She could testify that Jason wasn't there. And Sharon, if she wanted to, could corroborate."

I absorbed that. And when I talked again, my voice rose slightly, like a child. "But what's that mean? It's a participant criminal's testimony. So what?"

"Aha." He paused, looking strangely, and incongruously, satisfied. "See, that's why you're not a lawyer. That's *exactly* the point. If Mimi came out of twenty-two years' hiding and surrendered herself to the police, without a negotiation, without a lawyer, expressly to testify that Jason wasn't at the Bank of Michigan robbery, it would be what lawyers call a declaration against interest. In other words, she'd be giving testimony against her own self-interest, testimony that destroys her own possibilities of defense. For example, she couldn't claim that Jason was the ringleader and forced her to do it under duress, which would have been a very convincing argument in her defense. She also couldn't claim that Jason was there and she wasn't. A declaration against interest is very strong piece of evidence, Mr. Schulberg—it even mitigates the rule against hearsay evidence, which is huge. Then, if Sharon concurred, Sinai would be effectively exculpated. You see what I'm saying? He'd be found innocent—with his brother and sister-in-law attending to this case, he'd be reunited with his daughter in days."

My jaw may well have been hanging open. "So she would have to surrender . . . and Sinai is right now convincing her to give herself up to a jail term to save him?"

Again, the blandness of his tone seemed to be implying that he was telling me more than he was saying. "No. Not to save himself. That's the point. To save his daughter."

"But . . ." I was thinking hard, now, staring into this man's sky-blue eyes. "If Sinai's not guilty, why's he been in hiding for the past twenty-two years?"

He smiled, again, softly and without humor.

"You tell me."

Finally, I said: "To protect Mimi?"

"To protect *someone*." He was speaking very softly now. "To protect someone, Mr. Schulberg. Maybe not Mimi. The point, I think, is that this is a guy who has been hiding someone's secret for twenty-two years. Now, a bigger threat has presented itself. The threat of letting his daughter go to her mother. Think it out, Mr. Schulberg: if he thought that his daughter had any chance of being okay with her mother, would he be going through all this? Let me answer that for you, because you aren't a father. If he thought Julia was going to take good care of his daughter, he'd let her go. There are few things worse than what Sinai's doing to his daughter now. No. Jason Sinai's had to weigh his daughter's interest against the interest of the person he's been protecting all these years. And this is the way he's come out."

I licked my lips. "If Mimi exculpates Sinai, will it be true? I mean, these guys have been lying their whole lives. Is this just another trick?"

Now he smiled a rueful smile. "Tell me something, Mr. Schulberg? Which is it? Are you a really good reporter, or incredibly lucky?"

That one was easy, and I answered it honestly. "Both."

He nodded. "I hear you're staying at my house in Point Betsie."

"Yes, sir." I repeated my question. "Is Sinai innocent?"

"I'll call Rebeccah there with my answer this afternoon."

This was the first answer he'd given me that wasn't good enough, which disappointed me. I thought we understood each other. And so I spoke as follows.

"Mr. Osborne, what would the actual charge be against an FBI agent who failed to follow credible information about the whereabouts of a fugitive?"

It didn't work. He answered agreeably. "I think there'd be a variety, actually. Mr. Schulberg?"

"Yes, sir."

"You're about to do a lot of damage to a lot of people. You have no idea how much."

That wasn't fair. I said: "That's not fair. What choice do I have?"

"Just one. Give me five, six hours. The only thing that'll change by then will be that some innocent folk'll have an easier time in the storm you're unleashing. Trust me."

And watching him, I found that I did.

I didn't go back to Point Betsie, though.

What I did was, I filed my coverage of the Solarz arraignment by plugging my computer into my cell phone and writing it in the car.

Then I found a phone booth with a yellow pages.

I needed to find a camping store, and a car rental.

The camping store for some good topo maps.

The car rental to change the one I had for a four-wheel drive.

Date: June 23, 2006
From: "Amelia Wanda Lurie" <mimi@cusimanorganics.com>
To: "Isabel Montgomery" <isabel@exmnster.uk>
CC: maillist: The_Committee
Subject: letter 35

Your father and I made love that night. We bathed, ate. We drank the bottle of wine and smoked one of the joints. Then we made love. There was nothing awkward about it. Not to would have been awkward. What I wanted afterward was just to lie still on him with all my body weight. He must have understood that, because soon he stilled too.

There was no way to tell him: This is how you are to me. There was no way for him to know that it had always been like this with him, and although I had slept with strong and sensitive people, people whom I had loved or admired, it had always been true, it would always be true. There on the floor of the dark Linder cabin, a perfect continuity was established between the girl of eighteen who first slept with this man and the woman, now forty-five, whose skin lay next to his again.

He? For him, it was entirely different. He had not meant this to happen. I knew that as surely as if I were sharing his thoughts, as if the barely suppressed energy of his muscles were talking to me. I knew that if I looked, his eyes would be open, staring away at the moonlight in the window. This, it meant something other to him; he was doing it more *for* me than *with* me. I knew it with the surety of a prophecy.

Oh, I didn't doubt that I was as huge for him as he was for me, as legendary for him in the personal mythology of his life as I was in the popular mythology of our generation. I saw it all in reality, what was happening. I knew too that he had had a baby with another woman, and by that very fact that woman was never entirely absent from him. I knew that tired fact that old lovers learn when they meet again: that we never fully progress from one lover to another, that each real experience of love is in its own way a dead end, because each particular intensity is never found again. The twenty-two years between now and our last meeting was irrelevant. Nothing had changed. Except, of course, everything had changed. And lying there on him that night, after twenty-two years away and a single evening together, I knew that for Jason, what had changed was that I could never again be an end in myself. Not while his daughter was missing. I could only be a means to the single end that meant anything to him: getting her back.

So we lay there in the dark, he staring open-eyed at nothing, each hoping for the courage with which we had, as long as we had known each other, faced everything else.

I woke once to see the pink and blue of dawn, out the window, in the sky. My head was on his shoulder. Then I must have slept again, for when I opened my eyes the second time, he was gone, but the window was ablaze with light. And again I must have slept, because when I next opened my eyes, as if by appointment, the sun had risen high enough to throw that shaft of thick light past the sink and onto the floor, dust swimming in the brightness.

I felt I could sleep forever. I could do anything to avoid what was ahead. But I rose and dressed, jeans and a sweater against the chill morning. He was outside, in a thick plaid shirt, crouched over a little fire, on which he'd made coffee and oatmeal. He had a transistor radio, which he turned off at my approach. Wordless, I crouched next to him, thighs and shoulders touching, while he gave me coffee.

"What's the news?"

"Sharon was arraigned this morning. Pleaded not guilty."

"Has she said anything?"

"Nothing. No interviews, no nothing."

"What's her lawyer say?"

"Gilly? That her client's innocent. Gilly was one of us, you know." His voice was velvety, as if comforting a baby.

"I do know." I looked at him. "What's she doing?"

He met my gaze, and struggle showed in his expression. Then:

"Sharon's after a plea, Mim. She was trying to negotiate a surrender when those bastards got her."

"Um-hmm. Those bastards. Shame on them."

My tone was derisive. But your father shook his head.

"Don't go that way on me, Mimi. Please."

And suddenly, at last, I didn't care. As if finally, with Little J, I could complain. For the first time in nearly a quarter century. "Oh, what way, Jasey? Oh, what the fuck way?"

"Mimi. Mimi."

"Little J. Everyone has a daughter. Slovo. Che. Sandino. Allende. Everyone has fucking children."

"I know that. I know that." He answered miserably, looking down. "It doesn't make any difference to me. She's seven, Mimi."

"Her life's not ruined." My voice was low, urgent, like a pusher: first nickel's free, darling. "There's so much more of it, so much more. She has every chance in the world."

But your father shook his head. "That were true, I wouldn't be asking you to do this. I *know* this child, Mimi. She will never get over what's happened to her already. Sending her back to her mother is setting the stage for disaster. I mean serious, serious disaster. Drug addict, violent, miserable disaster, Mimi. Her mother has a disease that a few years won't make better. Maybe ten years, if she really really tries. As is, this child . . . Mimi, if I could take my heart out of my chest and give it to her, I'd have a chance of saving this child. If I can't, then she's finished."

I broke in. "Jasey, don't you think for a second it's the *sacrifice* that's stopping me. That I'm protecting my life? Fuck my life. Fuck my goddamn life. I could slit my wrists this minute. You know that, you of all people. You're asking me to do something *wrong*, something neither of us believe in. It's not *right*. You can't *make* it right that way. It's not *right* for Sharon to do time. Why don't the boys down to Kent State have to do time for their mistakes? Why do the ones who massacred Vietnamese become senators and the ones who screwed up a single time become fugitives? Why don't the ones who shot Freddy Hampton get jail terms? How about the soldiers who *assassinated* Americans *citizens* in the Phoenix Program? Why us, not them? For Christ sake, we've given our whole lives to the principle that the government can't excuse *them* and punish *us*. They have to *pardon* us all, or *punish* us all. Now you want me to give in, Jasey, Jasey, how the fuck can you ask me to do that?"

I was shouting, and he hushed me. "Mimi, Mimi. You don't have to convince me."

"Then why are you asking me this?"

"Because the principle doesn't matter." He was nearly whispering. "None of the principles matter."

"So you're one of those, huh. As soon as you breed, all your ideals go out the window. Suddenly it's a Darwinian universe, and you have to protect your young. Fuck everyone else's kids. Fuck racism, globalization. Fuck the people all over the world being massacred by our guns, by governments we put in power, we arm, we support. Fuck the black kids with no schools and no food and no future, all over this country. Fuck that we've spent twenty-five years proving that if people want to, they can be free of all these rules, of all this government power. Fuck that we've been the *only ones* saying fuck you to the march of this government, and *fucking everyone* has seen us do it."

He answered as if reciting a familiar point in a familiar argument. "If there were a revolution to sacrifice her to, I'd do it. I'd do it in a second. You know that."

"Well, the revolution didn't happen. That doesn't make us wrong. Every single thing we said then is true today. SDS, the whole New Left, it didn't make the slightest difference: just like we said. Imperialism, racism, warmongering. The government's stronger, and the people are weaker, that's the only difference."

"I know that, for God's sake." Now, for the first time, he let his intonation sharpen. "That's not what I'm asking."

I, in turn, hardened, my voice hoarse from shouting. "What are you asking, then, if it's not to abandon every ideal that means anything to us?"

"I'm asking for a trade. She's seven. You're heading for fifty. I know her, Mimi, you don't. I'm asking for the next ten years of your life against the rest of hers."

A long silence ensued in which I watched the high clouds drifting in from the north, felt the enormity of air mass moving against me, the rising wind that felt already like it was bringing, from great distance, rain. When I spoke, what I said scared me. It scared me that I was even capable of saying it.

Because of all the things I could have said, what I said was: "I saw her in Ann Arbor."

Your father nodded, but didn't answer. Then he said: "What's she like?"

I started crying again, just like that. "She's beautiful, Jasey. She's so, so beautiful."

Date: June 23, 2006
From: "Benjamin Schulberg" <benny@cusimanorganics.com>
To: "Isabel Montgomery" <isabel@exmnster.uk>
CC: maillist: The_Committee
Subject: letter 36

Two hours after I left Rebeccah's father, when my cell phone rang, I was in my new Mitsubishi Montero, parked in front of a camping supply store in Traverse City, studying topo maps of Michigan. It was Rebeccah on the line.

"Are you still in Traverse City?"

I told her I was, hoping I wasn't going to have to explain what I was doing.

"What happened there?"

"Nothing. Solarz was arraigned. I saw your dad."

"He told you his news?"

"No. What news?"

"God, Benny. My father just called. Both my parents have quit their jobs!"

I let that sink in, which it seemed disinclined to do. "What in God's name does that mean?"

Her voice was cracking with excitement. "I don't know. It's on the local news. My mother resigned too. They each did a press conference saying they were resigning for personal reasons. And then my dad sent a police car to bring me home. I'm on my way now."

"Is he sick?"

"No. He says not. He says he'll explain when I get there. And he left a message for you. He said to tell you that the answer to your question is 'yes.' Do you understand that?"

I answered slowly. "I do."

"There's more. He told me that I have to tell you something. Benny? Are you listening?"

"No, I fell asleep. Out of boredom. Christ sake, Beck."

"Calm down. He told me that I have to tell you that I was adopted. And one more thing. He said that you have a one-hour head start. Do you understand any of that?"

"No. Do you?"

Pause. "No. I was hoping you could explain it to me."

Do you know what the funny thing was, Isabel? The funny thing was, that when she said the word *I,* I couldn't.

But when she said the word *me,* I could.

I mean, at the beginning of her sentence, I could have explained a little. I could have explained the coincidence of her mentioning her father and Mimi Lurie and the family connection to the Linder estate to me when we first had drinks at the Del Rio and how, therefore, I knew that her father had lied to me when he said he had never met Mimi Lurie.

And I could have explained the intuitive leap I'd made when I learned Rebeccah's father was having the Linder estate surveilled.

I could have explained to Rebeccah how, therefore, I understood that Mimi Lurie and your father had gone to meet, again, at their old hideout, and realized that her father knew that too.

And I could explain my realization that there was something wrong in Osborne not chasing two known fugitives when he was aware of their whereabouts.

Finally, I could have explained that there was something Mimi could do that could exculpate your father.

All of that, I was able to explain to her when she said the very first word of her short sentence.

But by the last word, less than a second later, I could explain the rest, also.

All of it.

I don't know how, and I don't know why, and if you ask me till the end of my life, I still won't be able to tell you. But in that second while she spoke, I suddenly understood it all.

And so I answered, slowly, slowly: "Beck. I think you need to go talk to your father."

Date: June 24, 2006
From: "Amelia Wanda Lurie"
<mimi@cusimanorganics.com>
To: "Isabel Montgomery" <isabel@exmnster.uk>
CC: maillist: The_Committee
Subject: letter 37

I lay against his chest, the wool of his sweater against my cheek, heaving with tears. I couldn't remember crying like this before, ever; I couldn't remember ever before feeling so deeply purging an emotion. When it was over, sniffing, I sat up and crouched next to him, pressed against him, feeling Jasey's muscle next to mine, drinking his coffee in hot sips.

Big clouds were blowing in from the north on gusting winds, throwing the tree line in and out of shadow. I watched, and felt Jasey next to me, and dared not look at him. What would he do when I said no? I knew the harshness of what I was sentencing him to. He'd never see his daughter again. He'd have to go somewhere and start over. I knew what it was like to go somewhere and start over at our age. It was not a pleasant thing. Would he stay with me? The thought made my heart quicken. Why not? I had more than enough to live on. Could we not kidnap his daughter and take her with us? At this thought, I looked over at him, now, smoking a cigarette and ashing it into the little breakfast fire he had built. Then I said nothing. There was only one thing he wanted me to say to him. There would be nothing possible for us, nothing, after I said no.

Instead I stood and took his hand. Led him back inside the cabin, back to the nest of sleeping bags on the floor. He followed, willingly, as if he, too, knew that in the impasse between us there was only one kind of communication that was possible, or that made any sense.

Inside I knelt with him on the nest of sleeping bags. I held his face in front of mine. The dusky light, the high sun splashing light on the floor but leaving the corners in absolute shadow. "Little J." He nodded watching me. "I can't do what you've asked me to."

He nodded, again. "I know you can't."

"Then what are you asking me?"

"To become the person who can."

The sun dipped and deepened, dipped closer to the ground so its rays lengthened into the windows of the cabin, creeping up across our bodies; deepened in color so that the afternoon light that filled the cabin when I woke with Jason's head sleeping on my shoulder, it was a light that seemed to stain rather than illuminate. Slowly, I felt myself sinking into that light; slowly I felt myself traversing the whole range of emotions conjured by that light, the whole territory of emotions that had been waiting to have their way with me again these twenty-two years and more.

Then the process stopped short, and before even being able to think what I was doing, I shook your father's head and whispered.

"Jason, wake up. There's a car coming."

Date: June 24, 2006
From: "Benjamin Schulberg" <benny@cusimanorganics.com>
To: "Isabel Montgomery" <isabel@exmnster.uk>
CC: maillist: The_Committee
Subject: letter 38

The road up to the Linder cabin veered off the state trailhead outside of Rose City, and although it had not been used for years, by the look of it, it was passable.

I kept the Montero in four-wheel low, but even then I wouldn't have made it had not a guy in the camping store where I was buying my maps advised me to take a chainsaw and a towing chain in case of falling trees. Twice, thanks to him, I cut away trunks that would have stopped me dead from the road and pulled them to the side by looping a chain around them, allowing me to pass. What had taken Jason over two days to hike—he took the state trail—took me some four hours to drive on the old logging road.

I arrived at last in an overgrown meadow, bordered by a pond, with a little cabin turning its back on me. I turned off the engine and stepped out of the car into a late-afternoon silence filled with the rush of wind. It was, it felt to me, a lot of wind, and above the tree line I could see scudding clouds across the sky. As for the sun, low to the north, it both looked into my eyes from above and bounced off the surface of a pond from below. With a hand over my eyes. I stepped through the thick grass around to the front of the house. There was a small wooden porch to the open door, and inside I saw, when my eyes adjusted, two backpacks and a pile of sleeping bags. I did not go in but went back a few steps into the pasture.

I'd been wondering for hours how I was going to do this, but now that I was doing it, I found it coming by itself.

"Mr. Grant. Ms. Lurie. I'm here alone. I have not notified the police. I think I can help you."

I don't know what I was expecting. What in fact happened was that with no warning, your father was behind me. Speaking in a conversational tone.

"Help? You've sure helped me a lot so far, Benny."

"I haven't come as a journalist." I turned while I was speaking, and found myself facing your father. He wore a wool sweater over jeans, and was barefoot. And now, in his suddenly obviously Jewish face, I saw everything.

"No? What have you come as?"

Of course, I couldn't answer that, because I didn't know. And after a moment your father nodded, absently, as if thinking about something else. At last he said, "Okay, Benny. Let's just go sit out there by the pond, should we? I'd hate to miss the last sunset of my life."

He walked off to the pond, and I followed, speaking to his back. "And why would this be the last sunset of your life?"

"Oh, what with the chance of being in jail tomorrow night. Funny thing, Benny. Every time I see you, the chances of my going to jail seem to go up so."

I thought about that. "That's not a causal relationship, Mr. . . . Sinai. It's that, I only figure out where you are just before the police do."

"Don't think they haven't noticed that. Don't think they're not coming here, right now, because of you."

That surprised me. Could I have been under surveillance myself? "Hmmm . . . I guess it might seem that way. To a certain way of thinking. But I'm told that they're on their way anyway."

"Yeah, well then. Let's cut to the chase, shall we?" He let his voice get low for that one.

Was this guy actually joking with me? Now? I asked: "What are you going to do, Mr. Sinai?"

"Well, I was thinking of getting you to violate the ethics of your profession, for one thing. Then, of getting you to break the law."

So we went to talk by the pond. And later I realized that as we did so Mimi Lurie must have gone back into the cabin, prepared her things, and left the house on the logging road to the west, running quietly across the unmowed field around the house, right behind me, her passage covered by the noise of the wind, and into the tree line that seemed to be beckoning her as the wind blew the crowns of the tree, this way, then that.

Date: June 24, 2006
From: "Rebeccah Osborne" <beck@cusimanorganics.com>
To: "Isabel Montgomery" <isabel@exmnster.uk>
CC: maillist: The_Committee
Subject: letter 39

The patrol car pulled up, and from the backseat I saw my parents waiting outside their neat little house in Traverse City. My mother was still in her work clothes—a black pants suit that would be hidden by her judicial robe—but my father had already changed, jeans, sneakers, a white T-shirt. He came forward and shook the policeman's hand through the driver's window, then opened the door for me.

I felt tall, suddenly. Tall and awkward, walking between the two of them, these aging people, into their kitchen. It reminded me of how I'd felt as an adolescent, when I'd started to gain my height. An ungainly swan with a ridiculous neck.

At the kitchen table we sat, the three of us. For a time there was silence, and I remember a feeling of pure unwillingness to hear whatever it was they were about to tell me. Cancer, divorce, bankruptcy: whatever it was, I remember, I simply did not want to hear about it.

And then, almost exactly when, way up north, Jason Sinai was beginning to talk to Ben Schulberg, my father began to talk to me, and in both cases, they were telling the same story.

2.

1974. In mid-June, in a midwife's office in Ypsilanti, Michigan, assisted by her husband, a young woman called Sally Maynard gave birth to a daughter.

Two weeks later, on a Friday afternoon, just before closing, a man walked into the front door of the Briarwoods Mall branch of the Bank of Michigan. As he walked in, he put on a rubber mask. Inside, moving swiftly and efficiently, he closed the large drape at the bank's front window, while from behind the counter a teller—a black-haired woman—moved next to the bank's guard and put a handgun to his head, elbow pointing out. Then the man rounded up the customers in the bank, obliging them to lie down, with the guard, on the floor. While he did that, the black-haired woman returned behind the counter, ushering her colleagues at gunpoint into the bank vault.

When she returned, the masked gunman tossed her a canvas sack, into which she emptied the contents of all five teller drawers, what would later be estimated at $700,000. She hoisted this over the counter onto the floor. Then the gunman tossed her another canvas bag, which she took back to the vault. For several minutes, all was silent on the floor of the bank, the masked gunmen holding his hostages quiet. When the teller emerged again, this canvas bag was also filled, this time with what was estimated later to be another half million dollars. She managed to hoist that over the counter, then she climbed over herself. Now she picked up one bag, leaving the man covering the guard, and carried it out the door to a parked car.

A Dodge Dart.

With a single person in the driver's seat.

The black-haired woman, Sharon, stopped in surprise.

"Where is he?"

Moving steadily, Mimi climbed out of the car, opened the trunk, and the two put the bag of money inside.

"With the baby."

They got into the car now and pulled it around to the front door of the bank. As they drew up, the gunman came out, pulling off his mask as he came to show a laughing, happy face. Vincent Dellesandro. He threw the second bag of money into the trunk, then climbed into the backseat of the car, and Mimi pulled away.

For a time they drove in silence. Then Dellesandro, still laughing, said: "So, the little daddy bailed?"

It was a comment to which she made no answer. She drove carefully, slowly, while her passengers squirmed into fresh clothes, then stopped the car and traded places with Sharon so she could change herself. At the train station, in Ann Arbor, she pulled into a parking spot, and the three left the car. They transferred the money to the back of another parked car, which Vincent Dellesandro and Sharon Solarz then drove away. As for Mimi, she walked into the station restaurant and went into the bathroom, where she stuffed her hair into a hat and put on a pair of sunglasses. When she came out, she went to yet a third car and, alone, drove it away.

The money was with Sharon and Vincent. John and Sally Maynard, with their new baby, were to relocate the very next day to West Virginia, where John was to be working at the new Arcata printing plant—so they had been telling their neighbors, for weeks. In fact, what the Maynards had planned was a complicated series of identity switches that would leave them in northern Oregon, absolutely unconnected with the couple who had just left Ann Arbor.

The house in Ypsilanti was half packed.

Three-fifty-five. Baby would be waking from her nap just now, waking to the smells of Jason's last dinner in Ypsilanti.

The car's dashboard clock must have been a minute fast, because at four, when Mimi turned on the news, music was playing, "Magical Mystery Tour," the final bars.

Then came the news.

> "WGHJ, CBS Radio, Detroit, Michigan. A cop is dead in a bank robbery, and four suspects have been identified as members of a radical underground group. The leader, Vincent Dellesandro, is a veteran of the U.S. Army in Vietnam and a paroled state prisoner. With him were three others, all prominent in antiwar circles from the University of Michigan, thought to be members of the Weather Underground group. From Briarwood Mall, Ann Arbor, Ted Martz reporting."

> "Jimmy, it was a textbook case of a perfect plan gone wrong. Witnesses say that at approximately five minutes before clos-

ing, a masked gunman entered the Briarwood Mall branch of the Bank of Michigan and subdued the guard and customers. Meanwhile a teller, apparently a plant, pulled a gun from her cash drawer and took control of the other employees. According to witnesses, it wasn't until the whole robbery was nearly over that one of the gunmen shot the guard. Witnesses say that as he was leaving, he said to the guard: "I was a cop too, once. Military Police in 'Nam. Want to see something they taught me?" He then shot Sergeant Hugh Krosney from Chelsea, Michigan, at point-blank range in the chest."

A road in Ypsilanti, Michigan. Mimi Lurie, sitting at the wheel of a running car, moments from home.

She knew the consequences, knew them with brilliant clarity, and right away. Now she was an accessory to murder. Now she could never surface, never. Now she could never, ever come back.

And she knew what Jason would say. He had said it, in night after night of argument, as they went over every possible consequence of the robbery that was about to take place.

"Mimi, it's too risky. Let them do it without you."

"No. I've been with Sharon since the beginning. She saved my life in Chicago. I owe this to her, Jasey. This one last thing, I owe her."

"And if it doesn't work out?"

"Jasey, I'm just driving the car. We don't need to surface. Baby never needs to know that we were anyone else. We never need to change identities back."

"No." He had been lying beside her in the dark while he spoke, and now, like an animal surprised, he stepped out of bed and began to pace. "No. I've thought about that, and I'm not doing it, Mimi. You stay home, and if it goes bad, you take that child and you surface. You won't be implicated."

Mimi shook her head. "No way. You stay home. I do the job. It's my gig, and I do it. Besides, I'm better than you. End of story."

"And if it goes south?"

"Then you surface, with baby. Deny any knowledge of it."

She watched him pacing in the dark room, a slim, naked young man, his body covered by fine red hair. "It won't happen, Mimi. I'm an accomplice already. She'll be a year in a foster home by the time I'm cleared. If I'm cleared."

The child was two weeks old, and, as if it held magic power, they had not yet started calling her by her name.

For a long time, nothing. Then, Mimi, eyes focused on the baby, said very softly what she had known, all along, she was going to have to say.

"I had a friend when I was young. A kid. His father was a friend of my father's. His only friend."

"And?"

"I grew up with him. Until he went to 'Nam. He came back with a combat vasectomy. Do you understand?"

Jason turned on the light. "What the fuck are you talking about?"

"You do what I say, Jasey. You hear me? If something goes wrong at the Bank of Michigan, you take our baby to him." Still looking at the baby, she spoke as if in a trance. "His name is John Osborne. He lives in Traverse City. His father was good to mine, and he'll be good to her. He needs her. And no one will ever, ever in the world connect Johnny Osborne's daughter with us. She'll have the perfect new identity."

3.

Two o'clock in the morning, June 27, 1974. In the bedroom of his little house in Traverse City, John Osborne woke up next to his wife. Someone was downstairs.

My dad had always hated this house. There was no security in it, none, and even now that he was no longer undercover but an investigator in the Traverse City FBI field office, he knew that he needed more security than most. But the department had refused to underwrite his housing expenses, and this had been all they could afford. And, as he often thought, it wasn't as if they needed room. Vietcong Dong. Ho Chi Minh Birth Control. Happened all the time. He was luckier than most—with hormone replacement therapy, all he lost was his fertility, not his virility. Now someone was in the house.

Just like he had always known would happen one day. There was a criminal in his house. One of the hundreds of people in this state he had put in jail. One of the hundreds of people in this state with reason to hate him.

Lying awake, he processed the noises, quickly, before the roar of blood filled his ears, as he knew it was about to. The kitchen screen door had opened—that was the sound that had woken him—a pane had been knocked out of the window, and the inner door was being opened now, as he listened.

A wave of adrenaline went through him. When the screen door closed again, John climbed out of bed. In his underwear, he moved across the room to where his holster hung on the back of a chair, and took his gun. Then he began to make his way to the door, holding the gun in both hands, pointed down.

Which was when he heard a baby cry.

The sound woke his wife.

Flabbergasted, they made their way down to the kitchen, where they found a young man, barely in control of himself, sitting with a two-week-old baby.

4.

Twenty-two years later, in that same kitchen, I sat across from my parents as they finished talking. I turned in my seat sideways and stared out the window at the lawn. The poplars were bending in wind gusts; big clouds were beginning to jostle each other in the sky. I stared, and for minutes on end—literal minutes—said nothing. Until, finally, in a voice that surprised even me, I spoke without looking at them.

"I've never asked you about my birth parents."

"We know that." My father, but I couldn't look at him right now.

"It was a decision I made early."

"Yes. We understood."

"But if I had?"

My mother, this time, speaking readily. "Your father and I intended to tell you the truth."

"At least, we had intended to decide whether to tell you the truth." My father.

"And if all this hadn't happened? Then I was supposed never to know?"

"Never. We redid your identity. Papered a legal adoption. With the resources of the FBI at my disposal? Nobody ever needed to know."

"But what the hell were they thinking?"

"Thinking?" My father rose now, that massive man, and paced to the window. "Thinking? I don't think anyone was doing that much thinking, that night."

"And you? You had an accomplice to murder in your kitchen?"

"Sinai was innocent, Beck. He wasn't in that damned car. Any lawyer could have made the case that he didn't even know they were planning the robbery."

"Then why didn't he?"

My mother. "Because of you. Because if he did, you'd be the child of two legendary radical criminals. Sinai thought that even if he proved himself innocent, you'd still be sacrificed to the altar of the B of M for the rest of your life."

My father, disagreeing. "I don't buy that. Even if Sinai . . . your father, had turned himself in, no way he'd be able to prove his case—not without Mimi's testimony, or Sharon's. Dellesandro, after they caught him, he never said a word about it. In my opinion, your father was looking at seventy-five to life, hard time. And I knew Mimi. She was not going to turn herself in, not if all she was doing was giving you an inmate mother. All your life, that would never go away. Your fugitive mother. All your life, they'd be watching you, keeping tabs on you, looking for contact with your mother. You'd never have any normalcy."

"Normalcy?" For the first time I looked up at them. "What about you, Daddy? An FBI agent consorting with a federal criminal, illegally adopting their child?"

He answered without hesitation. "That's our decision, not yours. We've always been willing to face the consequences. I'm lucky it took this long."

"Mom, Dad. Okay." I sighed, tiredly, as if talking to children. "Okay.

I get it. Everyone has to have birth parents. These are mine. Can we stop talking about it now?"

"Well, yes and no, Rebeccah." That was my father, and his tone was soft.

"Which means?"

"Which means"—it was my mother answering, and the answer was not without bitterness—"we have to see what's about to happen. Your boyfriend's already figured it out. And he's a journalist. And then, the chances of Mimi Lurie surrendering to testify that Jason Sinai was not at the Bank of Michigan robbery, because he was away giving his daughter to us—they're virtually nonexistent, Beck, there's just no way she's going to do that."

"So? Then what's the problem? You've kept your secret this long."

"Well, darling, it's not that simple. If Mimi won't come forward, then we'll have to."

If it were possible to be more shocked, then I was.

"You're not telling me you two are going to exculpate Jason Sinai?"

They, too, looked at me in surprise.

"Of course we are, Beck. If we can."

"But why?"

"Because of his daughter, of course. His other daughter. Your half sister."

They watched each other now, each, no doubt, enumerating for themselves the consequences of that corroboration. And then, my mother smiled, and in that smile I saw the courage of people living purely in reality.

"Don't look so glum. Your father and I always looked forward to the chance to tell the truth. We're proud of what we did that night. And we're proud of every single thing we did that resulted in you."

Date: June 25, 2006
From: "Benjamin Schulberg" <benny@cusimanorganics.com>
To: "Isabel Montgomery" <isabel@exmnster.uk>
CC: maillist: The_Committee
Subject: letter 40

And as your sister's parents told her the deepest secrets of her life, way up north in the Linder cabin, Jason Sinai and I sat watching the two suns converge, one lowering out of the sky, one rising along the surface of the pond.

It had taken him perhaps twenty minutes to confirm everything that I knew. Twenty minutes to dot the i's and cross the t's; to give me the one or two details that I hadn't figured out.

Now, finished, we sat side by side in the doorway of the Linder cabin and watched the two suns converge.

I don't know what he was expecting me to say. What I did do, however, was acknowledge the one fact he was still keeping from me.

"Mimi's run, hasn't she?"

He smiled, wryly. "I was hoping to have a little more time with her."

"Why'd you let her go?"

"Oh." He took in, and then let out, a deep breath. "If she's to help me at all, she has to surrender. See what I mean? She can't be captured. So she needed the head start. When the FBI gets here, they can chase me. They'll think Mimi and I are together. I'll lead them astray to the west, and she'll escape to the east."

"Why'll they think you're together?"

"Because you'll tell them that. Won't you?"

I shrugged. "Will Mimi surrender?"

I watched him in profile for a long time now, this strange man, staring into the distance, squinting against the suns. Then he actually smiled, and wearily stood up.

"No."

"So what's the point?"

"Oh, well. Before she can *not* surrender, she has *not* to be caught."

We walked back to the cabin now, and while I watched, he began changing his clothes from his backpack: jeans to shorts, and a pair of new Montrail trail-running shoes. I watched from the door, hearing the wind ripping the trees back and forth behind me.

Then I said:

"You know, I'm planning on making you my father-in-law."

He nodded, not looking at me but at his running shoes, which he was lacing carefully. "I gathered as much. Not very professional of you, is it, Schulberg? Falling in love with your subject's daughter."

"Count yourself lucky, Mr. Grant. It's a slippery slope, these ethics concerns. Maybe I'll keep sliding down. Even mislead the police for you."

"I hope so." He rose now, and in his smile I saw suddenly who I was dealing with: a man who had been living without pretense or illusions for most of his life. He turned and busied himself with assembling a small collection of objects—a tin container, some matches, some food, and some water—to go into a little day pack. When he finished, for a time, your father held my gaze from the depth of his brown eyes, but I did not think he was really seeing me. Then he said to me the following, and I tell you, Izzy, I knew as I was listening that I was going to be able to remember what he was saying well enough to write it all down, so deep an impression was he making on me.

"You know, Benny, it was the best dream we ever had. That these motherfuckers could be made to stop. That the machine, the corporate machine, the government machine, the war machine, that it could be turned off. That real rights of real people could come before money. That ecology could come before corporations. It was the best dream we ever had, ever, and it put us in the same company as all the other people around the world who had the same dream; all the people who've dreamt the same dream in all the history of mankind. From the very beginning. Do you hear me?"

I nodded, and he went on. "You can listen to what everyone says, you can think what you want. You can listen to the right-wing sons of bitches or the left-wing phony pundits. There's no difference. You can think we fucked it all up, killed the antiwar movement, destroyed the New Left, whatever you want to. But when you remember me and Mimi, remember that no matter what any of our old friends say, the fact is that in every possible way—race, war, the environment—we were right. Our government has rolled over that dream, every single day since the sixties. Every single day it's gotten worse. The poor are poorer, the rich are whiter, and the world is a worse place than it's ever been before. And every single ex-hippie who occupied their Ivy League school's cafeteria or got hit in the head at a protest, every one of them sitting back with their copies of the *Nation*, watching their kids go to college and checking on their 401(k)s—every single one of them who tells you that tired bullshit about how badly we fucked up: they've lived their whole lives at the expense of what they once dreamed. It was the best dream any of us ever had, and that it failed, Benny, that the machine rolled on over the poor and the blacks at home and all Latin America and Africa and all of the people who so detest us abroad, it didn't have to happen that way. If this country had made the three central ideas of the Port Huron Statement—antiwar, antiracism, and antiimperialism—the law of the land, today we'd be living in a safe, just, and prosperous society. Probably a safe, just, and prosperous planet. All we ever asked them to do was to practice the fundamental principles of constitutional democracy, like they always said they would. And that they wouldn't . . . it's so sad, I can't tell you."

He looked steadily at me, and when I made no response, finally he nodded.

"The question you face, Ben, it's not, which side are you on. That was never the question. See, in this thing, no one's right, everyone's wrong. The question is, do you want to keep company with the folk who are wrong *my* way or the folk who are wrong *their* way? If it's them, hell, you know what to do. But if it's me, then you tell the FBI when they get here that Mimi and I took off together and that we went west. Okey-doke?"

With that he turned and started off at a slow jog toward the tree line, shaking in the wind and darkening in the clouding sky.

When he disappeared, for a long time I listened to the wind crossing over the forest.

It took the FBI, with the state police, perhaps another half hour to get there.

When they did, I told them that Mimi Lurie and Jason Sinai had taken off, by foot, together, and they had run west.

Date: June 25, 2006
From: "Daddy" <littlej@cusimanorganics.com>
To: "Isabel Montgomery" <isabel@exmnster.uk>
CC: maillist: The_Committee
Subject: letter 41

Midsummer, the logging road west from the Linder estate was generally dry, but large exposed rocks required constant adjustment to the step, either to jump over or to jump on. I was ready for it: no trail running anywhere is harder than the Catskills, either in the shape you have to be in to survive the physical challenges, or the grace you need to negotiate the obstacles.

The first couple of miles I resisted the urge to hurry, loping along slowly on the full length of my foot, heel to toe, body loose, taking the shock with the strong quadriceps muscles of my thigh. Although one set of impulses kept pushing me faster, I paid serious attention to staying slow, eleven-minute miles, letting my body warm up and balance for a very long run. What I could not afford, now, was an injury—any injury.

At 4:15, some five miles in, I stopped suddenly and turned around, pitching my hearing as far back down the trail as possible. Nothing: just my panting breath and behind it the gusty, angry wind bending the treetops hard one way, then the other.

Above, the white clouds blowing in from the north showed virtually no blue, swirling and whorling in the wind, enough weather, I thought, to keep helicopters away. That meant they'd be coming by foot, perhaps with dogs. I was wearing one of Mimi's T-shirts, the one she'd worn hiking in, because it smelled acridly of her sweat. This would be good for the dogs. But it also felt familiar, which now felt more important. And that made me notice, now, that there was inside me a great deal of anxiety.

That was not good: nothing could be worse timed than fear, right now. Fear, I knew, is quick to affect your judgment, sometimes in ways of which you're entirely unaware. It could sap all the energy I needed to run. It could cause me to trip, to fall, to injure myself in a way that, in turn, would stop me from ever running again. Molly never ran when she was anxious, for that very reason.

Molly. At the thought of her, my anxiety swelled again, and I grew not only afraid but, what was worse, afraid of being afraid.

Still breathing heavily, I reached into the trailpack for the little Army-Navy bullet case holding the dope I had buried at the Linder estate in 1973 and dug up the day before. In the saturated light through the clouds, above, the blue of the box's surface was a pastel. And suddenly I so clearly remembered buying it at a head shop on Liberty Street, just for this purpose, to carry joints in. And then something else occurred to me: from far in my memory, dimly, I thought: "I saw Sharon Solarz that night."

Sharon. I closed my eyes and saw her, her curly black head of hair, her aquiline face, wearing faded hip-huggers and a black leotard top, dancing to Junior Wells and Buddy Guy at the Blind Pig, a cigarette between her lips and a Miller longneck in her hand.

Without a second thought, as if I owed it to that twenty-two-year-old, I put the joint to my lips and struck a match.

While I smoked, now, I took out my survey map. There was another eight miles to the end of the logging road, where it intersected with a dogleg of the state trail: one direction came twelve miles from a trailhead along Route 25, due west, the other direction led due north to the Oscada, some fifteen miles. If they learned from Benny where I—and Mimi with me, according to Benny—had gone, they could perhaps be getting a second team out on the 25 right about now. That meant I had eight miles to do against their twelve to arrive at the trail dogleg.

I repacked the bag and looked up the trail. There was a steady grade up, now, and I thought I remembered that this would be the case for some time. As if doing an inventory of my resources, I checked my anxiety level and found it not lessened but somehow contained, painful but present in only one portion of my body.

That thought, however, I failed to connect with the joint I had just smoked, perhaps because, stoned, I had forgotten having smoked it.

Pack strapped on, I took a skip and began running again.

Again, having forgotten the dope, I did not question my immediate, enhanced sense of my body's balance. Knowing I was going too fast, I slowed and began running off my toe, using my gastroc to absorb the impact and to launch the leg, instead of relying on the tendon of my heel. The step was made all the easier by the fact that the little logging road had grown over with grass, a magically soft surface that folded beneath my running shoe and cushioned each step. When my gastroc, in turn, began to feel the use, I switched my gait back to a flatter-footed step that relied again on the tendon and sped up to tip the vectors of my weight farther forward. Tendon, I knew, would last longer than muscle even when injured. That it would take longer to get better, if it got better at all, in this case didn't matter.

Now the wind came to me as a huge curvaceous breath in the sky, shaped like a paisley, rustling precisely around me, the round orb of the fat end encircling my head, then gaily sending its energy into the thin twist of tail. My mind seemed to follow that tail right up over the ridge and then on west through the high sky of windy clouds, defining a precise topology of forest hill and dale, of lake and clearing, as it went. And across the distance of wind, I felt the chill waters of the Great Lakes in three directions, the water that was sending these big clouds tumbling inland on rushing wind, the water that was feeding this enormous canopy of the sky the high kinetic energy of storm.

A sudden movement attracted me, and I saw, for several bright seconds, the tail quarters of a coyote, heading away. I stopped, but just briefly, and then leaned back into the run. In the wake of the animal's escape I felt the metallic, sensation of its fear emanating like rings on a lake's surface when a fish jumps.

As I ran for my life in the Michigan woods.

The Michigan woods. I breathed in balsam with the wind, as if it could pass purely through my body, dissipating and carrying away fear.

But now, stoned, there may have been terror in all the reality around me, but I was cleanly aware of it, without feeling afraid. What had happened? Calmly, I felt my way backward until I arrived at the joint, and as I did, I began to laugh. Ah, dope. The dope of my youth, apparently, had lost none of its potency.

Then I stopped laughing and slowed my pace. On my watch I estimated that I had run off four of my eight miles.

The lowering clouds had all but hidden the sun, now, and the evening was coming fast into the windswept forest. The deep woods during the approach of a Great Lakes summer storm. The sinking sun lighted the woods around me like a stage set. The hysterical wind poured through the trees; the plastic, nearly cartoonish colors shifting around me; the sky of fast-moving cloud, the dryness of the ripening leaves, deep green now. The road had sunk again into wetter land, and in the rutted track I ran thoughtless, an easy pace, catching footholds on the trail with my balls of my feet, shortening and lengthening my step between flat areas, jumping, sometimes, across little runnels of groundwater.

I came to the end of the logging road in two and a half hours, just as the sun had disappeared over a low ridge of hills. The remains of the old gate were there, but there was also a beaver pond that I didn't recall. It was too dark to check the topo map. For a time I stood, hands on hips, feeling my breathing calm. Then I took off my shoes and socks and gingerly waded through the beaver pond. On the other bank, I set myself on a perch that looked back over the trail the other way.

Where would Mimi be? Eyes shut, as if the big wind could carry my perception, I imagined sweeping across the topography of the peninsula toward the western coast. She was traveling a marked trail and had a flashlight—she could reach the coast road by midmorning the next day. If she were going that way—Mimi, I assumed, was heading for the east coast, Oscada perhaps, where she had a boat, or access to a boat. What I needed to do was to keep the police following me until ten or eleven o'clock. Then she would be free.

If I could. The full night was coming in now, the wind lengthening and hooting through the forest. I was shivering. In the bag were a set of silk long underwear. I pulled off my sweat-soaked running clothes and put those on. Then I pulled a space blanket from the pack and made myself a little nest in the leaves at the side of the beaver pond, my little pack with my clothes and shoes against my stomach. Lying there, shivering slightly, I dipped a cup of water from the pond. With the water, I ate two PowerBars and some salted peanuts. I finished with an orange.

Now I had no food left.

The thought made me feel free.

Free.

An unexpected feeling to descend on me right tonight. Lying on my back, I lit another of the joints and smoked it quietly, like a cigarette, letting the pouring wind whisk the big lungfuls of smoke away. To be alone in a woods, with a wind to destroy all sound and the darkness to hide in. To be stoned, the good, old-fashioned dope—nothing like Billy's hybridized bud—easing my fear, massaging my anxiety.

When had I last felt like this? And at the question, it was as if a tunnel had opened into my own past all the way back to high school nights when my parents were out, alone with a joint and the television; and further: hotel rooms with my parents, before my brother was born, with a foldaway bed in the corner. I closed my eyes against the wind whipping the treetops, against the darkening sky of clouds, aware that I was seeing forty years into the past, far beyond the time when I had lost my daughter, all the way into the time before my father lost me.

I never went back to my family's house after March 6, 1970, not once.

It had felt like freedom, then.

Now, huddling deeper into the space blanket and the little nest of leaves in the forest at night, I let my mind go where for years I had kept it away. The house on Bedford Street, my parents' since the fifties, filled with objects from my grandparents' Mount Morris—Jewish Harlem—apartment: their Katubah, their kosher dinner service kept in their oak sideboard. Its very rootedness was what had driven me away. The vast family—Sinais, Singers, and Levits, three cousins come together to New York in the last year of the last century, risen in a single generation, my father's generation, to the pinnacle of what the country had to offer. The family richness that had gathered in accidents of history like puddles after a rainstorm—the hospitality of America to Jews, the continuity of life in New York through boom and bust—its very wealth, its very warmth. Like the march of a Greek tragedy, it turned out to be that a generation later, my generation, it would all be undone, as if the very richness of the family held its loss as a necessary consequence. In the roar of the wind I saw that I had had a vision of the end of a way of life, of my family dissolving like wood in water, crumbling with age, battered by tide.

The wind hurled itself above me now, an endless pouring of energy, as if forming an impregnable roof above me, roaring through the miles and miles of empty forest, each tree shaking like a hand with a tambourine, each giving its voice to the roar of obliteration, and in that roar I huddled further into the delicious warmth that held my body within the blanket, like a magic spell.

We go through life on a tongue of flame. The very basis of our existence is as insubstantial as fire. We think that love makes loss bearable, but that's not true. Nothing in God's creation made losing Rebeccah bearable, nothing ever would. Love makes loss not bearable, but beautiful, and the beauty of that child, the beauty of that child's happy life, the beauty of the few days of it spent with me, it could have sustained me until the day I died.

I saw her in Ann Arbor, Jasey. She's so, so beautiful.

I fell into sleep as under a magic spell, curled into the warmth of my space blanket, surrounded by the roar of the wind in the trees. And perhaps my beautiful daughters, after all I had done to them, perhaps they still sent their beautiful souls to share with me this last night of freedom, because it was a sleep as sweet and sound and as healing as any I ever had.

In the morning there was a thick, still mist, the wind having gone entirely away.

Six A.M. Not far from me I heard the snort of a deer. Was that a dog barking in the distance? I imagined the deer pausing to listen. Then I heard the steps of it startling and running away. The barking had come from the east.

That would be team one, the one that had left from the Linder Cabin.

I unwrapped myself from the space blanket, emerging into the chill air, and changed back into my wet running clothes. I left the blanket and the silk underwear where they fell—let the dogs find that, it would kill some time. In the backpack now were two joints left over, some caffeine pills, and some aspirins. I took the pills and aspirins, smoked half of one of the joints, and saved the other, with the remaining matches, in the little pocket of my running shorts. Then I walked around the beaver pond so as to leave a scent back to where I had slept, and then made my way back to the trail,

A dog barked. This time under a mile away, and that was sure. What was less sure was whether I had heard a man's voice calling also.

Hunger suddenly welled up in my gut like nausea, and I leaned over to retch briefly.

I was at the dogleg of the state trail now. Leaning over still, I took several deep breaths. Then I started the northern trail at a sprint, nearly my fullest speed, for twenty-one full minutes by my clock, three six-minute miles and a couple of minutes to spare.

As soon as twenty-one minutes was up, I stopped dead, turned east off the trail, and climbed straight up a small incline, then made my way from tree to tree for fifteen minutes by my watch: a half mile at this pace. I turned at a right angle and, still sighting from tree to tree, made my way south for fifteen minutes, another half mile. Now I stopped and sat on the far side of a tree trunk, elbows on knees, head in my hands.

Slowly my breathing calmed. Slowly my body temperature came down. In the wet clothes, I even began to shiver. In the fog, I sat and shivered for a very long time, perhaps an hour, making no sound.

Now the mess of dope and exhaustion, the depletion of blood sugar, the overwork of endocrinal balances: my state of my mind was virtually impossible to take apart. And when at last I managed to put a name to the overriding quality of my consciousness, it was, to my immense surprise, loneliness.

When had I last felt like this? Dimly I felt my way backward from place to place, year to year, all the familiar avatars of loneliness—Julia's departure, Mimi's flight—until, to my surprise, I arrived at the big, diffuse bruise of my existence, the time in my life when I, too, became a father who had abandoned a child.

Oh lord, that child. Oh lord, Rebeccah at two weeks old. Two weeks of that translucent skin, that milky smell, the blue of her eyes.

The morning after I'd left Rebeccah with Johnny Osborne, I went back to Ypsilanti for the last time. I cleared out the house, mechanically, without feeling, until I reached baby's crib anyway. I told the neighbors that Mrs. Maynard had gone ahead with baby, and I packed the car and drove away, just as if I were in fact going to West Virginia. Down in Kentucky, I stored the contents of the car in a storage unit, paying for three years, and sold the car. The switch car, parked at the long-term parking at Lexington Airport three weeks before, by Mimi, was still there—Mimi had not taken it. And it was in this car that I drove to Chicago.

Now, as I held my face in my hands, crouched behind a tree in a fogged forest, I remembered those weeks as if the present, when I had lost everything, had formed a tunnel through time to its counterpart, those days of driving west to Chicago. To my enormous surprise, I had found myself amazingly, endlessly homesick. And not for my house in Ypsilanti with my wife and child—they were gone now, a hole in my breast, too horrible even to contemplate, like a gunshot wound—but for my childhood home.

It had seemed so close. As I drove west. My parents were sitting at their kitchen table, reading, or in the living room. My brother Daniel would be up in his room with Klara, my adopted sister, recently come from Israel, Daniel and Klara doing their homework or reading or smoking dope in the strange, conspiratorial friendship that had sprung up between them. In the downstairs study, the old dog, Replica, would be sleeping heavily, his white-flecked snout on two paws. And now, in the forest, in the very last moments of the run that had started then, out of all the things that could have come to me, the smell of my mother's kitchen came to me with a shocking reality: lamb shanks with their thick marrow, briskets cooked in wine, baking breads.

And while I was thinking that, I heard, directly behind me and at not more than fifteen yards, voices.

I had not meant to be this close, for God's sake. They were practically behind me—I could practically hear the dogs' paws. The wind was against them; that was good. And there was no scent trail to me: they were on the path coming from the east, and I had looped down from the north. The thought was a comfort for the second or two before the dogs began to bark.

Now I clenched shut my eyes, my heart exploding. In the muffling fog the dogs' barking was everywhere, all around me. Would they stand at bay, showing me teeth, or would they bite? I had always, deep down, been terrified of dogs. Like a baby, I hid my head under my hands and waited.

Until, my panic subsiding, I realized the barking was moving west.

The dogs had caught my scent on the northern trail and were pulling their handlers up that way.

Quickly now I stood and bushwhacked south until stumbling out onto the eastern trail.

And then I began to sprint again.

There was no preparation now. There was no stretching, or bending, or slowly building up speed. They were going to catch me. The only question was when. And so I stretched my legs out as far as I could for every step, putting the fullness of my body strength into my speed, jumping from perch to perch along the trail, soaring over anything I could so as not to have to risk landing.

Everything I was doing now was buying Mimi not even hours, but minutes. Capture was imminent; the only question was when. But how long could I keep running? You can, I knew, run only so far on physical strength. After a time, you start burning mental energy: determination, intention, willpower, fear, ideas. All these can power you beyond your physical strength, but as you use them, you impoverish yourself. Using mind's resources for physical strength makes mind very vulnerable, and for the first time I felt, again, the distant noise of fear.

I'd expected the rising sun to burn off the mist, but in fact as I ran, the fog deepened, fading the colors of the trees, hanging in shreds from the sky and snatches along the trail, dropping big wet drops of water. Like an acoustic wall, it seemed to bounce the sounds of my steps toward me, deadening any awareness of anything but the immediate. I kept moving through it, though, splashing through puddles and sometimes having actually to walk through slippery spots on the trail. At ten o'clock I stopped to drink from a little stream. That was when I realized that I had left without my backpack, and that in the backpack were the compass and map. And at the thought, the forest—the wet, dripping forest—rose around me like a sea, vast, undulating, impenetrable, with all the threat that the dope had been, since I had left, been keeping at bay. Then a dog barked, not far, but also to the north.

What was left now was the time it would take the dogs to follow my scent up the trail to the north, then down through my bushwhack.

I pulled Mimi's shirt off and flung it into the woods. Eyes to the ground, breath pulling in through my throat, I set the fastest pace I could and flew along the trail.

In fifteen minutes or so I was at my vital capacity. Now, however, I'd run past most of my physical pains and could move more easily. I stretched out my gait to take as much as I could of the impact in my buttocks, setting my stomach muscles to absorb, also, the vectors of my weight from the hinge of my legs. I kept this up for perhaps forty-five minutes until the first dog reached me.

I had heard it barking behind me for about ten minutes. When it actually reached me, however, it changed to a low throaty growl and came after my feet, going in at my heels with its growl, then barking again. It was a German shepherd but not, evidently, trained to attack, because it never jumped me, just worried my feet. I kept running, and in time the dog began simply running keeping up with me, occasionally barking.

The second dog, when it arrived, was much more aggressive, making an immediate jump, jaws snapping at my hand. I felt a tooth tearing my palm, but I pulled away and put on a burst of speed. It jumped once or twice more, then joined the other dog in following at an easy lope, barking as it came.

By now my lungs were burning, I felt my head hunching between my shoulders, felt my shoulders working into my speed the way I hadn't run since a child in a game of tag. But that made sense, didn't it? That's all it boiled down to—a lifelong game of tag, keep running till they won't let you anymore, only, in this game, you don't really get a chance to be "It."

I don't know what made the dog lunge. Perhaps it was that little dip in my courage. One minute I was running, the next minute the dog's body was flipping over my shoulder, teeth hanging on in my neck.

I hugged it, instinctively, to release the weight from my neck, then fell and rolled over it and over it. When I stopped I had my elbow under its throat, pressing up against its quivering body. Without its teeth, the beast was helpless, and its eyes bulged big and white from the short fur of its bony cheeks. The sight made an enormous rage come across me, a child's rage, so pure that it seemed good. And I was that, wasn't I? I was a raging child, raging against those who had lost me, those who had promised me, those who had told me lies, those who had never told me that all I loved was to go away. My hand was in the dog's throat, grabbing the massive muscles in my fingers, all the while twisting the dog's big neck backward. Now it whimpered, and the other dog bit me, hard, in the thigh. Still I pushed and pushed, until I felt the dog begin to grow limp beneath me.

And then I let go and rolled over, too exhausted to move, thinking, Fuck it, killing this dog isn't going to save Mimi.

The dog I'd attacked fumbled to its feet, looked at me, then lay down next to me, panting. The one who'd bit my calf stood still for a time, baring his teeth and growling. Then it too lay down.

And that, Isabel, is how the FBI found me, some twenty-five years after they first started looking. A middle-aged man lying bleeding on a trail in northern Michigan, attended by two exhausted dogs.

Date: June 25, 2006
From: "Amelia Wanda Lurie" <mimi@cusimanorganics.com>
To: "Isabel Montgomery" <isabel@exmnster.uk>
CC: maillist: The_Committee
Subject: letter 42

I was in Ypsilanti, Michigan, driving home to Little J and Rebeccah, when I heard the news on the radio. That Vincent had shot the guard. Senselessly, stupidly—after the robbery was already a success.

The guard was dead.

First a long movement of horror went through me, so horrible that I did not care about my safety, and I simply stopped the car and stared at nothing. Dead. Dead. The horror went through me, again and again, a peppery burning in my groin and armpits, a shudder through the muscles of my stomach. I don't know how long it was until I came to myself, my hands holding the steering wheel, and realized that I was in a car, the getaway car.

Getaway. There was no getting away from this, ever. And I think I may really have just waited there to be caught, or given myself in—I just no longer cared.

It was only after minutes and minutes had passed that I remembered that I had to care, and why.

Rebeccah.

Oh, Rebeccah, the very weave of the world went out of any recognizable shape.

I knew the consequences. I knew them clearly, and right away. I was an accessory to murder. My daughter was going to be raised by Johnny Osborne. And if I wanted her to have a normal life, I could never surface again. She could never know who her mother was, and never know who her father was, and I could never come back again. There was no emotion in this. I had known it could happen, and I knew what I had to do. The car I had was a rental from out of state, taken on a credit card stolen by someone Vincent knew. I drove it upstate to East Lansing and left it behind a small, closed mall. Then I took a bus to Traverse City.

I had made someone die. Why would I be afraid of doing, myself, what I had made another do? Wasn't that what we had fought for so long, to bring the real experience of the real war, the terror we were raining down on North Vietnam, home to our towns and cities? Didn't we always say that we had to be prepared to experience the horror of the war we were prosecuting abroad? Then, it was theater: the explosions that hurt no one, the violence that left no dead. Now, it was real, really really real, and I found myself calm.

The bus let me off at ten o'clock at night, outside a closed gas station in Grawn, Michigan. That was all there was to the town: a gas station, a bar across the street, dim lights through a dirty window the only sign it was even open for the two, three cars parked outside. A streetlight buzzed to an audience of circling moths.

It was as if I had always known what I was going to do. Without a thought I made my way across the road and into the woods, following a dirt road that took me up, and up, and finally to a gate opening to what had been, in the fifties, a Girl Scout camp.

I made my way through the deserted camp, drawn by sentimentality, to the little lean-to I had stayed in when last I was a camper, years before. Nothing in it felt familiar, though: just a lean-to in the woods, falling apart. An instinct made me go to the corner. The same instinct made me curl into a ball.

As if I had always known how to do this. As if genetically programmed in me was the fact that one day, I would have to die, and this was how I would do it.

Four days alone in the woods. With the clothes I wore and no food. Four nights huddling in the little lean-to, four days wandering the camp where I had been a girl; the empty dining room, the counselors' cabins, the offices. Four nights of lying dry-eyed, staring at nothing. Four days of living on water that I had collected from the swimming pond, growing lighter and lighter, every day, with hunger.

On the fifth morning I woke at four, as if I had an appointment. The woods were still dark, the trees were clinging to the escaping night. I crossed the camp to its western border, then felt my way along the lake's edge to the north. Here the state trail passed, heading straight west to Point Betsie, and by the first light of the sky I began to follow it.

It was as if I always knew what I would do. I had taken a life, now I would give a life. I would walk into the woods, the dear woods that had been the one constant in my life, the woods next to Point Betsie where my father died. I would find a place to lie, and with my pocketknife I would open my veins and let my life drain into the ground, peacefully, comfortably. Slowly, feeling my way through the woods, just before dawn, like a fairy tale, it felt to me that it had always been meant to happen. The mist rising from the forest floor. The absolute hush before dawn. The summer air as fresh as if it were the first day of all time. First my father, then my brother, then my mother. Jason. And that dear, dear girl. It was as if it had always been meant to be this way: that I would be stripped down of all that was familiar to me, all that meant anything, until nothing was left but a girl, dizzy with hunger, walking into the fairy-tale woods.

Dimly, confused, I realized that I had, in the singularity of my hunger, actually come to think of myself as a little girl. Rebeccah, Rebeccah, Rebeccah. She was a gift for someone else, someone who deserved a gift, not for me, not for me. Now, it would be with my death that I would guarantee her life.

Rebeccah. I crouched now, on the path, and put my palm to the ground to stop from falling. Rebeccah. What I would do now, I thought, was lie down on the ground, on the path, with Rebeccah, and never get up again.

Perhaps I would have. I think I would have. But as I, weak and lightheaded, lowered myself to the ground, that morning, I experienced a potent hallucination.

I saw the sun come up over the trees, the weak sun of morning, and with sudden, absolute certainty, I knew that at that very second, my baby was seeing it too. In a very literal way, I knew she was lying on her back in her new home, at Johnny's house, and that she was next to a window, and that her arms and legs were moving in their uterine weightlessness and her eyes, her eyes that couldn't yet focus, were filling with light that she couldn't understand.

Watching the sun approach me through the woods, I knew that I had got it wrong. The boundless love that washed through me, through and through me, it was the only thing I had to offer my daughter. By its very existence, how could it not fill that child with confidence and possibility, with luck and with happiness? That my inability to imagine a circumstance in which she might need me did not mean that such a time would never arise. And I knew that nothing mattered, nothing mattered, but that I live out that love for her.

And then the sun crept across the sky and touched me, and when it touched me, like a little girl in a fairy tale, without thinking, I got up and began to walk, guided by a good witch through a magical forest, to the coast.

I didn't have to think about what I'd do. I would walk to Point Betsie, and wait for night. At night I would go down to the Yacht Club and roll one of the little training dinghies into the water. I'd rig it, and then I'd steal a compass, and then I'd set off west across Lake Michigan to the Wisconsin shore. If I made it alive, I'd find a bar, find a man, find a way to hide for a week, two weeks. Then I'd go up to Milwaukee. Donal James had IDs I could use, I knew that; he'd always had an excess of IDs. And he could get me the name of the contact we had, in what seemed another life, with the Brotherhood. My last contact with anyone I'd ever known in my life would be Donal James. And then I would disappear even to him.

It was a death, but a different kind of death. Everything about Mimi Lurie would die. But that love, that love that inhabited the very light of the spring sun, that light that held, and carried, my baby, that I would keep alive.

In case one day, one day I could show it to Rebeccah.

• • •

Twenty-two years later I came out of the trail in the morning at the town of Oscoda, the east coast of Michigan, nearly twenty-four hours after I left your father at the Linder cabin. I made my way to the marina and stepped into the office. When I came out it was with a key, and this I carried directly down the dock to a twenty-nine-foot Pearson, the *Evelyn I*, kept here by a couple who worked for McLeod. The key opened the passageway, and when I came back out of the cabin, it was in yellow slickers to protect me from the wet fog. On diesel, I pulled the boat out of its slip and quietly moved out without lights.

Offshore, the fog cleared, and a fresh north wind was blowing. I dropped anchor, then went below to wait for darkness. In the event, I slept: a heavy unconsciousness, conditioned by days of tension and nearly twenty-four hours on the trail.

When I woke, it was night, and a north wind was blowing at ten knots. For a few moments I put my face into it, eyes closed. Then I moved quickly to weigh anchor, start the engine, and turn the boat to the wind, leaving it a touch of throttle for steerage, and set the automatic steering.

Through the fore hatch I put out the number-four jib, a Genoa, and then scrambled out on the foredeck to rig and raise it. When it was up, fluttering in irons, I hooked the winch handle into my belt, moved back, and raised the main, winching it on the master. That finished, I moved back to the wheel and released the steering, but kept the boat throttling gently still into the north wind.

And now? Standing, my face to the wind, my hair blowing backward, the sails luffing, I unzipped my slicker.

Canada was due east on a beam reach; a single tack with the wind on a gently curved suit of sails would take me right into the Kincardine Marina. With running lights off, my passage would never be known to man or satellite. And from Kincardine a bus went to Toronto, Ottowa, Montreal.

Montreal has an international airport.

To the south was Detroit, due south, a run: wheel around, luffing through all the points of sail, 180 degrees, then put the sails wing on wing with the wind at my back and run straight in to Detroit.

Canada. Tess Sanders untouched by the whole affair. And if not

Tess Sanders, then another: Paige James, Jennifer Howard, Pat Cremins. It didn't matter what name I used. I was always myself, always myself. And the whole world waited on the other side of Canada.

Detroit. Sail into the Bell Isle Yacht Club, leave the boat, take a taxi into Ann Arbor to the police station. Giving a cabbie such a good fare, there are worse last moves before you go to jail.

Ha, ha. I laughed into the wind, but without much humor. West or south in a north wind: blue-water sailing either way.

It was a funny thing, wasn't it? Canada with its passageway to the whole world, to a whole life of freedom, that felt like a jail, but Detroit and jail, it seemed like freedom.

But then, I had never been afraid of jail. I had been in jail since the day I lost Rebeccah. Imprisoning me changed nothing.

And freedom?

The only thing at stake was the highest principle of my life.

For a last long minute I looked out into the vast possibility before me, Canada, savoring it in the taste of the north wind.

Then I cut the engine, letting the boat drift backward on the wind in the sudden silence, falling off to the east. The sails, slowly, filled into a beam reach, and as the boat pointed east, it gained speed. The wind came around to the beam, and I winched the mainsheet, reeling the sail in, catching the wind and accelerating east. Canada.

Only I could not seem to make my hands stop the wheel. I tried for a second, and then I realized I didn't want to. And so the boat veered farther to the south, and farther, until the wind behind the boat jibed the closehauled mainsail to the starboard side, and now my hands were working again, because I found them letting the sheet run out, steadying the boat into the most beautiful run a boat can make, wing on wing, mainsail on the starboard, jib on the port, before the north wind, running south.

Feeling, in a way I had not since the morning sun first guided me out of the forest in 1974, cleansed of every tie, carrying all the love in the world for a little girl, and a little boy, and knowing that nothing, nothing, would ever take it from me, free.

EPILOGUE

When we watch the children play
Remember
How the privileged classes grew
And from this day we set out
To undo what won't undo.
Looking for the grand in the minute
Every breath justifies
Every step that we take to remove what
The powers that be can't prove
And the children will understand why.

—Chrissie Hynde,
"Revolution"

Date: July 4, 2010
Filename: Izzy_final.doc
Author: Isabel Sinai Montgomery
Time: 02:08:58 GMT

I remember Saugerties, the Catskills, the Hudson Valley, always in the spring: a sea of undulating green stretching away forever to the horizon, always warm, always in bloom.

My father and I never went back there. Not to live. We went back to hike, to visit: Billy Cusimano—until he moved back to the city—Charlie and Naomi, a few others. But we never went back to live. And in time the place we lived when I was a baby—in time that whole summer—turned into a memory of green, the Catskills in midsummer, an endless and infinitely welcoming world of kind forests and magical trails, the place where I was a child.

I'm not supposed to be telling this. In fact, I wasn't supposed even to save the e-mails I got from what my mother called "the Committee," those weeks leading up to Mimi Lurie's parole date. I even worried that Big Billy's computer geek put some programming in them, causing these e-mails to delete themselves after I read them. A neurotic need for secrecy, in my opinion, has always characterized my father and his friends. Just to be on the safe side I printed a copy, and burnt a DV, and put that in a safe deposit vault. And as it happened, things went a bit wild after Mimi's parole hearing, and it took four years for the consequences all to play out. Which is why it is not until now, this very early morning in London in 2010, that I am finally doing something I have been meaning to do for years, that is, write down how everything ended up, that summer of 1996, when Mimi Lurie surrendered herself in order that I might continue to live with my father. And, more importantly, what happened when Mimi Lurie came up for parole in the summer of 2006, and what exactly they wanted me to do to help get her out of jail, and what I decided to do in the end. And then I'll put the whole thing away again and hope that someone will one day in the future want to read this and, more importantly, that the South Asia War is going to leave us a future in which they can.

That summer, after my father was arrested, I lived with my uncle Daniel and my aunt Maggie, the redheaded lady who had shown up in the hotel to get me. I've never really decided whether I remember what had happened that night in the Wall Street Marriott, or if I've just read so much about it that I think I do. I do remember my uncle's house by the sea on Martha's Vineyard. I remember the ocean that lapped up against the bottom of the lawn, I remember the slap of water against the hull of the boat my uncle and aunt took me sailing in, I remember the enormous ticking clock in the hallway with the writing on it, B-R-E-G-U-E-T, I remember my two beautiful and brilliant little cousins, Leila and Jacob, Jakey three, Leiley almost my age.

When Daddy was let out of jail, we moved in with my grandmother in New York City, which was a lucky thing, because I came to love my grandmother, and these turned out to be the last few years of her life. In the fall they put me in a school called Little Red Schoolhouse, which was where my father had gone, and because of that, I guess, everyone tended to gush over me somewhat, making me feel more like a historical artifact than an actual girl. More importantly, this was the time when I got to know my sister Rebeccah—my half sister—when she finished school and moved to New York. In fact, I spent a great lot of time with Beck after she moved to New York, but that's another story, and I'll tell it another time.

Later I found out all the facts, some from Beck, some from Molly, who were apparently the only ones who believed that I should be treated like a human being with a right to know some of the truth. Like, how after Mimi's surrender and confession, and Sharon Solarz's identical testimony, the state of Michigan dropped charges against my father for murder and larceny, and the state of New York decided not to pursue charges stemming from his life as a fugitive; and the old federal charges, which were corrupted by illegal wiretapping under the Nixon administration, had long been forgotten. As a result, even though my father was known outside of the rules of evidence to have been involved in all manner of crime, Yale University transferred James Grant's law degree to Jason Sinai. Jason Sinai, however, was never admitted to the bar: the Ethics Committee of the Bar was allowed to consider things that the courts weren't. He kept working by keeping a staff of litigating lawyers, which became in fact rather a legendary job, springboard to many eminent legal careers.

And how he was able to do this turned out to be very simple. During the time my father was underground, it turned out that my grandfather, Jack Sinai, had matched every penny he spent on his younger son Daniel—and on his daughter, Klara Singer, whom they took over when she was orphaned in Israel shortly after my father went underground—and put it away. When I tell you that both Daniel Sinai and Klara Singer went to Elizabeth Irwin High School and Yale for college and graduate school, not mentioning twenty-six years of other expenses, you can imagine what kind of money was involved. Every penny had been saved, and although my grandfather's principles forbade him investing in secondary markets, my uncle Daniel's did not, and under his stewardship it came to a considerable amount of money indeed. My father was therefore able to open up an office in, of all places, the Exchange Building, tenth floor. They did not, my father used to joke, have to change the sign on the door. When Mimi Lurie came up for parole, my father was able to set up an office in Michigan and work full time on her release, which is why all his e-mails came to me from Michigan that summer of 2006.

And me? I moved to England in '03, for a lot of reasons. One was that by then, it had become clear that my mother, Julia, might not ever be a Rhodes scholar, but she would be clean forever, and I had been spending summers and holidays with her for years—my father never tried to make me dislike my mother, though he never came to like her after he stopped loving her, and I admit I always did see Molly Sackler as my mom and my actual mother as more of a friend. Another reason was that I was not a particularly good adolescent, and that New York is a lousy place for an unhappy kid. And another reason might be that I, after a time, began to see my father as someone who had abandoned me just like, years before, he had abandoned my sister Rebeccah. At least, a shrink my dad made me see told me that, and who knows but that it's the truth.

But I personally see it this way: having a hero for a father is not an easy thing. And having a whole generation of hippies—whom I'd see at Billy Cusimano's famous SoHo loft after he became the organic king of the world—going all teary-eyed every time they see you gets to be a big drag too.

Whatever, by the time I was thirteen, it was pretty clear that Elizabeth Irwin—that's the high school of Little Red Schoolhouse—and I were not going to get along anymore. And because, by then, it turned out that my mother's sobriety was real, and true, and that her worst sin now was a lifelong commitment to shopping, and my father and she had reached some kind of peace, my father agreed to let me come over to Exminster, which I did. It was the right thing to do, as it happened. For one thing, I discovered that in many ways, I'm my mother's daughter too. I'm one mean shopper, and I like to dress. We pierced our eyebrows together, and I got my first tattoo with her. And lastly, as everyone knows, being a hopeless parent doesn't keep your kids from loving you. Mom, I had never stopped loving her, now I learned to like her, too—though why she and my father had gotten married was a mystery I'd never answer and which gave me one of my first insights into how childish adults are. And somehow, understanding that I was my mother's daughter, that made it easier to see the ways in which I wanted to be my father's, too. See, it was definitely my father's daughter who, one day when I was fifteen, trapped Benny Schulberg in a hotel room while he was visiting in London with my sister Beck and made him tell me a few key details about the summer of 1996, key details that had been left out, so far, from everyone else's account. And Benny, tough-guy reporter, caved in about twelve seconds flat.

What he confessed to me—what I wanted to know—was that for all the time my mother and father were married, my grandfather had known and concealed Jim Grant's true identity. Benny says, "The old bastard didn't have a choice, Iz. What was he supposed to do? On one hand, he turns your father in to the police, and he loses his daughter. On the other hand, your father goes back underground, and takes Julia with him. Either way, Montgomery loses."

Then he thinks for a while, looking miserable. And says: "These fucking Vietnam stories, Iz, 'scuse my French. I mean, every war has its war criminals, they're easy. But once you're done with the politicans and the murderers, it's not that easy to tell the good guys from the bad. Your dad? Take my word for it, he made some moves in Weather that make Mussolini look like Jack Kennedy. Your grandfather Montgomery? Can you really argue with what he did?"

Well, maybe not. Maybe, on the other hand, given how he used his good deed against my dad in the summer of '96, so.

Which leads me to what they were actually asking me to do about Mimi Lurie's parole hearings in 2006, and what I decided. And to tell you about that in turn, I have to tell you about the last thing that happened with all these people in the summer of 1996.

2.

Mimi Lurie turned herself in to the Ann Arbor police on July 10, 1996. She was taken into custody, pleaded guilty at her arraignment, and took—as they say—a twelve-year hit in state court on July 15, which she began serving immediately.

Several days later, the U.S. attorney announced that all criminal charges had been dropped against my father, and he was released from prison in Traverse City, where they'd been holding him. Naturally, he showed up immediately at John Osborne's house, not only because I was by then staying there with Aunt Maggie and Molly, who had brought me out to Michigan as soon as Mimi surrendered. And after they had all talked, and cried, and slobbered on each other or whatever they actually did, well, then they had a surprise. And that surprise came from John Osborne himself.

Want to know what happened? Benny—the open book—told me all about it. It was pretty brilliant, I guess. In its way. What happened was that when all the emotion had settled down, and everyone was sitting around at the kitchen table, John Osborne suggested something. He suggested that now that my father was cleared, there was no necessity now to reveal publicly the fact of who Rebeccah's birth parents were. No one had a lot of objection to that. But when, right after that, he suggested that another part of my father's story be kept secret, that was another matter altogether.

What Osborne suggested here, it turned out, was to have an enormous effect on the rest of my life. Sitting at the kitchen table with the core members of what I would later come to know as the Committee, Johnny Osborne looked around the table with a slightly sheepish expression. Benny thought, at first, that it was just the discomfort of having Rebeccah's birth father there in the same room. But, of course, there was much more to his sheepishness than that. Because, what he said, after getting the table's attention was as follows:

"You know, guys, there's something else we maybe want to keep secret. That is . . . well, you know, Jason, now that you're not under any criminal charges, there's no way Senator Montgomery's going to sue you for custody."

"No, of course not." Benny, had already worked this part out for himself. "You've got him by the short hairs, Mr. Gran—Jason. That old bastard. He was never planning on suing you. He was blackmailing you."

My father nodded. "Um-hmm. He's all mine now. I tell a reporter how he knew, all during his senatorship, that I was Jason Sinai. And how he consistently used his influence to keep his daughter, who made Jimi Hendrix and Janis Joplin look like Mormons, out of court. Then tried to take custody of my daughter? Yeah, right. So much for his ambassadorship at the Court of St. James, I'm guessing."

"And I know just the reporter to write it," Benny says. Except, to his surprise, that comment is greeted with silence. And then, John Osborne, in this agreeable voice, like he was talking to a child, speaks.

"Well, that would be one way to go."

It appeared there was also another way to handle it. And that was the subject of a pretty detailed analysis over the next half hour. And when they were done, Ben pursed his lips and whistled.

"Yikes. That's not legal."

"Nope. Nor is it fit to print." Both Osborne and my father regarded their future son-in-law as if wondering what he would do.

But Ben didn't need convincing. I can hear him saying it. *Truth or love? Fuck truth.* So he never wrote the story of Rebeccah Osborne's abandonment and adoption. And he never wrote the story of my grandfather's deceptions concerning my father and mother. And he never wrote the story of my mother's drug and alcohol addiction.

See, what John Osborne and my father understood, the one from all his years in the FBI and the other from all his years as a fugitive, was that keeping a secret, you don't necessarily have to have an actual reason to do it for the secret to have power. They understood that the very act of keeping a fact secret gives you options that you may never have had otherwise. In a way, what they did, that day, was metaphysical.

On the other hand, it was intensely practical. Because, by 2006, when Mimi Lurie came up for parole, Rebeccah Osborne had finished law school, and finished her FBI training, and to no one's surprise, had her own office in the Federal Building on Duane Street. She had been at the 2004 presidential inaugural, and sat on the National Security Council and the Homeland Security Staff. And therefore, when in the late winter of 2006 Beck requested an interview with the office of the senator from the great state of New York, she got onto the schedule of the chief of staff—a certain Michael Rafferty—the very same day.

To Rafferty's surprise, Rebeccah Osborne was there to discuss the impending parole hearing of one Mimi Lurie in the state of Michigan, a parole hearing that raised key issues of punishment and rehabilitation, of the scars of Vietnam and the imperative to forgive. It was an impressive presentation, and Rafferty listened. He listened to the circumstances of Mimi Lurie's minor accessory role in a crime, to the story of Mimi Lurie's life—a fiction, admittedly, given that Beck did not tell the senator's chief of staff that Lurie had been one of the most successful marijuana smugglers in history—and to the litany of wonderful things she had done with her ten years in jail. He listened and considered and reviewed the file Rebeccah Osborne had brought about this case that she felt so strongly about. And all the while he listened, he wondered what on earth Rebeccah Osborne thought could convince the senator to go to bat for a woman widely seen as a domestic terrorist.

And then Rebeccah, to Rafferty's surprise, changed the subject entirely. "Mr. Rafferty, I understand that Ambassador Montgomery is endorsing Todd Shawcross for the senator's seat in the midterm elections."

He stopped short. "That's right. What of it?"

"He has an awful lot of clout in New York State, the ambassador. An awful lot. I heard that he handpicked the senator for the job, and now he's going to handpick her successor. What was it those two disagreed about, again? Wasn't it when he kept the senator off of the Foreign Relations Committee because she refused to support the invasion of Iraq?"

Well, Mikey was not used to being talked to in this way, even by his old boss's daughter, and he was about to dismiss Rebeccah when his own political aide intervened, and suggested he continue to listen. At which point, still speaking in her quiet, polite voice, Rebeccah went on.

"Mike, here's the thing. Do you remember Ambassador Montgomery's press conference at the time of Jason Sinai's arrest? How he expressed shock and regret that all these years he'd been harboring a criminal in his house and his heart? And his regret that his ex-son-in-law couldn't be legally held accountable for his moral responsibility for a heinous crime? And his satisfaction that, at least, Mimi Lurie was to serve the maximum time for what she had done?"

As was the case when this kind of horse-trading took place and plausible deniability became possible, it was Rafferty's aide who answered. "Mr. Rafferty remembers, Ms. Osborne. Make your point, please."

But my sister, she was not subdued by this. After all, she'd testified before Congress and spoken to presidents by this point in her career. So what she did was, she went on in the same tone.

"Well, tell me this. What would you think if I told you that I have proof that Ambassador Montgomery knew, and concealed the knowledge, all through his three terms as U.S. senator, that his son-in-law James Grant was in fact the federal fugitive Jason Sinai? And that, furthermore, all through those three terms, he also interceded multiple times with the New York State police and court system to protect his daughter from criminal charges stemming from her drug and alcohol addiction? Do you think that this might change the terms of the midterm elections a little bit?"

Silence greeted this statement, Mikey standing by his desk and staring at the young FBI agent before him. And again it was, in the end, his aide who—with a constant and loyal eye to plausible deniability—answered.

"Ms. Osborne, no one's going to listen to that, coming from Jason Sinai."

"No, I agree." In the same exact voice, Rebeccah addressed Rafferty, pretending the aide was not there. "How about coming from the ambassador's granddaughter? In sworn testimony? At Mimi Lurie's parole hearing?"

Rebeccah says she could hear the water splashing in the fountain outside the Hart Building, so silent did it become. And the silence lasted so long that she began to talk again.

"The way I see it, it's pretty effective. Isabel Montgomery, testifying on behalf of Mimi Lurie, describes how Mimi's surrender saved her from being raised by her mother, a deeply addicted and incompetent person, and her grandfather, who had repeatedly, over years, abused the privilege of his office and concealed knowledge of a federal fugitive's identity."

"The ambassador will go to jail, Ms. Osborne." At last Mike said something, and at that point, my sister told me, she knew her work was done.

"Not at all. The statute of limitation's run out. And there's no charges on Sinai for the ambassador to be accessory to. But he won't be serving as kingmaker in New York State anymore, that's for sure."

"And what is it you require, Ms. Osborne?"

"The senator's personal appearance on Mimi Lurie's behalf at the parole hearing, and a supporting letter from the president. The president, Mikey, is no fan of Ambassador Montgomery either."

See? It was easy. And all that they needed to do now, the Committee, was find a way to make good on their promise.

To get, in other words, Ambassador Montgomery's granddaughter—

me—to agree to expose her own mother as a former drug addict and then, if that weren't enough, to ruin her grandfather's long and distinguished political career.

And so it was that June of 2006, in my room at Exminster, I spent two long weeks reading a series of e-mails designed to explain to me who my father was, and who Mimi Lurie was, and why, thirty years after the war in Vietnam was over, it should matter to me whether or not she goes free.

Matter so much that I would sacrifice two of the most loved people in my life.

On Sunday morning, June 25, 2006, I turned away from my computer and lit a cigarette, leaning out the window into the wet spring dawn.

I was a slight girl, at seventeen, brown-haired and brown-eyed, a pierced eyebrow and ear, a penchant for black clothes, lightweight materials. No one ever expected me to look the way I did, the dark daughter of ash-blond Julia Montgomery, the slight granddaughter of towering Robert Montgomery. There were other ways I seemed to defy genetics. And there were other ways I didn't deny them at all.

That morning, I called home and told my mother I was coming up for the rest of the day. Did she believe me? I don't know. I don't even know what she wanted me to do. I can tell you that in her voice, that day, there was a distant and wistful quality. And I can tell you that she said to me, before we hung up, the following, apropos of absolutely nothing I had said.

"Hey, baby? Listen, remember something. I take heat in the tabloids every week. You saw what they did to me when they got those topless pics at Brian's place in Saltaire? Didn't kill me, now, did it? You felt you had to do something public now, well, all this must pass, or some such thing, right, darling? You know how I love you."

I wasn't feeling too hot just then, but what I said was, "I know, Mom. But what about Granddad?"

"Granddad's made his own choices, darling." There was forced cheer in her voice. But remember, Mom, in her way, is from the sixties too. "He's had half the world in his pocket for half a century, hasn't he? That old bastard, he eats stuff like this for breakfast. What you have to worry about as far as Granddad's concerned, it's his bloody security personnel, you hear me? You got to find a way round the bodyguards he has on you, and Izzy, your Momma's no use to you whatsoever on this front."

See why I love my mom? But I, I knew what it would do to Granddad, though, and I knew what it would cost her, too. I guess I knew that somehow Granddad would weasel his way back into the corridors of power, someday. But what he was really after, at this point in his career, was not a job as much as a place in history and that, for sure, I was denying him now. It was a massive fucking enormous and *huge* drag, for the both of them, and that their daughter and granddaughter, respectively, was going to do it, it made it that much worse.

I packed an overnight bag, a very small backpack, and threw in my palmtop.

3.

The day was wet, a warm British spring day, the sky as if dissolving moisture onto the lawns and hedges. I took a taxi to the airport, then the commuter to Bournemouth, a long hop cross-country. Bournemouth, an international hub, was busy even this Sunday morning, whereas the local airport had been deserted, the ticket taker drinking tea in the waiting room. Our local airport, however, had made it easy to see Granddad's security. Here, in Bournemouth, I could not know who was watching. I knew, however, that the plane the Committee had booked me on—the plane to Michigan—left from the south Terminal. And because they had e-mailed the ticket, I knew that my grandfather's security teams knew too. Therefore, I walked up through the big glass corridor to North Terminal and took the London commuter.

We got in at Islington at eleven, and I stepped off the plane, through the airport, and directly into the Angel tube stop. I took the train one stop to King's Cross, and then changed one more stop for Russell Square.

I didn't care if I was being followed when I came out and walked over to a tiny little street off Gordon Street called Gower Court. Stores were open, though most of the folk out today seemed to be tourists—tourists never stop in London. I didn't pay much attention to the stores, though. I checked my A to Zed on my palmtop, and I made my way to number 2, Gower Court.

See, I'm no idiot. I don't go leaping on airplanes using tickets e-mailed to me when my granddad, the American ambassador, doesn't want me to and has a government-paid security detail to help him. You don't *do* things like that when people like my grandfather don't want you to. No, I had a whole other plan.

Years ago, when I first came here, my father had given me this address, 2 Gower Court. He told me that some day I might need some help with some little thing, and maybe my mother wouldn't be able to give it me. And he told me what I was to do if such a need arose.

Now, when I walked into a little office in the top of a Victorian town house at 2 Gower Court, I found myself, for a moment, in an empty reception room, with a black leather couch and, on the wall, a number of miniature city landscapes that I recognized—because my grandfather owned two—to be Horowitzes, and a massive abstract frame, floor-to-ceiling height, which I recognized—because my mother owned one—to be a James Nares. I waited in the company of these canvases for a time until at last a person came out: a blond woman in slacks and a beige silk shirt, perhaps thirty. She stopped short when she saw me and gazed with frank interest, then amusement. And at last, in a low, American-accented voice, she spoke.

"So. You must be Isabel Montgomery, for God's sake. How very, very nice to meet you."

I didn't answer, but she went on in her slightly amused tone. "It's so funny. Chevejon told me to expect you today. How the hell he knew . . . but listen my dear, welcome. You're so among friends here, I can't tell you."

I nodded to her, not quite knowing what to say. But she was unconcerned, talking pleasantly while she led me through a steel door, past cameras and a Plexiglas security booth inside of which stood a guard with a machine gun, into an interior office where, on the wall, I recognized a Matisse sketch, a Derwatt, and something—if I didn't know better—I would have thought a Caravaggio. "My name is Allison Rosenthal, Isabel. We have all kinds of things in common. My father and your grandfather are friends. And I summered on the Island when I was a kid. West Tisbury, just down the way from your uncle. I know your grandfather's house on Menemsha Bay, right next to Michael Herrick's. The Spanish Barracks, my dad used to call it, I never understood why when I was a kid. Now, my dear—"

We were in an office that smelled of tobacco and orange juice, both items on view on the desk, and when the woman sat down at the computer, she lit a cigarette and sipped from the orange juice carton. I sat too and smoked, watching her work. Her face, focused on the screen, was composed and serious; her eyes, amazingly green, alive in a way that I couldn't remember seeing before and which, somehow, like when I first met Rebeccah, opened new vistas of womanhood for me: strong, reliable, effective ways of being a woman; ways that diminished what any but the very finest men had to offer the world.

"Now, let's see." The woman was facing the computer screen but, apparently, talking to me. "Do you have papers?

I guess I looked confused.

"Travel docs."

"Oh. Yes."

"Alright." Allison lifted the phone, spoke briefly in Italian, at which two towering suited men came into the room. Then she rose, as if everything were already all arranged.

"Very good then, Isabel. This is Paolo, and this is Giorgio. Shall we go?"

"Go where, Ms. Rosenthal?" I remained seated, unwilling—I see now—to accept that she knew so much about me.

"Why, to Detroit, Michigan. Isn't that what you came for? Paolo and Giorgio, here, they're going to see that you get there without anyone interfering."

I stayed seated. "But who are you all?"

She looked surprised. "Why, we're friends of Chevejon, of course."

"And who is Chevejon?"

She stopped short. "My dear, there's so much to tell you. Chevejon is Mimi Lurie's brother. Come, I'll tell you all about it on the way to the airport. I'm not allowed into the States, damn it. But we'll talk on the way to the airport, and I'll tell you all."

And so I, Isabel Grant-Sinai-Montgomery, found myself, just like that, giving myself over entirely to this woman who smelled of tobacco and orange juice and her two bodyguards, and—my father's daughter after all—walking calmly away from everything familiar and into the unknown.

4.

And that, essentially, is the end of my story. Except I guess you want to know the last details of how everyone ended up, so let me fill you in.

Ben Schulberg moved east with Rebeccah, after having written the entire story—or, I should say, *most* of the story—for the *Albany Times,* and been been snapped up by the *World News New York*. And because Rebeccah and Ben both lived in New York now, they could be married and begin to breed, which they promptly did.

Sharon Solarz refused to take a plea bargain, insisting that Gillian Morrealle try the case on its merits, which Morrealle did. The result was a sentence of twenty to life for murder, and she serves it today in Baraga maximum security prison, where she teaches reading to inmates and the children of inmates and, recently, won an award from the State of Michigan Board of Education for Innovation in Literacy Pedagogy.

What Mimi Lurie did after being paroled, in late June of 2006, that is a story still being written, and you will need to hear it elsewhere. I will tell you that she spent that summer traveling in America, seeing old friends, thanking some of the many, many people who had come forward after she surrendered, to visit and to help. The trip started with a visit to the Krosney family—the family of the guard killed at the Bank of Michigan robbery—who had informed the board that they would not oppose her parole. Then she went on to McLeod's, and to Donal James, and to friends from Chicago to Albany and many points in between. With her, for much of that time, was her birth daughter Rebeccah, who had found a variety of pretexts to visit her in prison over the years—easily done, seeing she spent all her vacations with her much-loved parents in Traverse City, and does to this day—and had grown to know Mimi well. Then, that autumn, Mimi left for Italy to be with her mysterious brother, who had disappeared so long ago, and who reappeared, during the years of her incarceration, as an Italian businessman by the name of Peter Chevejon, showing that the taste for new identities can run in families. Chevejon had visited her in prison so often—despite the fact that he was coming each time from Europe—that he had eventually purchased a house outside Ann Arbor along Huron River Drive to stay in during his visits, a house in which his old high school friend John Osborne was a frequent visitor, as was Osborne's daughter and Chevejon's niece Rebeccah, with her husband Ben and, later, their children.

But I will tell you one thing Mimi Lurie did not do. She did not return to the great love of her life, for my father and Molly Sackler were married in the summer of 2002. A year after, Leo Sackler—Molly's son and my childhood hero—and his wife were both killed in a bombing at the USMC station in Kabul, where Leo was stationed during the war, which was by then over in Iraq but still smoldering in Afghanistan, and so as if my father hadn't screwed up enough daughters by then, he set out screwing up a few more: Leo's two infant daughters, my other half sisters, whom Molly and my father more or less raised from then on.

Who else is there? Well, Jed Lewis took some substantial heat for his role in the whole thing when a group of big donors to the university raised a fuss over the prominence of a former fugitive in the American History Department and withdrew quite a bit of money. The university, however, held firm, and indeed the *Michigan Daily* published an editorial by one Rebeccah Osborne, who pointed out that having been a revolutionary was a pretty appropriate qualification for an American history professor. Still, in retrospect, Dr. Lewis came to feel that the publicity had cost him the chair of his department, and rather limited the second half of what had been a pretty illustrious career, a fact that failed to move many other former members of Weather, whose lives had been limited to high schools rather than universities by taking orders from Jed Lewis in the days when Jed Lewis gave orders, and who thought that Jed had a lot to be thankful for—and sorry for—whatever happened.

Mac McLeod, with predictable prescience, began the process of extracting himself from the marijuana trade the moment Mimi Lurie left

California for Ann Arbor. His name never surfaced in connection with the whole story, which was a good thing, for it enabled him ultimately to funnel his fortune into a number of charities, where thousands of people all over the country benefit from it still, blissfully unaware that the money buying them medicine, or sending them to school, or helping them with their houses, or researching their diseases, started as a jagged, hairy, glistening leaf in one of McLeod or Cusimano's Seas of Green.

As for Billy Cusimano, with whom my father started this whole story and with whom, therefore, I will end it, he never grew a Sea of Green again. He was rearrested in the midsummer of 1996, and although his case was thrown out due to the illegality of the FBI's wiretap—the same one that caught them Sharon Solarz—when he got his house back he found that the harvest had been burnt, the planting beds smashed, the gro-lights broken, the computer circuitry torn out.

It was a sad thing for Billy to inspect the ruins of his summer harvest. His last visit to his basement Sea of Green, just before he moved his family out of Tannersville altogether, his house packed and the moving vans waiting, he was sentimental enough to take a J with him and smoke it down there, a last look at the ruins of his lifework.

Dope growing was the thing he had been best at, and he had been doing it for thirty years, spreading his bud all over America, where it made thousands and thousands and thousands of people, one way or another, see the world in a different way than they ever had before. It was a good thing for him, of course, that he was no longer a criminal, with McLeod altogether out of it, now. The future would definitely prove this: because Billy really couldn't plant the seed again, he was forced aboveground, and of necessity—he had three children in high school and one still in middle—founded Cusmimano's Organic Market, and from then on everything Billy touched, more or less, turned to gold. His kids went to college, one to Bard, one to Antioch, one to Skidmore, and the fourth, surprise, to Yale and then Oxford on a Rhodes scholarship. He and his wife lived in great comfort in SoHo, and then, after 9-11, moved out to Brooklyn.

But all that—all that was going to happen in the years to come. Billy didn't know any of it when, in the late summer of 1996, the moving vans packed and waiting, he climbed down to look at what was once his Sea of Green. And whatever he might have become later, that's how I will always see him: standing stoned, bemused, next to the ruin of all he had worked on for so much of his life, and knowing it would never come back. Perhaps he shut his eyes tight and saw, in their darkness, the resplendent, resinous thick growth of marijuana, hairy and seedless, shocking green, and somehow joyous, as a loud electric switch turns on the rain and water fills the air, water that the plants reach up to with their arms, bathing themselves, full of life. Then he opened his eyes again to his ruined aspirations and leaned heavily against the basement wall.

Knowing that he would never produce that kind of life again, nor would his product produce the kind of insight, and experimentation, and visions, that so much of his own life had been given to. And maybe that's the first time that Billy saw himself for what he had become, a man moving over to the other side of middle age, with children to raise in a world that he would, from then on, only live in, never think that he could change.

Well, what the fuck. He smiled a little, stoned, realizing where he was at. So was this, then, it? Like poor Oedipus, dying at Colonus, realizing that it was only now, because he was nothing, that he became a man? Settling all the big questions of life with the simple necessity of children? Giving up?

Well, maybe. With a huge, huge sigh he exhaled the last hit of his J and flicked the roach onto the floor. Fact was, the age his children were getting, it was about time he stopped smoking joints anyway, and why not stop now? The thought made his heart tear a little. Such a long time, defining himself by the things he believed, the herb he grew, the company he kept. Well, the company would never change, that was sure. But maybe it was time to let the kids grow their own dope and plan their own revolution, and who knows? With parents this good—parents like Jason, Molly, the Osbornes, McLeod, and even, in his own small way, Billy himself—maybe it would be their children who'd at last, at long last, do better with this rotten, corrupt world.

After all, everything they'd done themselves, it was like Chrissie Hynde said, right?

It's the children who'll understand why.

And it was with that thought that he climbed out of the basement and turned off the lights for the last time on what had for so long been the source for so many people of so many dreams, Billy Cusimano's Sea of Green.

Acknowledgments

During the writing of this book, a number of people agreed to speak to me about their experiences on both sides of the war in Vietnam. Foremost among them is Eleanor Stein, who was a steadfast friend to me and to this book throughout its writing. Like Ben Schulberg, I have been lucky enough to have the help and friendship of William J. Taylor. And I am deeply appreciative of interviews and insights given me by Bill Ayers, Chesa Boudin, Lieutenant Colonel John W. Capito (USMC, ret.), Joshua Cohen, Bernardine Dohrn, Lieutenant Colonel David Evans (USMC, ret.), David Gilbert, Ron Jacobs, Michael James, Jeffrey Jones, Vivian Rothstein, and, not least, the interviewees who spoke to me, with such generous honesty, on condition of anonymity.

Four books were indispensable to this book. Ron Jacobs's *The Way the Wind Blew: A History of the Weather Underground* (Verso); Judith Clavir Albert and Stewart Edward Albert's *The Sixties Papers: Documents of a Rebellious Decade* (Praeger); Harold Jacobs's *Weatherman* (Ramparts Press); and David Wallechinsky's *Midterm Report: The Class of '65* (Viking). Other published sources include Jane Alpert, *Growing Up Underground* (Morrow); Bill Ayers, *Fugitive Days* (Beacon); Tom Bates, *Rads* (HarperPerennial); Noam Chomsky, *The Chomsky Reader*, James Peck, ed. (Pantheon); John Castellucci, *The Big Dance* (Dodd, Mead); Frank Donner, *The Age of Surveillance: The Aims and Methods of America's Political Intelligence System* (Knopf); Todd Gitlin, *The Sixties:*

Years of Hope, Days of Rage (Bantam); Brian Glick, *War at Home: Covert Action Against U.S. Activists and What We Can Do About It* (South End Press); Larry Grathwohl (as told to Frank Regan); *Bringing Down America: An FBI Informer with the Weathermen* (Arlington House); Stanley Karnow, *Vietnam: A History* (Penguin); Kirkpatrick Sale, *SDS* (Random House); *Biographical Dictionary of the American Left* (Johnpoll and Klehr); David Farber, *The Age of Great Dreams: America in the 1960s* (Hill and Wang); Thomas Powers, *Diana: The Making of a Terrorist* (Houghton Mifflin); and Susan Stern, *With the Weathermen* (Doubleday). Filmed sources include *The Weather Underground*, directed by Sam Green and codirected by Bill Siegel (The Free History Project); *Rebels with a Cause*, a film by Helen Garvey (Shire Films); and *Underground*, a film by Emile de Antonio, Mary Lampson, and Haskell Wexler (First Run Features).

At Viking, I was and am in awe of my amazing, perspicacious, subtle, hilarious, brave editor, Molly Stern; and grateful to Peter McCarthy, and to Katherine Griggs. John Karp's early encouragement for this book was of inestimable help. In California, Michael Siegel gave this book a level of support so far beyond the call of professionalism that I am literally humbled, as did Priscilla Cohen. And finally, as always, to Eric Simonoff, my friend and agent, my deepest thanks.